THE TRAFFICKED

Lee Weeks left school at 16 and, armed with a notebook and very little cash, spent seven years working her way around Europe and South East Asia. She returned to settle in London, marry and raise two children. In those 15 years, she worked as a cocktail waitress, chef, model, English teacher and personal fitness trainer. She now lives in Devon with her two children and her dogs. Her debut novel, *The Trophy Taker*, was a *Sunday Times* bestseller.

Please go to www.leeweeks.co.uk for more information and visit www.BookArmy.co.uk for exclusive updates.

By the same author:

The Trophy Taker

LEE WEEKS

The Trafficked

AVON

AVON

A division of HarperCollins*Publishers*
77–85 Fulham Palace Road,
London W6 8JB

www.harpercollins.co.uk

A Paperback Original 2008

First published in Great Britain by
HarperCollins*Publishers* 2008

Copyright © Lee Weeks 2008

Lee Weeks asserts the moral right to
be identified as the author of this work

A catalogue record for this book is
available from the British Library

ISBN-13: 978-1-84756-083-4

Set in Minion by Palimpsest Book Production Limited,
Grangemouth, Stirlingshire

Printed and bound in Great Britain by
Clays Ltd, St Ives plc

Mixed Sources
Product group from well-managed
forests and other controlled sources
www.fsc.org Cert no. SW-COC-1806
© 1996 Forest Stewardship Council

FSC

FSC is a non-profit international organisation established to promote the
responsible management of the world's forests. Products carrying the FSC
label are independently certified to assure consumers that they come
from forests that are managed to meet the social, economic and
ecological needs of present and future generations.

Find out more about HarperCollins and the environment at
www.harpercollins.co.uk/green

I would like to thank my agent Darley Anderson and everyone at the agency for making me feel part of a winning team. Thanks to Maxine Hitchcock who is a good friend as well as a great editor. Thanks to my children, Ginny and Robert, for their insight and their help at tricky moments.

This book is dedicated to my mum

1

Philippines, March 2004

A child whispered in the darkness.

'Shhh . . . stop crying. The Kano will hear you. What's your name?'

'Perla.'

'How old are you?'

'Eleven.'

'I'm Maya. I'm eight. You from Davao?'

'Yes.'

'Me too. Where are we?'

'Angeles City.'

'Why are we chained up? Are we in prison? Why does that Kano hurt everyone? What will happen to me?'

'You will be sold.'

'Sold?'

'Sold to a man.'

'What will the man do with me?'

'He will have sex with you.'

'I'm just a girl. I can't. I'm going to run away. Let's do it, Perla. Let's run home to Davao.'

Perla stated to cry again.

'Don't cry. The Kano will come. He will hurt you. He will poke you with the buzzy stick.'

'My legs are wet. I am bleeding.'

'Don't cry, Perla. I'll be your friend. I'll tell you a Mickey Mouse story.'

By the time Maya finished her story, Perla was dead.

destination for every whorist and paedophile in the western world.

The Colonel sat with three other men on one of the four tables outside the Bordello on Fields Avenue. He paused, beer bottle pressed against his mouth, and watched Jed, a big black guy, swagger towards him, walking the walk, talking the talk, bling hanging from around his neck in layers of gold chain and a diamond crucifix. On his arm was a tiny Filipina named Peanut. Jed glanced the Colonel's way, nodded his head respectfully, grinned at the other men and then swaggered on past into the Bordello.

The Bordello was like all the other bars and hotels down the avenue – a facade. From across the road, face on, it looked like a mock-up of a western saloon, but from the side it looked like a cardboard cut-out supported by a scaffold and attached to a windowless concrete block. It was situated three-quarters up Fields Avenue, before the road widened, branched out and the hotels began. They weren't proper hotels. There were no five-star accommodations on Fields Avenue. Most hotels offered their rooms at an hourly rate.

The Colonel had called a meeting for eight o'clock in the Tequila Station. He had plenty of time till then. He drank his beer and surveyed his kingdom. In the thirty years he had lived in the Philippines, Angeles was where he'd always been. Firstly as a Chief Petty Officer stationed at the nearby American naval base at Clark, and latterly as the self-styled saviour of the city of fallen angels.

Brandon sat directly to the Colonel's right, British,

shaved head, ex-Marine, his voice thick with a Portsmouth dialect, akin to a gravelly cockney. He had tattoos of Chinese script on both his arms and an eagle stretched across his upper back. He was not a man to move hastily. He had learned to sit back and observe. It had kept him alive in the Marines; it would continue to keep him alive, as long as he never forgot it. Brandon had been with the Colonel for eighteen months now. His job was to control the women, make sure that the young ones stayed scared and compliant and that the others felt the back of his hand. Brandon had not found it easy in the beginning. Hitting women was not in Brandon's nature, but he had got used to detaching his brain from the work. That's all it was – work. They were merchandise. The Colonel liked him, he knew that. One day he wanted to take over from him. Of course, there were obstacles to that, and that's why Brandon had to be good at waiting and watching.

Next to him was Reese, an Australian who was stuck in the seventies – a string of love beads around his neck and flowery board shorts on his skinny legs. His surfer's curls that were once his pride and joy were now straw, and his once beautiful face was now thin and deeply lined. He sat cross-legged, swinging his suspended leg nervously and fiddling with his cigarette packet.

The fourth man called himself the Teacher.

A few westerners sat in the Bordello at the bar enjoying a late-afternoon beer. It was their lull time. The evening unfolded in a regular pattern. The needs of the whorists were always the same – eat, sleep and fuck – but they formed their own patterns according to their age. From lunchtime onwards the younger ones emerged in packs, tired and hung over. They needed food and a good few beers and to socialise with each other. They got rid of one date, sobered up and recharged themselves ready for another evening of heat and sweat and DNA exchange. The older whorists were loners, even if they had come along with another male they didn't feel it necessary to stay with them all day and all evening. They sat at bars on their own, picked up a girl early. They were after a companion to have dinner with and spend the night snoring next to. They preferred the calm surroundings and the melancholy country music of the Bordello. They needed to pace themselves.

A barmaid named Comfort kept the energy circulating in the bar with a big smile and a substantial push-up bra. Her laugh ricocheted around the walls as she bantered happily with the three men who had nothing else to do but sit and watch her.

Comfort looked up as Jed and Peanut came in and she moved down to the end of the bar where the signing-in book was. She leaned over the book, pen ready.

Jed didn't acknowledge the other men in the bar. He walked in as if he were on stage. He talked loud, laughed louder. He was showing the older men that he was a young stud.

'You got a room for an hour, baby?'

He rested his elbow on the counter and leaned over to get close to Comfort and look further down her cleavage. He grinned smugly; his gold teeth flashed in the gloom of the bar. She grinned back. Peanut stood waiting patiently for it all to be over. She was an un-educated girl from the countryside, and spoke very little English. She was unattractive: dark-skinned and rough-featured. Her scrawny legs dropped down from beneath a micro denim skirt like two sticks of gnawed liquorice. But Peanut was a hit with men who liked their women to look like undernourished girls. Jed towered over her at six foot four to her four foot nine.

Comfort flicked her hair back from her face and turned her large round eyes, as clear as amber marbles, towards Jed, ignoring Peanut altogether.

'You go-in' to need two hour, Big Boy.'

He raised an eyebrow and let out a laugh that boomed out across the bar. 'Damn! Is that right? How come? You plannin' on joinin' us?' He ran his hand down her forearm. 'You want a repeat performance?' He stroked the round of her breast as it rested on the signing-in book. 'You missed me that much you want some more of the big man?'

Comfort looked up at Jed and bit her bottom lip playfully.

'You spoil me. Give me ree-al good time larse time.' She reached out and ran her fingers lightly down his chest to his crotch. She felt the muscles in his abdomen tense. 'I'm go-in to have to give it to you for free, Big Man. You leave door unlock. I come up an' party wid you. Okay?'

He grinned inanely. 'Oh yeah, baby! Me and Peanut here are gonna be waitin' for you.'

He flashed his teeth and clicked his tongue, placed his hand on Peanut's tiny bottom and steered her towards the stairs at the far end of the bar. A door there led to the two floors of short-stay rooms. Above them slept the women who serviced those rooms. He turned back and winked at Comfort. She winked back, waited till he was out of sight then turned to look at the Colonel. He was watching her through the window. He tapped his watch at her. She nodded.

7

For a few seconds Amy didn't know whether her eyes were open or not – it was too dark to tell. She felt around the bedcover with her hands. It didn't feel like the soft cotton one that she was used to. It felt hard, waxy. She scrunched it in her fingers – no, it definitely didn't fold in her hand the way it should, it was like cardboard. She blinked again . . . yes . . . her eyes were open. She lay there in the darkness and thought hard. She tried to remember what had happened: Lenny picked her up from school; they drove to an apartment block next to lots of others, in the middle of nowhere where lots of buildings were going up all around. They came up in a lift. The flat smelled of paint and had hardly any furniture in it. It didn't look as if Lenny or anyone lived there. Lenny didn't know where anything was. He had opened the wrong door in the kitchen when he wanted the fridge. Then he had shown her her room. She remembered sitting in the lounge and watching telly whilst Lenny made a few calls. It was then that she had begun to feel very uncomfortable and she had looked for her schoolbag so that she could make a phone call. When he came off the phone she asked Lenny where it was. He said it was still in the car and that they'd get it in a minute when they went back out. But nothing felt right. Amy had drunk her Coke and pretended to watch the telly but inside she wanted to cry. Then she remembered feeling so tired that she just had to close her eyes for a little while. She gasped now. Was she naked? Had he undressed her? She felt under the bedclothes. It was all right, she still had her clothes on. She blinked again and this time she saw a faint orange glow in the room coming from beneath the door. She looked around; only moving her eyes, she didn't dare move her head. Yes – there was the desk, the chair, the old lamp. She was lying on a mattress on the floor, not in a bed; it was the room she had seen before. She must have got sick and Lenny had put her to bed. That was it. She could hear the sound of a television in the room next door.

'Lenny?' She sat up and called out. 'Lenny?'

The television went off. She heard the rustle of someone moving; she heard someone approach the door and turn the handle.

A man stood in the doorway. He was Chinese. Amy knew his type: rough Hong Kong low-life type. She had been around types like him all her life.

'Where's Lenny?'

The man didn't answer for a second and Amy could see that he had something behind his back. Only when he came into the room did she see what it was – it was a length of rope with a loop at the end.

8

Johnny Mann went back to his flat to unpack and repack his case before he headed over to Stanley Bay to see his mother and explain why he wouldn't be over for Sunday roast. He knew she would be looking forward to seeing him. He hadn't caught up with her for a while. The last case had kept him working twenty-four-seven and then the aftermath had left him needing to get away and recover his sanity.

'They're lovely.'

He stood behind her in the hall mirror and finished fastening the string of pink pearls around his mother's neck. She reached up and touched the hand he had placed on her shoulder and smiled at him in the mirror. Molly was about to hit seventy but she kept herself fit and active and stood erect. She was a good-looking woman, strong-featured with piercing grey eyes and a straight roman nose; she had high cheek-bones and ivory skin. Her hair was a beautiful mix of grey and silver interwoven with darker shades. It was long and thick and she twisted it into a bun and caught it with a clasp at the back of her head. Now that Mann stood behind her he realised how slight she was. Her shoulders felt bony beneath his hands.

'You shouldn't have spent your money on me, but it's very thoughtful of you, Johnny.' She patted his hand before turning away. Mann followed her through to the kitchen.

'Nonsense – it's a pleasure. How have you been, Mum?'

She put the kettle on. 'I'm fine. You don't need to worry about me.'

He watched her make tea. He liked the familiarity of her actions – her hands never dithered or wavered. Her actions were always measured and decisive and her fingers moved with grace.

She was not a gabbler or a waster of words. She was a woman who took her time and thought things through. She was a holder-in of emotions. He had never once heard her raise her voice in uncontrolled anger. Molly didn't boil over, she just simmered. She was prickly, almost, except her heart was soft – not everyone could see or knew that, but Mann did.

He looked around him. Something was missing in the flat – the maid hadn't come in to say hello to him as she always did.

'Where's Deborah?'

'Day off.' Molly didn't turn to look at him as she answered.

'Mum?' He could tell by her sudden busyness – looking for a teaspoon in a drawer for seconds that she knew where to put her hand on at once – that she was not telling him the whole story.

She glanced over to him on her way to get milk from the fridge.

'Well, I don't need anyone full time. What will I do if I have nothing left to occupy my time? I gave her some money to go back home to the Philippines for a while. She has kids she hasn't seen for months. It's not right. I am able to look after myself.'

'And you have enough money to afford an army of maids – it's Hong Kong, you have to have a few maids, Mum; it's just the way it is. You have all the money you could ever need in the bank. Why don't you spend some of it?'

She brought the tea over to Mann, who was sitting at the kitchen table.

'When the time comes you will inherit it, then you can decide what to do with it – for now I don't need the money.' She was getting agitated.

'I don't want it. I want you to make a point of spending every last dollar of it, leave me nothing. You are still young, Mum – you look great for your age. You need to get out more. It's time to make some more friends: join clubs, go on singles' holidays.'

'Ha!' she laughed. 'With a bunch of other oldies, you mean?'

'I am sure amongst all the incapacitated octogenarians you will find a few that are like you. Why don't you go on a cruise or go around Europe and look up family and friends. Use the money to have some fun?'

She stared into her tea.

'I don't want to touch the money. I have everything

I need.' She got up and went to wipe the work surface where she'd made the tea.

Mann could see that the time had come for him to drop it, otherwise she was going to clam up completely. He held up his hands in a surrender gesture.

'Okay, sorry. Let's drop it. Please come and sit with me. This must be the only kitchen in the whole of this expensive block of flats in which the owners sit and drink tea. Better make sure no one catches us or you'll be chucked out of the wealthy widows' club.'

'Ha . . .' she laughed. 'If such a thing exists, I don't think they would ever ask me to join, do you?'

'No, you're right – you'd have them donating all their money to the poor and making baskets to sell.'

A ginger cat appeared and wound itself around Mann's legs. Molly's face lit up when she saw it.

'Hello, Ginger – just woken up, have you?'

'I didn't think you'd agree to take on David White's cat . . . Never thought I'd see you with a pet; I always thought you hated them.'

'Nonsense, it was your father who hated animals, not me. I always had animals when I was a girl, back on the farm. I grew up with them.' She leaned her hands against the rim of the sink and stared out through the kitchen windows at the wooded hills that rose in a bank of emerald green opposite. 'My life was very different then.'

'I can imagine little Molly Mathews running around with straw stuck in her hair and mud on her knees.'

She turned from the window and smiled, but there was sadness in her eyes.

'That was such a long time ago, it feels like another life. I hadn't thought about my childhood for years until recently. Now something comes back to me almost daily – vividly – I'm not sure I like it.' She sighed and turned back from the window, buffing the taps with a cloth as she did so. 'Anyway, son, tell me . . . How is it with you? Did you get the rest you needed?' She came and put her arm around his shoulder and leaned over to kiss his cheek.

'I did a lot of thinking. As the saying goes, Mum – you can run but you can't hide.'

She sat opposite him and leaned forward to hold his hands in hers.

'You mustn't be so hard on yourself. You have been through such a lot these last few months.'

'It's nothing to what others have endured, Mum, and I feel responsible for some of that.'

'You mustn't blame yourself, Johnny. No one could have known that Helen would be killed.'

'But I let her go, Mum; I have to live with that.'

'You let her go because you didn't think she was the one for you. You didn't know she would be killed.'

'If Helen had never met me she'd be alive today.'

'Chan was the one to blame, not you. None of us could ever have imagined he would turn out like that. All those years we knew him as a child, we never realised how envious, how vindictive and downright evil he was.'

'Father saw it in him. He hated him.'

'Your father saw something in him: a ruthlessness, a mercenary heart. He knew the triads well and he knew that Chan had been enlisted.' Molly gave an involuntary sigh and picked up Ginger the cat and held him close to her. 'You have to be a bit kind to yourself. You have to let it go now. Time will heal, son.'

Mann looked at his mother and searched her eyes.

'I will never let it go, Mum. In my own way I got justice for Helen, and I will get it for father. I will find out who killed him and I will make them pay.'

'Your father made enemies. It killed him. We can't keep raking up the past.'

'And I cannot forget it . . . the sight of my father being executed will never leave me. I can see it so clearly. It is branded on my mind's eye, on my subconscious, in vivid detail. There is no forgetting for me until I get it explained. I want to find out why his death was ordered and I want to get the man who ordered it.'

Molly was staring at him, horrified. Mann felt instant remorse. He had not meant to worry her. He reassured her with a smile and stroked Ginger, who purred in her arms.

'I never knew that about Dad – that he hated animals.'

She looked at him and met his eyes with her piercing grey stare.

'There was a lot you never knew about your father.'

9

'What is that fucking awful smell?'

The Teacher sat back in his chair and waited for an answer. Reese sniggered.

The Colonel paused, beer bottle to his mouth. 'What smell?' He lifted his chin and sniffed the air from right to left.

'The all-prevailing smell of shit in this place.'

Reese giggled nervously. 'You get used to it, bro.'

'Don't you smell it, Colonel, or is your nose buggered from all that speed you shove up it?'

Reese and Brandon looked anxious. It wasn't often they saw their boss at the butt of someone else's jibes. He wasn't the best at taking a joke. But then, he didn't usually have to suck up to anyone. His word was the law in Angeles. He owned five of the big clubs there: Hot Lips, Lolita's, Lipstick, The Honey Pot and Bibidolls. They were the best clubs in Angeles with the youngest, prettiest girls – handpicked by him. He also owned several bars and hotels. The Bordello was one of them, the Tequila Station another. The Colonel set his beer carefully down and looked at the Teacher. He smiled.

'I thought the same when I first got here. I thought "what a shit-hole". Now I think "what a gold mine". The smell of shit and the smell of money have become one and the same for me.'

'Just as well, because this place is an open sewer.' The Teacher looked about him in disgust. 'Literally . . .' He was referring to the foul running water that ran the length of the street and followed a course beside the cracked and uneven pavement.

The Teacher gave up the conversation and sat back and drank from his beer bottle. There was too much noise to talk. Opposite the Bordello the mosquito drivers with their noisy motorbikes with sidecars, were trying to impress the girls who stood outside Bibidolls in their bikinis. They were competing to see who could rev their machine the loudest – the night was young and they were bored. They belched fumes and beeped at one another whilst the girls giggled at them – although both sides knew it would not end in a coupling. The boys didn't make enough money and the girls didn't give it away for free. The girls' sole aim in life was to marry a foreigner and get off the Fields. They were Guest Relations Officers, GROs. Their job was to entertain the tourists on Fields Avenue. Besides their yellow plastic bikinis they wore permits that hung long around their tanned necks and settled just below their pert cleavages – permits that had their photos and stated they were legally permitted to work in the clubs and that they were eighteen and over. Most of them weren't; their documents were forged. The girls swished back their hair and pushed their chests forward as they bantered with the whorists as they passed by.

Upstairs in the Bordello there were no GROs. This point on Fields Avenue was the boundary. Here marked the beginning of the descent into unlicensed bars and twenty-four-hour hostess clubs where the girls didn't wear badges. They often didn't wear bikinis. They were kept locked in a back room. They were children.

The Colonel flashed the group of mosquito drivers a look that silenced them instantly and they moved hastily away.

'What about the police? Have you fixed it? Blanco hates fuck-ups.'

The Colonel drank from his beer at the same time as he kept his eyes fixed on the Teacher. He was letting him know that whilst he would take *some*, he would not take a lot of dissent, especially not in front of his men.

He set his bottle down. 'Blanco doesn't need to worry. Over the years I have cultivated a good working relationship with the police. Some I have had to trick by providing them with a girl for the night and then informing them that they have slept with a minor. Others, I have had to give a small share of my profits to. Most of the time it has just taken hard currency.'

'Everyone here has a price, huh?'

'Not everyone . . . *he he* . . .' Reese was eager to show he could be part of the conversation and saw his chance to impress the Teacher. '. . . not the Irish priests.'

'Yes . . .' The Colonel stared disapprovingly at Reese. '. . . that is true . . . they are all over the fucking Philippines like a plague.'

'Yeah, man. They have a refuge just up the road from here and for as long as the Colonel's been pimping the girls the priests have been saving them. Twice the Colonel's been to court . . . *he he* . . . He had to pay off everyone: the girls' parents, the police and the fucking court judge.'

'I think you will find . . .' The Colonel glared at Reese and made sure that he understood that he had said enough before taking his eyes from him. ' . . . that it isn't just us bar owners who would happily pay to see the priests shot. Even the local church here doesn't want them interfering. After all, we bring in big revenue *and* we always give a fucking big donation to charity. But – nevertheless they remain a thorn in our sides. One that I hope you will remove sometime soon – very soon.'

The Teacher nodded. 'You honour your side of the bargain, I will honour mine.'

Comfort came to the table with a tray of four beers. As she set the drinks down the Teacher ran his hand up over her flanks and bare legs. She giggled, tried to stay upright but was pulled into his lap. She put her arm around his neck and tipped his peak cap up so she could get a proper look at him.

'Hey, you handsome man.' She looked at his sky-blue eyes staring back at her. 'You marry? Wanna nice Filipina wife?'

The Teacher held onto her hair and tilted her head backwards. He smiled.

'What's the offer on whores this week – two for the price of one? Buy one, get one free?' He grinned

45

sarcastically. 'Hello "Bogof". Now fuck off, you disease-ridden piece of shit.' He pushed her from his lap.

Comfort smiled the way that Filipinos always did whatever the situation. She understood the aggression, but not the words. She knew all about the Kano's temper. She bore the scars on her body from the Colonel's off-days. She looked at the Colonel for guidance. She had been his favourite when she was ten. Now that she was twenty, she was way past her prime, but she still felt an affinity to him. He had looked after her, in his own way. She still had her uses for him.

'Ready?' His expression hardly ever changed. He had been born looking pissed-off, red-faced, angry. His bulbous eyes were puffy above and below like a chameleon's. If his head was turned upside down his eyes would look the same.

She stood – 'Yes, Kano' – picked up the tray and went back into the bar.

10

Jed wasn't wasting any time. He'd been in enough of these places to know the score. What you paid for and what you got were two different things. The hotel looked great from outside, but inside it was just a windowless room with a dirty mattress on the floor and no air-con. Still, he wasn't there for long, and he had just one purpose in mind. He kept his bling on, nothing else. The heavy gold chains swung back and forth beneath his chest, knocking Peanut in the face with every thrust.

He had a hard job controlling himself. He was excited about Comfort. She was that rare Filipina – the one that was confident enough to work it – so many of them were just 'yes, no, pay now' girls, but Comfort knew how to be a very good bad girl. She liked sex. She enjoyed it. He was going to take his time, even though Peanut wriggled beneath him. He knew she was eager to get it over with. It was almost time for her to go back to work. He had bought her out from Lolita's nearly twenty-four hours ago. He'd had his money's worth. In another hour she would be back dancing in a g-string in front of strangers. The thought of the threesome he was about to have made him thrust harder. But he didn't want to come. He needed to wait. This was just a warm-up.

He paused, listened. He was sure he could hear Comfort in the corridor outside. There it was, her knock on the door, just like she'd said she would. He took some deep breaths, relaxed. He could wait for the fun to begin.

'Come in, honey.' As the door opened Jed felt the rush of air cool the sweat on his back. 'We bin waitin' for ya.' He turned, slow, kept himself hard and strong inside Peanut, who lay motionless beneath him with his crucifix resting on her eye.

'Where would sir like it? Up the arse?' The Teacher fired two shots from a Heckler & Koch P7 pistol with the silencer attached. He fired one into Jed's rectum to immobilise him. Boomph! He fell like a felled elephant on top of Peanut, who lay there, eyes wide, unable to move. Then he fired the other shot into the back of Jed's head. Brain and skull fragments splattered across the wall above Peanut.

11

Mann boarded the plane and settled down for his twelve-hour flight. Better twelve than eight, he thought. At least he had some hope of sleeping five or six hours and not being force-fed like a laboratory animal every couple of hours. But sleep wasn't going to come easy. He thought about what his mother had said. She had come to a crossroads in her life, it seemed to Mann. She was in a reflective mood. Today, for the first time ever, his mother had hinted that her marriage had not been as it should. Now Mann had the task of revisiting his memories from a different angle. He had to take away the child's perceptions, straighten their edges and see them through untinted glasses. It would be a hard task. The most time he had spent with his family had been the years before he was sent away to school – he had started boarding when he was eight – and then there were the holidays when he'd come back to Hong Kong. Was it true that their marriage hadn't been as strong as he had always assumed? His mother always left out more than she ever said.

He was in for a long night. Thoughts bounced

around inside his head. He hadn't been back to the UK for a long time – seventeen years. The last time he had stood on British soil his father had still been alive. It wasn't that he hadn't meant to return, but there had just never been a good time.

Mann practised his particular type of meditation – he shut his mind to all but the pursuit of sleep. Anything unwanted, even sex, that popped into his brain was booted out without being looked at. He pulled his fleece blanket up over his face and mentally put himself on the beach, with not a bikini in sight.

12

'*La La La. Love Love Love. Kiss Kiss Kiss Me.*' Eight-year-old Sophia sang along to the jukebox in the Tequila Station.

'Love that one, sweetie. You coloured that real pretty.'

Sophia turned the pages of her book and showed her father her efforts. Terry ran his hand affectionately over Sophia's soft brown curls, keeping one eye on her work and the other on the door. It was a quarter to eight. The meeting was scheduled for eight. The others would be arriving soon.

The Tequila Station was a large sprawling bar set out on three levels, the most popular bar on Fields Avenue. Just down the road on the same side as the Bordello and within spitting distance of all the best clubs, it was the perfect meeting place for whorists who, in between fucking and partying, came to play pool, relax and get something to eat. It was the favourite place for the younger of them – a home from home. Then, fed and watered, they partied solidly till three in the morning.

Terry and Sophia sat just past the main bar on the

right, down two steps in a private seating area that was screened from prying eyes. It had a RESERVED sign permanently on it, although most of the time that wasn't needed. Everyone understood it was not an area for the general public to sit in. Terry and Sophia were the first ones to arrive.

Sophia was still in her school uniform and was doing her homework whilst Terry talked on the phone beside her. His laptop was open. Terry had installed Wi-Fi so that he could connect with the world from anywhere in the bar.

Sophia sucked the end of her coloured pencils and paused frequently to survey her work. Occasionally she demanded her father's attention. She didn't speak – she pushed her face into his as he talked on the phone, and pointed to her work. He smiled and nodded, pretended to be interested.

'Wait,' he mouthed to Sophia. She tugged at his arm. He held the phone away from his mouth and covered the mouthpiece. 'Wait, sweetie. I'll be with you in a minute.'

She pulled a cross pouty face and went back to colouring, her tongue protruding just a little as she concentrated on keeping the colours inside the lines.

He continued his conversation, a smugly satisfied look on his face.

'She took a lot of finding. It was thanks to our men in black . . . Yes . . . She's being seasoned right now. Be ready in a week or two. I know, I know, *ha ha*, a nonstop fucking supply of baby whores – couldn't ask for more. Yes . . . So far, so good . . . The deliveries should keep coming regularly. They are standing by their word. But this *is* the Philippines; they might always sell out to the highest bidder. . . . Yes, the Chinaman, is he still buying up everything? We need to show them we mean business . . . It's in hand.'

Terry finished his phone call and gave his attention to Sophia, but she had lost interest in her colouring and had now got out Princess Pony to play with. She started combing its hair. The smell of raspberry-scented pink plastic nauseated her father as much as it delighted her, and he instinctively turned his back on her and watched the door. He knew that the others would all be on time. Only the main man would be late, as was his privilege.

Sophia was making clacking hoof noises and Princess Pony was trotting across the table when the door opened.

The security guard stepped aside to allow Reese through. He didn't get frisked like everyone else, none of the Fields' VIPS did. The strict 'no weapons' policy all around Angeles City did not apply to them. Brandon walked in behind Reese.

The four young black guys playing pool looked up and watched as the two men entered. One of them nodded in their direction. Laurence also worked for the Colonel and had the job of looking after four of the Colonel's clubs. The Colonel had taken him under his wing as ex-US army; he had felt a bond with him.

Reese and Brandon picked themselves up a drink, and then went straight over to sit with Terry and Sophia. Sophia looked up from her colouring. She knew them both but she never bothered to talk to them because they did not acknowledge her. Only Reese talked to her sometimes, when her daddy wasn't around.

Laurence finished up his game of pool and came over to join them. He sat down and checked his watch.

'Five to eight . . . same old fuckin' bullshit. We have to be early, but he rocks up when he fuckin' feels like it. Then he's gonna turn up with all that "time of reckoning" shit, spoutin' stuff from the Bible.' He looked at the others for support. Only Reese sniggered. The Colonel had a Bostonian accent that Laurence could mimic very well. Terry stared back, expressionless, and Brandon just looked around the bar. He could not afford the luxury of a gripe.

Terry looped his arm around the back of Sophia's seat. At fifty-six he was the oldest member here. He had been in the Philippines for eighteen years. He'd come as a backpacker and an opportunist and stayed. He had married a local widow with several young children and he had fathered one of his own – Sophia. Terry knew how to keep everything low-profile. He went about doing his work unhindered. He bought houses and then offered them for tailor-made paedophile holidays to people from all around the world. Terry was the Internet king. People contacted him from all over the world and he got them what they wanted. He found them a house, he even arranged for a child to be waiting in their bed when they got there. Not just any old child: one to order, one handpicked and pre-seasoned. Now, with his new contacts, Terry was able to have a bigger hand in child recruitment. He had control of a new gang who were delivering on time and on target. No longer did he have to rely on the small-minded gangs of feuding triads to recruit the girls, he was now in control of a slick team that could locate and capture any number of young girls. Terry was a happy man.

Reese tapped away with his cigarette packet, turning it over and over. He did not have room to cross his legs so instead he jiggled his left foot incessantly. Reese was Terry's 'gofer'. He did all the day-to-day stuff. He kept the customers happy. Reese didn't make a fortune from it, but it kept him in a lifestyle he loved. He got to lie on a beach, smoke weed and have lots of sex. Reese had spent his childhood in care. As the boy with the golden curls, Reese had had a *lot* of attention from the other boys and the wardens. Now he had finally found peace and tranquillity in the laid-back smiling arms of the Filipinos he didn't want to lose it and he was worried that he would: tension was creeping in everywhere. The Teacher had brought it with him and Reese felt that panic inside him just like when he was a child in the orphanage. He felt he was about to get shafted.

13

'He didn't have to hit me.' Amy's sobs broke through her words. 'I was only looking outside.' She touched her mouth; it was sore from where the rough Hong Kong man, who she now knew was called Tony, had hit her. She could taste the rawness where her brace had cut into the inside of her cheek. She couldn't stop shivering.

Lenny gave Amy a tissue and she wiped her nose.

'You are not allowed to look outside. There is no point in banging on the window anyway, the windows are double-glazed and there is an anti-glare film on them, so no one can hear or see you.'

'Why did he hit me then?'

'He hit you because he and Sunny', he gestured towards the lounge, 'are very angry with your father. You have to be quiet and do as you're told or they *will* hurt you.'

'Why did you bring me here?' She blinked tears from behind the pebble-thick glass of her spectacles. 'I don't want to stay here. I need to go back to school now.'

'You cannot go anywhere until your father pays up. Now, eat this . . .' He handed her a Pot Noodle.

She stared at it. She was really hungry. She had not had anything to eat since she got there. She took the carton from him.

'Can I have my bag please, Lenny?'

'You can have your bag but not your phone. You won't be talking to anyone for a long while. Play by the rules here and you'll be okay – make trouble and you will suffer . . . Understand?'

Amy nodded, her lip starting to quiver again. 'Thank you for the food, Lenny.' She stared at the Pot Noodle but it was no longer in focus as tears filled her eyes. 'Thank you very much.'

14

The Colonel walked down the street, surveying his kingdom. For most people it was difficult to negotiate the cracked and uneven pavement, but the Colonel knew every inch of it and never needed to look down to know what was there. The Shabu did that to him. The methamphetamine speeded up his reactions, made him super alert and gave him a feeling of elation and euphoria. It also heightened his perception of the world, peeling away the layers of reality like skins from an onion. He could take in and analyse every movement on the periphery of his vision. He floated along the street, watching everything and knowing all around him from the cockroach hiding behind the pipes in his bathroom, to the bartender stealing money from his till.

An old beggar woman, ghostly and barely more than a skeleton, stepped out of the Viagra sellers doorway where she lived, one arm outstretched and her hand open. She was swaying with the effort of keeping herself upright. She did not see that it was the Colonel until it was too late. For a minute he poised, hand raised ready to hit her as he had so many times, push her back into the alleyway to rot amongst the starving kittens and rat-bitten puppies, but, as she gasped, waiting for the blow, he didn't do it because he saw that today she wanted it. She was hoping today would be her last. He stayed his hand, lowered his arm and dipped into his pocket. He threw some coins on the ground beside her. If the Colonel wanted her alive, alive she must stay. He was God on Fields Avenue.

He stepped over the pile of dog excrement and passed the schoolgirls touting outside The Honey Pot. Two girls were being measured for their GRO outfits. The girls rolled their eyes towards the mosquito drivers and giggled suggestively at the tailor, who was taking their measurements from waist to crotch.

The Colonel stopped outside the shop. The tailor bowed respectfully, the mosquito riders pretended to clean their bikes and the girls smiled sweetly.

'Evening, sir,' they chorused. He didn't answer.

He walked on into the Tequila Station. He looked around. He was reassured all was as it should be – no unwelcome surprises, not for him anyway. Sophia looked up as he approached the table and smiled, but it wasn't at the Colonel, she had learned not to look at him at all. He scared her with his red eyes and angry face. She was smiling because her favourite song had come back on the jukebox and now she could happily take no notice of the men whatsoever.

'*La La La. Love Love Love. Kiss Kiss Kiss Me.*'

The Colonel always sat in the same place. He had the biggest vantage point. He sat facing his men, back to the wall, with a view to the bar and the street beyond. Nothing happened that he did not see. He looked around his assembled men and smiled.

He splayed his fingers out and rested the palms of his large hands on the table. They trembled without him realising. Almost as if he were a psychic about to go into a trance, his breathing was laboured. He sucked the air noisily in through his mouth and blew it dramatically out. Ever since he was a child he had been aware of his breathing. He had been a tall and gangly child and soon outgrew the cupboards where he hid from his daddy on a Saturday night when he heard him coming back from the bars – all fuelled up and no one to stop him hurting his son. Then, as the child squeezed into the small spaces, his knees pressed up against his chest, listening in the darkness for heavy footsteps, his breaths were quick and short and shallow. There was never enough room in the cupboards for him to breathe properly. So now, whenever he felt under stress, he filled his lungs right up; felt them expand as he opened out his rib cage, straightened his back, sat up erect: tall, strong and proud. But no matter how hard he tried, he could never fill them *right* up. They were always a *bit* squashed, a bit stuck together. The more he thought about it, the more obsessed he became and so the noisier was his breathing. Terry knew it. He'd seen the Colonel this way many times. At the moment, with all the stress and excitement, the Colonel was fully wound up and on the edge of exhaustion. He was continually hyperventilating. The Shabu wouldn't let him rest. The more hyper he was, the more Shabu he snorted.

'I have gathered you here because I have news on the shape of things to come: changes that will affect us all here in Angeles, in our world. In the kingdom that I created. Christ!' He banged his palms on the table. Sophia tutted as her crayons rolled off onto the floor. She scrambled under the table to pick them up. 'I shaped this place. From a scruffy little nothing that provided comfort to servicemen on the Clark military base, I turned it into a world-famous sex resort.' He looked at the men around the table. They stared back. Nobody was going to disagree with the Colonel, especially when he was in psycho mode. His face was rubbery and feverish. His eyes were the colour of a raspberry split. He licked his dry lips continually. He was as jittery as a fly.

'For some time I have been telling you about a man who will change things around here; a man who is going to help us turn this place into a five-star paradise. Blanco is coming. Today he sent us a show of faith.'

There was a general look of confusion and concern around the table. The Colonel's surprises were seldom nice.

'He has proved to me that he is committed to us. Now, this man wants you all to join him. This is our chance to go global. We can take our empire to the four corners of the world and make millions, or we can stay here in our small kingdom and count our pennies. He offers you the hand of friendship.'

'He can stick his hand up his own arse,' said Laurence, and looked at the others for support. Reese sniggered whilst Brandon sat stony-faced, watching and waiting. Laurence grinned and gave a deep chuckle. Terry glared at Reese. Reese, feeling suitably chastised for sniggering, went back to flicking his cigarette packet.

'We ain't givin' up nuttin', said Laurence. 'We got a good thing goin' here, don't we?'

The Colonel swivelled his head round towards Laurence and smiled his 'nearly smile'.

'Pro-tec-tion,' he over-enunciated. 'Should this world of ours need defending we will have a mighty army at our disposal. We have the government, for Christ's sake – you can't get much bigger than that.'

Laurence gave a snort of derision. Brandon stared at him. Terry couldn't believe that the big guy wasn't going to shut up. Reese stopped his twirling. Even he knew that the Colonel wanted an audience and wasn't asking for feedback.

'We don't need no fuckin' protection. Who's gonna fuck wid us here?' Laurence tried to redeem himself. 'In our own fuckin' country? We own Angeles.'

Terry looked at the Colonel, who merely stared at Laurence and waited for him to dig himself a bigger hole.

'Excuse me, boss, I mean *you* own Angeles, and we work for you,' he said, backtracking as fast as he could.

The Colonel always prized himself on being a good judge of character. He trusted these men in so far as he knew their limits and knew their price. Reese was stupid but predictable. Brandon was a thug. Terry was clever. But Laurence was sneaky. He had become a little premature in his ambitions. Laurence was not to be trusted – the worst of all sins.

Terry spoke up. 'Get smart here. This is no minor league. Blanco heads a syndicate so powerful that it will wipe all others off the board and we'll be part of it. Not just a part – we are key to its success, right, Colonel? We have been offered the chance of running the whole of Angeles, Olongapo, Cebu and Puerto Galera just the way we want. We will take out all opposition; wipe it off the board. We will set up new trafficking routes, build hotels and bars up and down the islands. The whole of the Philippines will be controlled by one syndicate and . . .'

'AND . . .' The Colonel turned back to Laurence with not even a nearly smile on his face. His eyes were piercing. 'If you are not *for* Blanco, you are against him *and* us.'

'Colonel, I didn't mean . . .'

The Colonel silenced him with his raised hand.

'I know what you meant. I know everything. When you came here you were a bum with nothing but pussy and beer on your mind. I gave you all that you wanted. You sit here in your fancy clothes that I paid for and you question my authority?'

The Colonel was spraying the table with spit. Sophia had stopped her crayoning to watch the patterns it made as it landed on the table.

Laurence shrugged and shook his head. He looked hastily around the table and realised he was on his own.

'I don't question it, boss. Just want to be sure, that's all. I like things the way they are.'

'Do you? You're happy with what you have, are you, Laurence, not thinking of branching out on your own?'

Panic flitted across Laurence's face.

'No way, boss.'

'Sure,' said Terry. 'We have a good life here. But there's always more. We stick together and we can achieve it. Is that right, Colonel?'

The Colonel relaxed. He could always rely on Terry. Terry was a shrewd businessman like himself. Terry was the brains in Angeles. The Colonel looked at each man in turn.

'Now it's our turn to prove ourselves to Blanco. We can't afford to make mistakes. We are supposed to be professionals, not fucking amateurs. We were given a job. All we had to do was get the women to the UK and liaise with the Chinese, then we would get our money.' He turned his head slowly towards Brandon and Laurence. 'What happened in London was a major error. It looked bad . . . very bad . . . We looked like fucking arseholes.'

Brandon stared back at the Colonel. Laurence looked around the table nervously. Sophia picked up Princess Pony and held it up to her face and stared at Laurence through the pony's pink mane. Sweat was overflowing from Laurence's frown lines and trickling down the side of his face. Sophia was watching a big droplet form at the end of his nose and she was counting the seconds it took to drop.

'What *did* happen in London, Laurence?'

Laurence flashed a look at Brandon. Brandon kept his eyes glued on the Colonel. Sophia giggled as the sweat drip landed on the table.

'We was caught out, is all. They caught us unawares.'

'How "unawares" exactly?'

'One of the women needed teachin' a lesson – causin' trouble. I was busy, didn't see them comin'.'

'And where were you, Brandon, when this *punishment* was being handed out?'

'I was called to a meeting with the Chinese, sir.'

Terry and Reese looked at one another. Everyone around the table knew the truth. It had been Laurence's cock-up, his fault. He had been left in charge of maintaining a watch over the women. He had been too busy sampling the merchandise.

Laurence's phone vibrated on the table. Laurence picked it up and read a text message.

'I have to use the john.'

'Anything the matter?' asked the Colonel.

'Nothin',' answered Laurence. 'Be back in five.'

He got up and walked across to the flight of stairs that led down to the toilets and the lower floor. The Colonel had the 'nearly smile' glued to his face as he turned his head first to the right, then the left.

'And where is Jed?' He drummed his fingers on the table.

Laurence walked past the seating area and the dance floor. A few couples were getting ready to party, a few others were just getting drunk. He read the text again. *Meet me in the john. I need to speak to you.*

Something about the text bothered him. A text wasn't just a text. You could tell who it was from by the way they phrased it. Did they use predictive? Did they abbreviate? The Filipinos were the fastest texters in the world, but Laurence's friend wasn't. He made mistakes. This text was perfect. Too perfect.

Laurence walked into the toilet area – the urinals, the two toilets with their half doors that never hid a big guy like him. Empty. Nothing unusual, just the foot bath was missing, that was all. They were clean people, these Filipinos, always washing their feet.

The Colonel looked at each man in turn.

'Any ideas where Jed is?'

Brandon looked uncomfortable. He didn't like surprises – 'be prepared' was his motto. He kept his eyes on the Colonel. Reese looked at Terry. Terry glared back and shook his head as if to say *don't even think about opening your mouth*.

'We are getting sloppy. Some people are making mistakes.' The Colonel's eyes rolled backwards, his fingers floated above the table. 'The time of reckoning is upon us . . .'

Sophia placed Princess Pony back on the table and silently mimicked the Colonel.

Laurence pushed the back door. It was stuck. There was something against it – a weight blocking it. He shoved it, a small sharp push. It moved. Four small shoves then it was open. Gun in hand, he looked out to the alleyway beyond. Nothing. Then he looked at his feet. There was the missing foot bath. He stood for a few seconds as his eyes made sense of what he saw. Jed's head was in it, the top of his skull blown away. His eyes were shut, his mouth hung open and his balls were inside it.

Laurence tasted the bile as it surged into his mouth. Adrenalin flooded his system; his legs began to give way. He turned. The Teacher was waiting right behind him. He held the gun against Laurence's heart, smiled and fired.

The Colonel sat upright. Sophia opened her mouth, held her breath, watched the Colonel and waited, ready to say it.

'The time of deliverance is at hand . . .' They spoke in unison.

15

Amy pulled the blanket up to just under her eyes and listened hard. She had come to know the sounds in the flat and what they meant. She could identify who it was by the sound of their footsteps and by the way they closed the door. There was the one who had gold teeth and stank of aftershave, who was always watching telly. His name was Sunny. He always had the volume up really loud. He was always eating and farting. The other man, Tony, had spots, and he was the one she had seen that first night. He always walked around a lot. He talked on the telephone. He watched soaps on the telly. Then there was Lenny and a woman. Amy hadn't seen her, but she had heard her. The woman was always shouting at the men. She only stopped moaning when Lenny arrived. Then she laughed like anything. She must fancy Lenny a lot, thought Amy.

Amy lay still and listened to the woman talking. The woman was Chinese – from Hong Kong – and spoke Cantonese. But Amy never saw her. The only person Amy saw to talk to was Lenny; she saw him every day. She liked him the best, even though he had been the man to take her from the school. He had explained all that to her and said that he had no choice. That he was, in his own way, a prisoner like her, and that when her father paid up they would both be free.

At least Lenny was nicer to her now. They had stopped giving her the sleeping pills every day, and Amy only looked out of the window now, she never banged on it. She understood the rules. She was used to rules. She was also used to fitting in to a pecking order; boarding for so many years had taught her that. She was an observant child and she knew how to watch and appraise others without being seen to do so. She knew how to get on people's good sides, even when she didn't like them.

It was a lucky thing that Amy had her drawing pad and her Macramé in her bag. Now she had nothing to do, she would do that. She sat on the chair by the desk. First of all she would draw a picture of Lenny. She sucked the end of her pencil as she thought hard about his face. She wanted to get it right. She wanted to get it so perfect that everyone would know who it was.

16

Mann made his way through Heathrow, picked up his small suitcase and headed out through 'Nothing to Declare', where he was handed his weapons' case, which had been carried separately, locked away in the hold, before he followed the signs for the exit.

The ragged line of people holding cards up behind the flimsy barrier looked hopefully at Mann. He had reached the end of the line when a short-haired blonde woman in her early thirties wearing dark trousers and a slim-fitting brown shirt rushed up to him, coffee cup in one hand and a sticky bun in the other.

'Detective Inspector Mann?'

He nodded.

She introduced herself. 'DC Rebecca Stamp, but you can call me Becky. You hungry? Need to stop for a coffee? Long flight?'

'I'm fine, thanks. I slept well. Lead the way.'

He followed her through to the car park. He watched her as she strode along beside him. She had that athletic gait that policewomen had, as if she were marching along with a rucksack on her back. Women competing in a male-dominated world didn't lose their femininity, it just changed – became more assertive – showed they knew what they wanted and how to get it. She was no more than five foot two and came to just under his shoulder, but she wasn't one of those women you should offer to reach things for.

She was still holding her bun in one hand and her coffee in the other when they arrived at level three of the short-stay car park. They stopped at a black Audi A2. She put her coffee on the roof whilst she looked for her keys.

'Shit! Sorry, my keys are somewhere. I had them in my hand a minute ago.' She put the bun in her mouth whilst she searched.

'Left-hand jacket pocket.'

She stopped and looked at him incredulously before aiming the rest of the bun at a bin ten feet away and scoring a direct hit.

'Thanks.'

She unlocked the car and got in, put her coffee in the cup holder in the centre of the red leather dashboard and started the engine. She switched the Bose sound system on and drove out of the car park.

'Thanks for picking me up,' Mann said.

She turned to look at him. He smiled.

'That's okay . . . you're welcome.'

'Did you have trouble recognising me?'

She giggled – deep and throaty, dirty, almost. She had a lovely broad mouth, strong laughter lines – a healthy tom-boy beach-babe look. She looked like she would be the last girl left at the campfire, drinking beer with the boys, long after the other girls had gone to bed.

'Six foot, Eurasian, snazzy dresser – no trouble. I did my research. I have booked you into a B&B near to where I live. I thought it would make sense for us to be close.'

'Sounds great.' He gave her a mischievous smile.

'Chief Inspector Procter – he's the man in charge of the kidnapping – wants to see you as soon as poss. I said I would fill you in on the way to the school. Then we go and meet the rest of the team. Hope that's okay?'

'It all sounds good. I bet the rest of the team can't wait.'

She swung him a look to check if he was joking, saw that he was and broke into that deep, rich laugh again. Her eyebrows and her eyes were a few shades darker than her hair, he noticed, which was the colour of gold, and her eyes were fringed with long, dark lashes. It gave her a striking Northern Italian look. She wore no makeup.

'Yeah, right! Pleased as punch. No one's quite figured out who asked for you. We didn't think we needed help.'

'Don't worry. I didn't want to come. Offer I couldn't refuse – that kind of thing. But it's nice to be here.' He looked wistfully out of the window. It was early and the air had that spring brightness, that expectancy to it that the sky was just waiting to burn off the morning haze and reveal a blue day. The roads were also just beginning to get choked with commuter traffic. 'I haven't been back here for a long time – too long.'

Mann stared out of the window. 'Where are we going first?'

'The school in Rickmansworth. In this traffic it should take us about an hour.'

'You've been out there already; what was your impression?'

'Posh school . . . awfully nice people but clueless. Let her walk out with a complete stranger. We get to see the Head at ten, thought you'd like to look around first.'

'Did you work on the other kidnappings?'

'Yes and no. We didn't even know about them till after the event. When Amy Tang went missing we sent out an alert around the boarding schools with Chinese kids. We got some information back about the abduction of two others – both boys, from two separate schools on the outskirts of London. One was ten, the other was twelve. Both were released after the ransom was paid.'

'Big money paid to release them?'

'Two million US each.'

'How did the ransom demands come?'

'All the same way – by email, via one of those scam sites for claiming an inheritance that you never knew you had.'

'Has it been traced?'

'We're still working on it. Someone knows his computers. He sent it around the world first. It came back with the logo of a bogus company plastered on it – BLANCO. We checked it out – there are a lot of companies called that, unsurprisingly. We traced it back to a Nigerian working in a taxi rank – he didn't have a clue how someone got hold of his dodgy identity. We decided it was a red herring.'

'Where was the money dropped?'

'In all three cases it was a different route, but same method. In Amy Tang's case it was dropped in a bin off Gerrard Street in Chinatown.'

'By whom?'

'By an employee of CK's, apparently, no one knows who. Getting cooperation from any of the Chinese families has been very hard. They would rather just pay up and shut up. A local crack addict was then paid to pick it up; he gave it to a lad on a courier bike and we think the courier had it taken off him at some lights. I don't know whether that was the end of the chain or not. It was elaborate and it worked. We lost it. We only got that much from CCTV footage.'

'Did he use the same method of abduction? Was it always the same man?'

'Hundred per cent it's the same man, though he was more cautious with the first two abductions. But the emails were written by the same person. The collection was virtually the same.'

'Were the other children able to give a description of him or where they were held?'

'No, they said they were kept blindfolded and that they slept a lot. Must have been kept sedated.'

'Did the others have triad links?'

'Both kids were from Mainland China – mega-wealthy parents but no direct triad links that we could find. The usual suspect business partners along the way, but nothing obvious.'

Becky beeped hard at a green MG that cut her up. Mann smiled to himself – he could see that she loved her car. She whizzed in and out of the traffic and she drove it with a passion – like a man – hard on the revs, aggressive, unapologetically.

'How's the investigation going?'

'We've drawn a blank. We've been out searching all vacant, newly rented properties in a ten-mile radius – so far, nothing. She could have gone anywhere from there. There are links to motorways north and south. She wasn't reported missing until Sunday evening – that's thirty-six hours after she left. She could be anywhere.'

'She wouldn't be being held where there are large groups of Chinese – she's much too hot a property. There would be quite a few people eager to ingratiate themselves with CK and tell him who's got her. She would be hidden somewhere nondescript, a bland mix of cultures. Maybe a satellite town or a new vertical village somewhere where people are anonymous. Do you have good undercover agents in Chinatown?'

'One really good one called Micky. He's infiltrated the Flying Dragons. He's been undercover for two years now. He doesn't break his cover for anyone and he keeps in touch by phone. I already talked to him, told him you were coming. He has no news about her whereabouts but says the feeling is that this isn't a home-grown problem – it goes back to Hong Kong.' Becky turned the radio off. She was perking up, the coffee had worked. 'Were you born here?'

'No. I am a Hong Konger, a Eurasian – half Chinese, half British. But I spent the best years of my life here, although you know that anyway – you've seen my stats.' He grinned.

'I only know the official stuff, plus I found out a bit on the grapevine. Micky told me a few interesting facts, he knew all about you. I guess as we are going to be working together for a while I will have plenty of time to fill in the gaps.'

'Let's hope so,' said Mann.

She gave him a sidelong glance and giggled, embarrassed.

'But, you're kidding, the best years of your life, really?'

'School – didn't you like yours?'

'Nope . . . Couldn't wait to leave.'

'Where did you grow up?'

'Islington – where I still live. Bought a flat there three years ago – in Highbury. Went to a local girls' school – I did okay, but I didn't enjoy it. I was a sporty kid. We didn't have the provisions for that in the inner city. I beat all the boys at their school when it came to cricket practice.'

'I noticed the bowling action with the bun, back in the car park.'

'Yeah, the trouble is all we ever did was *practice*. I did swim for the borough. I still keep my hand in – still go to the gym, swim a few times a week.'

'Is that what keeps you sane outside work?'

'Yes, plus I help out at a youth rehabilitation centre for young addicts and homeless women. I teach self-defence to the women. It's a major problem for them on the streets. They get attacked all the time, raped. I try to teach them how to diffuse it and, if they can't, how to defend themselves.'

'How long have you been in the police force?'

'Since I left uni. I did a degree in psychology. Then I joined the police force.'

'Been married long?'

'Ten years.'

'What does your husband do? Is he in the force?'

'Huh! That would never suit him. No, he's one of those entrepreneurial types; never quite know what he'll try next. At the moment, amongst a million other things, he is helping out a friend and running a language school. Don't ask me what the other things are!'

No sticky fingers on the dashboard. The car was tidy, neat, uncluttered – no kids, thought Mann.

'Actually, Al has a relative in Hong Kong.'

Mann looked at her and grinned.

'You're going to ask me if I know him, right?'

She gave that deep chuckle again; she still had a lot of the child left in her, thought Mann.

'Maybe. And you?'

'Marriage, you mean? Never felt the need. No kids. No commitment. Better that way.' Mann closed his eyes for a few seconds and leaned his head back onto the headrest.

Becky put a CD on – a homemade compilation that was a strange mix of dance hits and soul – reggae and Leonard Cohen.

Helen came into Mann's head. The film of her being

tortured, the sound of her screams. His eyes snapped open.

'Eclectic tastes,' he said, nodding in the direction of the sound system.

'Not mine – my husband Alex's – he loves Leonard Cohen. I don't – so miserable. The dance tracks are mine. We are ... very different. God knows how we ended up together. Chalk and cheese.' Her laugh disappeared into the air, 'So, no wife hidden away? No long-term girlfriend?' She nodded her head knowingly. 'A bit of a Jack the lad – obviously.' She flashed him a mischievous look.

'I prefer to keep my options open, let's put it that way. But I have a few ground rules.'

She raised an eyebrow. 'Tell me ...'

'No little girls lost. No newly divorced and still bitter. And absolutely *no* married women.' He grinned at her.

She smiled, despite trying not to, and blushed again.

'Like I said! Jack the lad.' She hummed along to Shakira.

They turned through the impressive school gates and followed a narrow winding road that was signposted to the main building and the visitors' car park. Ahead of them was a once-magnificent estate, now a very prestigious school.

'Great place,' said Mann.

'It's a former stately home, parts of it dating back to the sixteenth century. It stands in a hundred acres.'

'Let's just drive around first. Are there any other exits by car?'

'No. All traffic comes in one way and goes out the

same way. Behind the school are the playing fields. You can only exit there on foot.'

'Let's see how many other car park options there are.'

They drove past the visitors' allotted spaces and through a narrow section that opened out to a small lawn area and two large boarding houses. It was rush hour – eight-thirty lessons were about to start and there was the inevitable panic to make it to class on time. They waited whilst the last of the children dropped books, tucked shirts in and scrambled past on their way to lessons. Past the houses, at the end of the road on the right, was a larger overflow car park for teachers and match days. They turned the car round and headed back to the visitors' area at the side of the main entrance, parked and sat. A sudden stillness had descended on the place as the frantic rush to lessons on time was over. There was not a child to be seen. A teacher, dressed in a tracksuit with a whistle around his neck, passed and smiled in at them. Becky smiled back and whispered under her breath.

'Like I said, this place isn't exactly a fortress. Nobody has asked us who we are or what we're doing here.'

'It would have been really easy for him to check this place out first. All he needed to do was come at rush hour, like we have.' They watched the sports teacher disappear up a few steps and into a side entrance. 'There's not even any need to use the main entrance. All the action seems to come and go from over there.' He gestured towards the disappearing teacher. 'You ready? Let's go.'

They left the car and walked around to the front of the building, up the impressive sweep of granite steps and through a carved arched doorway. Then they followed the signs to reception. A charming receptionist – beautifully spoken, impeccably polite – asked them to sit whilst she went to find the headmaster's secretary. Two minutes later both women reappeared and the detectives were led to the headmaster's suite to wait. They skimmed through the usual literature about the school, the current glossy magazine full of sixth-formers' excursions to South America and poems by a six-year-old genius.

'Anything of Amy Tang's in here?' asked Becky.

The room was filled with the sound of the secretary's rustling skirt as she came bustling around from behind her desk. 'I'm not actually sure. Let me see. Amy is a fourth-former and I know she loves art.' She flicked through the magazine till she reached the photos of the art exhibition. She scanned the page. 'No. She doesn't appear to have any work in this issue. But I know she helped with these.' She went over to a tabletop covered in various items: raffia bags, string baskets, and macramé jewellery. 'The children learned how to make these wonderful things from a Fair Trade organisation that came over from the Philippines. They were here a few months ago. I know that Amy attended every class and produced some lovely pieces. She is such a nice little girl, quiet, thoughtful, *resilient*. The whole school is in shock. We just can't believe . . .'

The door opened and the headmaster floated in, his

black gown billowing out around him. He introduced himself as Mr Roberts.

Shit! thought Mann. *He's about the same age as me! Headmasters are supposed to be old and crusty. When did this happen?*

They all went into his study. Mr Roberts closed the doors behind him and asked them to sit. They declined his offer. The headmaster went to stand by the fire-place. It was obviously his favourite posing place. Behind him there were numerous photos of him shaking hands and smiling with famous speakers who had come to impart their wisdom to the pupils. He didn't look like such a happy man today, though.

'Thank you for seeing us, Mr Roberts. My name is Inspector Mann of the Hong Kong Police. I am here to assist the Metropolitan Police in the investigation into Amy Tang's disappearance. Could you tell me what kind of checking procedure is in place for exeat requests and who is responsible for making sure the request is genuine? I appreciate you have told others but I would like to hear it from you.'

'I am happy to help, so far as I can. I will do anything to get the child back. Her loss would be disastrous for the school. Most of our income comes from overseas children. It would be catastrophic if this situation were not resolved expediently and satisfactorily.'

Becky and Mann exchanged glances. The headmaster was not making the best of impressions.

'Sometimes the child will tell us that they have been invited somewhere, then we ask for it to come in writing in some form or another – an email has become an acceptable method. If we do not know the person then the usual thing is for the housemistress or master to contact them to ensure that they are prepared to take full responsibility for the wellbeing of that child whilst they are off school grounds. If we are satisfied that all is in order we authorise.'

'The child is collected from where? This office?'

'No, not generally. Ordinarily, the child has been invited to go with another pupil and is simply picked up at the same time. It's always on a Saturday after the matches and match teas are done. The children tend to gather in the various common rooms. Those that have an exeat get picked up from there.'

'And in Amy's case?'

'The request came in email form. I have it here.' He handed it to Mann. 'I believe she received a text telling her to meet her host at the side entrance that leads to the car park.'

'And in between those two things? Who phoned and checked this person out?'

'I am afraid it wasn't done. The housemistress forgot to do it. She has been having some personal problems recently and . . .'

'So none of your staff got a look at the person?'

'No. I'm afraid not. Can I just say that we have never encountered a problem of this type before. We would expect to be confident that the child was going home with someone they knew. Amy is twelve. We expect the child to be quite responsible by that age.'

Mann was not warming to Mr Roberts.

'What would have been going on at the school at that time?'

'It was Saturday afternoon so all the pupils would have finished morning lessons. They would have been either at sports matches – playing games against other schools – or unwinding in common rooms.'

'Do you have a photo of Amy?'

'Yes.' Headmaster Roberts went to his desk, dug into a file, and produced one standard Christmas shot for the child to take home to the parents in the holidays. He also had one of her and the other four members of the school chess club. The third picture was of Amy holding a picture she had drawn. It had *runner up* written beneath it. She was short and square – a plain child with glasses and a mouth full of braces.

'So, what kind of child would you say Amy is? Would she go with someone she didn't know? Someone she didn't feel comfortable with?' asked Becky.

Mr Roberts screwed up his face 'It's always possible. She wasn't so much of a loner, but she is self-contained – she is happy to go along with things. She is used to a system. She doesn't often step outside that. She's been boarding here since she was six. It was the first time she had ever had an exeat in all those years.'

They left the headmaster's study and turned to walk down the long, straight, flagstone corridor that led through the two sets of fire doors to the side entrance and the visitors' car park.

'So this is where the girls saw her?' asked Mann as they stopped just inside the side exit. 'Strange that none of them got a good look at him. Did they say if he was English? Chinese? Did he have a beard? Was he bald?'

'I'm afraid they didn't take much notice. They were on their way to tea after a hard-fought netball match. They were hungry.'

'Not the kind of child that stuck out then?' Becky asked.

'I suppose not, but she is a contented child – solid. She has her friends in the chess club. She is never alone for long.'

They moved outside to the top of the steps.

'One last thing.' Mann turned to Mr Roberts before leaving. 'Have you heard of CK Leung?'

Mr Roberts shook his head. 'We always dealt with Amy's mother.'

'Thought so . . . You'd have taken better care of his daughter if you had.'

17

They spent the afternoon at the office in south London. The building had been constructed in the sixties and hadn't been refurbished properly since then. It was seriously jaded: polystyrene ceiling tiles on the linoleum flooring. It was a warren of small offices and long corridors.

Becky worked in a unit of ten. Her usual partner was Sergeant Jimmy Vance. He looked like a seventies cop: his hair was dangerously close to being a mullet, short on the top, long on the sides, and he wore brown slacks and a paisley shirt. There were sixty others in the SOCO department, most of whom were working on the kidnapping.

Superintendent Proctor called Mann into his office to welcome him and have a one-to-one. Proctor was a tall, long-legged man with a head of short-cropped wavy silver hair. He thanked Mann for coming and asked him to pull up a chair.

'Sorry about the state of this place. We are waiting to be relocated to a purpose-built office a few miles away.' He had a straight-talking Yorkshire accent. 'We have assigned DC Becky Stamp to be your partner whilst you are here because we feel she has the insight into the case you are looking for. She was instrumental in finding out about the other kidnaps, befriending and liaising with the Chinese parents in those cases, and we are fortunate she managed to get the information she did – as you know, the Chinese community often chooses to keep itself to itself.'

'I'm sure we will work well together. She seems very competent, thank you.'

'We will be happy to cooperate with any line of inquiry you wish to pursue. Our sole aim is to get this girl back. We have allotted you an office, but basically we will meet here every morning and keep in touch by phone throughout the day. I don't expect you to be here more than you have to, but I do expect to be kept informed night and day. I hear that you are a man who likes to do things his own way – I have no problem with that, so long as you run things past me first.'

Mann thanked Proctor for his support whilst thinking, *Don't hold your breath. I'll phone when I want something – till then, don't expect to see me.*

Jimmy Vance was waiting for Mann in the corridor outside. He pulled him to one side and grinned at Mann.

'Watch her – she doesn't take prisoners.'

'Thanks for the advice.'

'Another thing . . .' He leaned in to say what he had really come to say – the reason why he was waiting for Mann in the corridor. The smile disappeared. '. . . her husband, Alex, watch him. Becky knows how I feel about him – he's a nasty bastard. He was done for GBH when he was young. Beat the other guy with an iron rod and almost killed him and it wasn't for lack of trying, if you know what I mean. I wouldn't put it past him to knock her about. She's like so many strong women. She's tough at work and soft at home . . .

Jimmy was all set to open the floodgates of information when Becky came looking for her new partner.

'Not telling tales on me, are you, Jimmy?'

He held his hands up in a 'Who me?' gesture and grinned.

'I wouldn't know where to start.' Jimmy stood and watched them leave.

'He's a nice guy,' said Becky. 'I am really fond of him but he doesn't have a family, just a dog, and he has adopted me to worry about.' She gave Mann a side-long glance that said she could guess what Vance had said. 'He really doesn't like my husband.'

'Really? He never said.' Mann shook his head. They headed out towards the car park. By the time Mann got back to his accommodation at six he felt the jetlag hit. It was a beautiful Georgian terrace at the top of Highbury Fields. He thanked Becky for the lift and got out of the car.

'See you for dinner at eight.'

'Thanks. I'll be there.'

He left her and went inside. She had done a good job choosing the accommodation for him. He met the landlady, exchanged pleasantries and went to his room. It was spacious, crisp, cool, and genteel; it overlooked the front of the house and the top of Highbury Fields.

There was a double bed – clean, starchy sheets, duck-down duvet. There was a small lounge area, two chairs and a coffee table. It had Earl Grey tea in the complementary tea service. There were real plants in the large en suite bathroom and a stack of towels on a rail in the corner.

Mann felt a tinge of nostalgia as he stood by the sash windows and looked out of the windows down onto Highbury Fields below. It was a picture-postcard of London in spring: new pea-green grass was sprouting at the base of trees in full bud. A steady stream of commuters were walking home and women were pushing buggies, with toddlers running alongside; a smoker sat on a bench enjoying the last of the spring light. He lay on his bed and stared up at the ceiling. He thought about Georgina. She had been on his mind ever since he landed on UK soil. She wasn't far away. He could get on a train, go down to Devon and see her. He wondered if she was still on the same number. He got out his phone and scrolled through the list. There she was – just seeing her name made him feel strange. He hadn't gone to dial her number for three months. His finger hovered over the call button but then he snapped the phone shut – now was not the time.

Mann unpacked and laid everything out on the bed. He had brought two suits with him – three white and two blue shirts, four white and four black T-shirts and a pair of jeans. He had also brought a light cashmere overcoat. Mann chose his clothes carefully. He chose his weapons the same way – handmade, bespoke.

He took them out of their leather pouches and laid them on the bed.

Mann had been collecting and customising triad weapons for fifteen years, ever since he had had his cheek sliced by one. It was a shuriken – an adaptation of a throwing star – and it had spun across his face, cutting a crescent-moon-shaped groove where the skin stretched tightest across his left cheekbone. The scar had done him no harm. The shuriken that had caused it fascinated him. Shuriken meant 'hidden in the hand' and was a collective term for sharp things that could be thrown: knives, spikes and throwing stars. Now Mann had added a few variations of his own. He preferred them to a gun: they were silent, just as deadly, but also served to maim rather than kill if chosen and they were objects of beauty and precise engineering. They could arc in the air, spin and curve around and over a building. They could kill an enemy even though he could not be seen. Each blade had its speciality. Each type was of a different weight, different thickness and needed different handling.

He unwrapped five double-ended throwing spikes, six inches long, five millimetres thick, from their cloth rolls, and strapped them onto a holster around his arm. They were for pinning down an opponent, disabling him, not necessarily killing him. Next he chose a set of medium-sized stars, each one a slightly different shape but all of the same weight so that he could stack them in his left hand and pass quickly to his right to throw them in quick succession or sometimes all eight at once.

Each of Mann's weapon sets had a pouch all of their own, but one weapon had a pouch all to itself. The Death Star – DS – was six inches in diameter, heavier than any other throwing star. Reinforced with steel rivets, its four points were curved and along its razor-sharp lengths were small teeth. It was a deadly thing of beauty that could cut through muscle and splinter bone. It was a perfect decapitating tool.

But Mann's favourite was a multipurpose shuriken: simple to look at, a thin nine-inch dagger, tassel-ended for fast retrieval and for continuous hits. It could be thrown or used for close combat. Its name was Delilah. He kept Delilah separate from the others in a discreet holster that he could tie around his wrist so that the blade was hidden inside his shirt, or around his calf so that it was hidden in his boot. Today he tucked Delilah into his boot.

Mann picked up his phone and looked up a number. It took a few seconds to get through.

'What's the matter with you? Thought you would have got yourself a Labrador and trained it to bring you your slippers by now.'

'Very bloody funny,' David White answered.

'You okay?'

'I tell you, Johnny, I'm not ready for this retirement game. It's too cold here. Can't see me staying in England for long. Maybe I'll head to Spain and start a new life dating widows.'

'I'm sorry it ended up like this, David, I'm sorry for my part in it.'

Mann had known White all his life. He had been a

friend of Mann's father, and when his father was murdered White took on the role of keeping an eye on Johnny.

By the time White had left the Hong Kong police force the once-big man rattled around in his uniform. The end had not been gentle; he hadn't been eased into retirement. His association with Mann, and Mann's disregard for orders, had cost him dearly, and White had jumped before he was pushed. White had disregarded orders and helped Mann to bring his kind of justice on Chan, CK's son-in-law. Everyone knew it was never going to happen otherwise. There were too many people pulling strings at the top. The only way justice was ever going to get done was Mann's way – but it wasn't popular.

'Don't be . . . We took a few heads with us. Besides, Johnny, I'd rather go out this way than just fade away. It's a pity we never got CK, but there we are – his time will come.'

'Maybe it has already. The case I've been sent over to help with . . . it involves CK. His daughter, by a girl-friend, has been kidnapped from a school in Hertfordshire. He paid the ransom but they haven't given her back. It looks less and less likely that they intend to. We don't even know whether she is still alive, or, if she is, whether she is still in the country. We are linking her abduction to the birth of a new trafficking society – a super group – bigger than the rest. Bigger than anything we've ever seen before. Stevie is involved, that's for sure, but we don't know how involved yet. It looks as if the group intends to go for immediate dominance over the others. It must have some serious money and connections. They are muscling in on all aspects of the sex industry in the Philippines, buying up every available beach resort.'

'Let me help you with the case.'

'Sure, if you want to, you can put your Internet skills to use and find out more about the new trafficking ring. Who's offering brand-new deals for sex perverts? Who's got the hottest deals on paedophile holidays? Still want the job? Will you be able to do it undercover? I don't want to read about an ex-cop up on paedophile charges.'

'I didn't help computerise the Hong Kong police force without picking up a few skills along the way. Don't worry, I can plumb the depths of the cyber-sex world without leaving my signature. I'll start straight away.'

Mann had been given directions to Becky's – it was a ten-minute walk at most. He left thirty minutes early, shutting the door behind him and cutting across the top of the fields. He was hit by the smell of energised air – the world was warming up: the tarmac, the trees, all collectors of that first heat of spring. He stopped just past the smoker who was sitting at the same spot that Mann had seen him twenty minutes earlier. He was a slight Chinese man in a grey polo shirt and jeans. His hair was cut short at the sides, left long and gelled on the top. He sat with his elbows on his knees, deep in thought as he dragged on a cigarette through a cupped hand.

'You must be Micky?'

The man looked up, surreptitiously checking out the space around Mann. When he was satisfied that it was as it should be, he nodded.

'You wanted to see me?'

Mann sat next to him.

'Yeah, I need some information. I need to know who has the balls to take on CK here.'

Micky tilted his head, looked sideways up at Mann and grinned.

'You tell me.' He shook his head and drew the cigarette from a cupped hand. 'Manufactured – new society – come from nowhere. Came out of fuckin' thin air! All Chinatown is asking the same question.' He shook his head again incredulously. 'How did someone get that big that quick?'

'Maybe several of the big guns have got together to mount a challenge.'

Micky grunted his agreement. 'Yeah, you'd expect it to come from existing triad societies.' He flicked his cigarette into the bushes.

'What's the talk?'

Micky shrugged and shook his head. 'It's nobody from the 14K or the Flying Dragons. It's not a recognisable style. Kidnapping such high-profile kids takes organisation – know-how. There has to be somebody home-grown helping with this. Stevie Ho was here. You been tracking him? He's always in the thick of it.'

Mann nodded. 'I followed him to the Philippines. He's expanding trafficking routes, setting up new bases. Seems that Stevie wants more than his fair share of the Asian run. He has some muscle behind him. He was in Boracay at the same time as three white guys. The Colonel was amongst them.'

'Would they take on CK? They're not triads, they're traffickers. Would Stevie cross CK?' Micky shook his head. He wasn't buying it.

'Maybe Stevie changed allegiance?'

'He was in the Wo Shing Shing all his life. His life will be over if he double-crosses CK.'

'Or unless CK has given him permission to ally with another society. Maybe CK is playing yet another game. Keep in touch, Micky.' Mann got up to leave.

'Another thing, Mann, before you go, the talk is that you are in CK's pay. They say that you helped him dispose of his troublesome son-in-law.'

'What do you say, Micky?'

Micky sat back, looked up at Mann and grinned.

'I know your reputation – the triad annihilator. But everyone has their price.'

'Maybe, Micky, but mine isn't money.'

18

Mann walked on around the top of the Fields to the end of a parade of shops and took a left. Halfway along the road he stopped at number twenty-five – a Victorian terrace. Becky Stamp greeted him at the door dressed in jeans and T-shirt.

'Is that for my benefit?' He gestured towards the T-shirt, which had a picture of Bruce Lee on the front. She looked particularly sexy and sassy tonight, thought Mann.

'Of course.' She grinned. 'Do you only wear white shirts?' she asked, ushering him inside and closing the door behind him.

'Not always – saves me thinking too hard, though. Anyway, it shows off my tan and my great physique.' He grinned.

She chuckled. 'You're a bit vain, you know that, Mann?'

She led him through the narrow hall past a neighbour's open door and the thumping sounds of techno, and up the two small flights of stairs into her flat. They passed a kitchen on the left and continued into the lounge straight ahead. She opened a bottle of wine and poured them both a glass.

'Just make yourself comfortable. I need to check the food.'

She excused herself for two minutes whilst Mann looked around the lounge. It was small but nicely decorated with a mix of modern and antique. On the walls were two very different paintings. One was an Andy Warhol poster. The other was a black and white photo of a couple saying goodbye at a train station. She liked her knick-knacks, thought Mann. There were two alcoves filled with a mix of souvenirs from around the globe: a carved black rhino, an African Maasai warrior, a collection of Russian Matryoshka dolls and a family of wooden wild boars in varying sizes, lined up along the shelf.

There were other photos, landscape shots of deserts and rainforest all in ornate silver frames. There was one of a younger fresh-faced Becky with flowers tucked into her shoulder-length hair, smiling out of a wedding photo. The man beside her was blond, good-looking. They made a handsome couple.

'You've travelled a lot then?' Mann said as Becky returned. He held the black rhino in his hand.

'I did before I was married. Then Alex and I went around India, safari in Kenya, that kind of thing. We haven't been anywhere much for a few years. Alex takes off on business trips. That seems to be enough for him. I keep meaning to plan a trip, but I've got a bit bogged down with work. You know what it's like? It's hard to book something in advance when you don't know what case is about to come up. I think about it a lot. That rhino you're holding is from Zimbabwe. We had our honeymoon there.' She looked sad, thought Mann, as he watched her move the smallest of the wild boars next to the largest. She looked around the shelves of souvenirs. 'I watch all those travel programmes – have a real wanderlust, just never seem to get anywhere any more. I have to go and finish the food. You can pick some music for us if you like, then come in and chat with me.'

Mann took his time choosing the Eagles' greatest hits before following her into the kitchen. She was busy peeling onions on a smart granite worktop. It was a well-designed kitchen, all wood, stone and chrome. It had a breakfast bar to the left of the entrance and a huge American fridge. Becky was stood in front of a window that looked out towards a distant block of flats and down to a row of walled gardens below. Mann sat on a stool and watched her.

'Can I help?'

'I don't know. What are you good at?'

'Grinding, chopping, opening bottles, multi-talented really.'

'Are you going to get your famous knife belt out?'

He laughed. 'So you have done your homework on me, after all?'

'I found out a few things.' She gave him a small smile.

'I usually save the knife belt for when I've exhausted all my other pick-up moves.'

'Well then, just sit and talk. You must be shattered.'

'I'm all right. Been thinking about that school. You know what struck me today? Something that secretary said. She used the word *resilient* to describe Amy. Odd choice of words, don't you think? What about her friends? Did you talk to any of the children in her dorm?'

'She shared with one other girl. There are two to a room. The days of long, windswept dormitories are over, apparently. These days they have a max of two and even an en suite bathroom. I talked to her room-mate. She was a jumpy little thing. She was also Chinese, new to the school. The teachers said she'd been put in with Amy to settle her in.'

Becky left the onions caramelising and came over to join him and refresh his glass.

'Do you think we'll find her alive, Mann?'

'I don't know. So far, someone has CK's money and his daughter – they are giving him the finger whilst issuing a challenge. This is much more than a kidnap. I think we are being used; we are pawns in a game and we are not being told the rules. If we follow the path they expect us to – normal lines of inquiries, etc. – then we haven't got a hope in hell. I saw Micky.' Becky stopped mid swig of her wine. 'On the way over here, he was waiting for me.'

'What did he say?'

'Chinatown's jumpy. No one knows who the new muscle is, but the implication is that CK has pissed people off or that there is a new domination war about to kick off. Either way, it spells trouble.'

'He's a big guy, CK?'

'As big as you get.'

'But he's a triad, that's illegal. How does he get away with it? Why isn't he arrested?'

'He has friends in high places. He's the head of numerous respectable, legit businesses. He launders money through film production, taxi firms, nightclubs, to name a few. Some of his ventures even have government backing.' Becky's eyes widened. 'Yeah, I know, and to top it all off he's suspected of being the biggest trafficker of people from Asia into the UK and Europe.'

'The flesh trade is replacing all the others. It's overtaken drugs, guns or money laundering, hasn't it?'

'Yes, it has. Human trafficking is big business and getting bigger ever day. Girls abducted on their way to school or sold by their mothers for the price of a new TV. Women chained to their beds, forced to work twenty-four hours a day. It's becoming an everyday occurrence all over the world.'

Becky shuddered. 'I know. We've even had it in tiny villages here. They are finding under-eighteen-year-old girls who have been conned and lied to and ended up as sex slaves. Mainly from the Eastern Bloc. I talked to one woman who had been rescued. She was a respectable woman, conned into going across the border to fetch some merchandise to sell on a neighbour's market stall, just to have the neighbour sell *her* when she got across the border.'

'Life is way too cheap, that's for sure. If we don't watch it, we will all become as mercenary as the Chinese, and that would be a big mistake . . .'

He looked at her, watched her reaction. At first she

didn't know whether to smile, but then she did. At the sound of a key in the door, the smile froze. She stopped mid-stir, hovering wooden spoon in hand, her eyes opened wide, puzzled for a second at the sound of the front door closing followed by a man's footsteps on the stairs.

'Hi darling – we're in here,' she called out, recovering quickly. Mann watched her reaction with interest and wondered what it meant. 'My husband, Alex,' she said, by way of explanation. 'Didn't think he would make it – that's nice . . .' she continued, as she gave Mann a fleeting smile before concentrating on her stirring again. Mann could see that she was ruffled.

Alex Stamp appeared at the kitchen door.

'Thought I'd come and get a look at my wife's new partner. Hello, I'm Alex.' He shook Mann's hand with a strong grip and honed in with frosty blue eyes that stayed on their subject a little too long. Mann grinned. He was used to people trying to read him – it was a good game but there would only be one winner.

First impressions: Alex Stamp was a monitor lizard. He was a well-turned-out one, though – an expensive dresser – but he was a little too bulky for the designer look. He obviously liked his weights more than his aerobic machines at the gym.

He went over to Becky and kissed her cheek. 'Hello, baby. Managed to cut the trip short . . . had one hell of a week . . . tell you about it later. Business meetings . . .' He rolled his eyes Mann's way. 'You know how it is? Work always gets in the way of fun. Even worse in the police force. I should know. Never marry a copper, hey, Mann? Anyway, what are you doing in the kitchen? Come into the lounge and relax. Becky will call us when it's ready. Won't you, baby?' He kissed her cheek again.

'Yes, sure.' She glanced uneasily at Mann, who couldn't resist a raised eyebrow and grinned.

Alex picked up the bottle of wine and carried it, along with a glass for himself, into the lounge. 'Crap,' he muttered as he switched the music off. 'Becky says you're here working on a case involving triads. Is that right?' Mann sat on the two-seater black leather sofa. Alex gave a derisory snort. 'I can't believe we have trouble from triads here in London. We are a million miles away from Beijing, for Christ's sake.'

'Wherever there are Chinese businesses there are triads extorting money from them, I'm afraid.'

'Becky tells me you are half-Chinese yourself. How interesting. What side?'

Mann got the feeling that Alex was only asking questions to give himself the opportunity to study his prey. Not so much a monitor lizard as a Velociraptor, thought Mann, testing out his victim's weaknesses.

'My father's.'

'And this triad-related case originates in Hong Kong – is that right?'

'In a roundabout way.'

Alex laughed. 'Don't worry, Becky doesn't talk in her sleep. Isn't that right, darling?' he said, as Becky appeared in the doorway, new bottle in hand.

'What's right?'

'I said you tell me *all* your police business, don't you, baby.'

Mann saw a flash of anger cross her face. She held Alex with an icy stare.

'I'm surprised you remember me telling you anything about Mann coming. You don't usually listen to anything I say.' She smiled, thin-lipped. It was a challenge rather than a smile, and she fixed her husband with a disapproving look before she filled Mann's glass and came to sit opposite him on a seventies retro armchair that matched the sofa.

'Mann went to school here, didn't you?'

'Yes, I did.' Mann was starting to feel uneasy. He felt like there was a domestic about to kick off and he was going to get caught in the middle of it.

Alex drank his wine so fast that his second glass had already disappeared. His nose was bothering him. He touched it constantly and sniffed in between.

'You have a cold, Alex? That's a bummer in spring – or is it hay fever?'

'What? Sorry?'

'The runny nose – hay fever or a cold?'

Alex shook his head and shrugged. 'An allergy to something, I expect – dust, probably. We need to get a live-in cleaner – don't we, darling?'

'Would anyone like hummus?' Becky jumped up and disappeared into the kitchen. Mann wondered if she was an exploder or an imploder. He suspected that it took a lot to make her lose her cool in public.

'Tell me? Are you all Kung Fu experts?' Alex said, pouring himself another glass and raising his glass to Mann as if it were a challenge.

'My colleague is.'

'Ahhh . . . of course . . . a young man's sport.' Alex grinned.

'Maybe, but I find knives much more interesting.'

Becky returned with a plate of pita and hummus.

'Mann is being modest. He's a firearms and martial arts expert and something called Eskrima.' She looked at him. 'I read it on your stats. Have you ever heard of Eskrima, Alex?' He shook his head and had a look on his face like he was waiting for the punch line. 'It's a form of Filipino street fighting. Is that right, Mann? Mainly defensive?'

'The opposite, actually. Attack first, is the Eskrima motto. Kill before you are killed. It uses knives, mainly. It's all about staying alive on the street.'

'More knives . . .' said Alex. 'Your speciality . . .'

Mann sat back on the sofa and grinned at Alex.

'We all have to have one, don't we? What's yours, Alex?'

'Ha ha . . . that's for me to know and you to find out. I am a model husband, of course, isn't that right, darling?'

'Dinner is ready.' Becky stood, flashed him an over-sweet smile and strode off to the kitchen.

Mann left soon after he'd eaten. He walked back through the Fields. A group of boys were testing each other's skateboarding skills on a makeshift ramp. The tennis courts were lit and in full use. Apart from giggling girls watching bravado boys and the sound of the tennis balls being thwacked, everything else was quiet; the commuters were safely back at home enjoying a glass of wine and waiting for *EastEnders* to start. He could imagine it would be noisy back at the Stamps' house. There would probably be an almighty row going by now. He also wondered why he disliked Alex so much. His attitude was confrontational. He was not a man to reason with. He was brittle, volatile. He was also a cocaine addict. He didn't even realise he sniffed constantly. He had obviously come back home just to check Mann out. He didn't trust his wife, though clearly he could. He didn't trust her because he was playing away himself, thought Mann.

His phone rang just as he reached the door of the B&B. It was Ng.

'You're up early, practising your Tai Chi?' said Mann.

'Just about to start. No, busy night – we have trouble here. Wo Shing Shing officers have rounded up at least eight high-ranking members of three other societies. It seems CK is targeting anyone he thinks may have any affiliation to the White Circle. We haven't seen the bodies yet, but we will.'

'Stevie involved?'

'That's another thing – as soon as the trouble hit, Steve left town. He's back to the UK.'

'Okay. I'll catch up with him as soon as I can.'

'How's it going there? Is it raining?'

'No . . . it's not raining here, and before you ask, a pea-souper is rare these days . . . You should stop watching all those old black and white movies. I just met my partner's husband.'

'Nice guy?'

'Slimy bastard . . .'

'She must be good-looking, huh . . . ?'

Mann said his goodbyes and went up to his room. The weight of the cool white cotton sheets made him suddenly too exhausted to think of anything else but sleep, and he slept his first night in the UK for seventeen years.

It was cut short – at five o'clock his phone rang.

'Sorry to wake you.' It was Becky. 'There's been a fire. Twelve people dead . . . all chained to their beds.'

19

Mann and Becky parked up opposite the Victorian villa
– a three-storey redbrick detached house. It had been
built at a time when the area was semi-rural; now it
was Bedsit Land and Student Ville. It had long since
lost its front garden to tarmac and extra parking spaces
and its back garden to a small courtyard and another
house.

A small crowd of onlookers was gathered around
the edge of the crime-scene tape. Mann and Becky
crossed the line and showed their badges to the PC on
the perimeter.

They were greeted by the fire detective in charge, an
Inspector Ray. They stood in the burnt-out doorway.
The door had been kicked in by the firemen.

'Deliberate.' It was Ray's job to ascertain the cause
of the fire and to make sure it was a safe environment
to hand over to the police and forensics team, whilst
trying not to swamp the place with water and thereby
destroy evidence. 'There are two heat seats, one here
and one at the back door.' He turned and pointed
behind him, past the stairwell and along a corridor.

'We found the incendiary devices. They're crude but effective . . .' He picked up the glass bottle that had been used. 'They went off simultaneously at approximately four a.m. this morning. Unfortunately the local fire station had a series of hoax calls that evening and they didn't get here for twenty minutes. By that time the place was well alight.'

Mann and Becky stood just inside the entrance. To the right and left were rooms. Beyond was the hallway leading through to the kitchen. Straight ahead was a blackened stairwell that had obviously taken the brunt of the fire.

'The stairway effectively acts as a chimney. The heat was so intense that even the plaster wall has started to give way. I'm afraid the women at the top of the stairs had no chance.'

They stepped carefully over the debris and stood in pools of black water and sludge, looking up at the charred remains of the stairwell. Parts of the ceiling hung down, wires swung open-ended, and swathes of wallpaper peeled from the walls like strips of scalded skin.

Jimmy Vance appeared from round the back of the house. Ray excused himself and left Vance to take over.

'The woman who dialled the emergency services was told that the place was empty by a black guy running from the house when the fire caught hold.'

'How did he get out?' asked Becky,

'There was a window open in one of the ground-floor rooms at the back.'

'So he saved himself and left the women to fry – nice bloke.'

'Did she get a look at him?' asked Mann.

'She said he was over six foot, thirty-ish, American or Canadian accent. She hadn't seen him before. She was outside looking for her lost cat when the devices went off. She said he ran past and to go back inside and that it was about to blow up.'

'I suppose he couldn't risk her hearing the women cry for help,' Becky said.

'She wouldn't have heard them anyway . . .' Vance had a face that looked like it surprised itself when a thought struck him. '. . . the place was double-glazed.'

'Did she know anything about who owned the place?' asked Mann.

'She said it had changed hands six months ago. She hadn't been able to work out who the owners were – she saw men coming and going at strange times of the day and night. The only people she saw regularly were two Chinese guys and a smartly dressed Chinese woman.'

'Was it the first time she had seen the black guy?'

'She said she'd seen him and another big white guy a couple of times in the last few days.'

Vance led them up the stairs. 'There were four bedrooms on each landing, two to the right, two to the left, and a bathroom straight ahead. Watch where you're standing and don't touch anything, it will probably give way. The firemen had no idea that there was anyone in here until . . . they reached here and found this . . .'

They stopped on the top landing. Vance stood back to allow them to peer inside. The biting chemical smell from burnt paint and melted nylon carpet had a new undertone – the smell of roasted flesh.

'Jesus Christ!' Becky reeled and instinctively turned away.

'It's not a pretty sight. No way out . . . horrible death. Each of the victims is chained to their bed,' said Vance.

The women's knees were drawn into their bodies; their arms were held up in front of their faces. Their jaws were wide open and their teeth glared in the black of incinerated flesh. 'The other room is just the same. Each of the rooms has six victims. Both rooms overlook the front, the others looks over the courtyard at the back, but they were both barred and shuttered.'

'What's in them?' Mann pointed towards the other rooms on the landing.

'I'll show you.' Vance pushed one of the doors open. Inside the blackened room, wallpaper hung down from the walls. To the right was an open-plan en ensuite bathroom. Soot and debris covered every surface. At their feet were large shards of broken mirrored glass.

'These rooms are both bedrooms and so are nearly all the other rooms in the house. There's a safe downstairs: personal belongings, travel documents inside, still intact. I'll show you.'

They went back down the stairs and walked along the burnt-out corridor to a small kitchen at the back of the house.

'No hob, no oven, just a microwave,' said Becky. 'Doesn't look like their guests stayed to dinner.'

One of the SOCO team was examining the contents

of a tabletop safe. It had survived the fire intact, only its red-paint finish was bubbled and peeled. Vance passed Becky and Mann some latex gloves.

'You'll need those. Some of it has fused due to the heat.' Vance began to carefully open the pages of a passport. 'But we will get the experts to unravel it. So far, we have twelve passports and twelve corpses. He held up a passport for them to see. This girl, recently issued passport – three months ago – says she's eighteen.'

'Yeah, going on twelve.' Mann studied the photo. 'She's a Filipina.'

'Here's a travel itinerary for them.' Vance passed a piece of paper to him.

Mann took it and studied it. 'Says they came in via Hong Kong: originally on a tourist visa; been here for two weeks.'

'Is this the first fire of this kind you've had here?' Mann asked Becky.

'Yes, it is.'

'We know they came via Hong Kong and we know they were supplied with travel papers there. We have Chinese and non-Chinese working together at this end. I think these women were brought in by the new boys. I also think someone much further up the chain was watching and not approving. There has been some muscle-flexing here. I think we are done here,' said Mann.

Becky nodded. 'Okay, thanks, Jimmy, see you back at the office.'

'No problem. If we find anything interesting I'll ring you.'

*　*　*

110

Back in the car, Becky took her time starting the engine. They sat in silence and stared at the scene. They could see the white-suited SOCOs moving behind the bars of the bedrooms on the third floor.

'Must be the worst way to go.' Becky shivered.

Mann didn't answer. He was busy watching a Chinese man standing on the other side of the road, behind the house, staring intently at the house and talking on his phone.

Becky rested her head back against the head rest and sighed deeply. She looked across at Mann then she looked past him to see what he was staring at. The Chinese man had disappeared.

'I just don't get it, Johnny. What about the man who ran away from the scene? Who could do something like that knowing they couldn't get out? Even if he didn't set the place alight, he's just committed murder anyway.'

'He definitely didn't set the place alight. My guess is he was left here to look after the women. When the incendiaries went off he saved himself and destroyed the evidence.'

'That stinks. Evidence? Is that all these women were?'

'We both know there is no mercy in the trafficking business, Becky. It's all about money for people. The women represent a massive investment. Their earning potential was huge; they would have been sold on and around this country and all over Europe, earning money for their traffickers as they went. Someone will be left with a big hole in their pocket after this.

A trafficker is being punished right where it hurts. Losing face and losing money, two sides of the same coin. Someone's done both here. We are in the middle of a global turf war.'

20

Amy looked forward to seeing Lenny. He brought her things – some GCSE revision books, much too hard for Amy but it was kind of him. He bought her another macramé kit to make several bead necklaces and bracelets. After the visit from the Filipino people to the school, she had taught herself to make really intricate and pretty things. He also brought her some felt-tips and a drawing pad. Today he said he would bring her something to draw – fruit or something. She wasn't much good at drawing fruit. She was better at drawing people. But it was nice of him to think of her.

She lay still and looked around the room. It wasn't a nice bedroom. It had a small windowless bathroom off it with a smelly shower behind a nasty plastic curtain. It was cold in there. The curtain wrapped itself around Amy when she showered. There was little furniture, just a scruffy old raffia lamp and a chair and table for her to sit at. There wasn't even a proper bed – just a mattress on the floor. No telly. The curtains didn't fit properly. Anyway, there was nothing much to see. There was a car park below and a block of flats opposite.

So Amy just stared out of the window and counted the planes that went over day and night. Amy would be on a plane soon – going home for Easter, a whole month. She was so looking forward to it. Then she realised that it might not happen if her father didn't give the men who employed Lenny what they wanted – what they were owed, Lenny said. Then she might have to stay here a long time. Amy sighed. She had never really spent any time with her father, she didn't really know him. But the one thing she did know was that he was rich and powerful and easily irritated. All this would really bug him. She hoped he didn't get so mad he just wouldn't pay. Once, she had seen him when he got mad with her mother. They rowed about getting married and about her spending too much money. Her mother had shouted all the time but her father had said little. He was like stone. He had just said what he had wanted to then walked away and left her mother shouting. They had had no money for weeks until her mother apologised, even though she said it wasn't her fault. Her mother said she always had to apologise.

Another click of the front door, this time louder. Amy strained to listen. Heavy but precise footsteps, a strong but careful closing of the door . . . Lenny was back – Amy was pleased. She heard him talking to the Chinese woman in English. Her English was very good, thought Amy, but she had a strange accent. Amy couldn't put her finger on it. She was giggling again. Footsteps were coming towards Amy's room. The door opened.

'Morning, Amy . . . Here, I brought you these.' Lenny

came in with a bag of pastries and a mug of hot chocolate. He set down another bag on the table.

'Thank you.'

Amy smiled at Lenny and began pulling the pastries apart. He was watching her. Her eyes flicked back and forth from the pastry to his face. He reached out and patted her leg. Amy stared at the hand. She wanted to knock it off but she knew she had to leave it there.

'Can I go back to school soon? I am missing my classes and my friends.' She looked up unblinkingly at him, her eyes enlarged by the thick lenses in her glasses, her face covered in pastry crumbs.

'Soon, soon.'

'Thank you,' she said as she followed his eyes to his hand, which was still resting on her leg. 'Thank you, Lenny.'

The door opened and the Chinese woman came in. Amy hadn't seen the face behind the voice before. She had had an image of her in her head, but it wasn't quite right. She hadn't expected her to be this beautiful, like a model. She had long black hair down her back like Pocahontas, red lipstick and nails. Amy stopped eating and stared. The woman didn't look at her. She spoke to Lenny. She was definitely the woman Amy had heard talking but when she was speaking to Lenny her voice became soft. She must be Lenny's wife, thought Amy. Although she didn't have a ring on her wedding finger and he did. Maybe she'd lost it and he was getting her a new one.

'Amy, this is Suzanne. Suzanne will be looking after you for a few days. I have to go away on a business

115

trip. I won't be long. When I come back, hopefully it will be time for you to go back to school.'

Amy said nothing. She smiled but felt a sense of panic. Lenny was leaving? Who would be nice to her when he was gone? Not that one who stank or the spotty pale one, and *definitely* not Suzanne?

'Suzanne will get you everything you need. She will stay here in the flat and look after you. All right?'

Amy nodded, but said nothing. It wasn't all right at all. She felt like crying. She looked at the beautiful Chinese woman and tried a smile. Suzanne smiled back, thin-lipped. The pastry had become stuck to Amy's brace. The chocolate was all over her teeth. Amy saw Suzanne look away in disgust.

21

Hong Kong

Stevie Ho walked up from Central to the Peak terminal and waited in the tunnel entrance for the tram to come to a stop. There were only a few people waiting. It was too early for the tourists and too late for the few workers who went upwards to the Peak to work. Stevie was going because he had been summoned.

He sat at the back of the school-like wooden benches and waited for the juddering tram to crank itself into life. As it grunted its way forwards and upwards, the gravity coupled with the incline pinned Stevie back to the seat. He felt the wooden back of the bench dig into his spine. He was a big man, broad and carrying a little more weight than he used to. His back ached and he had a touch of gout – he had to lay off the drink completely. He shook his head. Thirty-five, no drink, what a fucking life! But secretly he didn't mind: the lack of booze had made him smarter, more alert, and he knew that he needed every ounce of intelligence he could muster now. His life was on the line.

The tram ascended, leaving Central behind and inching its way upwards, slicing the Mid-levels in half. Stevie looked about him, peering into peoples' windows, roof gardens, front rooms, lives, as he went. Plenty of time to stare – the journey was fifteen minutes, it gave him time to collect his thoughts. He knew what CK wanted to say and he knew why he had brought him to the Peak to say it. He wanted to make sure they were alone. He wanted to talk about the taboo subject – the day his son in law, Chan, had died. He would want to know if Stevie had been there and if Stevie could have stopped it.

The tram came to a halt and he walked around the corner and onto Lugard Road, which was more of a pathway than a road. Almost immediately he was met by the view that so many came to marvel at every day. Past the shimmering bamboo forests was a wall of skyscrapers, magnificent against the blues of sea and sky. He stood and waited and watched Hong Kong. He didn't often get time to do that and he knew the man he'd come to meet would already be watching him. He knew he'd be walking over to him at that very second. He took a last look at the glittering harbour far below, before turning to the man who had come to stand beside him, and then he inclined his head towards him in a small bow of respect.

'Good morning, CK.'

'Walk with me, Stevie.'

The two men walked along the narrow road, which was cool and dark and had the smell of damp vegetation and the sound of noisy crickets. Around another corner and the islands appeared, sunbathing in a sea of glitter below them: Lantau, Macau, Green Island and Peng Chau. CK walked slowly with a measured pace; he would not be hurried.

'Look down on these islands, Stevie. Was it on one of these islands that Chan was killed?'

'I heard it was off Cheung Chau, sir.'

'But we haven't got a body to prove it, have we?'

'No, we don't, but if he drowned I think his body will have been eaten by the sea by now.'

'Do you?' He stopped and stared hard at Stevie. 'I want to know how Chan died.'

'I did not see it, CK.'

'They say you were there. You did not protect him. You did not save him . . . They say you betrayed him.'

They walked on. Below them the junks and sampans of Aberdeen were bobbing in the water like blown-in litter collected at the coves. CK stopped and faced Stevie. Stevie was taller by a few inches and he was twice the breadth of the older man, but he had none of CK's calm or coolness. Stevie's bald head was getting hot; his forehead was shining with sweat. His small eyes looked puffy in his bloated face as they squinted in the glare. CK's face was untouched, bone-dry, unmoved by earthly feelings.

'Here is the solution I propose. I did not care for my son-in-law, he was not an asset to the Leung Corporation. He was a man with many vices and faults. But I cannot ignore your desertion of duty, your lack of loyalty. I cannot be seen to allow it – it would mean "loss of face". We will make a deal, you and I, a private arrangement. It will be just for our ears. My daughter Amy is still missing.'

Stevie bowed again. He held up his hands in an apologetic gesture.

'I delivered the ransom, CK. They want something more than money.'

'Are we sure who has her?'

'I believe she has been taken by a new society that call themselves the White Circle. I know little about them, but I do know they are making trouble for us across the globe. They are taking over some of our trafficking routes in the Philippines. They are disrupting many of our shipments.'

'I need them stopped. The abduction of my daughter will give me this opportunity. I have involved Johnny Mann. He will soon realise that in order to get my daughter back he will need to destroy the White Circle. That will leave us free to snap up the routes that become vacant as Mann destroys them. That will be your job. Follow Mann, make your deals along the way, buy up everything you can and expose the White Circle for Mann to do his work. Make him think you have changed sides. Make him believe that you are working for the White Circle. After the job is complete, Mann will not live long. There are many people in Hong Kong, many amongst our brethren, who will pay well to see him dead. You will oversee it. That will be your first duty in your new command. You will be promoted to the rank of Paper Fan, the same rank Chan held, and you will have your own team to command. You will be in charge of the trafficking throughout the Philippines into the UK and Europe.'

'What about your daughter?' Stevie studied the old man. He had worked for him all his adult life, but still CK's callous nature never ceased to amaze him. He knew what he would say.

'If I were them I would have killed her by now. I don't believe she is still alive.'

'But if Mann manages to find her?'

'We will not consider that option until we have to. Many doors will open to us by then. Many others will close to him.'

22

'I could have come to your house; you didn't need to meet me in town.' Mann had been waiting for David White in Caffe Nero on Regent Street. He got up to shake his hand.

'It's okay – I don't get out much. I welcome the chance to sample the delights of decent coffee.'

It was nine thirty in the morning. There were only a few others in the cafe. Mann sat back in the lounge seats in the window and watched as White queued for coffee. He still found it strange to see David White in civvies, but he thought his old friend looked better than he'd seen him for years. The tension had disappeared from his shoulders. He watched him banter happily with the Polish girl behind the counter. He heard him laugh; he hadn't heard him do that for a long time. White came over to join Mann with his briefcase tucked under one arm, an Americano in one hand and a biscuit in the other. He set it down on the small circular glass-topped table before sitting down opposite Mann.

'It's good to see you, David. How's it going?'

'I stand by my decision to come back. I just couldn't

afford a decent standard of living in Hong Kong on my pension, but I am finding it hard to adjust, shall we say, but happy to be working again, albeit briefly. Where's the investigation at right now?'

'You heard about the fire in Hackney?' Mann dropped two sugars into his double espresso.

'Yes, I did.' White shook his head sadly. 'What a terrible waste of life. Do you know who the victims were?'

'They were young Filipinas. It is looking likely that they were brought in by the new trafficking ring I told you about. If that is the case then it can't be a coincidence. They must have died for a reason, and it must have something to do with why Amy Tang has not been released. The two things cannot be random acts. There seems to be a lot going on in the Philippines right now. I could do with an insider. Are you still in contact with that mayor, Fredrico something? He looked like Castro and was mad about rugby and tried to get us to tour?'

'Sorry.' White shook his head. 'Lost contact years ago. Any news on the girl's whereabouts?'

'No. We've heard nothing. It's two and half weeks now since the ransom was paid by CK.'

'Do you have any more leads?'

'The man slipped in an out without leaving a trace. The school is off the M25. She could have been driven anywhere from there. She could be out of the country. I feel like I'm trying to referee a game when I don't even know the rules. I want to know who the players are and what they want and what's the best way to stop them getting it, whilst getting this child back unharmed.'

'Who's your undercover guy here?'

'He is in the Flying Dragons, name of Micky.'

'Have you met him? Is he secure?'

'I think so. How are you getting on posing as the new paedo on the block?'

'I set myself up as a likely customer. I've had to submit pornographic pictures of kids being abused, supposedly by me and my friends, in order to join. They are checking them out right now. Once they trust me I should get somewhere.'

'Jesus Christ! Where did you get the photos?' Mann pulled his chair forward so that an elderly Italian could squeeze past with his coffee and paper. Outside Regent Street's shops were opening. The shop assistants were filing in to get their skinny lattes to go.

White lowered his voice and leaned in closer as the Italian behind them shuffled his papers and grated his coffee cup on the edge of the saucer.

'I asked a favour from an old mate here who works in child protection. He gave me some amateurish ones that had been confiscated. They won't have been seen before. Then I will be able to access the cyber-sex sites that specialise in Filipino kids. As soon as I get something I'll let you know. I have made contact with a few sex tourist firms. There are just a few main players. There's a whole range of services on offer, from going from resort to resort and being part of a thirty-strong whorists' package holiday, to hiring a house on your own for a week and choosing a child from the Internet to share it with you. I'm cross-referencing phone numbers, names and sorting out who does what. I keep coming up with two men from Puerto Galera.' White opened his briefcase and pulled out two plastic sleeves with press clippings inside. He handed them to Mann. Mann could see that White was pleased with himself. He had enjoyed being back at work.

'Here we have Bob English and Harry Moyles – alias English Bob and Fat Harry. They have a company called Paradise Beach. They seem to have an interest in just about everything seedy.' He waited whilst Mann speed-read the stories on them. 'Do you know of them?'

'I remember reading about Harry Moyles a few years ago. He was a sergeant in the Royal Ulster Constabulary. He retired early, some say he jumped before he was pushed, after a few too many scandals involving bribe-taking. He cashed in his pension and bought himself a bar in Olongapo. He was caught offering underage girls for sex, but he disappeared.'

'He turned up again in Puerto Galera. He married a Filipina, which is how he has the licence to trade. In the beginning it was marketed solely to Irish perverts, now he's branching out and, with his new friend – English Bob – is wanted for child sex offences in Thailand and in the UK. I managed to trace them via a website. Paradise Beach is quite an impressive organisation. It's no small enterprise but I still think they're getting help from someone bigger, and the company definitely has Hong Kong links. It even boasts of it on the website. Could well be CK. Get Ng to work on who actually owns it all – see if we can come up with a connection to any new players. What's the score on CK?'

125

'I will find out now when I get back. He's playing games with me, that much I do know. There are too many things linking up here. It's not sitting right. There's some global networking going on. I think he intends to use this as an excuse to wage war. I can't let that happen.'

'Maybe it's time CK was taken out, Johnny? He's just one man. You chop off the dragon's head and the rest of it dies. People like Fat Harry wouldn't get far without the triad gangs to get a supply of girls for them. And a lot of those gangs are members of the Wo Shing Shing.'

Mann gave him a wry smile. 'Huh! Yeah . . . in an ideal world. If he wasn't hiding behind the cloak of respectability it might be possible. But for now I will settle for stopping him trafficking any more women and kids. One thing at a time, huh?' He smiled. 'You're getting bolshie in your old age.'

White smiled back. 'This Internet stuff is getting to me. I am surprised how much of it is done on the Internet these days. People think they can do whatever they want and remain anonymous, invisible. We could do with putting some Trojans on their PCs.'

'Trojan?'

'It's a gift horse that contains something nasty – a program that delivers a virus, infects a computer. The Trojan can perform various tasks. We need a RAT – remote access Trojan. Then we will be able to log keystrokes. The virus kicks in when certain words are spelled. You can program it to respond to a particular word, in our case "child" or "Circle", whatever. When it hears that word it will show you everything that is being written at that time. You can read people's emails, get passwords, everything. You can spy on exactly what they are doing.'

'That's impressive. Can you do it remotely?'

'Yes, as long as the receiving PC doesn't recognise it as a virus, otherwise you need to type it in to their keyboard and upload it manually. Another thing – ask your man Micky in the Flying Dragons to start asking questions about Stevie Ho, see what he comes up with. Someone in Chinatown must know what's going on.'

'I will, but I don't think this is Chinese, David. How many Chinese do you know who would be stupid enough to want the money dropped in a bin in Chinatown, no matter how elaborate the scheme? Why not just have it wired to a Chinese bank and get a few favours called in to launder it? The person who has the audacity, the stupidity, to take on CK isn't Chinese – someone wants to make this *look* Chinese.'

White sat back in his chair and finished off his biscuit. The cafe was filling up with people looking to kick-start their day. Outside on the street, the shops were lifting their shutters. White looked like he was preparing to go. He zipped up his briefcase. Then he remembered something.

'Was Ginger all right? Did you check up on your mum before you left?'

Mann grinned and gave a slow nod of the head. 'Put it like this: Ginger has adjusted very well to life without you.'

'Ha . . . that's good to hear. What about your mum? How is Molly?'

'She's loving having the cat, but I don't know how she is really. She seems in reflective mood at the moment. When I went to see her this time she wanted to talk to me about my father. I mean *really* talk, about their marriage, about him as a person. But at the last minute she clammed up, the way she always does.' Mann looked across at White, who had put his coffee cup down, and watched him as he instinctively ran the palm of his right hand across his head, smoothing the hair that had long since disappeared. Mann waited for White to make eye contact with him.

The old man's pale blue eyes stared back as he shook his head.

'It's not for me to comment on your parents' marriage. I always thought that it was strong, that it was what both of them wanted. People remember things differently as they get older.' He drank the last of his coffee and picked up his briefcase. 'Now, I must get back to work. Ha . . . that sounds good. It's great to be busy again: I'm going home to surf the cyber-sex world.'

'I'm pleased I'm not the one having to do it. The thought of infiltrating that dark world makes me sick to the stomach.'

'Yes, it's yet another sad indication of the state of the planet – money *can* buy anything.'

'But at a massive cost, David.'

They shook one another's hands as they parted outside the cafe door. The old man held on to Mann's hand, stared straight into his eyes and smiled.

'Take care of yourself, Johnny.'

Mann watched him walk away, heading home via

the tube. He looked a small figure headed towards Oxford Circus and he was soon lost in the crowd of shoppers. Mann cut through side roads then he headed up Oxford Street. He was off to pay someone a visit, but he wasn't expecting to be welcomed with open arms. As he walked along he felt the cold steel against the skin inside his wrist. He smiled to himself. There were a few things in life he could always count on – Delilah was one.

23

As he passed Tottenham Court Road tube, Mann ducked into a sex-shop doorway to answer a call from Ng.

'Yes, Ng?'

'We traced some of the women. The applications to travel were made out in Angeles. But at least two of the women came from Davao originally. I have been looking into the colonels and his colleagues in Angeles. I have come up with a few names for you: Reese Pearce, an Aussie, Terry Saunders, an American, and Brandon Smith – British. They all work for him in one way or another.'

'I need to go to the Philippines, Ng. Get Shrimp to make a new identity for me. Tell him I want to use the name John Black. I need to have a couple of small language schools, maybe one here in London and another up country. I need to be part-owner of some seedy bars, massage parlours. Tell Shrimp I need to have a legitimate but dodgy record.'

'Okay, no problem, but it would be easier for someone from London to do it?'

'He will be. I am coming back to Hong Kong. This is not where the problem originates. Leads are ending here, but nothing is beginning. Amy Tang may or may not be alive or still in the UK, but I can't help her from here. I'm going to leave the Met to continue their search for her. I need Shrimp to take over here when I'm gone. He can work directly with the team and liaise with me. Do we know who the Dragon Head of the new society is yet?'

'Not yet. Shrimp's on the case.'

Mann finished talking to Ng, opened his wallet and pulled out the piece of paper Micky had given him. He punched in the numbers and left a message on the answer phone. Five minutes later, Micky phoned back.

'You want me?'

'There was a woman, smart, young, Chinese, seen at the Lea Valley house regularly along with a couple of other Chinese guys – any ideas? Have we got a female snakehead running things?'

'There was talk a while back of a woman snakehead. Young, beautiful – I will find out what I can. It's said that someone did the fire for CK, as a show of respect.'

'Yes, I agree. He's calling in some favours and making some serious threats – if he doesn't get his daughter back soon, *everyone* will pay.'

'CK knew where to strike. Maybe he knows his enemy.'

'Or perhaps he intends to torch every brothel in the UK until he gets to the right people. Maybe he just wants blood, and figures if he spills enough of it everyone will work with him and get his daughter back.'

'Whichever way this goes, Micky, it will take a lot of calming down. If he does know who the new group is he must have someone working for him on the inside. Did you know Stevie's back?'

'Yes. He's an arrogant fuck walkin' around Chinatown like he owns it.'

'Did he talk of the new society?'

'Yes, and I have a name for you – The White Circle.'

'White? The colour of death. Yeah . . . the Circle of Death.'

'It's a strange choice.'

'Maybe.' Mann pondered.

'Mann?'

'Yeah.'

'Stevie also says you're as good as dead.'

24

'You looking for me, Stevie?'

Even from the other side of the busy Chinese restaurant in Gerrard Street, packed wall-to-wall with Chinese diners enjoying a noisy dim sum lunch, Mann spotted him easily. Stevie had gone bald from alopecia in his mid-twenties, now he had grown fat and the skin folded at the back of his neck like a pork joint waiting to be salted. He was the one bald head amongst ten smartly dressed Chinese – all polo necks, sunglasses and dark jackets. They were seated around a large round table with a rotating centre, covered in newly arrived steaming dishes. It looked like they were settling in for a long lunch.

Stevie Ho didn't need to turn around to know who it was.

'Let me guess? Detective Inspector Johnny Mann?'

Mann and Stevie knew each other from old, they had been police cadets together, competitive in their grades, and they were equal first in everything. As soon as they graduated, Stevie had been given the chance to go undercover, and he had never come out. Apart from his broad shoulders there was nothing left of the good-looking ambitious young policeman that he once was.

Stevie signalled to the waiter to bring another chair for Mann. Mann held up his hand to stop the waiter from bringing it.

'You've obviously finished your meal, Stevie, let's go.'

Mann watched as Stevie shrugged, took his napkin from his lap, folded it neatly and placed it next to his bowl. Then he started to rise . . . slowly. The man on the far left side of the table cried out in pain, clutched his right hand and squeezed his fingers tight. It took three seconds for the blood to start pouring over the white tablecloth. A small throwing star had, very efficiently, cut the man's fingers to the bone just as he was deciding whether he would be first to find his holster. The star landed noiselessly on the carpet behind him.

Mann smiled at him. 'Don't be stupid. I could easily have taken your hand off.'

There was a dive for weapons, a shuffle of chairs from nearby tables as the rest of the clientele sought to distance themselves from the disturbance. No one went for a phone. All the patrons in the restaurant were Chinese. They recognised this was triad business. They knew it wouldn't involve them as long as they didn't involve themselves in it. They averted their glances and kept on eating.

Stevie held up his hands for calm: 'I'm okay . . . sit . . . sit.' He flinched – Delilah was talking to his kidneys.

'Yes, finish your lunch, boys, and Stevie will be back in no time. Anyone follows – Stevie *will* return – but not all in one piece.'

They walked through the hushed restaurant. Every head was bowed, intent on eating. When they got outside they walked towards Covent Garden. No one noticed them – they were two more businessmen taking a stroll, weaving their way through the crowded pavement.

'What is it with you? Wherever there's trouble, there you are. You never think you might be living on borrowed time, Stevie? How many years do you think you have left? What are you doing here?'

'I am a global traveller – you know that. I'm sure you've looked into my itinerary. I go all over the world. I am a business advisor to many people. That's how I make my money.'

'You mean you are a Grass Sandal in the Wo Shing Shing. If that office had a job description it would read: collector of protection money and triad debts, liaison officer with other triad societies, and the person in charge of handling overseas business transactions for triads. So, CK sent you? You're on Wo Shing Shing business?'

They walked across the cobbles and through into Covent Garden market. The pigeons nodded to one another and there was an overpowering smell of fresh coffee corrupted with handmade soap.

'To belong to a triad organisation is illegal, we both know that. But I represent the Leung Corporation in many of its business dealings, that's true. I am here to safeguard CK's assets. I was here before to broker the deal for his daughter's release. I have a personal interest in getting her back. We are all, in our own way, working for CK, are we not? Even *you* are in his employ. The word is you're taking big pay-offs from him these days.'

'Yeah, I heard that one too. We both want things. It's just that your needs always start and end with a dollar sign. We aren't all pigs on a truffle fest, some of us have principles and I don't see a Porsche parked in my bay back at the police station. Who did you deal with when you organised the ransom?'

'I received anonymous orders – phone calls.'

'Man or woman?'

'Woman.'

'Chinese or English?'

'Chinese.'

They stopped at the edge of the plaza and watched an opera singer lay out his velvet begging bowl and switch on his CD player.

'What were you doing in the Philippines? I hear you were acquiring land, meeting up with your pimp friends – the Colonel and his mates.'

'I don't know the Colonel. The Philippines is still a great place to buy cheap property, pussy and police. Of course, I have my own interests, aside from the Leung Corporation's. I have to think of my own future now. You know me – I am ambitious.'

'I knew you once. That man is dead and gone, you're just a shell. Your new friends will betray you in the end. You mix with the scum of the earth, you can't expect to come out disease free. Do you never think of your conscience, Stevie?'

'I make my peace with my own god, Mann, each to his own.'

'Let's hope your god recognises you when you get to the pearly gates because, when your new friends finish with you and CK finds out, you're not going to look so pretty.'

He stopped and turned to face Mann.

'I swore an allegiance to Chan, not CK. That ended in the waters off Cheung Chau. You saw to that. I have agreed to help in the search for CK's child. I will do all in my power to find her. Then, I will consider my obligation to the Wo Shing Shing satisfied.'

'Does CK see it that way?'

'I can take care of myself. I know how to play the game, work the system, but you? You're pissing people off on purpose. You want to watch it, Mann, you're making yourself into a walking target. There are several people out there who will pay a great deal of money to see you dead.'

'That's the difference between us, Stevie. Being a target doesn't bother me, but kidnapping schoolchildren and burning women alive does.'

25

'Yes – keep in touch, okay, I'll tell her . . .'

Mann closed his phone and smiled as he saw Becky coming, and got up to get her a glass of wine before coming back to sit opposite her in the Highbury Barn pub. She was wearing the same dark trousers as before, with a different fitted shirt this time, same style, different colour: this one was beige, large pockets on the breasts – girl on safari look – very wholesome with a hint of adventure.

She picked up the menu, and looked at Mann over the top of it.

'I could have cooked for you again,' she said, hiding a smile. 'We didn't have to eat in a pub.' She pretended to peruse the lists of what was on offer. She glanced back up to check he was smiling and knew he was being teased.

'As cosy as it was last time, I'd hate to turn entertaining me into drudgery for you.'

She grinned, embarrassed. 'I'm sorry. It wasn't the best of evenings.'

'It was great – really . . .'

She put the menu down and looked across to the 'specials board' behind the bar. In profile her nose was cute as it turned up slightly. Her lashes looked very long – he realised she had makeup on.

'You look very nice,' he said as she turned back to him. He held her gaze and smiled.

'Thank you, I'm hoping Alex will make it back in time to spend part of the evening with me – it's our tenth anniversary.' Her smile seemed strained as it disappeared fast.

'Is he at home now? You don't have to stay with me.'

'No, I don't expect him till late and he will be eating with clients – busy man. I'm happy to be here, honestly.' She gave a slightly awkward smile.

Mann finished choosing from the menu and closed it. 'Tell me about Alex.'

'Why?'

'I'm curious, that's all. We are going to be working together. It's called "getting to know your partner", but if you'd rather not talk about it, that's fine.'

'Of course I don't mind . . . What do you want to know?'

'How you met, his background, that kind of thing? But wait a minute – I'll go and order. Have you decided?' Mann got up to go to the bar.

'Lasagne and chips . . . with salad, please.'

Becky watched Mann walk to the bar. She had looked forward to seeing Johnny again this evening. She had thought about him a lot during the day. It was funny, they hardly knew each other, but she felt a real bond with him. If she was truthful the makeup wasn't for

Alex. She knew that Mann would notice it, and that made it worth doing.

He walked back over. 'Okay, I'm all ears,' he said.

'Well . . . he was privately educated but got chucked out when he didn't make the grades. Sporty rather than bright. He went to a comprehensive after that. The thing is, he has a real competitive streak in him that came out on the sports field. Ruthless, I think they said. He was a really good footballer. Anyway, in the end he got injured in a tackle, tore all his knee ligaments and that started all the other injuries off. It scuppered his hopes of turning professional as a footballer. He left school with a few GCSEs and went straight into the workplace. He had a brief spell of working as a salesman for pool equipment. He did well at it. That's when I met him. We got married quite soon after we started living together. The thing is, he got made redundant and since then he's tried loads of things. He's the kind of man who will make a business out of anything. There, that enough? Now it's your turn.'

He grinned at her. 'I am an open book, Becky – surely you can see that?'

'Yeah, right!'

'Okay, ask away.'

Becky waited whilst the waiter brought their cutlery over and placed it on the table before she spoke.

'I have to be honest – I followed the recent Butcher case you had in Hong Kong. You were involved person-ally, weren't you? I am sorry.'

Becky watched as Mann took a few seconds to think

about whether he was going to talk about it. She could see he did not do it lightly.

'Her name was Helen Bateman. She was murdered by one of a syndicate of wealthy men who paid to have her killed in a snuff movie.'

'The report said her killer is still at large. That must be very hard to deal with?'

Mann looked at her but his eyes were glazed and his thoughts were elsewhere. Becky could see that it wasn't a nice place to be. His face had become solid and dark.

'The report is wrong. Both men are dead. The man who organised it all was both an old friend and a bitter enemy. He drowned in the waters around Hong Kong and Helen's killer died the night I recognised him.' He refocused on Becky. 'I saw the movie. I watched her die. He died of injuries very similar to those inflicted on Helen.'

Becky was shocked. His expression said it all – the stories about him were true. He did things his way. She could see he was capable of anything. He had an anger in him, a quest for justice that was un-compromising.

'You must have loved her very much. Were you together long?' she asked softly.

'Five years.' He sat back and studied Becky to see her reaction to the news that he might have had something to do with the men's death. He knew he had taken a risk. But he knew he was right to do it. She was on his wavelength. She understood. 'In my own way I did love Helen very much. But she wanted things that I couldn't give her – the whole kids and marriage thing – I didn't think it was for me. She got tired of waiting and she called my bluff. Two years ago she packed her case and got in a cab and left. The problem is – that cab ride was the last she ever took.'

Mann had to turn his head away for a few minutes. The truth still sounded strange and terrible to his ears, and the remorse never lessened.

Becky broke the silence. 'How do you deal with that, Mann? Do you keep asking yourself why?'

'No, I know why: wrong place, wrong time, right maniac. But I ask myself "what if?"'

'Can you see yourself with someone else?'

Mann looked hard at Becky. He wasn't used to so many questions about his personal life, but something made him trust her, made him want to be square with her.

'There was someone, an English woman named Georgina. She brought me back to life, briefly. I think maybe I could see myself with her, but . . .'

'But . . . ?'

'I'm not ready. Not sure if I ever will be.'

'A commitment-phobe?'

'I suppose I am. I don't ever want someone to die again, just because they know me. I would rather live alone. I am not sure I can take the responsibility of looking after someone else.'

'Is it all about responsibility for you, about protecting the people you love?'

'Maybe . . . I can't answer that.' Mann was feeling

decidedly uncomfortable by this point. The day that Mann witnessed his father's execution had changed him forever. Whatever hopes and ambitions he had once held were shattered at that moment, as a chasm appeared beneath Mann's feet where he had thought there was solid ground. Now, although Mann talked to others and lived and worked with others, inside he existed alone. He was irrevocably damaged. Helen had seen it. She had known there was nothing she could do to change it.

Becky watched him. His large soulful eyes were full of sadness. He bowed his head and twirled his glass in his hands. His black hair fell over his eyes. She knew talking about it had upset him. She knew he had told her more than he had probably wanted to, and she knew he had been completely honest. She felt a wave of affection for him – he had shared something diffi-cult and precious with her. He was much more honest than Alex, who was devious by nature. How different the two men were. She looked at Mann and thought it would be chilling to be on the wrong end of his wrath, but it would be wonderful to be loved by a man who would face death for you. She waited until he raised his head before she looked into his eyes and held his gaze.

'Sometimes you forget why you are with someone and stay for fear of being alone. You don't have that. I admire that in a way.'

They stared at one another, both aware that they had shared something personal and that now they were no longer work colleagues, they were friends. Becky smiled, a little embarrassed by the fact that they seemed to have moved physically closer during the conversation. Their hands were almost touching. To the relief of them both, the waiter arrived with their food and the closeness was broken.

Becky set about unrolling her napkin and searching for the mustard on the condiment tray.

'We are checking seat numbers on the plane and passenger lists to see who escorted the trafficked women in,' she said. Mann's hand hovered over the tray until it came to rest above the mustard. She nodded and he handed it to her. 'It will take time to work through everyone. Something else – the house was registered as belonging to a man named Brandon Smith. Guess where he lives?'

'Angeles?'

'Good guess.'

'Who is he?'

'Ex-military. Honourable discharge, served fifteen years in the marines. Came out, didn't work much in the next two years. He did a couple of short stints as a bouncer, a security guard. He moved around a lot. He has a record – assault charges in various forms, none of which got him put inside. Mainly drunken and disorderly stuff. He has been living in the Philippines for the last two years.'

'So he didn't adjust to life in Civvy Street. Not the kind of man who could afford a property after two years of squandering his pension. Someone else must

144

have put up the money and he agreed to let his name be used. Silly boy. Has he been contacted?'

'Still trying. The local police are not the most conscientious bunch.'

'The records show that some of the women have left children back home. I don't know what would willingly make them leave their families. How can it be worth it?'

'Poverty makes people do desperate things. It's become the norm for Filipinas to work in another country to support their own back home. There's a whole generation of Filipino children growing up without their mothers, who are working overseas to try and give them a better life. The children are looked after by their grandmothers, also being supported by the one overseas. But, I agree. I think, given the choice, those children would rather grow up with a mother and no money.'

'CK knows who has his daughter. He's hitting them where it hurts. Are you a fast packer?'

'What? You don't think he's been straight with us? And what do you mean fast packer?'

'He's definitely not been straight with us. I am going back to pursue it in Hong Kong. Your boss says you have to come too.'

'What?' she beamed.

'He agrees that we can do more good by chasing the source of all this. I am bringing my colleague Shrimp over to stay this end and liaise with us. He will be on the same wavelength as me, plus he's been working on this new society for some time – he knows more than anyone about them . . . Becky?'

She was already on her feet and halfway out of the pub door. He shouted after her:

'I guess I'll see you at the airport then.'

26

Becky got back to the flat in a great mood. She couldn't believe she was flying out the next day – by lunchtime she would be on the way to Hong Kong. And then she remembered she hated flying – shit! The thought of it made her stomach go weak. She was going to have to block it out of her mind till the last minute and she was going to have to have a few drinks to get to sleep tonight. But, hopefully, Alex would be in the mood . . .

She dialled his number again – it went straight to answer phone. She didn't look at the clock but she knew it was late. She knew if she glanced that way and saw what time it was that she would instantly feel tired, feel regret. She had to get up at six. She must get to the office by seven and get sorted for her trip. She took another drink and switched the music up a little louder. She looked at her reflection in the kitchen window, moving her hips slowly and sensually. She liked the way she moved in the silk slip and the way the candle-light caught the folds of the fabric. She liked the way it felt against her skin. She ran her fingers down her cleavage – *not bad* – the push-up bra had worked. It fascinated her to see that she had a sexy body. She didn't make this kind of an effort to show it off very often. Mann was right. She did look nice.

She sighed, stopped dancing, and took another gulp of her wine 'Cheers,' she said to her reflection. 'Here's to ten *fucking* years of *fucking* marriage.' She lost her balance slightly and banged her hip on the side of the worktop. *Should have stayed in the pub with Johnny.* Becky giggled drunkenly. 'Now that would have been a lot more fun,' she said out loud.

She stopped. *Bugger! What the hell was she thinking getting so pissed? Now she was even talking to herself!* She put the glass down on the kitchen worktop and went upstairs to the bathroom to study herself in the mirror. She stared hard at her face – her eye makeup was heavy, smudged, her eyes looked bloodshot and her face was ashen. She took a deep breath, sighed and turned away. *Not quite as sexy or appealing as I thought, then!*

She checked her watch: twelve twenty-five. She fumbled in the bathroom drawer and found the paracetamol, swallowed two and drank two glasses of water. She felt the pain in the top of her nose and her eyes began to water. *Not when she was pissed as well . . . why the hell did she have to cry now?* She was only crying because she was pissed. She never did it normally. She didn't dare look into the mirror. She held on to the sink and looked back through the open bathroom door down towards the kitchen. The music was still playing. *Bastard . . . why did he always do it to her?* She looked into the mirror. *So fucking stupid – stop crying – your eyes will be puffy tomorrow and everyone will know.*

A sob broke the silence. It was a horrible guttural sound. Becky hated the sound of it, What was she getting in such a state about? She didn't know why it hurt tonight more than any other. It didn't just hurt it make her fucking angry. She took a deep breath and splashed water on her face. He was working late. He was ambitious. She had known he was when she married him, she said to herself as she furiously brushed her teeth. She'd also known he didn't want kids, but she'd thought he would change his mind about that. It had begun to irritate her when he called her 'baby'. She wasn't a baby; she was a grown woman who should have her own baby by now. But she certainly didn't want a child with someone who didn't want one with her. After years of badgering him she had finally realised he was never going to change his mind, so now she had her career and Alex had his, and they saw even less of each other. She couldn't say she hadn't seen it coming. But here she was on their tenth wedding anniversary, getting pissed in her best frock, on her own. She looked at her reflection and shook her head sadly. Yep – definitely should have stayed in the pub with Johnny. Her smile briefly returned, then she heard the sound of a key in the front door.

27

Mann arrived at Terminal Three at Heathrow airport. He was early. He wandered around the departure lounge thinking how much better it was in the Philippines where you could sit and get a relaxing massage whilst you waited and didn't have to be subjected to slot machines and perfume counters. He restored his sanity by browsing books in Smiths, and now, with the latest Lee Child paperback in hand, he was looking over a black Ferrari 360 Modena that he *could* win if he wanted to part with twenty pounds for the ticket, but Mann wasn't that kind of a gambler. He preferred to make his own luck.

He looked up and saw her striding purposefully towards him. She was wearing jeans and a blue T-shirt that had a picture of a cowgirl lassoing a calf on the front. She was pink-cheeked and breathless. Her messed-up hair shone flaxen. She grinned at him but she looked slightly anxious. *She has no idea how attractive she is,* thought Mann, as he watched heads turn and she passed oblivious.

'It's all right, you're not late,' he said as she reached him, out of breath. 'You don't need to hurry.'

'It's not that . . . it's just I wanted to ask you if you mind if . . .'

Alex came from behind the other side of the car with a lottery ticket in his hand.

'Did Becky tell you? I'm coming too . . .' He grinned – there was the challenge in his eyes again as he waited for Mann's reaction. 'Just so happens I have business in Hong Kong – I was about to fly out anyway. So I thought I'd tag along. That's okay I presume?'

'Of course.' Mann glanced fleetingly at Becky. She smiled back but she didn't look too sure. 'Do you want me to organise somewhere for you to stay?' Mann asked her.

'Thanks,' replied Becky, 'that's kind but we are booked into a hotel called the Metro – in Causeway Bay.'

'It's a good hotel. Close to the underground. Good choice.' Alex wandered away from them. He looked like he had been seriously overdoing it, thought Mann. His face was sweaty and rubbery looking. He was too coked-up to maintain eye contact for long and he sniffed incessantly. He was back looking over the Ferrari and flirting with the promotions girl.

'I'll leave you to it then. See you in Hong Kong. I'll ring you later, see how you're settling in, okay?'

Mann walked away and resisted the temptation to glance back. He knew she'd be watching.

He slept most of the way back. When they landed he kept a discreet eye on them at Lantau Airport but basically he left them to it. They'd find their way perfectly well by themselves. But, hours later, back at his apartment he phoned Becky to make sure.

'You okay? Is the hotel all right?'

'Everything's great, thanks, but I am ready for work whenever you say. Do you want me to meet you somewhere now?'

'No, you're all right, enjoy your evening. I have some personal stuff to do tonight; I'll send a car for you in the morning.'

Mann put down his phone, poured himself a vodka and watched the sunset. He had a couple of hours to wait before he had to go to his appointment and he was restless. His flat always did that to him. It made him want to leave it. Not its fault – it was full of memories and a good few regrets. He looked around him at the sparsely furnished lounge – just one armchair, the telly and a small table. 'Minimalist' it had been called by someone – but it wasn't minimalist it was minus its heart. It had been womanless since Helen had left. He rummaged through the pile of newly laundered clothes and found a fresh pair of jeans and a blue Armani shirt, then he headed into town, to Central district, to SoHo, the cobbled streets of the area south of Hollywood Road.

It was a lively area with a diversity of chic bars and restaurants all crammed together. In a world where he was neither Chinese nor English he fitted in Soho – Italians, Swedish, Spanish – foreigners of every description came there to find a little bit of home. It was a place of refuge for Mann. He always returned there when his spirits were low.

He sat in the supernatural, filmic surroundings of the Cantina, a bar dedicated to the whims of sci-fi buffs. The waitress brought him a large Zubrowka vodka on the rocks, with a dried seahorse wedged on the rim of the glass. He looked at the seahorse and frowned at her. She shrugged and walked off. Was he getting old or was the world just becoming a little too disrespectful of its living creatures?

He took the seahorse from its perch and placed it on the bar, next to the bowl of peanuts and his phone, which he had set to vibrate. He was one of a dozen others dotted around the Cantina, which had alcoves around its perimeter and a starry floor in its middle. As you walked across it, the stars twinkled brighter for a few seconds as if suspending you in space, then they disappeared and dropped you straight down a black hole – it was the perfect way to disorientate you when you'd had a few too many seahorses.

Mann looked over and raised his glass to the R2-D2 model robot who winked and chirruped back from the corner of the bar. 'Cheers.'

A woman's rich, deep laughter came from behind him.

'You do know he's not a real person?'

Mann smiled to himself and turned round.

'He's more real than a lot of people I deal with. How's it going, Miriam?'

He kissed her cheek. Miriam was an Englishwoman in her late forties but she had a face that belonged in the *nineteen* forties: dark eyes, deep red lipstick and full mouth. There was a touch of Ava Gardner about her. She wore a tight-fitting sheath dress, belted in the middle – it showed off her great figure.

She rested her elbow on the bar beside him.

'Hello Johnny. Where were you last week? You missed our *Star Wars* fancy dress party. I reserved you a costume and everything.'

'Damn! Lost my chance to be Darth Vader then?'

'No, had you down as Chewy.' She winked at him.

That was one of the many things Mann liked about Miriam – she made him laugh. He had known her for ten years. He had first met her when he was investigating her husband's death. He had been Japanese with Yakuza connections. The Yakuza often worked with the triads to achieve a common goal. Her husband had died during a bungled drug-smuggling deal. Miriam bought the Cantina with the money she got. She also inherited Yakuza protection that kept the local gangs at bay. She and Mann had been intermittent lovers for the last two years. An occasional lover was all Miriam needed or wanted. Both knew where they stood. But, in the last few weeks he had sought out her company often and she had gotten a bit too used to having him around.

'Where did you go?'

She had that look on her face that said she was asking one question but really wanted the answer to another – was there another woman involved? Yet she knew she didn't have the right to an honest answer. They had never laid claims on one another. She only wanted appeasing.

'UK – on business.'

Happy, she ordered a drink and pulled up a stool next to him.

'Some of my husband's old friends came by whilst you were away. They wanted to warn me. They said there would be a turf war that would involve all the triad societies. They came to say that they would not be able to protect me if it happened. They were leaving it to a new society to sort out. Is it true, Mann? What's going on?'

Mann's phoned buzzed before he could answer. He excused himself and checked the screen. Then he slid off the stool and slipped on his jacket.

'Sorry, Miriam, got to go. I'll tell you all about it later.'

'You only just got here and now you're leaving me?'

'I'll pick you up on my way back though – about twelve.'

'You're a cocky sod!'

He leaned towards her and breathed in her ear.

'And you are a beautiful, irresistibly sexy woman. And I aim to show you just how much I've missed you – later.'

Mann waved and set off, checking his phone again on the way out. CK was waiting for him.

28

The traditional dark wood and red leather dining room in the private club in Kowloon had plenty of tables set with crystal and silver ready for the dinner service. It was 9 p.m. and the place should have been packed, but there was only one diner. Two of CK's bodyguards met Mann at the door and escorted him to his seat. CK was sitting with his elbows on the table, fingertips pressed together, a man in careful deliberation. As slight as CK Leung was, he had the presence of a powerful man. Like Mann, he was an immaculate dresser, although he favoured the traditional Mandarin-collared suit.

CK had been the Dragon Head of the Wo Shing Shing for as long as Mann could remember. He had already been in his mid forties when Mann joined the police force. Then, he was a freshly hatched Dragon Head – building up his empire. Now, at sixty-two, due to his business expertise, his foresight and his total lack of ethics, he headed the largest triad society in Hong Kong, with ambitions to take over the triad world. Mann hated CK and all he stood for, but the animosity between them was more complicated than that.

Someone within the Wo Shing Shing had been responsible for ordering the death of Mann's father. Mann believed that CK knew who it was.

Mann walked across the empty dining room and sat opposite CK, who handed him the menu.

'I recommend the Japanese dishes – the fugu is a personal favourite.'

Mann snapped the menu shut.

'The fugu it is.'

It took seven years of training for a chef to hold an official licence to be able to prepare the deadly paralysing puffer fish for the table. One fish could kill thirty people – it was a thousand times stronger than cyanide. It poisoned at least six diners a year by paralysing the nervous system. The victim could neither move nor breathe, but remained fully conscious till death.

'Why have you returned without my daughter?'

'I don't mind playing a game when I know the rules. You sent me halfway across the world when you knew the dice were thrown here. The only thing we both know for certain is that the stakes are high. All leads come back to you. It seems you hold your daughter's fate in your own hands. What is it they want from you, CK?'

'I have told you all I know.'

'That's not entirely the truth, is it? There is a lot of talk around town. There's a new society stepping on toes, not least yours – if they are responsible for the kidnap of your daughter, we need to know what they want.'

CK sat back in his chair and waited whilst the waiter unfolded the thick starched napkin, flicked it out, laid it neatly across CK's lap and stepped back.

'I have heard of this new society, the White Circle. Yes, I believe that they are responsible for the kidnap of my daughter, but I do not know what they hope to gain from it and I do not know anything about them. I have not been crossed in this way before. It is . . . new territory for me. You are the detective, you find out.'

The fugu arrived; the fillets of white fish were still twitching. They were arranged in the shape of a chrysanthemum – the funeral flower.

CK looked at Mann and smiled.

'Tonight we have two chefs to prepare the dish. One of them has been preparing the dish for years, the other has just started his training today.' Barely a smile flickered across CK's face. 'Life is precious, but it is not worth living if it has no risk involved, don't you think?'

'I will always take the risk if it's my life I stand to lose, but I don't gamble on the lives of others. What do you know about the arson attack in London that killed twelve young women?'

'I heard about it – tragic.'

'Did you order it?'

CK met Mann's stare. Mann picked up the convulsing fillet in his chopstick and dipped it into hot green wasabi and soy sauce. It shivered as he placed it into his mouth. He swallowed. 'Twelve women and children burned to death – sex workers trafficked from the Philippines to Hong Kong and on to the UK. If you knew where to light the match . . .' CK held a piece of fugu fillet suspended in his chopsticks and watched it twitch '. . . you must know who your enemy is. But by forcing their hand with the fire you may have caused the death of your daughter. Not everyone responds well to intimidation.'

CK's eyes fixed on Mann. His face remained expressionless, but a light of anger flashed into his eyes.

'If I knew the man who had my daughter I would strip the skin from his flesh in small sections and feed it to my whore's lapdog whilst he watched. I know nothing of the fire. I heard about it but I did not order it. I agree it was bad timing. I would not have made such a mistake.'

'So, someone else ordered it to please you. Did you release Stevie Ho from the Wo Shing Shing?'

'Stevie knows what he has to do to fulfil his oath to me, then I will release him.'

'The oath is for life. When was it changed?'

'Times are changing, Inspector. We have to change with it. Many societies that were once enemies are now friends.'

'They work together only when it serves a common purpose – that's not friendship. I hear your members have been annihilating senior members of other societies.'

CK's face was stony. He sat back in his seat and stared hard at Mann, who stared back.

'Why did you involve me, CK, if you don't intend to work with me? You are playing with your child's life.'

The last dish to be brought to Mann was a soup made from the fish bones and head and anything else that could possibly be left. As Mann finished it he felt his tongue tingle and his lips go numb – a small amount of the poison had escaped into the stock. He felt nauseous and dizzy. The fugu was working its way into his system – the poison was giving him palpitations. He ordered a large vodka on the rocks. When it came he held on to the glass, felt the cool of the condensation. He looked over at the door. The bodyguards were still there. He saw CK watching him. There was no antidote, but if he hurried he might be able to empty his stomach, stop it getting worse. But he wasn't going to do that. He wouldn't give CK the satisfaction of seeing him squirm; instead he practised his breathing, held the ice in his mouth and hoped the poison would stabilise. He hoped he would be able to speak.

'Let us conclude this meal with an understanding,' CK said. 'You are a man I trust, and I trust you to find my daughter in whatever way you decide, and . . .' he sat back '. . . I will pay you whatever it takes . . .'

Mann could see that he was being studied. CK was watching him cope with the poison.

'If I get your daughter back I would expect something else in return – not money.' Mann felt his pulse stabilise, his lungs relax, his heat quieten – the poison was dissipating, just his mouth still tingled. CK inclined his head in an 'I'm listening' mode. 'That the Wo Shing Shing ceases all human trafficking. That you shut down the whole chain right from recruiters to snakeheads.'

'If I admitted to such a thing as the trafficking of human beings that would be a high price . . .' CK lowered his head in a gesture of agreement. 'You have three days – seventy-two hours from midnight tonight, Inspector. If my daughter is not returned by that time I will presume that she is dead, and I will wage the biggest war ever seen here. The streets of Hong Kong will run with blood.' CK rose and bowed.

Mann stood and faced CK. He returned the bow. Even faced with a man he hated, etiquette had to be observed.

'That is not all I want. There's something else.'

29

In the morning Mann could still feel the tingling from the fugu when he ran his tongue around his lips. He rolled over and studied Miriam. Classically beautiful, her porcelain skin was hardly touched by the sun. Her dark hair splayed out in waves across the pillow. She smiled sleepily, aware that she was being scrutinised.

'Mmm, morning.' She sighed contentedly.

'I have a present for you, Miriam.' Mann slid his arm beneath her and pulled her closer. 'I brought something back for you that I picked up at the restaurant last night.'

'Is it flowers?'

'No.'

'Chocolates?'

'Not quite.' He turned her on her back and pulled her down the bed a little. 'You'll enjoy it, though.'

Becky climbed out of the rooftop pool and stood drip-drying in the gentle breeze. The sky was milky blue. Hong Kong was just waking up. All around her were other rooftops, some with helicopter pads, others with pools or roof gardens. Immediately below her, people were playing tennis and practising Tai Chi in the green spaces. Further away she could see glimpses of the narrow streets already filling with morning traffic. In front of her was the deep-water harbour, dotted with container ships and fishing boats, and then came the glittering ocean all the way to the horizon.

It was a magical sight. The ocean and the land faced each other, defiant and yet harmonious at the water's edge. Giant tower blocks threw up their arms to the heavens and tried to reach higher than all the others around. Each building was unique; a thing of beauty, created with the elements in mind, sculptured and multi-faceted like cut diamonds, now touched by the first rays of morning sun that turned their mirrored sides golden.

She stood gently drying in the warm breeze and watched the world come awake. She finally understood how you could fall in love with a vertical city. She felt like she was on top of the world. She was suddenly glad Alex had come. This might be just the space they needed to find the fun in their marriage again. They hadn't made love for over six months. That thought shocked her, she hadn't realised it was that long until she calculated it – then she remembered that the last time was after a drunken bonfire party. They had stayed up to watch the fireworks and they had drunk too much scotch. She smiled to herself when she thought about it. They had giggled like teenagers. She had let things slide for too long, thought Becky. She had to make more of an effort to make it better between them.

After all – she had signed up for life – no one said marriage was easy. Her parents had had it rough sometimes and they stayed together. Becky had never invested so much in someone else before. She wasn't about to admit it had been a mistake. If they had it good once they could have it again. But then Alex had to want it too, he had to make an effort and she wasn't sure he was capable. She didn't know how to please him anymore and he never tried to please her. Then a thought flashed into her head that maybe Alex was having an affair. The very idea stunned her. Becky shivered as the breeze got up. She pulled the towel closely around her and went back inside to their room. She found Alex in the bathroom, shaving. No time like the present she thought and slipping out of her bikini, she put her arms around his waist and pressed her cold body against him.

'I need warming up.' She looked over his shoulder at them both in the mirror. 'It's early. Coming back to bed for a while?'

'I need to finish shaving.' He held his hands away from his sides. 'I have a busy day.'

Becky released him at once, almost as if he were too hot to touch. She went into the bedroom and lay naked on top of the bed. The rays of sun filtered in through the open curtains and flittered across her. She sighed heavily.

'I can hear you,' Alex called from the bathroom. 'Stop sighing. Make sure you're around later then we'll have time to spend together, okay, baby?'

Becky didn't answer; instead she lay back on the

pillow and stretched out on the cool cotton sheets and enjoyed the warmth of the sun on her naked body – warming her through to the bone. Alex came into the bedroom.

'I thought you were getting dressed?'

'The car isn't arriving for another hour. I have plenty of time. I am going to get some breakfast in a minute – I'm starving. Aren't you eating?'

'I'll grab something later.'

She watched him get ready. He was always so meticulous. His attention to detail was frightening. 'You look very smart,' she said, as he finished getting ready and put the final adjustments to his hair.

'It's important here; people care what you look like. They judge you by what you're wearing.'

'Oh shit!' she giggled. 'I'm stuffed then.'

Alex finished looking at himself in the mirror and turned to her.

'Maybe you should buy yourself some clothes whilst you're here. Actually, I don't think you'd find anything to fit you. They're all size zeros here.'

'Ah well, shan't bother trying then.'

As soon as she said it she knew it was the wrong thing to say. He closed the wardrobe door abruptly and came to stand at the end of the bed.

'That's your philosophy for life, isn't it, Becky?' Alex picked up his jacket and briefcase. 'I'm off. See you later.' He didn't wait for a reply. He was gone.

30

Mann was sitting next to Ng at his new desk when he saw Becky walk into the main PC area, escorted by the young policeman who had picked her up from her hotel. She didn't see him straight away. The way the open-plan office fanned out from the central rectangle of PCs made it impossible to distinguish one area from another.

She looked lovely, thought Mann. She had swapped her trousers for a cream-coloured cotton skirt that ended just above her knee, and she had on a white open-necked blouse and carried a blue jacket.

'You ready for a day's work?' He greeted her and thanked the young policeman who was steering her towards him. 'Meet the team . . . Detective Sergeant Ng . . .' Ng stood up to shake her hand. 'Watch him – he has a way with the women – I've never worked out what it is.'

'I'll tell you later.' She winked.

Shrimp walked in at that moment. 'And this is DC Li – we call him Shrimp. Speaks English like a Yank, dresses to impress, but we haven't worked out who.'

Shrimp looked very seventies today with his tight black stretch shirt and his black trousers. 'He'll be catching the plane over to join your team in the UK later tonight.'

'Pleased to meet you, yes, I'm looking forward to it . . . Nice outfit, by the way. Love the shoes.'

'Pleased to meet you too . . . Thanks.' She looked down at her feet – she'd got it right by accident – they matched. 'I'm amazed everyone speaks such good English here.'

'English is still the main language in here for police work, ' said Mann.

'That's handy. What have we got planned for the day?' she asked.

'I'm going to give you a tour and we need to take in a couple of stops. We'll start by buying some luggage. We're going to need it.' She looked at him, waiting for an explanation.

'We need to go to the Philippines. We don't have a lot of choice and time is not on our side. If we want to discover who has Amy and what they want in return we need to go where it all seems to be kicking off.' Mann paused and looked at Becky. 'What about Alex? How will he manage without you?'

She thought about it for a second and then shrugged and Mann could see she couldn't resist a little smile. 'Perfectly well, I'm sure. He has loads to get on with here. Anyway, the thing is, it's work . . . If we have to go, we have to go. I'm ready.' She could barely conceal her excitement at the prospect despite a short-lived twinge of guilt that the thought of heading off with

Johnny Mann was much more appealing than spending any more time with Alex.

'Okay then, all I have to do is convince that man in there...' He nodded in the direction of the Superintendent's office. 'Ng – fill Becky in on what we found out this morning while I go and have a chat with my friend in there.'

Mann knocked on Wong's office and went straight in. Becky sat down to listen to what Ng had to say.

'Stevie Ho left England just after you,' Ng explained. 'He was seen at the airport changing his ticket. So something unexpected must have come up. He went straight from Manila to Negros. We know there is a triad stronghold on that island. We think he will check in there, then head up to Angeles where the main traffickers are based. The answer must lie in the Philippines – it's the only reason for Stevie to move so fast. He must be under new orders.'

'Yeah!' added Shrimp, who was emptying his bag of drink tins and lining them up on his already untidy and cluttered desk, ready for the day. 'Stevie is putting some deals down. He knows Mann has come back here and he hopes to slip through the net and get his business done quickly before we can catch up with him. We're sure he's going to lead us to Amy Tang's kidnappers. Now, Mann just has to convince the Super.'

Becky stood with Ng and watched Shrimp fire up his PC and bring up images of the Philippines, for Becky to get a glimpse of what she was going to. All three glanced surreptitiously towards the Superintendent's room, trying their best to gauge what was happening between the two men. It seemed to be all over in seconds as Mann emerged looking nonchalant.

'Can we go?' Becky asked.

'Yep!'

They all looked at the glass partition. Wong was shaking his head – looking a very worried man. Then he realised he was being watched and gave an embarrassed wave at Becky, who waved back.

'We'll leave on the night flight. We have to change at Cebu, a two-hour flight from here. Then we will fly to Davao and move up to one of the tourist resorts of Puerto Galera, before we head up to Angeles. There are a few places we have to go to, some men we have to talk to. We have to cover a lot of ground very quickly. We will be going as a married couple – Mr And Mrs Black. Shrimp will fix us up with our new identities and book the accommodation,' he said, glancing at Shrimp's face. Shrimp grinned. '*Suitable* accommodation,' Mann added. 'No three-in-a-bed romps with a couple of horny cockroaches.'

'Leave it to me, boss.'

Mann escorted Becky out of the building and into the staff car park.

'Let me see if I can guess which is yours.' She scanned the half-empty parking lot. 'I think it will be one of two things – either something sporty and vintage, or a mini with a big engine.'

'Will a BMW convertible do?'

She smiled. 'Good choice.'

They left Central, heading through the tunnel across

169

to Kowloon and away from the harbour. They drove up Nathan Road, the Golden Mile, and into the small back roads of Mong Kok. It was a bustling old world of narrow streets and disappearing pavements, known by westerners for its markets: night market, jade market, bird market, they were all here, but so were the choppings – the attacks between triads using meat cleavers. Most tourists were blissfully unaware that the area was run by triad gangs. It didn't affect them – triads killed other triads.

It was still early morning. The night market was packing up and the piles of the previous night's rubbish were waiting to be collected. The shopkeepers were just setting up their stalls and opening their shutters in preparation. Although most of the shops would not open till ten, the street was still crammed with people. The office workers, in their smart clothes, were dodging the debris left on the pavement. A Caucasian business-suited man walked by with a Starbucks coffee in his hand. He stuck out like a sore thumb.

'What was it like growing up for you?' Becky asked as they were stuck waiting to move on a side road, inching their way along behind moving stalls and street vendors.

'The main divide here in Hong Kong is not the colour of someone's skin, it's how much money he has. I was lucky enough to belong to the "comfortably well off" race.'

'Are your parents still here?'

'My mother is. She lives out at Stanley Bay. My father was murdered by triads when I was eighteen.'

They stopped outside one of the old tenement blocks. 'Here we are.'

He was already out of the car before Becky could question him.

'What?' Becky got out of the car and hurried after him. 'So that's what Micky meant. When I told him you were coming he called you the triad annihilator. He was right – this is personal for you.'

'Yes, it's personal.'

One day he'd tell her how he'd been held down by two men and made to watch every chop that brought his father to his knees and finally split his skull. How he'd looked into his father's eyes and known that he had failed him. One day he'd talk about the part of him that blamed himself for not being able to prevent it.

They followed a man inside the building. He disappeared left. They headed right towards the elevator. Mann pulled at the heavy metal grid door for Becky to step inside. Four more people squeezed into the tiny lift. They alighted at the third floor and walked past open doors with the din of televisions blaring out and the sound of children being scolded, and then stopped at a door halfway along the corridor. Mann knocked. A few seconds later a woman opened it. She looked at the couple, smiled and bowed as she stood to one side and ushered them in. The place was stacked with cellophane bags. Louis Vuitton, Chanel, Gucci, all piled high to the ceiling. The room smelt of plastic and new leather.

'Come in. Come look . . . plenty good bag. Good price.

Make me offer. Give discount. What you want?' She beamed eagerly at Becky.

Mann glanced around the room, at the mountain of counterfeit bags, purses and suitcases, all wrapped in cellophane.

'Where's Ponytail?'

'Not here.' The woman turned back to Becky and began her sales pitch again. She picked up one of the bags, ripped off the polythene and pushed it into Becky's hands.

'Tell him to come.' Mann took the bag from Becky and turned it over in his hands, inspecting the stitching. Then, disgusted, he threw it back onto the pile. 'Crap. We're not buying crap. Get Ponytail or we go.'

The woman rushed over to a different pile and began to tear off more plastic covers.

'This one. This one velly best. Look!'

She thrust this new one at Becky, still hoping that Becky would take over the negotiations. Mann took it and threw it across the room like a Frisbee. It landed on top of a pile of others.

'Let's go,' he said to Becky. 'It's all crap.' He motioned towards the door.

'Wait. Wait . . . I ring Ponytail, sure he come for special customer like you.' She bowed, blocking their exit.

Mann stepped back. 'Okay.'

Two minutes later an unhealthy-looking young man slipped through the front door, still eating his breakfast. His lank hair was tied back and tapered to a rat's tail at the nape of his neck, his face was greasy and pock-marked. He was wearing grey jeans with darkened patches down the front of his thighs where it looked like he'd rubbed his greasy hands.

When he saw Mann he stopped, mid-shovelling. His eyes flicked to Becky then back to Mann. He lowered the bowl and wiped the chicken stock from his chin.

'You wanted to see me?' he said in English.

'We were told you have top-quality bags. We haven't found any yet.'

'Sure. I have top quality, genuine, made same factory as originals. Follow me.'

He handed his noodle bowl to the old woman, who gave a disgruntled moan at having to involve a third party and lose part of her commission. Ponytail ignored her and led them through to a small room at the back. He closed the door behind them, turned and grinned at Mann.

He looked Becky up and down. 'Fuck, Johnny, not bad!' he said, in Cantonese.

Mann grinned. 'Have some fucking manners and speak English, you peasant. Becky – this is Detective Tin . . . Ponytail. He is one of our best undercover cops and an old friend. Becky is working with me on a case. She's from London.'

Ponytail wiped his hand and then shook Becky's.

'Pleased to meet you.'

'I got your message. What have you got for me?' asked Mann.

'I guess you heard the rumour about you working for CK?'

173

'I heard.'

'There's an even better one than that. The talk is that you're working for the new society – the White Circle.'

'Is that the best you have for me, Ponytail?'

'They say that CK has set the whole thing up. He wants this war so that he can wipe out all the opposition in one go and take over all the profitable trafficking routes. They say he is in charge of the new group using the Caucasian traffickers who are already established in the Philippines to do all the work for him, and then he will get rid of them.'

'Why would he order the arson attack on the trafficked women in London?'

Ponytail shook his head, screwed up his face. 'To throw us off the scent. To make it look realistic. I don't know, but I know anything is possible with him.'

Mann looked at Becky and gestured toward the pile of bags.

'You can't leave without one.'

'Take your pick.' Ponytail pulled a sheet from a pile behind the door, pulled off a Kalashnikov rifle from the top of a pile and revealed high-quality Chanel replica bags. He put the gun to one side. 'Here, have this one – it's the best. Goes with your outfit.' He handed her a dainty cream clutch bag.

'Thanks.' Becky took it reluctantly but looked secretly pleased. Mann wondered when was the last time she had been given something.

'That's five hundred Hong Kong, Mann.'

'Fuck off! I'm not paying for that shit. Three hundred, tops.' He grinned.

Ponytail shook his head. 'Four.'

'Throw in a couple of matching travel bags and it's a deal.'

31

Suzanne sat on the chair at Amy's desk whilst Amy brushed her hair. Suzanne said the brush was made from real boar bristle. Amy wanted to ask Suzanne where the bristles came from, and did she mean a wild boar, like a pig? But she didn't ask because Suzanne got cross when Amy talked. She liked Amy to be quiet and concentrate on the brushing, and if she didn't then Suzanne would be horrible to her again. She would make her drink the salty water like the day before, and then Amy had been sick all night. Amy had had to sleep by the toilet because she mustn't be sick in the bed, because Suzanne would hit her.

The bristle brush was soft. That meant that Amy could brush Suzanne's hair with long hard strokes, the way she liked it. Suzanne closed her eyes.

In the next room, the spotty one, Tony, had left the telly on when he'd left, and Amy could hear *EastEnders*. Amy recognised the theme tune. She didn't watch it normally. It came on at a time when she was doing prep, but she had sometimes seen the omnibus on Sundays.

Suzanne was getting drunk. Amy had seen people

drunk a few times. She'd even seen her own mother drunk. She would start happy, laughing and singing, and then become miserable. Sometimes Amy had been fast asleep and her mother had come and woken her up to tell her how much she loved her, and Amy had smelt the booze on her breath. But, she did love her – that was the main thing. Amy could tell that Suzanne didn't even like her. And Suzanne had such bad moods. Amy didn't know what she was going to be like from one minute to the next.

'Suzanne?'

'Yes?'

'Are you married to Lenny?'

Suzanne closed her eyes again and took a swig of gin.

'I will be, just as soon as he dumps his wife. He promised me he'd have it done by now, but he still fucking hasn't.'

Suzanne waved her hand in the direction of her glass and Amy picked it up.

'How did you meet Lenny?'

'I met him at home in Nanjing. He had business there. I was working as an interpreter.'

'That's why you speak such good English.'

'Yes . . .' She gave a drunken giggle. '. . . and I've been fucking western guys since I was not much older than you. I lived with a German for three years from when I was sixteen. That's why my English has an accent.'

'Yes, you have a strange accent. Not strange . . .' Amy corrected herself quickly as Suzanne opened her eyes and glared at her '. . . but different . . .'

Suzanne tapped the glass with her false nails. She was still waiting for Amy to go and refill it. Amy took it from her and went out into the kitchen to do it. Amy had become an expert on gin-mixing in the few days that she had been left alone with Suzanne. She had even been allowed to go next door, into the lounge and the kitchen, to fetch the gin and tonic and to refill the ice tray when needed. Now Amy knew where lots of things were. She saw where they slept, when they took it in turns to stay over in the flat; she saw where Tony hid his porn magazines; and she saw where the spare keys for the front door were.

Amy came back in with a fresh drink for Suzanne, who was waiting for her.

'Every woman has to make the best of herself, Amy. I have had to – you will have to. In this life women need to make use of *all* the assets they have to make it.'

'Yes.' Amy started reeling off a list. 'Women need to be strong, intelligent . . .'

'Of course we're fucking intelligent.' Suzanne's eyes snapped open and she swung an angry look at Amy before settling back into her seat and signalling for Amy to continue brushing. 'We've always been more fucking intelligent than all those pricks . . . Women need to know how to work the system, Amy: use your . . .' She opened her eyes and looked Amy up and down. ' . . .use anything you have. That's what I will teach you, Amy. I have plans for you. Things have changed. Stand over there, Amy . . .' Suzanne pulled Amy's arm roughly, making her stand in front of her. 'Take off your clothes. Let me look at you.'

Amy batted her eyes and her brace got dry and made the sucking sound.

'Take that fucking brace out of your mouth. You're not going to need it any more anyway.' Suzanne sighed, exasperated, and looked Amy up and down. 'And don't even bother to take off your clothes – I can see exactly what you look like; we need to put you on a strict diet. Come here . . .' Amy inched towards her. 'Give me that thing in your mouth . . . spit it out.'

Amy reached into her mouth and dislodged the plate.

'Throw it in the bin – *do it.*'

Amy went to the bin and dropped it inside.

'Suzanne – let me do your hair now. I love your hair. You're so beautiful, Suzanne – like a model. You are the most beautiful woman I have ever seen. Please let me do your hair . . .'

Suzanne's phone rang. She answered. Amy knew it was Lenny on the phone because of the way Suzanne's voice changed. Then Amy saw her smile disappear as she listened hard, concentrating on what Lenny was saying. Something wasn't right.

'Yes. Yes, I will do it now. Yes, okay. You know I will.' Suzanne closed her phone.

'Was that Lenny?'

'Shut up and hand me my bag.'

Amy did so reluctantly. She knew what that usually meant. She watched Suzanne dig into the large leather bag and bring out the bottle of pills that Amy had seen many times since she arrived at the flat. Suzanne tipped out one into her palm.

She passed Amy the glass of gin and tonic.

'Take it.'

Amy screwed up her face as she tasted the gin, but she knew better than to cross Suzanne.

'Now lie down and go to sleep.'

Amy did as she was told. Suzanne watched her take the sleeping pill, then she went into the lounge to get ready. Amy lay down on her bed and pulled up the duvet. She waited for the familiar heaviness to come down on her. She listened to the sound of Suzanne tidying up the kitchen, washing the coffee cups. She heard her moving around the lounge; occasionally she heard her come back to Amy's door, feeling her presence as she looked in to see if Amy was asleep yet, then went back to the lounge.

It wouldn't take long for Amy to fall asleep. It never did. Suzanne peeped in. Yes, Amy was snoring away. She really needed to get her adenoids seen to, thought Suzanne, as she went back into the lounge and checked her watch. She should have been gone by now.

Fucking men! They couldn't do one thing right. Suzanne didn't understand why Lenny kept changing his mind. She didn't see why they were bothering to keep the child alive now. What was Lenny stalling for? That was the part that worried Suzanne. The side of Lenny that was capable of double-crossing anyone and everyone. Did that mean he would do it to her? She didn't really believe that – they were the same type, him and her. They were meant for one another. He wouldn't double-cross her. He must want the child alive in case the plan changed. He was smart; he was rich; he was good-looking – she didn't need to worry. But she did need a contingency plan, and she had it. If things went wrong, Suzanne had it all worked out what she was going to do. Amy was her ticket to freedom. With the money she could sell Amy for, she could retire.

She headed over to check on the new arrivals. She had better keep a more watchful eye on this lot. She couldn't trust the men where the women were concerned; they weren't using their brains to think. They were easily distracted. They had been responsible for the loss of the women in the fire – she had warned them that it was only a matter of time. She had told them to move the women earlier. But had they listened? Now Lenny was gone to try and sort it out and she was left to manage the idiots. Things had not turned out the way they were supposed to.

She locked up the flat and called a cab. The journey took her twenty minutes as she headed north off the M25. She reached her destination – a scruffy end-of-terrace on a road that was high up on a demolisher's list.

Tony answered the door. Suzanne went past him and straight through to the kitchen. 'It's freezing here. Put the heating on.'

'It doesn't work.' Tony followed her through to the back.

'I thought you were going to tart this place up after we sold the other girls on.'

'The Albanians screwed us over. We didn't get a lot for the girls, in the end. They weren't worth much – they were finished.'

Suzanne looked at him. She knew he was lying, but

181

it didn't matter to her, she hadn't handled the deal – if the shit hit the fan it wasn't her mess to clean up.

'Well, get the heating fixed before we start getting punters in here. They're going to be too cold to get their clothes off. Ring someone and get them round . . . no, wait, leave it – I'll do it tomorrow.'

Suzanne had decided that the men were best given minor tasks. She couldn't risk another disaster. She set the bags of bread, pasta, jam and milk down on the kitchen table. A bare electric light bulb swung down over their heads. A small portable television was blaring out from the corner of the worktop. The house was ex housing association. It had been bought at an auction and needed a lot of money spending on it, which it wasn't going to get.

'You have four hours max. I have had to dope the girl as there is no one there to look after her.'

Tony was disgruntled. 'We can't manage them, just the three of us. It's too much.'

'It's not too much if everyone does their fucking job. We're already fifty grand down with the loss of the others.'

'That had nothing to do with me.'

'Yes, it did. You should have known the Chinese would come. You should have backed me when I said to move them on quicker and you should have kept an eye on that black guy. He wasn't thinking with his brains.'

Tony shrugged. He was looking sheepish. He was up to something or he'd done something, thought Suzanne.

'Where are the girls? Upstairs?'

Tony nodded. She could see by his face that he was hiding something.

'What kind of condition are they in? They've been cooped up in the back of a lorry for a week. Are any of them sick?'

Tony turned his back on her and started to unpack the groceries.

'Not sick, but they were playing up – making a noise. I had to get rough with them. Had to make them do as they were told, show them who's boss.'

Suzanne could see by his face that he'd had his fun. She went upstairs to look at the girls.

The house had four bedrooms. Six girls slept in one room and the other three were going to be used to entertain clients.

As Suzanne made her way up the stairs there was an eerie silence coming from above. The front door sounded loud as it juddered shut behind the exiting Tony. She opened the door to the girls' bedroom. Two of the girls were sitting on their beds, facing each other, talking. Two more were lying curled on their mattresses. The other two sat together on the floor, their backs against the wall. The room smelt damp and dirty. Suzanne blamed the mattresses. Tony had found them on a skip. He was a cheap little hood, but Suzanne had to work with what she was given. She was still a minor player in the league but was working her way up the ladder. She and Lenny would be a great team one day, a formidable team. But for now she must look after a few frightened Filipinas – schoolgirls, kidnapped and sold to the highest bidder, which just happened to be Suzanne's new boss.

The girls on the bed turned and stared at her as she entered. She went over to the two on the floor. One of them was the youngest of the six girls, at thirteen. Her fifteen-year-old sister had her arm around her. Tony had done a good job by raping the youngest first – they looked frightened, traumatised, *exactly as they should look*, thought Suzanne.

32

'How long are we in the air? Do you think the plane is safe? It seems really old to me . . . and what are those drops on the wing?'

Becky and Mann were sitting on a small domestic aeroplane heading for the island of Mindanao.

'Just relax – just takes a couple of hours, that's all. I can't believe you are frightened of flying. I thought you loved travelling.'

Mann was having a hard job keeping the smile off his face.

'I love to travel but I hate getting there.'

'Just relax, close your eyes, try and sleep.'

'No way – at any minute I might have to fly the plane.'

Mann laughed. 'This plane is made out of bits of chicken wire and soggy cardboard, God knows how it stays in the air as it is – if there's any trouble we are going down fast . . .' He looked at her panic-stricken face – her eyes were huge. 'I didn't mean it. This airline has a better safety record than Qantas – believe me, there is nothing that can go wrong – why don't you read a magazine and forget about it.'

Becky slumped in her seat and took the in-flight magazine from Mann, but continued to stare at the water droplets that ran in ragged paths across the wing.

They were on the second leg of their journey now. They had stopped at Cebu, sat in the suffocatingly hot departure lounge, paid boarding tax, luggage tax, departure tax and now they were sitting on the connecting plane that would take them to Davao, the capital of Mindanao. It was a small old plane with one very short-skirted hostess and a pilot who coughed incessantly. Becky was wearing cut-off jeans and a vest top. She looked at the hostess and was glad she had chosen not to wear shorts. She wouldn't want to *begin* to compete with those legs.

They flew out of the cloud and Becky looked down below to see white-rimmed islands floating dream-like in the transparent turquoise ocean. She felt calmer. They had a chance now they were over water. She had rehearsed the escape from a plane in the sea many times in her head. She was a good swimmer; she could afford to relax for a while. She opened the magazine and started reading about Mindanao. She turned to ask Mann a question but he was asleep. His sunglasses were resting on his head; his black hair and choppy fringe were pushed back from his forehead. She studied his face. His broad forehead had a permanent crease, a frown line across it, even when he was resting. His eyebrows were black and thickest where they arched over the centre of the eye. The scar on his cheek sat right over the cheekbone in an otherwise quite beautiful face, thought Becky.

She looked at the way his faded blue T-shirt folded softly around his bicep and his washboard stomach. He was a lot like Alex, thought Becky, in the way he liked to look good, but Mann was understated, he liked to be well-groomed, not flash. Alex liked people to know how much his suit cost; Mann liked to keep them guessing.

Mann knew she was looking at him. He was resting his head and trying to take his mind off the fact that he was so tall that his knees were jammed against the seat in front. He was aware of her turning towards him and he felt her soft breath on his face – a hint of mouthwash. He snapped his eyes open.

Becky quickly turned back to her magazine.

'Says here that Davao is one of the safest cities in the Philippines. I thought Mindanao is where the rebels are?'

Mann leaned over to look at the magazine on her lap.

'Some parts of the island are no-go areas – terrorist strongholds – but Davao has been transformed into a crime-free zone. It's held up by the government as a model city, crime rates falling, vagrancy dealt with.'

'How come?'

He sat back. 'It's called the forty pesos solution. Forty pesos is the cost of a bullet. Davao has a death squad. Two men dressed in black ride shotgun on a motorbike – the Davao Death Squad. They target anyone undesirable. It used to be rebels but now it's petty thieves, drug dealers and vagrant kids who live off the streets.'

'They kill *children*?'

Becky looked past Mann and became aware that she was speaking too loudly, as across the aisle an old Filipina was staring at her looking annoyed.

'The Philippines has a massive vagrant child population.' Mann kept his voice low and smiled over at the woman who smiled hesitatingly back. 'The country is eighty per cent children. The average size of the family here in the Philippines is six. The streets are clogged with children, they live off refuse and they sleep on the pavements. They have no papers and no identity. Lots of the kids don't have any birth records. They don't exist, so far as this city is concerned.'

'And so they just get rid of them?'

'The DDS do. The kids are either stabbed or shot by them. They are bad for tourism, unsightly. Their bodies are dumped in a killing field outside the city.'

'My God! That's awful. Why are we going there? What has it got to do with this investigation?'

'Because, recently, they seem to have *stopped* killing them. There have been reports of children being snatched off the street. There are rumours that they have started trafficking them instead. Making money from them instead of just killing them for fun.'

'Does no one care about these kids?'

'Some people care. They risk their lives to care. We are going to talk to one of those people right now.'

'Oh God, are we landing?' She swung round and pinned her face against the small window at the same time as there came the familiar clunk of the wheels being lowered. 'More planes crash either taking off or landing than at any other time.' She sat back and quickly fastened her seat belt.

'I wouldn't bother doing that – when it catches fire you're going to want to get out fast.'

Becky thumped him hard on the arm.

Ten minutes later she was following Mann out through Davao's light and airy arrivals lounge.

There was no air-con, but the place was open fronted and the high ceilings, and cool stone floors kept the air circulating and the temperature down.

Outside, the day was idyllic: a constant breeze, rustling palms and an azure-blue sky. There was a throng of people waiting at the exit. Mann stood for a few minutes and scanned the crowd. He saw who he was looking for and waved. Becky saw a slight, wiry man, late fifties, salt and pepper hair, with a checked blue shirt, who was standing with his legs apart, his hands on his hips, like a military man. The man waved back and walked purposefully over to them. He shook Mann's hand with both of his.

'Good to see you, Johnny – can't stay away, no?'

His voice had a charming, almost comical quality to it. It started soft Dublin then ended in squeaky Filipino as it rose at the end of every sentence.

'Good to see you again, Father, this is for you . . .' Mann handed him a bottle of single malt. 'And this is my colleague – Becky Stamp, from London. Becky, meet Father Finn O'Connell.'

'Both you and the scotch are very welcome.' He shook Becky's hand. He had a film-star charm about him: his twinkling emerald-green eyes were striking against his tanned face. He had deep laughter lines around his mouth. His eyebrows were as thick as black caterpillars. He shook her hand and gently steered her out of the way of a runaway luggage trolley. 'How is everything back in the UK? Must be summer, no?' he asked her.

'Nearly, Father, but it's been a long time coming.'

'Tell me, this is your first time to the Philippines, no?' He was already on the move, steering them away from the exit.

'Yes. I have done Thailand before, been to Bali, Goa, but never been here. It's a beautiful place.'

'Yes. Beautiful place, wonderful people. They have the most trusting, happy disposition. They try and please. That's probably their downfall, no?'

'What about you, Father? You're a long way from home. What's a priest doing out here?'

'Ha . . .' His laughter came quick and fast, exploding into the air. 'I hope it's God's work. It keeps *me* busy anyway. I will tell you all about it in great length when we get into the shade. It's good to have you here. Now let's go.'

Becky looked around her as Father Finn led the way at speed across the car park. There were lots of people just milling about or sitting in the shade of the palm trees that ran around the perimeter of the airport. It reminded her of a music festival, where there was nothing to do but mill about. To the left was the palmed perimeter of the airport; to the right was the public transport area, where queues were forming to get on the Jeepneys to take people into town. The main form of public transport in the Philippines, the Jeepneys were highly decorated and customised open-sided buses. Father Finn was a few paces in front; he was a fast walker. Becky stayed back with Mann.

'Are there lots of priests here?' she asked Mann as they walked past the people joining queues for Jeepneys.

'Yes, they've been here for many years. They are all over the Philippines – mainly Columban order. They do a fantastic job at guilt tripping the government into facing up to a few of the problems. Father Finn here runs a refuge for the kids that get into trouble, one here and one in Angeles City, north of Manila.' Mann called to Father Finn, who was a few strides ahead. 'I was expecting Father Vinny to pick us up. I didn't think you'd be down this way. Here on business, Father?'

'Yes, I am here to pick up a child – a boy, Eduardo. He is in hiding at the moment. We rescued him from the jail. We found him in there – wrongfully accused of stealing and imprisoned there for two months. He was shut up with men, some of them paedophiles. He was terribly abused. It will be the first case of taking the Philippine government to court. He should have been protected and he wasn't, no? He will testify against them. They will drag it out for as long as they can. The trial will take a couple of years. I am here to escort Eduardo back to Angeles, where I can protect him. But that is not the only reason I am here. I got a call from a young woman who used to live with us, in our refuge.' He stopped and turned towards Mann. 'You remember Wednesday, Johnny?'

'I remember Wednesday. Cheeky little Amerasian

girl, she was with you at the refuge in Angeles for a few months, wasn't she? That must have been, what, seven or eight years ago, Father? She must be grown up now.'

'Yes. We rescued her from a paedophile ring when she was twelve. She stayed with us for a few months and then she ran away from our shelter – it is not a prison and we cannot force the children to stay with us. Well, sadly we lost contact. I didn't know what had happened to her until she phoned me. I assumed, wrongly, that she had gone back to the bars, like so many do, but it wasn't so. When she phoned me she told me she left because she found out she was pregnant and she felt she couldn't tell us. That saddens me; there is nothing more joyful to us than the birth of a child, whatever the circumstances. Anyway, she came back here – to Davao. She was thirteen when she gave birth to a little girl. She has been a good mother. But her child has gone missing.'

They reached the car – a battered old maroon-coloured Toyota. Father Finn went round and opened all the doors quickly, whilst Mann lifted the boot and made some room inside for their bags. The heat was sweltering inside the car.

'We need to leave it to air for a few minutes. We'll turn on the air-con once we get going.'

'You have air-con? I'm impressed,' said Becky as Mann slammed the boot shut.

'Ah, well, I might have exaggerated that slightly, no?' he said with a mischievous smile. 'We have Filipino air-conditioning in the car. When the windows are down that means the air-con on. When they are up its off so, if you wouldn't mind . . .' He gestured towards the back windows

Becky smiled. 'Of course.' She slid into the back seat and set about winding the windows down as fast as she could. Her legs were already sticking to the hot leather.

Mann sat in the front beside Father Finn, who grated the old car into gear and waited for it to stop juddering before pulling erratically on the steering wheel and heading out of the car park. Becky smiled at the armed guards, who grinned back from their sentry boxes at the car-park exit, their rifles resting just inside the entrance.

'I read a report about the DDS, Father,' said Mann, his elbow resting out of the open window, his sunglasses on. 'They seem to be growing from strength to strength. They are still killing anyone the authorities deem to be undesirable. I thought that the world press would have shamed the powers-that-be into stopping them.'

'You'd think so, wouldn't you? But it's the very opposite. They are being praised for their good work. The government is encouraging all other cities to do the same – get rid of the unwanted from their streets. It's even been suggested that the government are funding them indirectly. How else would they exist?' Father Finn crossed himself and shook his head in disbelief. His erratic driving seemed to fit in perfectly with everyone else's. Cars beeped, swerved and braked continuously. 'The government is holding the city up as a shining example of a caring, crime-free city that loves its children! Something has happened to the Death Squad – they are under new management, I think. They have taken a step up. They are an organised body now. They have a bigger team – not just two men on a motorbike. They now have new cars, black, plateless, of course, and they have been seen carrying the children away.'

They passed an ambulance with no windows. Curtains were flapping, and inside a man sat slumped forward, a blue mask over his nose and mouth. He was facing backwards, towards the road. A nurse held his T-shirt from the seat behind, to stop him collapsing and falling out of the back of the vehicle.

'Is it true that the younger children are being trafficked? Is that what you think has happened to Wednesday's daughter?' asked Becky as she leaned forward between the two front seats. There were no seat belts in the old car.

'We think so. At the refuge, we have heard many stories from the children whose friends have disappeared. They have seen the black riders appear, kill one or two of the children, then force the others into a car that accompanies the riders. They are selecting the very young girls. I'll take you to talk to Wednesday. She'll be happy to see you, Johnny.'

They left the wide streets of six-lane traffic, flanked by long low factory outlet buildings and squatters' villages that had attached themselves to the factory walls and occupied every gap. The roads became congested as they split and narrowed and wove over and under-passes and they neared the city. Beside the roads litter blew and became snagged on the barbed wire that ran alongside the road. The billboards were old and tattered with flapping grey paper bits peeling away from the images. A woman advertising sanitary towels smiled apologetically out from a big sign.

For Your **Red** *Day.*

The roads were congested with Jeepneys. Drivers hanging out of the sides all honked at one another. They beeped their horns constantly to communicate with one another, not aggressively, just passing on information: *I am coming out whether you want me to or not. I am a VIP, look at my car. You are an arse.* They had their own language.

'Things are no better than the last time you came, Johnny. We seem to take ten steps forward and eleven back. There are more children living off the streets than ever before.'

'How do the children end up on the streets? They must have caring families?' Becky asked, shouting to be heard above the traffic noise.

'Poverty is a terrible catalyst for misery. They consider a life on the streets is preferable to being hungry. Sometimes the parents just can't afford to feed them and the instances of abuse in the home are high here. It's a mainly Catholic country. The lack of contraception doesn't help. I have tried to introduce the idea – but it's not popular. Condoms are still not used much, even in the sex industry girls have to work without them.'

They stopped at some traffic lights and were immediately surrounded by a group of children. Their hair was matted, their skinny arms and legs emaciated. Their little dark bodies were clothed in just a few rags. Large, desperate eyes stared out from dirty scabbed faces, but lit up when they saw the three westerners. The children were especially delighted to see Father Finn. Their tiny black hands reached inside the car like monkeys after nuts, palms outstretched and begging for change. They peered into the back and beamed at Becky. Father Finn rubbed their heads and talked to them in Tagalog as he fished in his pockets for change. Then they smiled and waved farewell as the lights changed and the car drove off. Becky looked out of the back window and watched the small ragged group as they stood at the side of the road, waiting for the lights to change to red again.

'Surely the death squads are not killing little children like those?' she asked, as she watched the children scamper out of the way of the moving traffic. She shook her head sadly. 'Someone in the world would love one of those children, would give them a home. I would,' she said quietly to herself.

Father Finn turned off the main road and made left and right turns as he headed down towards the river. Becky was still thinking about the children when they turned down one street. At the end of the road there was a rubbish dump. They were heading straight for it. But then she realised that the rubbish dump had doors and walls.

She leaned forward, between Mann and Father Finn, and stared out of the windscreen.

'What is that?'

196

'A Davao housing estate. That is where eighty thousand of the city's workers live – the waitresses, the shop assistants, the janitors, the labourers, even some teachers and professionals live here.'

'What do they do for sanitation? Water?'

'The government provides them with a standpipe for water. Sanitation? That's easy. They use a bucket and empty it straight into the water below them.'

They parked up.

'Please do up your windows,' said the Father, 'otherwise our seats will be someone's new three-piece suite when we come back.'

They followed Father Finn as he walked along the mash of cardboard and rusty tin until he found the entrance he was looking for – the alleyway that marked the beginning of the slum town, on the edge of the Davao River. They left the sunny street and walked into darkness and stench as they entered the Barrio Patay, the Place of the Dead.

33

Mann walked behind Becky. He could see that her shoulders were rigid. She kept her eyes straight ahead. They slipped down an alleyway and were immediately plunged into darkness and stench – a stifling world of raw poverty – a living rubbish heap. And yet, children ran past, laughing and playing amidst the putrefaction. A sleeping woman dozed on a platform next to the alleyway. An old man squatted on the ground and washed himself. In the rubbish heap was a normal world.

The slum was a myriad of tunnel roads and windy narrow paths that were built without a plan. They had grown upward and outward organically. Sometimes they opened out to allow the sky in, other times they delved into a dark hole. It had areas where more care had been taken to keep the dwelling smart. It had festering places that housed the near dead, who lay in their doorways and had not the energy to even blink as they watched the strangers walk by. They wandered deeper and deeper as Father Finn wound his way through. Becky followed one step behind him. She was glad she had trainers on; she'd hate to slip and fall on the walkway. There was a hollow sound as they crossed over narrow planks, anchored in the water by bamboo posts. Below them the river appeared, seething with garbage, refuse. Methane bubbled from the untreated sewage that fermented at the water's edge and settled as black sludge. Two-storied dwellings hemmed them in on either side. Precarious planks were bridges and ramps to the upper storeys. A rope ran beside them to hold on to.

'Don't touch the handrail,' warned the Father, and Becky could see why. It was covered in excrement that had come directly from the windows above.

Becky wanted to cover her mouth to avoid the over-powering smell of sewage, but the look on the children's faces as they ran past her told her that this was their home; they didn't notice the smell and neither should she.

They turned left and headed down a narrow path that took them along the water's edge. Each dwelling was no more than twelve-foot square, rising up in layers of corrugated iron and cardboard. A thin stream of sunlight came through the six-foot-wide lane.

'Wednesday lives here alone with her daughter. She takes in washing for a living.'

Father Finn stopped outside an entrance crisscrossed with washing lines. They were strung across the alleyway and ingeniously hung from every available point. T-shirts, pants, shorts and sheets hung down and blocked the path in places. He pulled back a yellowing piece of net at the door and called out.

There was no sound from inside, and it was dark. He called again. A woman came out from behind the neighbouring curtain. She looked at the three Caucasians with surprise and suspicion, but at the same time she gave the obligatory smile. Father Finn addressed her in Tagalog. She listened, staring curiously at Becky and Mann, and then she turned her head, pointing in the direction of the river and one of the paths that led to it. A young woman was making her way back along the planks carrying bags of washing. Her sinewy arms looked used to carrying heavy loads. She had a thick blunt fringe; the rest of her hair was tied back from her face and caught in a ponytail at the nape of her neck. She wore a red T-shirt and shorts. She was barefoot. She looked up and saw the Father and gave a sad, grateful smile. Her large eyes were set in a triangular face. Becky saw that she was mixed race. When she saw Mann her face looked puzzled for a few seconds, before it lifted into a bigger smile and tears came into her eyes.

'There she is.' Father Finn went forward to help her with the washing. He took the heavy baskets from her and set them down near the entrance to her house.

'Hello, Wednesday. Do you remember this handsome man?' He nodded in Mann's direction. Wednesday smiled up at Mann, and then she quickly looked away as her eyes immediately spilt the tears she'd been holding back. 'And this lady is Becky – a policewoman from the UK.' Wednesday looked from one to the other, her eyes shining through the tears. She wiped her face and then her hand on her shorts.

'Thank you,' she said, clutching Becky's hand. 'Thank you, sir, ma'am. You come find my baby?' Her eyes were black-rimmed, bagged below from sorrow and lack of sleep.

Father Finn spoke to her in Tagalog. She listened and bowed her head respectfully at the Father's words. He finished in English.

'Johnny here, and his colleague, Becky, will help us look for her. We will do our best, Wednesday, you know that. You must hold out hope. Be brave, be strong . . .'

'Please come in . . .' she said as she pulled back the net curtain for them to enter. Inside she switched on a light. One bare bulb hung down. The wire ran along the ceiling and disappeared. The walls were made up of flattened cans and pieces of plywood. A piece of plywood on bricks served both as a sitting platform and a bed.

The Father spoke to her again and she nodded her agreement.

'She thinks her daughter was being watched by the DDS. She thinks that she was targeted by them. Other children have told Wednesday that they saw the men in black several times before Maya disappeared. She has been to the killing field, where the bodies are usually dumped. Her daughter is not there. She says many young girls have disappeared recently. No one knows where they go, but there is talk of them ending up in one of the sex resorts.'

Wednesday started to cry. Father Finn hugged her again and spoke softly. She took a photo from her pocket and handed it to him. He passed it to the others.

The little girl sat, hands in her lap, school uniform on, and smiled at the camera. Her oversized front teeth were slightly crossed, which gave her an elfin look. She looked a lot like her mother – same big eyes, triangular face. She was a pretty child.

'Can we keep this?' Becky asked gently.

Wednesday nodded and smiled. A small spark of hope entered her eyes. She looked at each of them, then she took Becky's hand and held it with both of hers.

'My little girl – so small.' She wiped the tears from her eyes.

Becky put her arm around her.

'We will do our best to find her, Wednesday.'

Father Finn spoke to her again. She listened, but halfway through the conversation she lowered her eyes and looked at the floor as she shook her head.

'She has heard that her little girl has been taken to Angeles. I told her she must stay where she is. I will go there myself and look for her.' Wednesday nodded and looked at Becky and Mann – dread in her eyes.

'The Father is right, Wednesday,' Mann said. 'Stay here where she can find you. We will look for her for you.' He turned the photo over. On the back was written Maya's name and her age. 'We will look for Maya for you.'

34

Maya looked at the bed next to her where Perla had been. The mattress had been washed by the women and laid on its end against the wall to dry. Maya had watched them do it. The Kano had spread the blanket over the floor and pulled Perla onto it. Perla had been left in the middle of the room whilst the women washed the floor. Maya had looked at Perla for a long time. Perla's body was stiff and strange-looking and she lay awkwardly. The Kano had shouted at them and he had hit her when she looked at Perla, but still Maya had not been able to take her eyes from her. She could not help thinking how uncomfortable she looked.

Now, three days later, Perla was gone, but her blood crept back out of the cracks in the floor and formed a black ragged line. Maya could smell it. Like bad meat. She kept staring at the line. It was as if every time she took her eyes from it, it moved closer.

35

Back on the street, Father Finn started the engine and turned the car around. Mann insisted Becky sat in the front this time. He knew she would want to ask Father Finn a lot of questions, he could see it in her face. She might have seen poverty on a backpacker's trip to India but there was nothing like having this kind of real insight into a world that most would never want to know.

Mann opened the windows in the back and looked long and hard at the slums that they were all so grateful to leave behind.

'Has she lived there since she left the refuge, Father?' asked Becky.

'Yes, she came back here when she found out she was pregnant, and she brought her daughter up here. She lives for that little girl. It's not easy on your own, but Wednesday has done a good job with Maya. I talked to the teachers at the school and they say Maya's a bright little girl and always clean and tidy. Wednesday's own mother sold her to a bar owner when she was seven. He was, and still is, a known paedophile in the

Angeles area. He promised he would send her to school and that she would grow up in his household. I don't for one minute expect the mother believed a cock and bull story like that – but it eased her conscience, no?'

They headed towards town. The city began to build up around them.

'Wednesday has done well to make it, once the girls are broken it is very hard to make them whole again – they often run back to the bar owners when they are rescued.'

'I know all the reasons on paper but I will never really understand how a mother can sell her own daughter?'

'Poverty. Ignorance. It's hard to understand, but it goes back further than one generation. It isn't easy bringing up any child, especially an Amerasian. Wednesday's father was an American sailor who left when the Clark naval base shut down and he deserted her and her mother.'

'Doesn't she have any rights?'

'The American government ruled that they were the children born from prostitution, but it isn't true – lots of these women were common-law wives.'

'But the children, can't they find their real fathers now?'

'I have helped some track their fathers. I have helped them write letters. Of the dozens we have sent, only one has come back and that was because the man wanted to put his affairs in order as he was dying of cancer.' Father Finn was clearly moved and angry as his voice climbed in pitch and his face reddened. 'The men who abandoned these women and children simply don't care.' He banged his palms on the old leather steering wheel and caused a volley of beeping horns as he veered to the left. Mann sat up in the back and moved forward. 'The American bases did untold damage here,' Father Finn continued. 'I believe it also ruined the men themselves – they came over here as young, impressionable lads, they witnessed the demeaning of women, the rape of children, and they became desensitised. In those days it wasn't uncommon to witness spectacles such as boxing matches staged between the girls. You have to ask yourself what that would do to the mind of a young man, no?' Father Finn shook his head sadly.

'What do you think has happened to Maya, Father?' asked Becky.

The father sighed. 'I know it's an odd thing to hope for, but our best scenario is that the child is a victim of traffickers and that she is still in the Philippines. The alternative is that she is already dead, killed by the DDS or has been trafficked abroad.'

'But, if she's alive and still in the Philippines, she could be anywhere by now, couldn't she, Father?'

They came to a standstill in the rush-hour traffic heading through the city. Exposed bunches of black cables hung down like destroyed spiders' webs and crisscrossed the street above their heads. All around them workers were hanging out of the side of Jeepneys. Becky no longer needed to shout, but her chest felt tight with the fumes coming in the open window. People smiled at her as they watched her from the traffic jam. She couldn't get over how friendly they were.

Mann bought a breadfruit from a man walking along the rows of stationary traffic selling a variety of goods from fruit to feather dusters and fishing rods.

'Luckily . . .' he leaned in between the two front seats '. . . it does not affect the whole of the seven thousand islands – there are distinct sex tourism areas. I think Angeles is where she'll be – it has the seediest reputation.'

'I agree,' said Father Finn. 'There is one man there worse than the rest; he calls himself the Colonel. He is the man who pimped Wednesday all those years ago and he is still there.' Father Finn shook his head in disbelief. 'He has set himself up as a God in Angeles; it should not be allowed to happen.'

Mann turned the breadfruit round absent-mindedly in his hands as he spoke.

'I know the Colonel. I've been watching him over the years. His network of paedophile businesses has been allowed to continue for so long that now he believes no one can touch him. But he's made a mistake siding with his new friends – the White Circle – they are a new trafficking group who are muscling their way in. The kidnap of the girl in the UK is linked to them and their power struggle. He might think he's about to hit it big, but he's wrong. His time just ran out. We will find Maya, find out who has Amy Tang, and then we will shut him down, Father, once and for all. If the locals won't do it – we'll do it for them.' He looked at his hands – he had ruined the breadfruit.

'If Maya is alive then she could well be hidden there, no? She will probably be being seasoned.' Father Finn glanced over at Becky. He did not want to have to explain the term – he didn't need to.

'I know what "seasoning" is,' said Becky. 'It's a softening-up process preparing them for the ordeal, making them ready to be sold for sex, to accept it and not give any trouble. It involves different stages: intimidation, isolation, disorientation, bullying and violence. Then, when their spirit is broken, they are sold. Who would be most likely to buy her?'

'A wealthy Asian or Caucasian,' answered Father Finn. 'She will be kept under lock and key and used for a week by him exclusively. Their virginity is the premium. It has all sorts of beliefs tied up in it: of course you're not going to get AIDS from a virgin. Some of them even believe it can *cure* AIDS,' added the Father, shaking his head incredulously. After a week their price drops, but they are still valuable. For the next two weeks they will be offered to select customers who can pay. After that they go into a brothel, chained to the bed like all the others. She will be servicing eight or more men a day and kept in nothing more than a cage. They get very sick. The life expectancy of a working girl in Angeles is not good, it has been reported as being twenty-five but no one can be sure. They don't get enough food and they get beaten. TB still kills many, as do untreated STDs. AIDS is just starting here, but everyone is in denial about it. No one wants to admit to being HIV positive because that is the end of their working life then, and there is no help for them.'

All the time the Father was speaking, Becky held

Maya's photo in her hand and stared at it. 'How will she survive all that?'

'What is your plan now, you two?' Father Finn changed the subject abruptly. He never liked to dwell too long in melancholy. He had lived with the poverty and degradation for so long that he knew it would break him if he didn't hang on to hope.

'I suggest we stay here tonight, Becky. See if anyone at the refuge can come up with anything to help us. Then we make our way up to Angeles.'

'Thank the Lord!' Father Finn crossed himself and flashed a mischievous look at Becky in the mirror as the traffic freed up and they were able to move slowly along the road. 'My life wouldn't be worth living if I came back to the refuge without you. When they knew Johnny Mann was coming it started them all off. It's all the girls were talking about today. Where is Johnny? What time will he get here? How is my hair? Does my bum look big in this? They'd started bickering and fighting over who was going to wear what by the time I left.'

Mann started to protest. Becky laughed.

'I bet they had.'

'So, spend the night with us. I have a friend with a plane. He is at your disposal. You will like him. Remy was a priest, now married with too many children for me to count and a small airline business. He helps keep the mosquito population down by spraying insecticide now and again, and he is also the flying doctor when needs must. I will ring him now and organise for him to fly you up tomorrow. I have a few more days' work here, then I'll be heading back to Angeles to continue the search for Maya.'

They passed a sign on the road: a young girl in a tight white bodice was holding a bottle of whisky:

Have you ever tasted a fifteen-year-old?

36

Maya needed to go to the toilet. She was hungry and she was dirty. She was not chained up like the other girls, but she was too frightened to move in any case. Maya was not allowed to leave the room. She was only allowed to walk as far as the toilet. She was not allowed to talk to anyone, and she was told that if she stepped outside the windowless room she would be killed straight away. The other girls were older than her and had been there for a long time. Maya listened to them talk to one another. They had to go with men all day long. Downstairs, where there were rooms. The men would come and then all the girls had to go and sit in a room and the men would choose which ones they wanted. The girls were never allowed to leave the Bordello. When they were finished with one man they had to go back in the room and wait for another. At night-time they came to sleep for a few hours and the Kano chained them up.

Now Maya must wait until the Kano came to unlock the chains and then she could go to the toilet. At the end of the room was a sick girl. She did not go to work with the others – she was too ill. The more Maya looked at the girl, the more uncomfortable Maya became. She seemed to just be laying there staring at Maya. Was she dead too, like Perla? Then the sick girl coughed and Maya jumped. The sick girl smiled at her and held her hand up to beckon Maya to her. Maya looked at the arm – it stayed suspended in the air, thin and black like a spider's leg. The girl started coughing again. She turned away from Maya and coughed for several minutes, spitting blood out over her blanket before laying back down, exhausted. For a few minutes Maya watched the girl's chest rise and fall and listened to the squealing noise of her difficult breathing, then the girl turned and beckoned Maya forward again.

Maya walked gingerly towards her. When she got to her side Maya saw that she was not much older than Perla had been.

'My name is Rosie.' The girl pointed to herself and then pointed at Maya. 'You?'

'Maya.'

'Come,' Rosie smiled.

Maya climbed onto the bed and lay down beside her and Rosie wrapped her arm around her and drew her in close. They lay like two spoons in the murky darkness of the quiet room and listened to the sound of the other girls sleeping.

'Listen to me, Maya,' Rosie whispered. 'And I will tell you what you have to do to stay alive . . .'

37

'It's a lovely place, Father.'

They pulled up outside the white-painted villa, shaded with mature palms that left their shadows on the white walls. A mosaic front of blue tiles gave the place a Moorish feel.

'We renovated an old government building, but it has a beautiful Spanish feel to it, and it's important that we are in the city where the trouble is. But it is not as beautiful as the refuge in Angeles – that is built on the side of a mountain, surrounded by forest – you will see it, I hope.'

'And how many children do you have here?'

'Five more than we should – thirty-five, at the moment. We have expanded the refuge so many times over the years and still it never is big enough, but we are always working on ways to improve it. We have created small centres in the countryside. We realised early on that it was not enough just to rescue the children from the brothels and the prisons and streets. There was no point in just returning them to their families. The whole family needed to change. We are providing them with an income by reviving traditional techniques, basket-weaving, coconut-shell jewellery, that kind of thing. We sell the things over the Internet and to trade fares. It has really taken off in the last two years. We now have five hundred families supported by the scheme. Supporting themselves and supporting each other.'

'Where did most of the children come from?'

Father Finn's face turned distant and troubled as he turned to talk to them.

'From the streets, from the jails. The children are not supposed to be imprisoned any more. They have their own detention centres. But they are, sadly, not much better than the prison. They have very little to eat and no exercise; there are eighty to a cell that was only meant to house twenty. They have to take it in turns to sleep and the place is regularly flooded.' He shook his head sadly. 'We *still* find children locked up with adults, even though the government promised that it would stop. We go around regularly, usually every Saturday night, and see if there are any children locked up. We find it often.' The Father looked back to the door to make sure he had time to tell them before they got inside the refuge. 'When we found Eduardo he was locked in a cell with twelve men, made to clean their faeces around the stinking hole that is the toilet in the corner of the cell, and he was passed from lap to lap, raped in the corner of the cell. If he refused to let them have sex with him he was beaten and starved. If he cried he was beaten and starved. When we found him he was lying on the floor of the cell, covered in sores and septic wounds, bitten by cockroaches and mosqui-toes. He wasn't even allowed the dignity of clothing . . .' Father Finn banged his palm against the steering wheel and the anger returned to his face. 'That's why it is important to bring Eduardo's case before government. They must be held accountable, no?'

Excited faces had begun appearing at the windows as soon as Father Finn parked up. Small hands waved furiously at them. The Father excused himself and marched off in his usual military fashion, as he went inside to organise the staff and children to come and greet their guests. Mann got the cases out of the boot and walked around to the front of the car. Becky stood and stared at him over the bonnet.

'How can he bear it?' She shook her head incredulously and shrugged her shoulders.

Mann could see that she was shell-shocked by the volume of human misery that they had encountered in one day. Maybe he had become desensitised over the years.

'It's one horrible story after another,' she said quietly.

They heard the sound of excited children being organised at the front door. Then Mann thought it was not so much that he had gone numb; more likely he had been infected by Father Finn's relentless hope.

'He can bear it because he has enough love and hope to see it through. He will never stop trying. As long as the world allows it to carry on, Father Finn will keep fighting, and along the way he makes a big difference to people's lives. He saves so many of them.'

'But it's hard to believe that such things go on here,

the place is so beautiful and the people so positive and happy. It just seems so wrong. They are lucky they have the Fathers to fight for them. I'm surprised that they are not deported.'

'People try and get rid of the priests all ways. Some of the Father's friends have been murdered, others have been beaten up. Father Finn has the scars to prove it, that's why he walks so fast everywhere. He lives under the constant threat of assassination. The paedophile westerners that he attacks would just love to see him dead.'

Father Finn came back to hurry them and escort them into the refuge. He was obviously immensely proud of it and all the people inside it.

'Come on, Becky, I would like to show you some of the work we do here and introduce you to the staff.'

'That would be great, Father. I would love to see around.'

By the time they reached the door, Becky had ten girls hanging off her arms.

'They think you're a film star!' said Father Finn. The staff – a group of four women and two men – had been patiently waiting to be introduced, smiling hope-fully at Becky and Mann. Father Finn ushered them forward. 'Mann, you remember most of these people, I am sure?'

'Of course.' Mann did the introductions. 'Becky, these two lovely ladies at the end are Jenny and Clementa, they do the cooking.'

Clementa was a robust-looking woman in her sixties. Her ample breasts were contained in a pink T-shirt but not supported by a bra and were resting on the waist-band of a white apron tied around her waist. She was head cook. She spoke very little English but was so overcome and embarrassed that she hid her mouth as she smiled, to disguise the fact that she had two front teeth missing. Pretty-faced Jenny, her assistant, gave them a big toothy smile and a small curtsey.

'Here is Maria – she is the housekeeper, keeps us all in line,' he said, whilst introducing a woman no taller than a child but with the sinewy outline of one who never stopped working. 'And this is Philip, the gardener, the newest addition to the refuge, who does a great job, as you can see . . .' The young man eyed Becky over as he thanked Mann for his praise. '. . . and this wonder-fully pregnant lady is Mercy, with her husband Ramon.' Mercy was a no-nonsense-looking woman with the strong, pretty features of a woman of Spanish ancestry. Her husband, Ramon, was a man in his prime, with broad square shoulders and a handsome face. Mercy looked ready to pop. Her tight round stomach was a source of great joy to all those around, including the children, who kept rushing up to touch it.

'Mercy and Ramon met here at the refuge, they were street children. Now they are responsible for setting up all the resource centres around the country. We now have twenty-five working cooperatives in the rural areas – all as a result of Mercy and Ramon's hard work.' Father Finn was obviously immensely proud of the couple. 'You will see them when you come to Angeles. Like me, they are only visiting here in Davao and we have to get Mercy back home before she pops.'

They stepped forward to shake Becky's hand. Mercy smiled and shook her head. Her English was very good. She remonstrated with the Father: 'It is always a team effort. Please, come in, and welcome to our refuge.'

Mercy led the way through the first building into the second, which was a large high-ceilinged room with paintings and posters that the children had produced all around its walls, along with handicrafts they had made.

'It has taken a few years to really take off, but now we have outlets all over the world. And we send representatives to tell schoolchildren about our work.'

'Come inside and meet the rest of the children,' said the Father.

From the corner of her eye Becky saw a small boy standing in the corner. He did not rush forward with the other children. He had a broad forehead and newly shorn hair that stood up bristly and black. His eyes were dark and smudged. His thick eyebrows were pinched together, giving him the look of someone carrying a weight of sorrow and pain on his small shoulders.

The father caught sight of him and went and knelt in front of him. 'Eduardo! How is my brave boy today?'

Eduardo did not speak.

'He is doing fine, Father,' Mercy answered.

Father Finn turned the little boy's arms over and examined his wounds.

'Getting better already, Eduardo. Soon you'll be as handsome as that man over there . . .' He pointed to Mann.

Mann held his hands up in a surrender gesture. 'He's much better looking than me.'

Eduardo was not taking any notice of the Father or Mann, because he was staring transfixed at Becky.

Father Finn traced his line of vision. Becky smiled and mouthed 'hello'.

'You have an admirer,' Father Finn said when he came back to join her. 'Eduardo can't keep his eyes off you.'

'He's so little to have suffered so much. It must be heartbreaking for you, Father, he looks so ill.'

'The scars will heal, and one day he will smile again and then my heart will break with joy. One day we'll have justice for him. I fear for his life unless I can make sure he is by my side twenty-four-seven. It's going to take years to bring the government to justice. They are going to make it as difficult as possible.'

'Is it really possible to recover from an ordeal like he's been through?'

'He will never forget, and we cannot undo the damage that has been done, but we will give him a home for life and look after him, that's the best we can do, no? Come, Becky, we don't often get visitors and the children want their autograph books signed. Sit here please.'

Becky thought he was kidding until she saw the children and the open books and eager pens waiting for her. She dutifully sat on the battered sofa in the open-plan lounge area, which was tile-floored and white-walled. The children had created a Filipino history frieze that ran around the walls. As she sat and chatted to them and looked at their pictures, Eduardo inched closer until he was sitting so close to her that he was touching her, and all the time he kept his eyes glued to her face. When she stood to follow the children and be shown around the refuge, he slipped his hand into hers.

Mann left them to show Becky around; he'd been to the refuge many times. 'Have you got Internet here, Father?' he asked. 'I can get it on my phone but it's painfully slow.'

'Of course, when it works – brown-outs are still the plague of the Philippines.'

Mann was in luck. The Internet was almost as slow as his mobile, but it was working. He checked his email and worked through it all until there was one left in Mann's email tray. He almost deleted it as spam – he didn't recognise the sender – but decided to open it.

BLANCO sends you greetings and he has a present for you . . . press **Here** *to collect your gift.*
Your time is running out.

Mann clicked and waited. An image appeared. It was Amy Tang with a noose around her neck.

38

Maya lay very still and listened to Rosie.

'Do as you are told, Maya. Do not fight the Kanos. Give in. But not in here . . .' She tapped her head. 'Keep in here safe. Then you will see your mamma again. Do whatever they want, then you will live . . .' She smiled and reached around Maya and pulled her closer.

Maya's eyes were wide as she stared out at the dawn that was trying to break through three small slats. They were too high and too narrow to see out of properly. They were meant purely to feed air into the stifling room. Rosie resumed her coughing so fiercely that she shooed Maya away with her hand and spat blood into her blanket. When she was finished she smiled at Maya's concerned face and reassured her with a shake of the head. She waited a few minutes until she regained control of her breathing, then resumed her whispering.

'When you see the Kano coming towards you with the buzzy stick you must put something in your mouth quick, before he pokes you with it. Put anything you can in your mouth – even your hand if you have to – because otherwise you will bite your tongue and you

221

will break your teeth. And, listen to me, Maya – keep a picture of your mama in your head. She will be looking for you, Maya. I know that she will be.'

'Is *your* mama coming, Rosie?'

'I don't think so, Maya. My mama sold me to this place. It is too late for me. There is no one to come for me. But yours is on her way, I am sure. Never give up hope, never.'

Then Rosie fell asleep with her arm around Maya. Maya knew she should go back to her own bed now that the Kano would be coming soon, but Maya did not want to wake Rosie and she could not bear to leave. When she heard the Kano's footsteps on the stairs she hoped if she laid very still the Kano would not see her. But the Kano saw everything. It was too late for her to run back to her bed. Now they would both pay the price of disobeying.

39

Wednesday had not slept. She lay on the piece of hardboard that was her bed and watched the dawn filter weakly through the cracks in her cardboard house. She heard the children outside getting ready for school. She heard the baby crying opposite. She knew that right now she would usually be watching Maya sleeping soundly beside her, and she would get up first and light the stove ready to make them tea and heat water for rice. There was only work for Wednesday to get up for now. Her eyes were sore; her breathing hurt in her chest; her stomach ached for her child. Her whole life was pointless without Maya. The love for her child was the only love Wednesday had ever known. She did not remember the mother who had sold her to the Colonel. She had no memories of any affection. She had grown up sitting on the Colonel's lap, sleeping in his bed. She was like a lap dog. One night the rage overtook him and when Wednesday awoke the sheets were covered in her blood and her stomach was agony. He had drugged and raped her. From that moment on she was no longer his pet. Wednesday was sold to a Japanese man with tattoos all over his body. He had been horrible to her – he had shouted at her and beaten and raped her until she learned what she had to do. She had to crawl on her hands and knees to him and tell him that she was his dirty little Filipina, she was not worthy of him. Then he would show her some gentleness.

After the Japanese came the old Caucasians, the young ones, the blacks, the whites, the Asians, and anyone else who could pay. Wednesday lost count of how many she had sex with and she lost all hope . . . until the day when Father Finn banged on the Dutchman's door and rescued her from his bed. Until that day Wednesday had thought her heart was dead. But when Father Finn had picked her up and marched out of there with her under his arm, he had changed her life forever and showed her what it was to care for another person, to risk for another and to open your heart and love another. On the first night she had sat with the other children at the refuge she had known her life was just beginning. It was the happiest she had ever been. She learned to play. She learned to laugh. Father Finn was her world. He was a hero to her. He taught her to read and write. He told her how smart she was and made her believe she could be anything she wanted. The Father was always telling her she could stay at the refuge as long as she liked, and she would have done, had she not discovered she was pregnant. She had no idea who the father might be. She had only just begun to have periods and had not known to use contraception. She felt her stomach grow hard and become round and she knew she could not spoil it all now. She felt the shame of it. She had to get rid of it. She knew the Father would never agree to an abortion. She knew he would want her to have the baby. But this was Wednesday's chance of life. She had to get rid of the baby. She ran home to Davao, to a woman in the Barrio Patay whom everyone knew as an abortionist. But Wednesday's flight was in vain. When she lay on the woman's floor, her legs open and the woman's fingers inside her, she felt the baby flutter. Wednesday knew it was too late for an abortion now. The baby was calling to her. It knew it had a mama and Wednesday knew she was it. Now she prayed with all her heart that Father Finn could be her hero again and rescue her baby.

She sat on the edge of the bed. It was then she heard the clamour from outside in the alleyways. Someone was calling her name. A small boy that she knew as Pepe was standing at her doorway.

'What do you want, Pepe? Is it washing for your mama?'

He shook his head. 'I have a message for you.'

'Who from?'

'A man stopped me – a Kano. He said I was to tell you something.' Pepe hovered at the door. 'He told me I was to say that you must go to Angeles, the Colonel is waiting and he has your daughter.'

'Aye!' Wednesday clutched her fists to her chest. 'Maya? He has Maya?'

Pepe nodded.

'What else did he say? You must try and remember everything, Pepe, *please* . . .'

The boy rolled his eyes skyward as he tried to recollect word for word what the Kano had said.

'He said tell her to come alone – no priests. If you come with priests he will slit her throat.'

40

Maya pushed back the hair that fell over her eyes. It was morning and she knew that she should wash her face and brush her hair. She knew her mummy would not let her look like she did. She could see the bathroom but she had to wait for the Kano to come and unlock her cage, then she would carefully carry the bucket from the back of her cell and empty it in the toilet. She pushed her hair back and tried to make it stay behind her ears. She missed Rosie. She knew it was her own fault that they had got caught. She had known the Kano was coming but she didn't want to leave Rosie's side and so the Kano had seen her and he had beaten her and put her in the cage. Maya's cage was opposite the bathroom. It was four foot deep and three foot wide. At the back of it the cockroaches ran. The Kano came twice a day. He brought her food. Maya had to reach through the bars to get it – the Kano put it too far for her, so that just her fingertips could touch it. It hurt her arms to stretch so far. He shouted at her in English. Maya did not understand what he was saying. She had only learned a few words in English.

She could count to ten and sing a song called 'London Bridge' and she could tell someone that she was from the Philippines and that her name was Maya. Every day the big Kano came into her cell and poked her with the buzzy stick. The pain was worse than the jelly-fish that had stung her when she went swimming with her mother. Afterwards her teeth hurt and her bones ached. She shivered. She tried to hold thoughts in her head for as long as she could. Maya could see her mother's face when she closed her eyes. She squeezed them shut and tried to think of nothing else.

Maya watched the big bald Kano come up the stairs a few feet from her cage. His massive legs were like a monster's. His back was bare and a huge bird flew across the skin. He glanced her way then he went on into the bedroom where the women were. In a minute Maya would hear the chains clanking as he released them; soon she would see the women pass by to wash. But today there was screaming. Maya covered her ears. It was a terrible sound to hear the Kano beating someone like a dog being whipped. Maya shut her eyes and ears as hard as she could. When she opened them she saw that the Kano had Rosie by the hair and he was dragging her into the corridor. Maya held tight to the bars as she watched Rosie being punched and kicked. Rosie was not making any sound. There was just the noise of the Kano hitting her. Maya looked out from her cage, watching wide-eyed. Then the Kano stopped hitting Rosie. Rosie was lying on the floor; she was not moving any more. The Kano's chest moved up and down as he breathed hard. The veins in his head stood out like worms. The other women were crying. Maya moved to the back wall, where she sat as small as she could in the corner. The Kano knelt down in front of her cage and beckoned her forward. Maya didn't move. She pulled nervously at her T-shirt and chewed her lip and pressed herself back hard into the wall. He beckoned again.

'Come.' His fingers snapped open and shut.

The Kano had to be obeyed. Rosie had told her; *always do what he wants and then you might see your mama again. Never disobey the Kano.* Maya inched forward. *Only keep your heart your own. They cannot take what is inside your heart and head, but give them the rest, give him the body, otherwise they will take it anyway and they will kill you.* She took one step forward, then another. When she was near enough the Kano reached through the bars and pulled her by her T-shirt until she was squashed against the bars, then he reached behind and pulled Rosie forward by her hair and pushed her face against Maya's. She had no eyes left with which to see Maya. Maya's seasoning was nearly complete.

41

'You understand there will be no turning back.'

Two men faced one another in the damp-smelling basement that had tables and chairs stacked in the corner, spares for the restaurant above. People passed by on Wardour Street outside. Only their calves were visible as they walked by the barred windows set at pavement height.

The younger man was bare-chested and his feet were shoeless. His skin was smeared in dirt.

'I understand. I have made my choice. I come before you a poor man with nothing.'

The older man wore a white tunic with a red stole around his neck, and around his waist was a white sash. On one of his feet he wore a grass sandal.

A third man, dressed in black robes, stood in front of an altar covered in a red cloth, on which stood an idol of Kwan Ti, the patron saint of triads. Joss sticks burned jasmine incense in golden holders. Triad weapons: eight throwing stars, four bone-handled shuriken and a spiked chain were spread out upon the red altar cloth, their bright steel incongruous in the gloom and dirt of the makeshift triad lodge.

'I have made my choice.'

In front of the statue of Kwan Ti was a rolled piece of parchment on which was written an agreement, a treaty, an allegiance. It had been witnessed by the three men and now it needed to be signed. But no pen would do the act, blood must be their bond. Each man would spill his blood into a cup and it would be sipped and shared amongst them. Then the parchment would be burnt and the contract would become binding. Two men had already bled into the golden bowl – one remained to commit the act that would seal his fate. The older man handed the small carved-handled shuriken, its tip especially sharpened for the job of cutting flesh, to the young man. His face intent on the job, his muscles tense along his arm, he swiped the blade across the inside of his forearm and held it out for the older man to catch the drips.

Now, the smell of the burning paper filled the small room as its cinders floated in the air, and Micky's arm still dripped blood.

42

'Come, sit on my lap.' The Colonel patted his leg. The Colonel and Terry were sitting on the balcony at Lolita's. They sat by the metal railings, looking down. The place had been done out in a builders'-yard style, there was a lot of sheet metal and iron cladding.

It wasn't the Colonel's usual seat, but he liked to surprise himself now and again and see his world as a punter might see it – from all angles.

Brandon pushed the child forward and then left to check on things. Maya walked slowly towards the Colonel. He pulled her onto his lap.

It was early but Lolita's was busy. There were several tour parties of young men in. All eighty-six GROs were out, winding their ways around poles, dancing in couples. The girls smiled at Maya. She stared back. Maya wondered how the girls could like wearing what they did: yellow thong bikinis and black high-heeled boots. All the women Maya knew would be very uncomfortable dressed like that. They would never show their stomachs and their legs.

'You look like your mother.'

It was her first time out of the Bordello in two weeks. She hadn't seen Rosie since the day the big Kano had beaten her. The other women said she was dead and that the big Kano had taken her body and thrown it away.

When the big Kano came to get her she thought he was going to kill her. But then he made her wash and brush her teeth. He gave her a clean T-shirt and some shorts to put on and brought her here. Maya looked at the man whose lap she was sitting on; she didn't like the look of him at all.

'Yes, you are just like your mother,' said the Colonel. 'I took her cherry too, it was on a Wednesday.' He laughed at the child's bewildered face and rocked so hard on his chair that Maya nearly fell from his lap. 'You are right, Terry . . .' He stopped and leaned forward; his face was sweating and his eyes yellowed. '. . . they are a whole fucking generation of baby whores.'

On the main circular stage downstairs, ten girls dressed in schoolgirl outfits trooped out to perform a choreographed dance routine. They swung their hair and lifted their miniskirts to reveal frilly thongs. Ten minutes and three routines later they came off the stage to whoops and hoots from the men. The place was charged tonight, throbbing with testosterone and youth. The young men banged their fists on the table and wanted to see more. So did the Colonel. His head snapped from side to side as he leaned over the railings and watched the goings-on. His eyes shone as he laughed like a lunatic and called out from the balcony. Trouble was brewing – sporadic fights were breaking out everywhere. Their youthful energy made the Colonel mad. Young men demanded more action. They were content in the first few days with just being whorists, and then they wanted to go that extra mile. They wanted to be entertained. Tonight Fields Avenue was packed with them.

Brandon came to join them. One look at the Colonel told him they were in for trouble. It made Brandon very uncomfortable when his boss was in this mood. Brandon glanced at Terry. Terry didn't respond and kept working on his laptop. Anyway, he had seen it all before. The Colonel needed him – it was Terry's name on the property documents and on the licences. Brandon had a lot to learn. Unless it benefited Terry in some way, Terry was not quick to help him. Why should he? It was every man for himself in this world. But Terry was uncomfortable with Maya jigging about on the Colonel's lap. Terry didn't care what people did behind closed doors, he didn't mind that most of the girls dancing around him were under sixteen, but at least they could pass for older. The child on the Colonel's lap was a baby. Someone in the club wouldn't like that, he was sure.

On the lower floor the men were having drinking competitions. One of the tables was getting carried away with some of the GROs.

'Fuck her. Go on . . . fuck her . . .' screamed the Colonel from his lofty position as he watched the scene below becoming lewd – two of the men were holding a girl's leg open whilst a third was simulating sex. The girls looked at him and giggled nervously. Boundaries might be crossed that could not be uncrossed. *No sex in the club. No lewd acts in the club*. Those were the rules, but the Colonel had made them and he could break them.

'We need some more fucking action in this place, Terry.'

Terry didn't answer, just tapped away at his keyboard.

The Colonel turned to Brandon. 'Make them fight.'

Even Terry looked up from his laptop at the Colonel to make sure he'd heard right. But the Colonel wasn't looking at Terry; his bulging red-rimmed eyes were fixed on Brandon. He repeated his demand.

'Make them fight.'

He had blobs of spittle collecting at the corners of his mouth and he was spraying as he spoke. There was no placating him now. They had left it too late. They'd have to roll with it now – no choice. Terry would have to have a word with Brandon later, tell him how to work the Colonel better next time – otherwise it would go badly for them all. An out-of-control speed freak was not what they needed to front their rise to power.

Fight? Brandon didn't know what the Colonel was talking about, but Terry did. The Colonel wanted a boxing match. He wanted the girls to fight. Terry remembered the boxing matches of old. They had nearly brought about the end to the club scene – they were a step too far. The priests in the refuge had organised pickets and some of the girls had been foolish enough to join them. In the end, inevitably, the ring-leader had their throats slit and the pickets stopped, but so did the fights, and it had been bad for business as people stayed away until the fuss died down. It had been fifteen years since Terry had seen the last boxing match here. Now the men had to content themselves with watching girls fire corks out of their pussies at each other, or write Lolita's whilst holding a pen inside their vaginas. But now, courtesy of the Colonel, they were in for a savage retro treat.

'Clear some space. Tell the manager to get the boxing ring out of storage. It's time we gave these guys a show. It'll be like the old days when the Americans were here. We need an Amazonian contest. We need proper entertainment again.'

Within half an hour a boxing ring was assembled on the multi-coloured stage.

The Colonel called the mamasan over and told her to fetch Comfort and Peanut. It was an unequal contest – Comfort was by far the stronger. Peanut, puny but wily, was still in shock from having been left under Jed's dead body for an hour before being rescued. But, just looking at her pissed the Colonel off, and he had a soft spot for Comfort – an uneven fight would give a better result. Peanut would be battered to within an inch of her life, the men would be fired up for the night ahead, and the Colonel had plenty of girls waiting. That was the good thing about the young men: they could go through a few different girls a night, they weren't there to make conversation. The old ones wanted a companion for twenty-four hours. Even with help from the Viagra sellers outside, they still wanted to talk about it first.

Fight, fight!

The Colonel banged his fist on the table and sprayed beer over Terry, who quickly closed his laptop. The Colonel moved Maya nearer to the railings so that they could get a better view.

The men downstairs took up the Colonel's cry. *Fight, fight*. The ring was made ready and the betting began. The girls paraded out in their shiny boxing shorts. Peanut was in red, Comfort in blue. The shorts were too big for Peanut's skinny legs and had to be rolled at the waist to stop them coming to her knees. The men screamed their bets as the girls struck their poses. Brandon held up their puny arms with the weight of the massive boxing glove attached. The men in the club whooped and clapped and bayed for the fight to begin.

The Colonel was brought a large hand-bell. He leaned over the balcony and roared at Brandon that the time had come. Brandon climbed into the ring to announce that all betting had ceased. A noisy hush descended. The men sat sweating and excited. The Colonel, Maya on his hip, the bell in his hand, raised it and it sounded. Brandon stepped up to the ring. His presence was enough to start the girl's feet moving. Their skinny legs in shiny boxers' shorts started shuffling. They reached out and tentatively touched one another with the boxing gloves that sat almost comically on the ends of their puny arms.

A chorus of catcalls went out. 'You can do better than that. Fucking hit her.'

Comfort swung a left hook and caught Peanut on the side of the head. Peanut staggered backwards, lost her balance briefly and Comfort lunged forward again.

She caught Peanut full in the face with a second punch. The cheers went up. Peanut staggered to the corner. Her eyes were watering; blood filled her nostrils and then ran in two straight streams down to her mouth. She tried to wipe it away with the big glove but only succeeded in smearing it across her face. She looked around her in a panic – trying to find a way out of the ring. The wall that was Brandon's chest stopped her. She turned back to the ring. Comfort was waiting. She was shaking with adrenalin and excitement. She knew she could come out of this the winner if she kept at Peanut. She was sad it was Peanut: they weren't friends but they knew one another, had seen one another every day, seven days a week, twelve hours a day, for the last year. But they both knew they had no choice. Peanut came forward gingerly. She made no attempt to put her guard up.

'You can hit me – go on,' Comfort whispered.

But Peanut was not seeing straight. She didn't know where she was or what she was doing there.

The men began stamping and screaming.

Peanut closed her eyes, swung her arm out and missed. Comfort punched back as hard as she could. Peanut was hit square in the face. She fell backwards against the ropes and landed near Brandon's feet. Peanut managed to climb up Comfort's legs and clung there. Comfort tried to push her off. Peanut clung tight. The men stood up, crowded around the ring and applauded as Comfort started kicking out at Peanut. She kicked Peanut's head just as she had kicked the green coconuts when she was a child and the anger and the frustration got too much.

The men chanted: *Kill her, kill her.*

Brandon pulled Comfort off and raised her gloved hand.

'And the winner is . . . Comfort.'

Peanut lay in an undignified pile, trails of blood across the floor behind her. There was blood over Comfort's legs where Peanut had clung to them. It dripped from her shiny blue shorts. The crowd applauded.

As Brandon held up her arm in victory the rest of her body slumped. She was hysterical, laughing, crying. The men cheered. The ring was hastily dismantled. Peanut was carried away. A cleaner came out with a bucket. The men turned back to their beers, a little sheepishly now. The dancers came back out – girls in plastic yellow bikinis gyrated expressionlessly around the dance floor whilst the cleaner mopped up Peanut's blood.

The Colonel was elated. He sat back heavily in his seat and rocked it back and forth on its back legs. He felt his lungs open, expand, big, full of air. He drew his shoulders back and snorted from flared nostrils. His body glistened with sweat. He looked at Maya. For a moment his eyes softened. He looked at Terry. He knew what Terry's eyes said – they said wait – she is not ready. But the Colonel did not want to wait. Fuck *and* fight – he could have both tonight.

43

The next morning whilst they were waiting for Remy to fly them to Puerto Galera, Mann left Becky interviewing the children who had had dealings with the DDS whilst he went to check his emails again. The PC was in Father Finn's study. It was a small white-walled room overlooking the courtyard at the back. It was wall-to-wall books and thick files, all documenting the years of bringing western paedophiles to justice or trying to get permission to build his refuges.

Mann sat and punched in his email address. The first thing he saw was another message from BLANCO.

Did you enjoy the Barrio Patay?
Give Father Finn a message from me . . . PRESS

Father Finn's image appeared with a naked child sat on his lap and a comic-strip cartoon of an exploding gun by his head – *Bang Bang.*

'I'm sorry if I woke you, David,' Mann said down the phone.

'It's okay, I was working anyway.'

'I got a couple of emails from the kidnapper. In one of them he sent me a photo of Amy Tang with a noose around her neck.'

'She's already dead?'

'No, I think it was a dress rehearsal.'

'What are they waiting for? Why don't they just do it?' asked White.

'It's all part of their strategy to keep us looking and to give them time to achieve their real aims – but what they are I don't know yet. That little girl is just bait in the centre of an elaborate maze, and we are manoeuvred this way and that down one alley just to find it leads to another. We are part of the game. The kidnapper knows where we are, David. He knows who we are, where we've been and where we are going. He knows our every move.'

There was a small pause at the other end of the phone.

'Do you think Becky is the mole?'

'I hope not, but I'll limit the information I give to her for a few days. I need to get some inside help with this. The White Circle have the DDS in their pay, and we all know who hires the DDS. Someone in government is making a lot of money from the trafficking. Can you try and find that mayor of yours, Fredrico?'

'I will try my best. But I am surprised they can be so brazen.'

'They don't care. They are still locking kids away in jails, even though the world press has seen them do it on CNN. The Columban fathers are looking after a

young lad who is willing to testify against the government. He is in hiding.'

'Where?'

'Here at the refuge.'

'Probably as safe as anywhere. About the mole – I
will contact Shrimp and warn him – we are all in
danger.'

44

Soho, London

Shrimp took a sip of Real Ale and decided it *might* grow on him, but probably not. He was sitting in the history-seeped wood-panelled surrounds of the Marquis pub on the corner of Rathbone Street, watching two Albanian pimps work the pub with their troupe of scruffy-looking girls, whilst a portrait of the young Dylan Thomas looked on. Outside, in Soho, the world ambled past, looking for restaurants and company.

It was eight thirty and the person he had agreed to meet was late. She was supposed to be here at eight. If she could tell him where Amy Tang was then it would be worth it. He tried to visualise her from the call she had made to the office that afternoon. She sounded young, and she spoke English with a European accent – maybe German, he thought. Now he was waiting, a slight figure sitting just inside the entrance to the pub at a dark and cosy corner table.

The Albanian pimp decided to try his luck, looked

over at Shrimp, and took a step towards him, pushing a girl before him. The girl smiled at Shrimp. He looked at her face – the thick makeup did a poor job of disguising the beating she had taken. He shook his head apologetically. As they walked away the girl looked back at him and fixed her eyes on his face. It was a look, not in recognition of his sympathy or a look of anger at his rebuttal – it was a warning signal.

He watched the two Chinese men approach him from behind the girl and the pimp. Shrimp was on his feet and out of the door before they got within arm's reach of the table. He dodged between the groups of meandering people as he sprinted down Percy Street. He looked behind him as he quickened his pace and headed out onto Tottenham Court Road and towards the landmark thirty-two floors of Centre Point building. He knew that marked the junction with Oxford Street. He thought he'd be safe there.

He tried to hop on a passing number 19 bus as the doors were closing, but didn't make it and bounced off its side. All he had to do was run past the fountain at Centre Point, cross over, and he'd be swallowed up by the teeming mass of Oxford Street. That was the plan, but as he reached the fountain he saw David White emerging from the Centre Point subway that led to Tottenham Court Road tube. For a second Shrimp froze. He turned and saw the men barge through the crowds waiting outside the Dominion Theatre. He looked back at David White and knew in that instant that they had all seen each other and he had no choice. David White stood transfixed for a few seconds as he tried to make out what was happening and looked back and forth from Shrimp to his pursuers. Shrimp stopped dead in his tracks, then he turned and ran back towards David White – he had no choice, he pulled him back down the subway.

They ran down the dark and dingy corridor with its two runway strips of fluorescent lighting along the ceiling that gave off a green glow. The smell of urine was ever-present. They ran past the drunk and the desperate as rough sleepers prepared to bed down for the night. The eeriness in the tunnel was permeated by the sound of running feet. Shrimp could hear them gaining. David White's legs were slowing. Shrimp realised he had no choice but to stand and fight. With his back to the wall and David White standing behind him, he prepared for the fight of his life.

45

'How old are you?'

'Twenty-one, ma'am.'

Mamasan Mimi examined Wednesday's hands.

'Washer woman hands,' she said in a derisive tone, and let them drop.

Wednesday looked at them. They were strong hands but not manicured, it was true. Wednesday always put palm oil on them before she went to sleep, to stop them drying and shrivelling, but they weren't pretty hands.

'Take off your clothes.'

Wednesday looked at the three doormen.

'Go away,' she said.

The mamasan laughed. 'They will see all they want soon and more, but okay – if you wish . . .'

She shooed the men away with a wave of her hand. They pushed one another out of the door, giggling like schoolboys. Wednesday slipped out of her sundress for the mamasan's appraisal.

'You have had a child. I can see by the round of your stomach. Still, you have good breasts and a curvy figure, the men will like that, and you are light-skinned with a pretty face. Start tonight. In three hours. Go and get your bikini made in the tailor three doors down from here. Tell him Mamasan Mimi from Lolita's sent you, hurry, and here . . .' she gave Wednesday some change '. . . get something to eat whilst he's making it. Come back to me in two hours, I will show you where you sleep and where you wash.'

Wednesday took the money and thanked the mamasan. She felt sick to the stomach but it didn't matter. Nothing mattered any more. She had brought Maya into this world and she was all the little girl had. Wednesday would find her and bring her home whatever the cost.

Tonight she would start the search for her daughter.

The tailor stopped eating and took up his tape measure. Wednesday glared at the boys who leaned on their tricycles outside.

'Wssss . . .' they called, to get her attention, and nudged each other as they eyed up the new girl in town.

The tailor measured around her waist, hips and bust. He measured the length of her crotch and his hand lingered. 'Hurry up,' she said. 'I am hungry.'

'I will get you something to eat and you can sit here and eat it if you like.'

Wednesday waited till his eyes met hers, as he was folding the measuring tape, then she looked deep into them and mouthed the word *No*.

He shrugged and told her to come back in an hour. She went down the street to a cafe she had known as a child. The old woman serving looked twice at her.

She went to sit at the counter and waited until the old woman came shuffling over to serve her. The woman stopped and scrutinised Wednesday.

'I recognise you. Long time ago.'

Wednesday smiled and shook her head. 'Just arrived.'

'Where are you from?'

'Davao.'

The woman went and returned with a bowl of rice and fish.

'What about you? Have you been here for long?'

The old woman set the bowl in front of her and snorted.

'Long? Thirty years. I was a bar girl myself, when the Americans were here. Things haven't changed much. Not so many of them here, but plenty of others. That's where I thought I knew you from – long ago there was a child who looked like you. Then, I thought I saw you again, the other day. A child who looked just like you or the person I thought was you. She was with the Colonel. Just the way you . . .' The old woman stopped and looked hard at Wednesday. Wednesday reddened and looked away. Her heart was beating so fast she thought the old woman would see it pounding. 'Oh well . . . old eyes play tricks, huh?'

Wednesday smiled and thanked her and got down from her stool. She looked at the old woman who was now busy frying chicken. Wednesday knew she had been recognised. Now her time here was going to be very precious. She picked up her bikini from the tailor's and headed back to Lolita's, ready to spend her first night as a dancing girl.

46

At its busiest time, between ten and twelve, Lolita's had over eighty girls working the floor. They took it in turns to dance for the clientele in groups of fifteen. They had choreographed routines, matching outfits, and they took centre stage in turns to perform. The rest of the time they milled about waiting to be invited onto tables. When the girls weren't dancing, and there weren't enough punters in to warrant them all being out, they sat in a crowded room at the back of the club. They chatted in groups, some dozed, others fanned themselves – there was no air-con and their bikinis were sweaty.

The talk tonight was of the fight. Peanut was still not able to work and Comfort was blamed by the other girls. Comfort had a corner all to herself and an empty seat next to her. Wednesday instantly recognised her when she walked in. They had been children in Angeles together. It was Comfort who had replaced Wednesday in the Colonel's affections.

Wednesday hoped Comfort wouldn't remember her. Comfort had seen so many girls come and go, maybe she wouldn't. She went to sit with her.

'Hi. Mind if I sit here?'

Comfort gave a shrug.

Not even a second look, thought Wednesday. *I'm safe.*

Comfort glanced over at the other girls to see if she was being set up – by their lack of interest she assumed she wasn't. She figured she could trust the new girl not to attack her. Comfort wasn't feeling good about the fight either. She had already agreed to give Peanut some of her wages, otherwise she would have nothing to send home to her mother who was looking after Peanut's baby boy.

'Why aren't you in a bikini?' asked Wednesday.

'I don't dance here. I work the bars at the end of the Fields.'

'Are they all owned by the same person?'

'Yes, the Colonel owns most of this street.'

'What's he like? Is he good looking?' she asked, feigning ignorance.

Comfort laughed cynically. 'No. He's mean and he's ugly, but he's the boss.'

'Have you been here a long time?'

Comfort buried her face in her hands fleetingly, then sat up and gave an ironic smile.

'Forever. This is my home.'

'Does the Colonel have a wife?'

'Huh!' Comfort's shoulders shook with laughter. 'Yes, he has. She is a little girl; he carries her around like a doll.'

Wednesday couldn't help the gasp that stuck in her throat, and for a moment she could not speak. She looked away for a few seconds so that Comfort might not see how that little girl's face matched Wednesday's.

'And will he be here tonight? Will he watch us dance?'

'Who knows? Probably not.' Comfort got up to walk away. 'But if he is in, he'll want you. He wants everything new.'

The ten girls filed out and stepped on to the elevated bar that they were expected to dance on top of. Most of the men sat around the long, oblong bar. A few of the tables were occupied. Wednesday was the fourth in the row; Mamasan Mimi had told her what she had to do. They had four poles between them; they took it in turns to dance on them. She would have to wait her turn for the pole. She didn't mind. They hadn't had poles when she used to dance, but her moves were the same. She began gyrating her hips slowly to the beat. She was a good dancer. She caught the attention of a noisy table of young men from the UK. They were indulging in the hair of the dog, talking about the previous night's escapades and getting themselves in party mood. When she finished her dance she was called over to their table. They made room for her to sit in-between one of the drunkest and a sullen one. She tried to make conversation but was ignored by the sullen one. The drunken one touched her breasts.

'No can touch.'

'Yes can touch,' he mimicked. 'Can touch as much as I want.'

He fondled her roughly. Wednesday squirmed from his hands and pressed him firmly away. His face was purple with drink. His breath stank. He nuzzled into Wednesday's neck and tried to remove her bikini top. The others around the table laughed. She pushed him away harder this time.

'Hey, you're a strong girl. Look at these muscles!' The lad across the table reached over and held up Wednesday's arm. 'Fuck me – that's more like it! Come and sit over here and I'll give you an arm wrestle.' The lad pulled Wednesday out of the clutches of his drunken mate and she scrabbled over laps to sit next to the arm-wrestler. He cleared the table and set his elbow on it. He held tightly to Wednesday's hand.

'Ready steady *go*!'

They both held each other's eyes and Wednesday could see that he was going to let her win. She played along and finally she pressed his hand flat to the table. A cheer went up. They kept drinking. It was getting late; she had to be out by the time the Colonel came in. Wednesday had to make a move on her lad. She slid from the table and began a private dance for him. His eyes fixed on her as she spun her body around the pole. She never took her eyes from his. She walked onto the centre of the stage and leaned her back against the pole and slid down it, opening her knees wide. She had been taught to dance by the Colonel and the mamasans when she was a girl. She could still open her legs into the splits. She dropped into a straddle and turned into a scissor splits. She rolled over and pulled herself up on the poll before arching her back and bringing herself slowly to standing. She wiggled her hips like a belly dancer as she moved towards him and jiggled her breasts in his face as she straddled his lap. His face was lost in lust. He pinned her to his lap and ground her to him. She could feel that he was hard.

'You better take me home, big boy. I gonna private dance for you.'

Mamasan Mimi was called. Negotiations were made and Wednesday was bought out for five ladies' drinks – the system that got around the supposed illegality of bar fining, which was the payment given to the bar to buy a girl out for sex. She went to change. Her heart was in her mouth. She had run away from this work nine years ago, now she was back where she started, but one of these lads might be able to help her. If she told them her story, one of them might help.

Back at the hotel she tried to get the sex over with, but he was in no hurry. Wednesday tried to engage him in conversation in the hope that he would want to know something about her, that he would care what her life was like, that she could tell him about Maya and he would help. But when the sex was over he went to sleep. At dawn he awoke and wanted sex again. At nine she decided to leave. She felt the hopelessness of it all. Soon the Colonel would find out she was here, and she didn't know if she could face him again. It had been years since she'd seen him, but inside she would always be that little girl he had owned. The Colonel would come and get her and she would never get her baby back. He had told her to come alone and not to contact the priests. Those had been the Colonel's orders

—Pepe said: 'tell her to come alone – no priests. If you come with priests he will slit her throat.'

But now, Wednesday realised that she could not do it alone and she could not afford to face the Colonel; she did not have the strength to do it alone. She would call the only person she had in the world to help – Father Finn – and ask for help from Mann and Becky. But she would try one last thing before she did that.

She dressed quietly and slipped out of the hotel room. She walked down Fields Avenue to the police station and asked to see the officer in charge. Three police officers watched her walk in. They stood and watched as she gave an account of Maya's disappearance to the sergeant and what she knew about her whereabouts now. The sergeant wrote down what she said.

'Okay. Wait here.' He left Wednesday standing at the counter. The three policemen stared at her. One of them tried a conversation.

'What do you do back home in Davao?'

'I take in washing.'

'Your little girl goes to school?'

'Yes, every day. She is very clever.'

'You are a good mother to come and find her. You have a husband?' Maya shook her head. 'You should – pretty girl like you.'

The door of the police station opened. The sergeant reappeared from his office. Wednesday turned. The Colonel was standing behind her.

'You bastard!' she screamed. 'You pig!'

'Call me what you like,' said the sergeant. 'You are nothing but a whore, and you insult the man who pays our wages. Get out of here. We will not help filth like you who can't even look after their own children.'

47

'Enough! It's time. Go and fetch her . . .'

Brandon left.

'No one ever escapes me, Wednesday, you should know that.'

The Colonel lifted Wednesday's head so she could look at him. Her face was puffed up like a football. One eye was completely closed, burnt by a cigarette in the eyeball. The hair had been torn from her head and left her scalp bleeding and raw. The door opened and Brandon walked in, pulling Maya by the arm.

The little girl stood for a moment, startled by the terrible thing she saw before her – unable to recognise her mother. The Colonel lifted Wednesday's chin and it took Maya a few seconds to realise it was her mother. Then she cried out and desperately tried to reach for her.

Wednesday looked at Maya and tried to speak but she could not; her mouth was swollen, her teeth broken from the electric shock torture. Brandon hadn't put the piece of plastic in her mouth to stop that happening.

But then, he didn't have any reason to worry if her teeth were broken and he ruined her looks. She was never going to be for sale again.

She tried to smile at the child. *Poor Maya, to see her mother like this. Poor Maya,* she thought. She could see that the child's eyes were full of fear as she whimpered. *Mama, Mama.*

The Colonel picked Maya up by one arm and held her aloft like a rag doll, then he pretended to drop her before catching her around the waist and holding her tightly to him. She screamed and cried out for Wednesday.

'You want your daughter back? Here she is.'

'*Mama. Mama.*'

The Colonel laughed and nodded in the direction of Brandon, who went to stand behind Wednesday's chair. Wednesday looked at her daughter and tried to speak, but no words came – blood spluttered from her mouth and ran in a trickle. But she had the strength of the dying and the determination and focus of a mother knowing that she is the only chance to save her child. She thrashed and bellowed – hoarse and strange her voice came out, distorted in her anguish and desperation. She shook violently.

The Colonel tutted.

'What can you offer me, Wednesday? You had your day. I took your cherry and I took your daughter's – one whore begets another.' He licked Maya's face and laughed as the child sobbed in small breaths.

'*Mama . . . Mama.*'

The Colonel walked to the far wall.

'But, you came alone, as I demanded, so I will give you one last chance to win your daughter back . . . it's only fair . . . If you can get here and kiss my feet, you can have her. If you don't make it – then she's mine.' He ordered Brandon to cut Wednesday's bonds and free her from the chair. 'Come and get her, Wednesday.'

Wednesday lunged forwards. Brandon stuck his foot out and tripped her and she hit the floor. He placed a foot on her back. He took his knife and sliced the long blade through the back of her right thigh, just above the knee. The hamstring snapped and curled. Maya screamed and turned away as Wednesday let out a muffled scream and clutched the injured leg as she dragged herself onwards towards Maya. She tried to stand on her left leg but Brandon kicked it from beneath her and she crashed to the floor again. He stepped forward and sliced through the other hamstring. She let out a tormented cry of anguish but still she pulled herself along with her hands like some freakish animal, bald, bloodied and crippled, she pulled her weight on her hands and elbows. She stopped within reach of the Colonel's feet and looked up at him. Maya held out her hands to her mother. '*Mama, Mama.*'

Wednesday extended a hand to touch his feet. Brandon dragged her head backwards.

The Colonel stared down at her. 'Look at me, Wednesday. Look into the eyes of your God.' He kissed Maya on the mouth. 'And take a last look at your daughter and know that I will have her, body and soul, until she is no more use to me, then I will kill her.'

Wednesday let out a cry of anguish but no sound came out; her vocal cords were cut as Brandon slit her throat.

48

Shrimp turned to look over at David White who was slumped against the wall behind, doubled over in pain, White glanced up and raised a hand as if to say that he was all right, just winded. Shrimp studied him for a few seconds to reassure himself that was the case before he looked back at his two assailants. They had landed a few metres apart. One was now doing his best to stand and crawl back towards the Centrepoint exit, dragging his right leg where Shrimp had delivered a sweeping kick that had smashed his ankle bones. Blood ran freely from a ragged wound on the side of his shaven skull where there was still a clear outline of Shrimp's boot. The other man lay still with his eyes shut, his chest barely rising and falling.

Shrimp made a move towards White and helped him stand upright. He looked shaken but not hurt, thought Shrimp. Shrimp looked down at himself and instinctively brushed the debris from his new jeans. He looked both ways of the tunnel. There were footsteps coming from the Centrepoint end but they were small strides, slow pace – not threatening. He looked to the other end of the gloomy tunnel that stank of wee. The three small groups of rough sleepers blinked back in the gloom.

Shrimp steered White towards Tottenham Court road tube. A drunk stood swaying as they passed

'Hey you . . .' He waved his bottle in Shrimp's direction. 'You put up one hell of a fight, so you did . . .' he grinned.

Shrimp looked back over his shoulder to make sure there would be no more fighting needed that day. One of his assailants had already made it out of sight; the other was just trying to stand. 'Fucking good fight, I said.' The drunk's words followed them down the corridor as the rough sleepers mumbled their agreement and turned to watch them go.

49

Mann and Becky sat in the old four-seater Cessna 172 and watched Puerto Galera come into view. In the distance they saw a faded purple banner draped lopsided across the roof of the small airport terminal. Becky had been very quiet all through the journey, and when Mann checked on her she looked ashen.

'Thank you, Remy. The lift is much appreciated.' Mann was sitting in the co-pilot seat.

Remy looked more Mexican than Filipino. His luxurious thick black hair, lightly dressed with coconut oil, sat on his head in waves of black. He also had an impressive handlebar moustache 'No problem. I have to see my wife's cousin who lives here. I am always happy to help the Fathers; they do a great job. I was a priest myself, you know. Got caught up wid a woman – same old story, huh? Ha Ha . . .'

He started singing the words to 'Come fly with me'.

Remy Bulgaros was doing his favourite thing – singing Sinatra songs and flying his planes. They were in safe hands; Remy knew how to fly almost any small plane there was. This was one of two he owned. The other was used for crop spraying and extinguishing the odd small fire. He lined up the plane with the runway and put the flaps down.

'Don't worry if it's a bit bumpy, huh? It's a good wind today, great for the beach, not so good for small planes.'

Mann glanced behind and saw that Becky's knuckles were white as she clutched the seat belt. Her head stayed absolutely still whilst her eyes flicked side to side as the tops of trees came into view. He heard her sigh with relief as they touched down and taxied off to the hard standing area. Remy parked up and switched off the engine.

'I will be ready to fly you to Angeles whenever you want. Just call me on my cell phone. You have the number, no? You can get a phut phut from here to the resort. Ask anyone inside. Okay? Juz call.' Remy burst into song again.

Mann and Becky stepped out. Before they'd gone ten paces from the aircraft they were surrounded by a dozen men all gesticulating and grinning, all wanting to carry their bags.

'It's not heavy,' Becky told them.

'It doesn't matter – it's their job,' Mann said, smiling as he handed them over. 'There's not enough work to go round so they invent jobs – keeps them in food for the day.'

At the airport door the bags were passed on to another set of men whose job it was to carry it another twenty metres to a line of phut phuts which were bigger versions of mosquitoes with more roof space and larger luggage baskets at the back. Some of the phut phuts were already loaded with children on the roofs as well as on every available space on the bike itself. Sometimes up to six managed to sit with the driver, clinging around each other's waists. The phut phut drivers sized Mann and Becky up and the biggest trike driver stepped forward, chosen to balance the load. He offered to take them to their resort, and put their bags into the seat at the back of the bike whilst they squeezed into the sidecar.

The road ran down narrow lanes, past scooters and tricycles with loaded side cars. A long, narrow road was flanked on both sides with stalls, workshops, the odd house and small hotel. It was all lush and green with forest in every gap between the houses and as far into the island as could be seen. The twenty-minute trike ride came to an end when the road ended and the beach began. There were several porters waiting. Mann recognised the man with the Paradise Hotel shirt logo.

'Welcome, Mr and Mrs Black. I will take you to the resort.'

BONG was written on a name badge and pinned to a blue and cream floral shirt, which made up his uniform along with ivory-coloured shorts and flip-flops. He took both their cases from them and marched in front to a waiting *barca* – a boat that looked like a large insect sitting on the water. The boat had *Paradise* written on the side. They loaded Mann and Becky onboard and set off.

'I can't believe we've got our own boat. What a place!'

264

Becky sat back and smiled. It was impossible not to. Under the shade of the canvas roof she looked out across the water to the island that lay some way off.

'It's a tropical paradise – swaying palms and white beaches – such a contrast to the city slums. So, this place we are going to, it's not for your average sex tourist?'

'Some areas are made for sex tourism; others are purely for the divers and the families. It's a great resort – spread out, covering several beaches. We are going to Sabang, which is not the prettiest place – lively and trashy; not really for families but we need to look up a couple of people – two men on the list of prominent westerners working the system out here. The good places, unspoilt, are not far from where we are staying – just a twenty-minute walk away is La Laguna – some of the best diving in the Philippines. Some of it is so unspoilt it's breathtakingly beautiful. But can't see us getting to see it, sorry. This is a one-night stop-over. It would be nice for you to come back and see this place properly one day,' Mann said.

'Definitely.' Then she thought about it. 'Don't think Alex would get it, though. He'd be irritated by the slow pace. He just doesn't do "lying around on beaches" stuff. For him it's all action and decisions.' She closed her eyes and settled back against the wooden seat. 'But I love it – it's stunning – like a postcard: white sands, tall, swaying palms.'

'What's Alex up to whilst you're away?'

'This and that. He's fine. Says he's busy making money. He didn't seem to mind.' She opened her eyes, looked at Mann and looked away quickly. His expression said it all. 'All right, Detective – he said it was the same old bullshit. Work always comes first. And maybe he's right.' She dipped her hand in the water and watched the wake. 'I am not really trophy wife enough for him. Nothing I do is right. My hair is too short, my hips too broad. My bloody eyes are probably the wrong colour. I can't do anything right any more. Maybe I never could.' She sat up and smiled sadly as she looked out to the turquoise water. 'I can't get over how beautiful it is here.'

'Nature's an awesome thing. I have the utmost respect for her. She can give you life and she can snuff life out in a second.'

Becky opened her eyes a tad. 'Like triads, you mean?'

'Yes. I guess so.' He looked quizzically back at her. 'But, if you have certain values, believe in certain things, then they are worth dying for.'

'That really *is* you, isn't it, Mann?' She sat up. 'You are willing to give up your life for others – people that don't even exist in other's heads, nameless victims – you will die for them. Why?'

'Because I understand what it's like to be helpless – to be vulnerable.'

'What about personal happiness, Mann? What about you finding contentment in *your* life?'

'I get my happiness where I can. A lasting love is not for everyone.'

'Alex told me that when he first saw me he knew I was the one.' She stared out at the glistening sunlight

266

on the water. 'Not sure I believe in that kind of thing either, really.'

'Are you faithful?'

'Of course.' She was flustered, almost insulted by the question. 'When I spoke my wedding vows, I meant them. Till death do us part, all that stuff. I am not a quitter, Mann. '

'What about him? Is he faithful to you?'

There was a pause. 'Truthfully? I don't know. I hope so, but I am not sure. There have been times when he's come back from a business trip and he's been different.'

'In what way?'

She became flustered.

'Well, in bed for a start. He's made love differently. Almost as if he was making love to someone else. But everyone wants to be with someone – no one wants to be alone. Except for you, it seems. Have you never fallen so hopelessly in love that you would have cut your arm off for her?'

'Never wanted that kind of love. I don't want love that you can't control. My father's death, Helen's, it's not worth loving someone at any cost. I would far rather never love than feel that loss again. And anyway, I don't believe in love at first sight. I've had plenty of other feelings at first sight. So far none of them were love. Maybe I'm not romantic enough.'

'Huh! I bet you are, really. You notice things.'

He looked at her. In the sunlight her face was honey-coloured and her cheeks were pink from the sun. 'So you don't think you are ever going to find love again because you don't want to. What happens if it just happens?'

'Things don't just happen – you have to let them happen.'

'You blame yourself for Helen's and your dad's deaths, don't you? You must have loved your father very much.'

They sat in silence for a few minutes and stared out at the ocean and the looming shoreline. As Mann stared out into the water, the blue filled his eyes and senses; the fresh sea spray cleared his head and he realised something he had never admitted to before. The thought jumped out at him and it shocked him. He turned back to Becky and looked at her concerned face as she waited for an answer; he knew she had unlocked another piece of the puzzle for him.

'I never really knew my father – I never got the chance.'

A jolt interrupted them and a commotion ensued as half a dozen men waded in to pull the *barca* up onto the sand and moor it alongside a dozen others. Becky reached into her pocket and handed the man a note in exchange for her bag. He held it up in triumph for the others to see. His workmates slapped him on the back and congratulated him.

'What was all that about?' Becky looked confused.

'The rounds are on him tonight. You gave him the equivalent of a month's wages.'

There was a jostle amongst the porters as to who would get to carry Becky's bag up the beach. She left it to them to sort it out and followed Mann. Bong hurried off to make sure all was in order, whilst Mann and Becky walked along the beach. It was a narrow strip of sand that was already congested with moored *barcas*, small hotels and bars that crept almost as far as the water's edge. There were a few couples sunbathing, and a few more sitting in the shade of beach umbrellas. Excited children were kicking up water at the ocean's edge.

They headed up the beach towards one of the beach-front bars, which were built on stilts resting half onto the beach. A few tables and chairs were pitched into the sand. Laid-back beach music drifted out from inside the elevated bar area. Becky caught up with the porter and took her bag from him. She dug in her pocket and, not wishing to appear mean, produced the same note as last time. It caused great whoops of triumph from the porters. Becky plonked herself on the stool in the sand. They were immediately surrounded by men wanting to sell them diving adventures and sailing trips.

The barman left his seat, on the steps of the bar, and sauntered over to their table to take their order. The touting locals moved on and up the beach.

'Two San Miguel.' Mann ordered their drinks.

'Yes, sir.' He came back with the tray. 'You staying at Paradise Hotel, sir?'

'Do you know somewhere better?' answered Mann.

'I know d best place in Sabang.' He grinned and pointed to the second floor rising above them. Washing and wetsuits hung down from the balcony above and the sound of heavy-duty bass came thumping out from the open balcony. 'We have rooms above d bar.'

'Yeah, right, now tell us somewhere where we can actually get some sleep.'

'Okay. Okay. I see you want d best for such a beautiful lady.' He grinned at Becky. 'Paradise Hotel – it's real nice, at d end of d beach, quiet, own by English guy, name Bob. It is good place for you.'

'Tell you what . . . we'll see how it works out. If it's bad we'll come back to you. Okay?'

'Is that one of the men you were talking about?' Becky asked after the waiter had left.

'Yes. English Bob, or Bob English, is an expat wanted for armed robbery and firearms offences back in the UK and in Thailand. He has twice managed to avoid prison for underage sex. He isn't fussy – girls or boys.'

'Nice bloke. He gets away with it here by paying people off?'

'That's it. He pays off the police, the parents and the politicians, and he sends the child back to the countryside, lost forever. Bob has been here five years. Seems to have found himself some useful friends, one of whom owns a few of the bars along this beach. It's probably a good place for us to start asking questions.'

The waiter came back. 'Your man, Bong, is coming back in five minutes – just making the room ready. You want another beer?' He pointed to Mann's empty bottle. Mann declined.

'What else do you know about this English Bob?' asked Becky when the waiter had left them and was working his way across the sand and up the wooden steps to the bar beyond.

'He owns a few clubs here. He is bound to have been approached by the White Circle, and I know he has

270

had dealings with Stevie Ho . . . Here's our man, and . . .'
Bong appeared to inform them that all was prepared for
their arrival. They followed him along the beach as he
carried one bag on each of his broad shoulders. He was
in no hurry at first, but he sprinted the last bit as the
hot sand got too much to bear. They arrived at the beach
entrance to Hotel Paradise, whose boundary was marked
by posts and three rows of sturdy-looking sun-loungers,
set out in pairs, with thatched sun umbrellas between
each set. There was a sentry post, a small windowless
box, and a smartly uniformed officer grinned and waved
at them from inside, his rifle over his arm.

'Why is *he* armed?' Becky smiled and waved back.
'I can understand the airport security, but why here?'

'They have had problems with terrorists for so many
years. They are used to a high level of security. They
have a "better safe than sorry" approach.'

Two women met them at the boundary of sunbeds
and presented them with their welcome pack – shell
necklaces and fresh papaya juice. They had garlands of
flowers placed around their necks and were ushered
towards reception.

The reception area was being swept, the sand was
being brushed out; it was a continual process. There
were three girls behind the desk dressed in tightly fitting
flowery uniforms, their hair tied up, glossy and black,
caught at the back of their heads with a flower. They
were flustered and giggly at Mann's presence. Becky
realised it was a fact of life that he was the average
Filipina's winning lottery ticket.

'Hello sir, ma'am,' they chorused. 'The manager,

Mr Bob English, apologises but he has had to go into town for business. He will be back later. He asks you please to have a drink with him this evening.'

'Please tell the manager we would be delighted.' Mann smiled at the girls.

Bong escorted them up to their suite on the second floor.

It was a nicely laid-out complex that sprawled back from the beach for an acre. Its main building stretched up for three floors of balconied rooms that looked down on an inner courtyard. There were also private villas, in different native styles, dotted around. The hotel faced the sea and its restaurant and bar was a broad balcony, with table and chairs and a lounge area for watching the sunset.

Their room was one of the better ones. It had a fiercely active air-con and a double-sized balcony equipped with chairs and a table. There was a bottle of wine in an ice bucket waiting for them and the bed was covered in petals. It was the honeymoon suite, they both realised at the same time.

'Ah!' Becky stood in the centre of the room and looked around. 'That would explain the giggling girls on reception.' She suddenly felt really awkward. It was the first time they had been on their own with no one else around.

Mann looked at Becky. He could see she was embarrassed.

'Don't worry, I will get them to put up a spare bed.' He smiled reassuringly. 'And I *will* kill Shrimp when we next see him.'

She smiled and shook her head. 'Okay – that's great, about the spare bed, I mean.' She felt a little stupid for getting flustered. As if Mann was going to make a move on her anyway? She rebuked herself. 'On the plus side – we get free champagne,' she said. 'What's the plan now?'

'Catching up with Fat Harry and English Bob later on, and I have made an appointment for us to view a place at four. A local estate agent is about to show us some sought-after property. I think it's best if we fly up to Negros from here tomorrow – not Manila – change of plan.'

'Why do you want to do that?'

'There's a big triad stronghold there. I think we have to check it out. We could find out more about CK and we might learn who's holding Amy. But we have a couple of hours to kill before any of it starts, so I suggest we go and inspect the beach. You ready to check it out? And, one more thing,' he shouted as he headed into the bathroom, 'you can be as loving as you like to me, Becky, as newlyweds we'd better make our cover convincing.' He came out once he'd changed into his board shorts and winked at her.

'Yeah, you can bugger off.' She hid a smile and carried on rummaging through her suitcase.

'Okay, baby – see you on the beach in a few minutes.' He ducked and dived out of the door as she threw a flip-flop at him.

He got outside the door. He didn't like deceiving her. He had no intention of going to Negros, but he had to see where that lie would lead them. They definitely had

a mole, someone had been aware of all their move-
ments so far. Mann didn't believe it was Becky, but he
had to be sure. He checked his phone; he had a text
message from Ng:

*Alex Stamp no longer in Hong Kong. He didn't board
a UK flight . . . Suggest he is in Philippines.*

Then again, thought Mann, maybe Becky didn't
realise she was the mole.

50

'He's an arrogant fuck . . .' Reese looked over to where the Teacher was sitting on a sun-lounger in the shade. 'I'm sick of fucking nursemaiding him.'

They'd been on a whistle-stop tour of the Philippines, which should have been fun, except the Teacher spent his whole time hiding away. He hid from the sun and he hid from the fun. He was fast getting on Reese's nerves. Now that Terry had joined them, things were a little better.

'Stop complaining, Reese. Try and look like you're having a good time.'

Terry came out to bring Reese another beer. Reese took it from him and continued his bitching. 'I have people waiting for me back home, mate. I have a house, all geared up for a visiting group of Aussies. I have to be there when the kids are delivered, otherwise I'll be cut out of the deal.'

Reese was a homebody. He was itching to get back to his house on the beach, his endless pursuit of new prey in his bed and his weed-smoking. He liked things to stay simple.

'Relax. Stop stamping your foot like a girl. There'll be plenty more deals, better ones. It's time you looked at the bigger picture, Reese. Smarten up.'

'I still don't know why we need it, bro, we have everything here already.'

Reese didn't know what had got into them all. He was still trying to work out how it would possibly benefit him to expand – his life was just perfect as it was.

'Because . . . as I've already explained, nothing stays still in this world. We have to move with it or we will lose it all. If you don't accept changes are coming, my friend, they will come anyway and you will be phased out.'

'How? What the fuck is phased out?'

Jed's and Laurence's deaths had left him feeling very nervous. The Colonel had said it had to be done, and that they had been planning to take over the whole operation. Reese didn't see it. Sure, they were ambitious, but not that much, and why did that add up to killing them? Greed was what it always seemed to come down to, and Reese didn't feel the need to make money the way the others did. He was all about the other stuff: the sunshine, the beaches, the kids.

'I don't know why we need his money, this weirdo Blanco. He can't even show himself in person – what's with all this cloak-and-dagger shit? We've done all right as we are. Not sure I want it to get any bigger. It will be harder to control. In the end we might make less money. Anyway, who gives a shit? We have a nice lifestyle, don't we, Terry?'

Terry knew that what Reese said was true, but he also knew they had no choice. The Colonel had been swept along by his delusions of being God. He saw this as his chance for world domination. Reese and Terry had been given the job of showing the Teacher how it all worked. They were taking him around and helping him spend his money buying up houses that they could turn into holiday lets to create new sex resorts in unspoilt areas. Equally, Reese knew Terry was making sense. Reese had nowhere else to go. He must go along with the rest of them. He could never return home. He was wanted back in Oz for buggering a small boy, and that meant it was too risky to go anywhere in the age of Interpol and eyeball ID. Reese's world had narrowed to the seven thousand islands of the Philippines . . . just as well he liked it so much.

'Anyway, we know nothing about this Blanco. We only know he's the head of the White Circle, and we don't know much about that. Why all the secrets? What is it he's afraid of?'

'He doesn't want people to prejudge him – who he is, I suppose. He wants to be given the chance to prove himself first. He is waiting until everything is in place.'

'Has the Colonel met him?'

'I don't think so. All communication comes through email and phone, or usually the Teacher; he is Blanco's right-hand man.'

'Yeah, well, that's not looking so fucking hopeful, is it, Terry? The Teacher's a psycho who is now killing us off one by one.'

'Don't exaggerate, Reese. Laurence and Jed spelled

trouble. They would have disposed of you in time. The Teacher did us a favour. Anyway, make yourself indispensable. That's what I intend doing. I have taken steps to cover my arse.'

'How many more houses do we have to show him? He's bought up half the bloody island anyway.' Reese was watching Sophia play. She was dipping her toes into the pool and flicking the water out, seeing how far away it landed. Reese smiled as he watched her. He would like to join in the game. He would love to play with Sophia.

'Reese! Take the Teacher and show him the latest house you're buying with his money. Show him his investment . . . Reese!' Terry was in his face now, blocking his view. 'Wake up, you fucking dope-head.'

Reese wasn't listening. He had switched to watching the young whore from Angeles. Terry followed his line of vision.

'Cool it, bro. The Teacher's finally startin' to unwind. He's about to get a lesson in Filipina.' Reese grinned.

Terry followed Reese's gaze and watched as the whore rubbed her crotch against Teacher's knee. Terry smiled. 'The thing about the Colonel's whores is that you know they will cooperate. They were so accustomed to his violence . . .'

'. . . and his massive cock . . .'

'. . . that they are happy to settle for anything slightly less.'

They watched the pair disappear inside the villa.

'Do him good to relax,' said Reese.

Within ten minutes they heard the sound of the girl

not finding the love-making session quite as loving as she had hoped. The Teacher emerged thirty minutes later with a fresh beer and a ghost of a smile on his face.

'Let's hope that did the trick.'

'Go and check on the girl, Reese.'

'Don't think so, bro. Whatever he did, wherever he made her take it – it will be nothing to what we'll get if we criticise. Anyway, she's a whore. More than that, she was the Colonel's whore, she's used to it.'

Terry raised his bottle of beer in the direction of the Teacher, who raised one back as he lay on the sun-lounger again, under the large umbrella.

'We've got him laid . . .' Reese smiled and whispered under his breath '. . . now we need to work on his tan.'

Terry grinned. 'That's not gonna happen. He's staying white at all costs.'

The Teacher got up and went back inside. The heat was getting to him.

'I better go with him. Keep an eye on Sophia for me.'

Terry picked up his beer and followed Teacher inside the villa. Reese drank some more beer and grinned to himself – *paradise* – it certainly was. He watched Sophia wiggling her legs in the water.

51

Becky sat on the bed for a moment after Mann had left. She felt a wave of guilt. She realised she wasn't really missing Alex. She took her phone from her bag and tried phoning him; he didn't pick up and it went straight to voicemail. She phoned Jimmy Vance. It was 7 a.m. in the UK, and she knew Jimmy would be getting ready to leave for work to make Proctor's meeting by eight.

'I am just slightly concerned, that's all, Jimmy, I haven't heard from him for a few days. He might ring you if he has an emergency of some kind. Also, can you pop into the flat for me, make sure everything's okay? Thanks, Jimmy.'

She finished speaking to Vance, changed, slipped on a beach robe and closed the hotel-room door behind her. She walked down the stairs and through reception and was just about to head towards the beach when she had an urge to explore the rest of the resort.

She turned left instead of right and headed round the back of the reception. She followed the sandy lane that wound past the villas and then opened out onto a shaded pool. It was surrounded by tall palms; leaves rustling like paper as they shimmied in the breeze. There was a row of sturdy wooden sun-loungers, with thatched umbrellas between each pair to the left of the pool. To her right was a low wall that marked the boundary of the pool area, and straight across the other side of the pool was a pool table shaded by an awning. Becky could hear the sound of a girl laughing, but she couldn't see the child.

She left her beach bag on one of the empty loungers and walked over to the pool and down the ladder, dutifully obeying the rules not to dive, even though she was tempted. She submerged herself beneath the cool, crystal water. All sound was muted into a dull roar as the cold water filled her ears and covered her hot scalp in blissful cold. She swam a length then emerged at the end and floated on her back. She closed her eyes and let the filtered sun coming through the palm leaves warm her face, before swimming a few lengths of front crawl. She stopped to catch her breath at the far end. Two girls had come out to play pool. The small one was the giggler that Becky had heard before. The elder girl wore a tiny silver bikini and matching silver stilettos. Her small breasts were padded out and forced into a cleavage. The bottom of the bikini had panels cut into it, revealing almost all that she didn't yet have. She arched her body over the pool table, looked up and giggled at a western man who had come to sit on the low wall beside the pool. He wore small, round 'John Lennon' type sunglasses. He sipped his beer and watched Becky. The older girl giggled and wiggled around the pool table, leaning over and forcing the younger girl to laugh with her. She was watching the man watch Becky. He sipped his beer, slow and languid, and as he leaned his back against the palm trunk behind him, his baggy shorts gaped. His balls showed white against his tanned leg. He shouted to someone who appeared briefly in the villa entrance, next to the pool.

'Come on out and get some sun. The pool looks great.' His eyes followed Becky's every movement. She swam to the end, climbed out of the pool and took the towel offered to her by the pool attendant. The man on the wall took a swig of his beer and lifted his head almost in a gesture of recognition as he grinned at her.

In recognition of what? thought Becky. *How dare he . . .*

It hit her and she was angry that just because she was white it somehow associated her with him. She was boiling with rage by the time she reached Mann. He was waiting on a lounger. She stomped towards him, wet and angry, the towel pulled tight around her.

'What's the matter?' He sat up as she approached.

She threw the towel down. Mann watched her march off towards the sea. Her arse was too round to stop the bikini from riding up as she tried to walk fast in the hot sand. He sprinted down and caught up with her.

'What is it?'

She strode into the water, knees high.

'Some perve at the pool. Obviously with an underage girl, she's dressed up like a tart. Plus – a really small girl, mixed race.'

'What did he look like?'

'Old . . . surfer type, bandana around his head and hippy sunglasses – a real creep. He had someone else with him but I didn't get a good look at him – another white guy he was calling to. They're staying in a villa right next to the pool.'

Reese had no objection to the woman's frostiness. It excited him in some way and she looked like one of the girls he's known when he was young, back home. She made him feel nostalgic for the chase. He slid down from the wall, adjusted his shorts, and stared over at the man who had arrived and now stood at the other end of the pool. Stevie Ho stared back.

52

Becky and Mann had finished looking around the beach property that they had agreed to view at four – it was a bit dilapidated but ripe for conversion into a small hotel – and were now waiting for the owner to return. He had disappeared to consult his partner about the price. Becky had a message alert on her phone. It was from Alex . . .

Hi Baby. Sorry keep missing your calls. Reception crap. Am fine. V busy here in Hong Kong. Will call you in a cuppla days. Love Al. Xx

She was in the middle of texting him back when her phone went.

'Hi Jimmy? Anything wrong?'

'I think so. I've just been around to your flat and there was a woman there. She said she was a friend of a friend. Said she'd been told her that you were thinking of renting the flat out and that she was given the key to come and have a look whilst you were away. I told her who I was and she gave me back the key and left. She definitely didn't like me finding her there, Becky.'

'I don't have a clue what that's about. Did she give you a name?'

'No.'

Becky finished the call and went to rejoin Mann.

'Anything wrong?' He looked at her face and saw that she was troubled.

She frowned. 'Not sure really. Is the phone reception in Hong Kong bad?'

'The best there is – we practically invented it, for Christ's sake. Why?'

'It's just that Alex has been trying to get through. He says the signal's bad there.'

Mann shrugged. 'I've never known it to be.'

'And there was something else strange going on back home . . . but I'm sure it's nothing . . . Jimmy's looking into it for me.' She gave a flicker of a smile but Mann could see she was worried.

Becky didn't want to say any more. She had to try and work out what it meant. Why was there a woman in the flat? The owner returned with his brother-in-law.

'We are sorry, sir, but we have already sold the house. It is no longer for sale.'

'You have had an offer?' asked Mann.

'Yes – a very good offer.'

'Who made you that offer?'

The two men looked at each other and spoke in their dialect.

'A Chinese man.'

'The offer was made today? Did he come here?'

'No. He made the offer by phone.'

'And you accepted it? He could cheat you. I can give you a payment right here.' Mann pretended to fish in his pocket.

'No, no . . .' They shook their heads and looked decidedly edgy. 'We know this Chinese man. He has made a good offer. We accept.'

'You have done business with him before?' They nodded. 'Okay. No hard feelings. I bet you've had a lot of interest in this house, huh?'

The men looked at one another and held out their palms in wonderment. 'We could have sold this house three times today – any price. But we only have *one* house.'

'Lucky Chinese man. What's his name?'

The two men sensed a trick. They shook their heads and started to walk away.

'Just Chinese, that's all. Bye bye.' They waved and walked back into the house.

Becky looked at Mann.

'Stevie Ho?'

'It could be elusive Stevie, who suddenly has enough money to buy the world it would seem. But they did the transaction by phone. The man must have wanted them to know he was Chinese. I am not convinced they have done business with him before; they looked like they were saying what they thought I wanted to hear. We need to get a better look at those westerners you saw. I'm thinking of sending you in, under cover. Could you work the bars, do you think?'

'Yeah, that'll work!'

'Hey, look . . . a woman has a lot of pulling power here. Especially a western woman – they're going to think all their Christmases came at once.'

'Yeah, right! They are going to think *reporter*. They

come here to escape women like me, not have sex with them. Anyway, we've been seen as a couple.'

'Just winding you up.' He grinned. 'But can I just say – if it was me, I wouldn't have a problem with that.'

She thumped his arm. He ducked out of the way to answer his phone, It was Shrimp.

'You all right? What happened? David White emailed me. He said you were both set up.'

'It was nothing, boss. I dealt with it – a couple of wanksters – would-be gangsters. Basically I kicked ass.'

Mann knew that Shrimp had come off well but not unscathed. He was a great martial arts expert but he wasn't used to having to protect at the same time. He had had a hard job defending David White and fighting, but he'd done it well.

'Who were they?'

'White Circle. They told me before I kicked the shit out of them and sent them away crying.'

'We can't move without them knowing.'

'There's something else Boss – Micky's missing.'

53

'You have a party of westerners here – with a little girl and a young woman? Must have been, what, four or five of them altogether. I met them by the pool earlier. I'd like to invite them for a drink, can you tell me what name they are booked under so that I can say hello?'

The girls exchanged glances. Mann was standing in reception. He picked out the one who hadn't taken her eyes off him and flashed his most charming smile. 'I know they are staying in the villa by the pool. We talked for ages but I forgot to ask for a name.'

'Do you mean the three men; one man is with his daughter and another girl?'

'Yes. That's the one.'

The other two receptionists flashed her a look. A momentary look of concern crossed her face. It disappeared as Mann leaned across the desk. 'I don't want to appear rude, but I have never seen such pretty receptionists.'

She smiled and lowered her chin, batting her eyelashes at Mann.

'It's booked under the name of Mr Reese Pearce, from Angeles.'

Becky was waiting for him in their room. It was furnished with rustic touches. It had rattan cabinets either side of the French doors that led to a small balcony. Above the bed was a tapestry – a native scene with coconuts and volcanoes.

She watched Mann finish unpacking his bag and hang up his clothes in the white louver-doored wardrobe.

'What do you think I should wear?' she asked.

He answered without thinking about it. 'Cut-offs. Flat shoes, nice top – chic casual – the purple silk top, that's nice.'

'How come when I ask you that, you have an exact image in mind? Most guys would just say "Put anything on".'

'Because it's important, we want to look right. We don't want to stand out too much, but we want to look moneyed. We want them to believe that we are a newly married couple used to exotic holidays.'

Becky was still sitting on the bed, surrounded by the spewed-out contents of her fake Louis Vuitton holdall that Ponytail had thrown in with the handbag deal.

'Whatever you wear you'll still look as sexy as hell. Someone with your looks can't help it.' Mann disappeared into the bathroom with his toiletries.

She looked at him curiously when he came back into the room. 'You actually mean that, don't you?'

'Of course – bound to get told I'm a lucky man more than once tonight.'

She shook her head in disbelief. 'That's the nicest thing anyone's said to me in a long time.'

Mann turned around to see if she was joking and realised she wasn't. He was about to add that it was a privilege to be seen out with her, but he could see that he had probably said enough – she was busy over enthusiastically tidying her things away.

'What's the plan this evening, Mann?' she asked, not looking at him.

'We will have to split up for the first part of it; strangely enough, you wouldn't be that welcome in the girlie bars, I am going to look for Fat Harry. He owns a few of the most expensive bars here.'

'Why do you think he's involved in the new society?'

'Because David White mentioned him and both Ng and Shrimp say his name has cropped up with any new ventures of the seedy kind with Stevie Ho. Besides being a bar owner he is also the appointed head of the local "Trade Organisation", which exists solely to protect the other western perverts who set up businesses here. I remember years ago, he was in the news in Hong Kong, and David White pointed him out. He had some connection to a syndicate that owned taxi firms. He escaped charges then, when he paid off the parents of three juveniles he'd been overly friendly to. He's a big enough fish to have been at least courted by the new gang.'

'What do you want me to do?'

'Find an Internet café and get in touch with the

team. See if they're getting any further with finding Amy Tang; see if Micky has turned up. Ask around here – see if anyone knows anything or has seen anything that can help us. But be careful, journalists die at an alarming rate here. Questions will not be welcomed. However, as a woman, you can move around easily; the Filipino men are very respectful. It's only the westerners that you have to watch out for, but then you know all about that . . . On that vein – first, let's see if we can find your poolside friend – Mr Reese Pearce and co.

54

Reese focused on them from far away. He could tell when people were new to the Philippines. They smelt different. Their clothes didn't have the smell of dust and damp. He recognised the woman from the pool, hard to forget. It had been bugging him for the last few hours. He had hoped their paths might cross again. He hardly saw western women any more. Becky's blonde hair made him nostalgic for home. She looked like a surfer girl. His eyes focused on her and he nudged Terry, who was, as ever, on his laptop.

'There's that woman I told you about – the one by the pool. I'm going to introduce myself. Maybe I can interest them in a guided tour or some such crap. Maybe they want to stay in one of the houses?'

Terry looked up from his work. 'They're just a young couple. Do you think we need any hassle right now? We have enough going on with the Teacher and . . .'

'Why isn't he out here now? He spends his whole time locked away in that villa. What does he do, just sit there and drink beer and stare at the walls?'

'He says he'll come and find us in a minute.'

'He can take all the time he wants – miserable bastard.'

Becky looked up and saw Reese staring at her.

'Think that's him,' she whispered, whilst pretending to whisper something nice in Mann's ear. 'At one o'clock, he's at a bar table with another man. He's seen me.'

'He hasn't seen *me*,' Mann said under his breath, and grinned. 'He can't take his eyes off you.'

'Let's mill around, take our time to work the street. Let him get a good look at you. Let's look in doorways, pretend to shop.'

He steered Becky towards the T-shirt souvenir shop. She thumbed through the racks of innuendoes and slogans, mainly referring to a diver's prowess in the sack, and looked over to see Reese grinning at her.

'It's definitely him,' she said to Mann, who was looking through a rack of leather-thonged shark's-tooth necklaces.

Mann looked over at Reese and Terry. They were sitting at a bar on the right side of the beach bar, outside a small hotel. He could see that Reese was still watching Becky's every move.

'Let's head for the bar opposite them – and be nice, let him down gently – he obviously likes you.' Mann held up a T-shirt in front of his face as he grinned at Becky. They made their way across and perched on stools at the end of the small bar just ten foot away.

Terry looked up and followed Reese's gaze across the lane to Mann and Becky.

'Stop leching after every piece of ass, especially some white woman's who's with her big boyfriend. The last thing we want is trouble.' Terry tapped away on his keyboard.

'No trouble.' Reese picked up his drink and sauntered over. Terry stayed where he was.

'Evening, folks. Just off the boat?'

Becky giggled.

'How can you tell? We were just about to order. Can I get you a drink?' asked Mann.

Reese kept his eyes on Becky as Mann was speaking. Becky smiled coyly back.

'Sure can.'

'What about your mate over there? Would he like to join us?'

'Terry!' Reese called over to him. Terry looked up and Reese beckoned him over. He shut his laptop and sauntered across.

'Hope my friend's not bothering you.' Terry rolled his eyes Reese's way. 'What brings you two here?'

'We are on honeymoon, actually. This is my wife, Lucy, and I'm John.'

Reese let out a whoop, did a panting-dog imitation and then wet his lips as he winked at Mann. 'Lucky bloke. Honeymoon, huh? I could do with one of those. Tell me, young lady – is he everything he promised he would be?'

Becky giggled. 'I am a very satisfied customer, thanks for asking.'

Reese burst out laughing.

'Good answer,' Terry said, grinning as he sat down on the stool next to Mann.

'And what about you gents? What brings you here?' asked Mann.

'A bit of property acquisition,' answered Reese before Terry could respond. 'Show them the pictures, Terry. Terry has lots of places to look at. He's downloaded photos of houses, I'm sure John here would love to see them, wouldn't you?'

'Love to.'

Terry wasn't best pleased with Reese's ruse to chat up Becky unhindered, but he guessed it wouldn't do any harm. He turned his laptop towards Mann and showed him some of the beach-front properties available. There were several on the screen.

'How do you scroll down?' asked Mann as the waiter arrived with their drinks.

Before they had time to drink them, Terry got a text. He read it, knocked back his whisky and got off the stool.

'Drink up, Reese, we're gone.' He took his laptop back from Mann, closed it and tucked it under his arm. 'Let's leave these nice folks to enjoy the evening. Reese . . . let's go.'

'Huh?' Reese was extremely disgruntled at having his flirting interrupted, just when he was about to try his hand on Becky's leg, although he would only have done it the once. Becky was fast losing the smile cemented to her face.

Reese took her hand and kissed it. 'Till we meet again . . .' He drank up and followed Terry, who was already several feet away. When they were out of earshot he hissed:

'What the fuck is wrong with you?'

'I just got a text. It's the Teach. We have to go. He

wants out *now*. He's not looking for excuses, move your ass.'

'Why? Thought he was on the way here?'

'Not now he isn't.'

'What the fuck is the matter with him? He was supposed to be on the way to come and find us for a beer.'

'He was, apparently; he turned back for some reason. Fuck knows! He's shitting himself about something. He says we have to leave *now*.'

55

Becky gave Mann a kiss on the cheek. 'Better make it look convincing.' She reached up on her tiptoes and pretended to whisper in his ear. 'Text me when you're done.'

'Will do, babe. Take care of yourself.' He winked at her and was about to step away when she caught his arm and pulled him down to her level to whisper in his ear. She started to say 'Don't call me . . .', but she didn't get through it all because Mann kissed her in the middle of it. He hadn't meant to. It had been an instinctive reaction; the second her cheek touched his, his mouth had turned and sought hers. It wasn't a long kiss but it was the first time they had kissed one another on the lips.

Shit, thought Mann. *That's all I need. She's married, she's a work colleague, and if she is the mole, she could be about to get me killed.* He looked back at her as he walked away. She was smiling in that special sweet, shy way she had. *Yep . . . I'm in trouble . . .*

He left her and made his way back along the beach. The small strip of sand was now crowded with *barcas* pulled up on the shoreline for the night. There was the sound of dance music banging out from the crammed strip of bars, and the coloured lights from their signs flickered on the water. Mann ignored several catcalls and continued walking until he saw what he was looking for, a bar called Pump It.

Once he got in range, the girls in their red hot-pants and silver boob tubes linked arms with him and led him inside the bar to find a table. It wasn't a bad place, thought Mann. It would look filthy in the light of day but it did well on this litter-strewn end of paradise. Mann looked around. The clientele were younger than Angeles. This place wasn't so much for the middle-aged lonely businessman but for the rowdy lads here to dive, sunbathe and have sex. The casual sex tourist – the man who just finds himself paying for it at the end of the night, without realising that it was always going to end like that.

Mann was looking for the owner. He didn't think he would be difficult to spot and he was right. Fat Harry was holding court at one of the circular tables, papers in front of him, drinking a beer. He had a constant stream of girls coming to pay their respects to their 'daddy'.

Dance music played whilst a girl in a cage, dressed in a bikini and fur boots, wound her athletic thighs around a pole. Mann found himself a space at the bar that ran around the elevated dance floor and watched the girl. She noticed him; he knew she would. He was dressed a lot smarter than everyone else in the place, who looked like they had come straight off the beach.

He smiled at her and she made her way over to him. From the corner of his eye he saw Fat Harry watching as she performed the next three minutes for Mann's entertainment. When she had finished her number he tucked a large tip inside the rim of her boot. He ordered another drink and sat back on his stool. On his third drink a mamasan came over to him with a tray and a vodka on ice on it. She pointed to Fat Harry and said:

'Fat Harry say would like you to join him.'

Mann nodded his thanks, picked up his drink and wandered over to Fat Harry's table.

Mann looked Harry over. His shoulders were broad, his arms large, once muscled, and his neck was thick. He deserved his name now. He had several chins hanging beneath his babyish face and even more massive stomachs bursting the buttons of his plain calico shirt. His face was red, babyish. His silver hair was thinning and swept back by oil or by sweat, Mann couldn't decide. Harry filled most of the circular seat meant for four people. His head came high above the others around him. He must be at least six three, thought Mann. He reminded him of Jabba the Hutt.

Fat Harry spoke to the girls who were sitting with him, all clad in matching white miniskirts and black strapless tops. They squeaked their goodbyes to 'daddy', giggled their girly hellos to Mann, and left to make room for him to sit.

Fat Harry did not stand as Mann approached, and Mann did not expect him to. This was not England or Hong Kong. Etiquette was not top of the list here; congeniality was. And Fat Harry was Mr Congenial. He smiled non-stop. He waved to the party on a neighbouring table. They had a hostess lying on the table and were taking turns drinking vodka shots from her naval. He laughed so enthusiastically that his stomach reverberated.

'Regulars . . .' he said, raising his beer to them. 'Come back here every year. Nice to see a new face, though. I am the proprietor of this den of feckin' iniquity. What's your name, fella?' Fat Harry's voice still had a hint of Ulster brawl to it.

'John, John Black. I must congratulate you – you have a good business here, Harry.'

Fat Harry studied Mann. He obviously liked the cut of Mann's clothes. He looked at Mann's wrist to see what make of watch he had. It was one of several that Mann owned – a Pateek Philippe. He was obviously passing Fat Harry's test. A fellow policeman was always going to keep an eye on small details.

'You here on business, John?'

Mann shook his head. 'My wife will kill me if I answer yes to that . . . I'm here on honeymoon. Why, is this club for sale?'

Fat Harry laughed. 'I like you already – a straight-talker – a man after my own heart. And no, this club is not for sale, although I could probably point you in the direction of one that is.'

Mann picked up his glass. 'Cheers to your good health.'

Fat Harry picked up his beer bottle and clicked it against Mann's glass. 'And yours.'

'So, what business are you in, John?'

'All sorts.' Mann grinned. 'This and that. I have a

few investments. I own a few language schools in London and Manchester. A couple of massage parlours and a few other things that I'd rather not admit to.'

Fat Harry laughed. 'Language schools, huh? Who are your main clients?'

'From Asia, mostly: China, Japan.'

'What about the girls in your massage parlours?'

'Well, not surprisingly, we have a fair few Filipinas but mainly Eastern Bloc girls. I recruit them through the school.'

'Good business, huh?'

'There will always be girls looking to make money and always men looking to spend it.'

The table next door had moved on to watching the girl perform a sex act with a specially designed ice-cream cone. There were loud appreciative hoots and claps. Fat Harry waited for the antics to be finished before he tried making himself heard again.

'You don't have any problem with the girls, they don't mind working?'

'A few of them do take a bit of persuading. Some of them owe money for their passage over, they're working it off – you know the kind of thing, I am sure. The young ones need to be controlled, shown who's boss.'

Fat Harry's greedy eyes fixed on Mann's face. Mann could see that he had taken the bait.

'How long are you staying here in Puerto Galera, John?'

'Just a couple of nights. We have friends in Manila; we'll go there after here. We fly home to London in a week.'

'Would you be interested in meeting one of my business partners? Bob English? We may have something you'd be interested in, and he'll be very keen to know more about your UK businesses.'

'Sure. Why not? I'm always open to offers.'

'Give me tonight to organise it. I'll call you in the morning; let you know what I've managed to set up.'

Mann hoped that Shrimp had done a good job on his and Becky's new identities. Fat Harry would be scrutinising it tonight. And they would want Mann dead by the morning if Shrimp hadn't.

56

'Hurt, ma'am?'

The evening had come in fast. The sunset had arrived in smoky plumes of billowing purple cloud against a backdrop of turquoise. That was just a few minutes ago, now it was as dark as midnight and the first stars were appearing. Becky sat in the middle of a row of five chairs inside the Paradise foot spa. Her feet were in a wooden bowl of warm water, being soaked and washed whilst another woman massaged her shoulders. She was drinking sweet ginger tea. Outside there were a dozen open-air stations for massaging backs and feet.

She was thinking about what had happened with Mann. They had become such good friends in so few days that it felt like forever. They laughed at the same things and they cared about the same things – basically he was a soul mate. Becky shook her head at that revelation – her *soul mate*! That's what she had thought Alex was at one time. But, more than that – Mann made her feel like a sexy woman again. Then there was the kiss.

'A little,' she replied, thinking to herself that these

women had developed incredibly strong fingers as they brought her back to reality and she felt the innermost muscles of her shoulders twang.

Becky had come into the spa, which seemed to be the largest women's workplace on the beach, thinking that if anyone would know what was new, they would. The women were all wearing black shorts and pink T-shirts with '*Paradise*' written on them. The masseuse who was washing Becky's feet was pregnant. She squatted in front of Becky, resting her bottom on a short-legged stool, her round stomach protruding so far that Becky wondered that she could still see her customer's feet in the bowl. She looked like one of Gauguin's Tahitian women. She wore a red flower tucked behind her ear and her hair fell over her shoulders in a thick black glossy sheet. Her face was broad and flat, as was her nose. She had a calm, earthy beauty. When her hair fell in front of her busy hands, she flicked it away in a move that was slow, deliberate and elegant. She wore a name badge with '*Rosario*' on it. Despite her beauty, she looked very sad, thought Becky.

'Why you no grow you hair, ma'am? Colour like gold.' Tina, the masseuse kneading Becky's shoulders, spoke.

Two other masseuses came in to get their feet done whilst they were not busy outside. One sat on the end of the row, whilst the other fetched the bowl. They all nodded their agreement with Tina.

Becky had just come from the Internet café. She'd heard from the team back home. More of the victims' identities were coming to light. Two of them had been traced to this area. It seemed that they had been brought together and shipped over to Hong Kong, then on to the UK.

The evening was only just beginning to get busy. People were still passing by in purposeful mode, off either to eat or drink. They were not chilled enough to think about a foot massage yet. At midnight the spa would be packed. Then the girls would set up camp beds in the sand opposite and give massages to passers-by. For now, the half a dozen girls whose job it was to tout, took it in turns to come and get their nails done, whilst outside the masseuses with the leaflets joked with people passing, made idle conversation with those they knew along the sandy parade. Becky wondered how so many women managed to eke out any kind of living from the spa.

'I like it better short,' she said smiling so as not to sound offended.

The girls' faces showed that the notion of short hair was way beyond their comprehension.

'Is Puerto Galera your home?' she asked Rosario, who was quieter than the rest. Becky felt sorry for her having to squat when she was so pregnant. She had begun rolling a smooth pebble along the underside of Becky's foot. It was an almost pleasant sensation.

'No, ma'am. Home far away from here.'

'Did you come here for work?' Becky knew she was making Rosario slightly uncomfortable by her questions, but she also knew that she would answer – it would be rude not to, and Filipinas were never rude if they could help it.

'Yes, ma'am. Not in here, work in club first, then here.'

'Is club work good here? Is this spa work better than the club?'

Rosario looked at the others who were listening to the conversation. There was a silence in the room.

'Too old now for club. Have to be young girl, you know?'

Becky looked at her. She couldn't have been more than twenty-five.

'When is your baby due?'

'Two months, ma'am.'

'Is it your first baby?'

'No, ma'am. The girl paused as she rubbed Becky's feet with the hot stone, drawing it between Becky's toes. She glanced at the masseuses and back at Becky. Have two more children, but . . .' Her voice trailed off as the other women stopped their work momentarily and looked at her. Tina resumed massaging Becky's neck and in a smiling voice that belied the contents of her words she spoke in Tagalog to her companion.

'Don't be stupid, Rosario, shut your mouth before it's too late. They told you not to speak of it.'

Rosario looked up; Becky could see her eyes had filled as she looked fleetingly at Tina and the others, then at Becky. She went back to working on Becky's feet.

Tina dug her fingers harder into Becky's shoulders. Becky resisted the temptation to flinch. Rosario gave a massive sigh. It made her bump rise and fall. She stopped her foot-washing and looked up at Becky. Her large brown eyes were wet.

'My children, ma'am. They . . .'

Tina interrupted in Tagalog; there was a sharpness in her voice.

'*You were warned; say nothing and they will be returned.*' Becky watched them as they looked from one to the other.

Rosario looked at her workmates. Her eyes were burning with injustice and misery. '*You must wait,*' said Tina.

'*Wait? How long? It will be too late for waiting soon.*' *Rosario's voice had risen and she glared at Tina and the others. She shook her head and with another sigh came more tears. She sniffed and wiped her nose as she continued rubbing Becky's feet.* '*They will be dead inside. The way we were. I don't want it for my children. I did everything to stop it happening to them. My girls are going to be lawyers, not prostitutes!*'

Rosario bowed her head again and a large sob heaved itself from her exhausted body. Her baby kicked inside. Becky saw Rosario's belly grow tight and move and a tiny heel protruded as the baby listened to its mother's sobbing. Becky looked at it in wonder. Rosario instinctively shifted on the stool to allow the baby to turn. Her voice rose. '*I cannot bear it. I don't want to give birth to this baby to see it taken from me the way they were.*' She looked defiantly around the room. Becky watched the other girls in the shop look anxiously at one another, worried as Rosario cried openly. '*I cannot bear it.*' Rosario repeated. '*They will be sick and scared and they will never be the same if we don't get them back soon . . .'* Rosario held her hand against her heart. *'Inside they will be dead . . .'*

'Don't endanger all our children for the sake of yours. They will kill us.' Tina looked around anxiously. She was nervous of onlookers from outside. *'Keep working . . .'* she ordered the women in the salon. A false busyness started up.

The woman who was having her feet pumiced by her workmate spoke up.

'But how do we know that our children won't be next?' she asked in a hushed voice. *'We cannot trust them. We need to tell someone else. She looks like she has a good job, plenty of money, maybe she could help.'*

Becky saw all eyes turn on her. She didn't know what they were saying but she knew they were weighing up whether to tell her something, something difficult – this might be her chance.

'Please listen.' She looked around at them all, then her eyes settled last on Rosario. 'I am a policewoman. I have come here because a child has been stolen in London. I am here to try to find that child. Maybe I can help you find yours too.'

Everyone turned to look at Tina, who was their spokeswoman. Tina always made the decisions.

Tina shook her head. She stared out of the window, her thoughts captured by the horror of losing her own children.

'I have to, Tina,' Rosario pleaded. *'I cannot bear it.'*

Tina ceased her neck massage. Her voice softened. *'All right, all right, say it.'*

'*I will make sure none of the others come in,*' said another girl as she signalled to her workmates outside that they were to keep out.

Becky waited, aware that something was about to happen.

'My children are gone, ma'am.' Rosario's dark eyes blurred with tears and she spoke to Becky in English. 'They were taken from me – two girls, thirteen and fifteen – good girls, pretty girls.' At that statement her workmates muttered their agreement and shook their heads sadly. 'I do not know where they are. Bad men have taken them.'

The women glanced nervously outside to the rest of the team who were staring in, perplexed at the serious nature of the talk inside the shop, but playing their part in pretending that nothing unusual was happening. Tina reassured them with an all-purpose smile. All the girls were jittery. All of them felt the pain and terror that Rosario was being forced to endure, and all of them knew that it could easily be their children next. None of them wanted it to happen to them, but they were powerless.

'Here in Puerto Galera, many girls go missing now. Not come back.'

'How long have they been gone?'

'My girls gone three months now.'

'Twelve girls gone, not come back,' added Tina. 'From here and from town nearby.'

'Who has taken them? Do you know? Tell me about the girls, maybe I can help,' said Becky.

The women looked nervously at one another. Tina

309

looked at Rosario and nodded permission for Rosario to speak.

'Kanos. Bad white men.' Rosario kept her eyes down, wiped away her tears and continued massaging Becky's feet. 'These Kanos know who took them. It is their friends.'

'Do the Kanos live here in Puerto Galera?'

'Yes. Very big men here. Very important.'

'What are their names?'

A man had come to talk to the women outside. It had made them jittery. They turned one by one to discreetly attract their workmates' attention to the fact. Becky looked at him. He was in his late fifties, with receding white-blonde hair caught in a ponytail that was streaked with grey. He had the deportment of a man unused to exercise and had a cigarette in one hand. The other was thrust deep into the pocket of his shorts. He was a man who had shrivelled inside his clothes. They looked out of place on his frame. He would have suited the dirty old biker look, thought Becky. 'One name Fat Harry, and the other that man . . .' Tina's head gave a small incline towards the window, where the man with the ponytail had moved on to talk to a man selling pearls opposite the massage parlour. 'That man – his name English Bob.'

57

'Just cool it, bro.'

'I told you to get packing, Reese. We're leaving.'

'There's no point, bro. We may as well sit it out, relax, no one's lifting off tonight. There are no planes taking off till tomorrow. It's a mañana moment, bro. It happened here – it's not civilisation as we know it.'

'No shit, Sherlock! If I want your input I'll ask for it . . . now get the fuck up and start packing.'

Reese lay back on the bed and rolled another joint. He watched Sophia play with Princess Pony. Terry was packing his things into a bag. Secretly, Terry agreed with Reese, there was no point in moving now – where were they going to go? They would have to sit in the airport for the night. But he wasn't going to say anything, not for a minute. Reese was doing his usual trick of not fully understanding when someone was at breaking point. He just never knew when to shut up. The Teacher looked like he was scared – Terry hadn't seen him like that before. Mr Cool, Calm and Collected was properly shitting himself about something.

Reese lit the joint and drew heavily on it, keeping

the smoke in his lungs as long as he could before exhaling. He offered it to Terry, who shook his head and continued packing. There was a stark light in the room. The Teacher had insisted that they close the doors. The room was gaining heat – it didn't bother the locals but the Teacher was sweating. His forehead had become speckled in glistening beads. His shirt was showing signs of wetness where it stuck to him.

'Put the fucking air-con on – who the fuck switched it off?'

Reese shrugged and kept rolling. 'It happens here, bro, it ain't a conspiracy.' But secretly it made Reese smile. He was going to roll himself a stash of joints. He thought he would need them tonight. He was damned if he'd do without everything – no sex, even his flirtation with the English blonde had been cut short – no fucking way was the Teacher going to spoil his entire night. If nothing else, he would get stoned.

Sophia stopped trotting Princess Pony over the furniture and stared at the Teacher, who had sweat dripping from the end of his nose. Her eyebrows knitted together. Then she started to giggle. Terry stopped his packing, looked at her and smiled, amused. Reese lay back on the bed and started laughing hard. His body was shaking with it. The hand holding the joint was banging on the bed and the ash was flying over the cover. Terry started laughing. Sophia continued her manic giggling. The angrier the Teacher looked, the more they laughed.

The Teacher went for Reese but he hadn't bargained on him being so quick on his feet. Reese was nimble whilst the teacher was bulky. Reese could outrun him anytime. As the teacher went for him, Reese was out of the door. He ran the first stretch, till he was clear of the hotel and the lane and on the far end of the beach, then he dodged between the boats. The stars were out; the sky was frosted with them. He crouched and listened as he peeped over the top of the *barcas*. He never thought to look behind him. Noiselessly through the sand a man walked in the darkness. He came within three feet of Reese's back before he lifted his dagger by the hilt and brought it down into Reese's neck. It went right through, and came out of his Adam's apple.

58

Becky left the foot spa and walked down the beach. It was as dark as midnight and the stars were out. She checked her phone – still no text from Mann. She stopped at the first bar she came to where she liked the music – 'Hotel California' by the Eagles. The Flamingo beach bar was open on all sides. It had a few life-size plastic flamingos peeping out of plant pots at its corners and what looked like leftover Christmas lights across its palm-thatch roof. It was the local drinking hole for all those from the PADI diving school. On the beach end of the bar there were stacks of diving equipment and rinsed, dripping-wet wetsuits draped over a rail pushed into the sand. The men and women sat in their board shorts and swimwear, recounting the day's thrills. Their sunny faces were alive and tanned but their lean and muscled bodies were white from lack of sun.

Becky sat at a stool at the bar. The news about Rosario's daughters and the added information from Shrimp had made her adrenalin start racing. She knew now that Fat Harry and English Bob weren't just hangers-on, or cashers-in, they were an integral part of the new trafficking ring.

She checked her phone. She had a voicemail message. She dialled and listened. A group of leering Brits began edging towards her but she stopped them with a look. A lonely, liver-lipped old American tried to tell her his life story but soon retreated back into the shadows. She pressed the phone to her ear and listened to the unfamiliar voice.

'*My name is Suzanne. I want you to know that I have been having an affair with your husband Lenny for a year.*'

Becky ordered a margarita and drank the first one fast. She ordered another and drank it faster. She stared at her phone. What was that about? Suzanne? She had no idea who this Suzanne and Lenny were.

'Mrs Black? May I join you?' A man's voice interrupted her thoughts. She was about to bite his head off when she saw who it was. 'Can I call you Emma?' The man with the ponytail appeared beside her. 'Sorry, I missed you and your husband at the hotel. I'm the owner. My name is Bob English.' His voice was raspy from years as a heavy smoker. His accent still had a hint of northern to it, but it was a clash of styles and adopted accents. He smiled at Becky.

'Of course.' Becky nodded and smiled sweetly. 'Please sit. Nice to meet you. You have a great hotel.'

She shook his hand, repressing the urge to wipe hers afterwards. He had smoker's fingers and a deeply lined face from the sun. Inside his open shirt his white chest hair looked albino against his tanned chest. His body appeared almost emaciated. He ordered a scotch and soda and another margarita for Becky.

'How do you like it here? Is the hotel matching up to your expectations? If there is anything you need . . .'

Becky held up both hands and rolled her eyes skyward.

'The place couldn't be more perfect, thank you. It's such a welcoming place. It's amazingly friendly here.'

'They are a happy nation, aren't they?' English Bob grinned. He obviously didn't trust dentists; he had terrible teeth, uneven, broken and yellowed like a horse's. Becky looked long and hard at English Bob – she felt a huge shiver of repulsion. He was as hideous inside as he was out.

A group of giggling teenage girls passed by along the beach. He took his time studying them. He watched them leisurely, lingeringly, like a lover would.

'That's what I love about them.' He snapped back to her and picked up his drink. 'No matter what happens to them in life, they are always such happy, positive people – foolishly optimistic in a way.' He picked up his scotch and licked his lips as if it burned. She looked at him curiously. 'Oh yes, they allow themselves to be taken advantage of. They practically rely on it. A very naive nation, loving, trusting. Even the bar girls – sorry – the guest relation officers . . .' He winked conspiratorially. 'These girls really believe that someone loves them, even if it's just for a night. They dream of a foolish western guy falling in love and marrying them. It's not a business to them.' He laughed, loud and cynical. 'It's not a business to them like it is to the girls in Hong Kong or in Thailand – here it's a vocation. Ha ha . . .'

Becky smiled politely and waited for him to stop laughing at his own joke. 'They must be easy to take advantage of,' she said, signalling to the barman that she would like another margarita.

'They are a very physical people.' English Bob steadied his gaze and locked her eyes to his. 'You can't apply the same rules as we do back home. You wouldn't dream of having sex with a thirteen-year-old back home – here, it's different.'

'Really? You think they develop differently?'

'Yes, that's it. They are much more . . . sexualised.'

'Is that due to the sex tourism?'

'Oh no. It has been like that for ever. Most of it starts in their own home. People feel sorry for the bar girls. Let me tell you – it's far preferable to cutting cane.'

'Of course – now I get it!' she said, trying to hide the sarcasm from her voice. She wondered whether he could be any more loathsome.

'Yes! I used to feel sorry for them myself. But then I married one of them. Now I have half a dozen of the little smilers running around. So I'm never sure who took advantage of who.'

'How lovely – a family man!'

'Wouldn't swap it for anything. It's a great life, I'm sure. What about yourself? You been married long?'

'We are on our honeymoon. So far, so good.'

'Ha . . .' He made ready to go. 'The honeymoon period . . . Make the most of it, and when you discover he's been cheating, come and see me. I have a very sympathetic side.' He grinned at Becky. His eyes went liquid, his lips went wet. 'And let me know if you need another foot massage. I'll do it myself, happily.' He backed away grinning, then his lecherous eyes turned hard and he glared at her. 'And if you need to ask any more questions about local matters, things that only concern the people who live here, you come and see me. You can ask me as many questions as you want. You have to watch who you talk to round here . . .' He stood up. '. . . loose tongues and all that.' And, with that, English Bob disappeared up the lane.

59

Johnny Mann appeared from the other side of the bar. He leaned in and kissed Becky's cheek.

'Did you have a nice chat?'

'Huh! He came *this* far . . .' Becky pinched her forefinger and thumb together as if she were picking up salt '. . . to getting a punch in the mouth. If I hadn't been afraid I'd need a tetanus jab afterwards, I would have . . . Sorry I took so long. I took a detour back to the room to see if our fish had taken the bait, and . . .'

'Had it?'

'Hook, line and whatever. Bags gone though. Well, your bag was gone. My stuff was obligingly set out in neat piles. They would have found everything they needed. Ng has created a great profile for us – you're a beautician, by the way. On paper I come out as a dirty bastard and you come out as a trophy wife. By the time they finish checking us out tonight I will be just what they are looking for.' Mann nodded in the direction that English Bob had just departed. 'You think

319

he's bad – you should meet his best friend, Fat Harry. How did you get on?'

'I'm afraid he knows I was asking questions.'

'Can't be helped. We don't have time to pussy foot now I have an appointment with them both tomorrow. We will soon find out if they know who we are.'

'I had disturbing news from home. Two of the women in the fire were traced here. And I talked to the women in the spa, down the beach. One of them has similar-aged girls gone missing. I got some details and faxed them over to Shrimp. He's seeing if any of them match the burn victims. The women here are very scared. They told me that there have been a lot of girls going missing over the last year.'

'How?'

'Kidnapped on the walk to school. A windowless van turns up. Three men jump out, none of them local, apparently, at least one Chinese. They bundle the girls in the back. Onlookers have reported that when the doors are opened at the back, they see other girls sleeping, doped, in the van. And, surprise, surprise . . . who warned the girls off reporting their missing children?'

'Our British pals?'

'Precisely, and the women daren't go to the police around here because the chief is part-owner of most of the bars along the beach.'

'So I gathered from Fat Harry. Okay. We'd better make sure tomorrow is our last day here. We need to get up to Angeles. I meet them at eleven; we'll be gone by twelve thirty. I'll text Remy now and make sure he is ready. We might want to get out in a hurry. Another thing – I found a friend of yours . . . Reese the friendly pervert. He is sunbathing on the beach right now.'

'Strange timing . . . does he know it's night?'

'It's going to be permanently night for our friend Reese. We better get out as soon as we can tomorrow. They aren't going to take long to find him, maybe longer to recognise him – the crabs were having a midnight feast when I left.' Mann checked his watch – it was midnight. 'We have twenty-four hours till the deadline is up.'

'What if CK is setting us up to fail? What if he wants this war more than he wants his daughter's life?'

'CK will honour his pact. But others may not.'

'Wait a minute . . .' She stopped and turned to him. 'You said we were going to Negros, didn't you?'

'Change of plan.'

She tilted her head to one side and scowled at him.

'Don't fucking bullshit me. You don't trust me, why? Why did you lie?'

'Okay – I have had emails from someone calling themselves Blanco.'

'The name of the bogus company on the kidnap emails?'

'Yes. He is playing a game with us. He knows where Amy Tang is being held and he knows where we are and what we are doing. He probably knows we are on this beach right now. I don't know how he does that but I do know he holds Amy's fate in his hands.'

* * *

Stevie Ho was watching them from the balcony of the hotel where Terry and Reese had sat having a drink. He finished dialling a number and pressed the phone to his ear.

'Finish it. Kill her,' he said, and closed the phone.

60

Amy watched the planes overhead. They were so near she could count the windows along the side. She waved to the pilot, even though she knew he couldn't see her. She listened for the sounds outside. She had learned the routine of her captors very well. She knew exactly what time they relieved each other of their babysitting duties. She knew what time they would have lunch. She knew what television programs they listened to outside in the lounge. They chattered away on their mobiles, forgetting that Amy was able to understand them. Impossible for the Cantonese to talk quietly. Amy knew a lot more about them now.

Since Lenny had left, Suzanne had been in charge and the men didn't like it. She talked to them like idiots, thought Amy. The one with the spotty face, Tony, had left, and now there was a new one. His name was Pat. He was nice to Amy. He let her come and watch telly on his shift and he bought her pizza. He played chess with her.

It was seven in the morning. Pat would be gone soon. The nasty, ugly one, Sunny, would take over.

He spent the whole time talking on the phone and watching porn movies on the telly. Amy could hear it in the evenings, all the moaning and grunting.

Suzanne came and went less rigidly than the men. By now Amy understood that this was not the only place where Suzanne looked after people. There was another house that she and the two men took it in turns to go to. Amy wondered who was at that house and whether there was a girl like her. Sometimes Amy started crying. She was so bored and fed up, only Pat brought her books to read, and she couldn't relax. She never knew what mood Suzanne was going to be in. Amy knew it was her by the way the front door closed. They all did it differently. Suzanne was precise – she clicked it shut, rather than slamming it the way Sunny did. In between was Pat. He closed it strongly but without banging. Suzanne seemed to creep in.

There were just the two men this morning. Amy sat there listening. Pat and Sunny were talking about Lenny's trip. They weren't happy that he'd been called away. They didn't think that Suzanne was competent to handle the job. They were getting nervous about it. Amy listened hard.

She was sitting at her table where her macramé kit was laid out methodically. Beads were kept in the box lid, to stop them from disappearing. The cord was laid out in its varying lengths and different colours. There was a frame on which to stretch the necklace whilst you worked on it. Amy was putting all her energy into making one item. It was a necklace for Suzanne.

Pat left and Sunny sat down to watch the telly. The

door clicked – it was Suzanne. She greeted Sunny with a ticking-off for not taking out the bin whilst it was still early and there was less chance of being seen. Now she had to do it and it was already nine o clock. Why was everything down to her? Amy listened. She knew what Sunny would say. It was what he always said every time Suzanne had a massive go at him.

'I am not your fucking servant. You don't like it, I'll go. You're lucky I'm still here. No good will come of things. We'll all be in the shit when they find us. So, go on – get rid of me, fire me, please.'

Suzanne answered: 'Just do the few things you are asked to and do them well, then we'll all be happy. And leave the merchandise alone.' That bit puzzled Amy. 'Knocking them about is one thing, but this isn't your dream come true, Sunny. You want to get laid, pay for it like you usually do. Stop fucking the girls, especially the young ones – you're damaging the merchandise. She's split inside already . . .'

'That wasn't me, that was the two punters.'

'Leave them alone – got it?'

Sunny grunted that he had. 'What about that one?' he asked. Amy's eyes went wide and her brace formed a vacuum at the roof of her mouth as she heard the question directed towards her door. 'Why not that one?'

'Ha ha, you are fucking priceless, Sunny.' Suzanne lowered her voice. 'The day I decide to put Miss CK's cherry up for sale, the place will be swarming with rival triad bosses. You don't think I'm going to let you have it for free, do you?'

Amy heard her throw down her coat and bags and

stomp off with the rubbish. Then the click when she came back. Sunny stomped out soon after, muttering under his breath about having had enough. Amy listened to Suzanne's footsteps approaching her bedroom door.

She looked up from her macramé table. She smiled as the door opened.

'Morning, Suzanne.' Her heart was hammering.

Suzanne didn't answer. She grunted something about making her bed. Amy jumped off her seat and hurriedly pulled the covers up over the mattress.

Amy smiled at Suzanne. 'You look lovely, Suzanne,' she lied. Suzanne wasn't bothering with makeup any more now that Lenny had gone. 'Yesh. You look really pretty and so slim, like a model.'

'Yes, well, time we got some fat off you. I'm thinking of moving you somewhere else, to a different house where there are other girls.'

Amy started making nervous sucking noises with her brace.

'And why is that fucking brace back in your mouth?'

'Sorry, Suzanne, it's just I will get into trouble if I don't wear it.'

'Come here.'

Amy took a few steps towards her. Suzanne slapped her hard across the face. Her glasses flew off. Amy cried out, flinching as she clutched the stinging side of her face.

'Sorry, Suzanne.' She took the brace out.

Suzanne sighed, then rubbed her forehead as if it itched.

'My fucking head is pounding.'

'Sit down, Suzanne; I will give you a neck massage. I can brush your hair for you if you like. And look, Suzanne . . .' Amy rushed to the table and showed her the half-constructed necklace. 'This is for you.'

Suzanne didn't look impressed. 'Okay, let's get on with the massage, and then you can brush my hair.'

'Oh, yes please, Suzanne.'

Amy scurried to find the brush to keep it close by for when she needed it. She didn't want to risk irritating Suzanne any more than she had done. She started kneading her strong little fingers into Suzanne's shoulders.

'Suzanne . . . what's your favourite colour? I need to know for your necklace.'

'Mmm . . . green, no, blue, no, red! Red, that's it.'

Amy looked over to her bead collection. The biggest of all the beads was red! How lucky was that?

'Pass me my bag?'

'What are you doing?'

Suzanne rummaged inside and found her phone.

'I am ringing his wife. I am fucking sick of waiting *and* of babysitting you. I am going to speed things up. I am going to tell her what her husband really thinks of her, the fat, ugly cow . . .'

61

The phone rang. It was Fat Harry.

'We checked you out – very impressive – we have quite a few similar interests, it seems.'

'You mean we tick each other's boxes?'

Fat Harry laughed down the phone. He had a laugh that carried on too long after the joke was told. 'Eleven o'clock, then.'

'Where?'

'The Flamingo bar – and Black . . . no wifey. This business is strictly for boys.'

Mann closed his phone. He strapped his armoury on. His spikes were now moved to the harness around his ankle, next to Delilah, and his throwing-star belt was under his armpit, concealed beneath a baggy shirt. He had a knife belt around his waist – with four short-handled shuriken knives tucked inside

He handed Becky a piece of paper.

'We have to be sure that one of us gets to Angeles. Remy will be waiting for us on a small airstrip, a kilo-metre away from here. Here is the address . . . Take the bags and go there now. Remy will wait for two hours.

Any sign of trouble, he will lift off and take you straight to Clark and to Father Finn's refuge. You will have to coordinate things from there. We have just two days left. We have to find the Blanco and force his hand. We have to find his weakness and exploit it, everyone has one. I'm not even sure that CK wants us to win. I think he wants an excuse to start a war. I don't want to give him one now. This might all be a game to these people but we're going to do our damndest to spoil it for them. Don't worry Mann. You will be on that plane, but if not, rest assured that I will do whatever it takes.'

'Save me a seat on the plane – no running off with Remy.'

She laughed but he could see how scared she was. He didn't want to but he left her standing in the centre of the room, his heart melting a little.

He walked out through the hotel lobby, which was open on all sides and ended on the beach, and headed for the Flamingo bar. It was a ten-minute walk. He took his time. He was early – always early – but they did not know that about him. In the distance he could make out the pinks and peach of the Flamingo bar, its canvas flapping gently in the breeze. He was thirty metres away. Beyond that he saw a hint of police action – they must have found Reese. He could see Fat Harry, sitting with his back to him, along with English Bob and a third man with a bald head. That must be the contact they had talked about. They still had not seen him. He slowed down. His feet dug into the sand. Something didn't feel right.

62

Becky looked at her watch. Mann had said to give him twenty minutes, to make sure he was well into conversation with them before she left. It had only been eight.

She made the last check around the room and then pulled out a piece of paper. There was a sketch map and the name of the airfield. It was so lucky that all the signs were in English. It all looked straightforward. It was just a couple of kilometres away, basically up the lane towards the neighbouring town, then take a left. Mann had already settled the bill the night before, so all she had to do was pick up the bags, walk out and get a trike to take her to the airstrip. In that case, why was her heart pounding? Why did she feel so anxious? She looked at her watch again. It would only take ten minutes from the room to the Flamingo bar, and that was at Filipino pace. She moved the bags to the door. It was time to go. Mann would nearly be there by now; she could leave without arousing suspicion. She turned the handle and pulled the door open. As she bent down to pick up the bags she saw legs, feet and expensive trainers – *no one round here would wear those*. She didn't

look up; instead she launched Mann's bag forward at
the legs and heard the man groan as he fell backwards.
At the same time someone else pushed her back into
the room. Becky looked up to see four Chinese men.
She blocked a punch and turned side-on as she made
a run for the door. A man stood in her way, his arms
raised to stop her; she hooked her wrists over his and
brought a knee up to his groin. He doubled over in
pain then she felt the flash of pain as a fist slammed
into the side of her head; then an arm tightened around
her throat. Her feet were kicked from beneath her
and her head smashed against the side of the bed as
she fell to the floor.

63

Mann began turning at the same time as Stevie Ho stood up and left Fat Harry's table. Mann began running before Stevie could see him. If Stevie was there, it meant they knew who he really was and his cover was blown. But they had lured him there for a reason. Then it hit him with sickening clarity – Becky was the target.

Mann sprinted back up towards the hotel. He didn't need to look back to know that Bob and Harry would give him ten minutes before realising he wasn't going to show up and that he knew. Then they would alert their friends. Mann's blood ran cold. All he could think of was Becky. He ran through the empty reception – no staff, and no guests. Something was going on that no one wanted to see. Whatever it was must still be happening in the room. Mann took the staff stairs to the third landing and walked halfway along until he judged he was just above their room; then he slipped into an open door whilst the chambermaid was cleaning. He crept out onto the balcony and listened. Diagonally across and down he heard Cantonese being spoken, the noise of excited, raised voices. He estimated there were four or five men. There was no sound from Becky. Mann stepped onto the ledge and jumped across to the neighbouring balcony. Now he was directly above the room. As he looked over he saw that the French doors to the balcony were open. He could just see inside.

He saw Becky on the floor. A man was over her. She was being raped. He felt the anger roar through him and felt as if he would spontaneously combust if he could not control it. He knew he must control it, because, more than anything, he wanted to rescue her. His senses became heightened as every fibre in him was preparing itself for a fight. He was poised on the railing, ready to swing down. He needed all the force he could muster to get through those balcony doors and into the centre of the room in one massive jump. He took a deep breath in, and on the exhale he held onto the ledge and propelled himself over as hard as he could. His feet contacted with the door frame. The door flew back and banged against the rattan cabinet to the right of it.

Mann crouched low and aimed high. From one hand he threw all five throwing spikes that had been strapped to his ankle. Three of them landed in the face and neck of the man nearest the door. Two were stuck through the shoulders of the man doing up his flies. He was now pinned to the hessian frieze above the bed. The third man had Delilah through his heart and was in the process of dying on the floor. Lastly, from Mann's left hand he released the Death Star. It span through the air and sliced through the back of the neck of the man who was in the process of raping Becky. It severed his spinal cord, as Mann knew it would – he couldn't risk injuring Becky in the process. He had to take the man out this way.

Mann watched him topple slowly sideways, then he walked over and picked him up with his foot and kicked him away from Becky. He checked her breathing; she had been badly beaten but she was alive. He pulled her trousers up and pulled her t-shirt down. Now Mann could let his anger loose. Now, as he turned to her attackers, he knew that he was the last man they would see on this earth. Anger was built in him that would not be quelled. Now he would have justice at any cost. He could never undo the harm they had done to her, but he could make them pay . . . and he would. She was still unconscious, but she was alive and she could wait one minute, one moment was all it would take for him to settle the score.

64

He walked out of the room and down the stairs,
carrying Becky in his arms. The alert would have
gone up by now, he needed to hurry. He passed the
bemused receptionist who had taken a shine to him
earlier. One look from Mann told her not to touch
the phones. He strode straight to the front. He carried
Becky up to the trike riders. He threw his full wallet
at a driver, grabbed his keys from him and slid Becky
in the sidecar whilst he took off in a swirl of sand.
He looked across at Becky. She was stirring. She
looked a mess. Her face was bloodied and swollen.
He wished the trike had gears, its max speed was
thirty and that was on a downhill. He looked behind
him. He could see a saloon coming at speed, hurtling
down the sandy lanes behind them. Mann looked
into the mirror. He saw Fat Harry sitting in the front,
English Bob in the back, but the driver wasn't Stevie.
No sign of him.

They were gaining. Mann would have to outwit
them. The road was busy. Mann drove up on pavements, took out fruit stalls. The car hooted for people

to move. The trike was smoking, screaming. The road was straightening out, the car gaining. Then Mann turned the corner and saw the runway. To the left was the tank for the aviation fuel, to the right was the small row of hangers, and Remy was at the end of the runway, making his last-minute checks outside the aircraft.

Mann saw him focus on the trike, his scowl changing to a smile when he recognised the driver; and then it changed to a look of alarm as he heard the volley of bullets coming from the car that had just screamed around the corner in pursuit.

Remy jumped inside and started the plane's engine. It cranked into life, spluttered, coughed, and then the propeller started turning. A second later Remy appeared, standing on the door frame of the pilot's side, pistol in hand. He fired at the car and blew out the tyre. It caused the car to veer slightly away and swerve. Mann reached the plane, threw Becky inside and took the gun from Remy as he jumped back in the pilot's seat and began taxiing along the runway. Mann jumped into the plane as it was moving and fired out through the open passenger door. The car was within twenty metres. The plane's ascent was slow. Remy's hands were strong and steady on the yoke as he gave it full throttle. Still it didn't lift from the runway. The car was pulling level with the tail of the aircraft. Mann steadied his shoulder against the door frame, aimed and fired. His shot shattered the car's windscreen. It swerved away momentarily. They came again. Fat Harry had a gun levelled at Mann. Mann had a choice: kill the driver, or kill Harry. *Take out the dragon head, and the body will die.*

Harry was thrown backwards by the shot. He had been hit in the face. The car skidded, the driver lost control; it was veering towards the far side of the runway. Remy pulled hard back on the yoke and the plane began to lift off. Mann had one shot left. He stretched one arm across the doorway and used it to keep his other arm steady as he aimed his gun at the fuel tank and fired. Three seconds after the bullet left the nozzle the tank exploded in a ball of fire; the heat buffeted the small plane as it lifted off the ground. Mann yanked the door shut.

Remy shouted to him from the pilot seat. 'Is she alright? Look behind. There's a medical kit on the wall.'

Mann took the kit down from its strap. 'Thanks Remy. You're a handy man to have around.' He began a search for antiseptic and pads.

'We should go to Manila airport, it is bigger. They could be waiting for us at Clark. No?'

'Manila is best, I agree, Remy. I just need to get her cleaned up before she comes round and . . .'

When he looked back at her, her eyes were open. She was staring at him. He felt his heart rush for a second as he looked at her. 'Hello babe. You had a rough time but you'll be okay, tough nut. Come here.' He eased her towards him and she rested against his chest. 'It's all right. You're going to be okay.'

He could see by her expression that she was trying to piece together what happened. She lay very still for a few minutes.

'Mann? Johnny?'

'Yes?' He kissed the top of her head.

'Are they dead?'

'Yes.'

'Thank you.'

65

'Is Becky all right?'

Father Finn was there to meet them at Manila airport, waiting for them on the apron. He was being blasted by the prop wash from the propeller as he opened the passenger door and stuck his head inside.

'There is a doctor waiting at the refuge.'

Mann had telephoned ahead. The Father knew what to expect.

'I'm all right, Father.' Becky sat up and eased herself out of the seat. She hovered, dizzy, at the door. Mann held on to her and steered her out. Father Finn supported her when she got outside.

'Thank you for coming to fetch us, Father,' she said, squinting in the sunlight.

The Father held up his hands. 'No trouble at all.' His eyes were on her and then he reached out and hugged her.

'Thank you, Remy.' Father Finn waved goodbye to Remy; he was eager to make a fast exit – as always, he thought on his feet. 'Now, let's go. I need to talk to you on the way. These are very difficult times, no? Can you walk?'

Becky nodded but she was looking very pale and unsteady on her feet.

'She doesn't have to.' Mann picked her up.

'I will run on and get the Jeepney.' Father Finn jogged across the car park and returned driving the Jeepney belonging to the refuge. It had slices of juicy-looking mango on the side and a Mercedes replica emblem on the front.

They left Manila airport and headed north. All three of them sat in the front. The back was filled with sacks of rice that would last the refuge several weeks.

Becky sat by the window and stared out. She had a scarf wrapped around her mouth to ease the pollution that bit the back of her throat and burnt her lungs. She closed her eyes. She knew she was safe now. Next to Mann, she always felt safe; she could close her eyes and rest.

They hit the MacArthur Highway northbound. The sign at the side of the road read:

No Dilapidated Vehicles
No Smoke Belchers

Father Finn glanced over at Becky and could see that she was resting. She wouldn't hear him anyway – they had to shout over the noise of the traffic and the Jeepney had no glass in the windows. He did not want her to hear what he had to say in any case.

'There's been terrible news from Davao, Johnny.

340

Wednesday is dead. Her throat had been cut. She had been tortured. Her body was dumped back at the entrance to the Barrio Patay. It was left as a warning to others not to come looking for their children.'

'Why didn't she wait for us?' asked Mann, shaking his head with sorrow. 'Such a bloody shame, Father. She deserved so much better.'

'She was contacted. Someone frightened her into doing it. You should have seen her, Johnny – made my heart break. She had been scalped; there were cigarette burns all over her body. It's the same cowardly way that those men always do it . . . But her legs were sliced through at the back, above the back of the knee, right through to the bone. I don't know why they did that.'

'She was hamstrung, Father, to stop her running to or from something.'

'Jesus, mother of God.'

Mann felt his heart fill with an overwhelming sadness. To him, Wednesday had embodied all the hope and decency of someone who had dug themselves out of the gutter and made a new life for themselves. All she had asked for was a little help along the way.

'Did anyone see who dumped her body?'

'Yes, a boy, Pepe, he saw her body thrown from the car. He said it was a big Kano from Angeles. He told me that he had talked to him before. It was Pepe who had delivered the message to Wednesday to go and get her daughter. "Come without the priests," the boy said they'd told her. You know who that is then, Johnny? It's the Colonel. No one else hates me like him.'

'That miserable fucking bastard will pay for this. Sorry, Father.' Mann apologised for swearing.

'Please . . . if I could say it, I would.'

The car fell silent as Father Finn concentrated on driving and farms replaced factories and the urban squalor. The land stretched out flat until it rose in the distance to the volcano beyond. They left the highway, to find houses crammed together in clusters at the edge of the road. They had no uniform style. The outsides were bright, gaudy and mostly looked half-finished. They were made from a variety of reclaimed and new materials: thatch-palmed roofs, corrugated iron and breeze blocks. Washing was hung over barbed wire and goats grazed beneath.

Mann had so much to think about. He needed to try and piece it together. Why had Becky been targeted? They hadn't expected Mann back for an hour. They were taking their time, but they intended to kill her and leave her in the room. Otherwise they would have moved her straight away. It was not a kidnapping, it was a murder squad who thought they had time on their hands. But why Becky? Stevie Ho must be the reason. Those were Wo Shing Shing officers that Mann had killed. They were under orders from Stevie. But still, why Becky? Was it just because of her association with Mann? That was the last thing he wanted to believe, but it was the first thing that came into his head – *yes, in my own way, I am responsible again.*

Becky stirred as the noise from the road disappeared and was replaced by the sounds of insects and birds, then the noise of children laughing.

'We are here.'

They turned into a steep driveway that led up to a large multi-level building. It was made of wood and had a large balcony at the front. 'Welcome to the Angeles refuge.'

'It's a lovely place, Father.' Becky smiled at the sight of the children all running out to greet them, as before.

'We are lucky that we have permission to build over this entire hill, so many of the workers live just a minute's walk from here, in their own houses. Mercy and Ramon, that you met before in Davao, have a lovely house just on the other side of this hill.' They were surrounded by children immediately. 'Here is Mercy . . .'

As she came to greet them, Mann thought how she looked bigger than ever. In just a few days her shape had changed slightly, the baby was resting lower.

Mercy looked at Becky, concern in her face. 'You need to rest, come . . .'

'No, please, I'd rather not.'

Mercy looked at Becky and read her eyes. She saw that she meant it. She needed distraction. She did not want to be alone to think about things.

'Come, then, someone is waiting for you.'

From the corner of her eye Becky saw Eduardo standing apart from the others, waiting to be seen. She smiled and beckoned him over. He took her hand.

'He is still traumatised. We have therapy sessions where the children are encouraged to let go of their feelings, cry, scream, whatever it takes, but he is still not ready. It is early days for him.'

Becky sat down next to him on the porch. His eyes

were full of concern and his brow was furrowed as he looked at her battered face. She smiled, shook her head and pulled him closer.

Mann's phone rang. He stepped out of earshot to answer it.

'Yes, Ng?'

'CK is on the move. He has been calling in officers from everywhere. He is preparing for battle. There are hundreds ready to go in London, Hong Kong and the Philippines. We have already had a few spark-offs here. Somebody tried to torch Miriam's bar.'

'Is she all right?'

'She's okay. Minimal damage, but the yakuza took it personally. Instead of stepping away from the fight they are stepping up to it. The place is buzzing with tension, Mann. I don't think CK will back down, whatever happens.'

'I still have till midnight.'

'He doesn't care about his daughter. He has been waiting for this day all his life.'

66

'Yes, I understand what you're saying – by tomorrow morning it will all be over, but, if I don't hear from you, I will do what I have to.'

Suzanne was talking to Lenny. Amy could hear it in her voice. She must be talking to him because she was speaking English and it was in a softer, higher tone than when she talked to others. But Amy could tell she was irritable. After she had finished the phone call, Amy listened to her pace around the flat, and then she burst into the room making Amy jump. Amy was sitting at her table working on the necklace for Suzanne. She had constructed the best necklace ever. She had put a lot of thought into it.

'Get off that chair and come here.'

Amy blinked hard, slipped her brace out of her mouth and surreptitiously slipped it into the bead box, hoping that Suzanne wouldn't notice.

'Yes, Suzanne?'

'I've bought you some clothes to wear, put them on.' She threw some things at Amy. Amy caught them full in the face. She was the worst catcher in the world.

When they had to pick teams for netball she was always the last one to be chosen.

Amy picked them up and looked at them: two items – a denim mini-skirt and a white cotton stretchy boob tube.

'They'll be tight on you, but they should do the job. Put them on.'

Amy blinked up at Suzanne.

'Go in the bathroom then, just get on with it.'

Amy disappeared into the bathroom and came out with the outfit on. Suzanne picked up the chair and dragged it to the centre of the room where there was good light and she could see what she was doing.

'SIT.'

Amy did as she was told.

Suzanne pulled out her makeup bag from her handbag and began examining Amy's face. She took off her glasses. Amy sat patiently whilst Suzanne made her up. When she'd finished, Suzanne sat back to admire her work.

'There, that ought to do it . . .' she giggled.

Amy didn't know what to say. She was waiting to be given permission to move.

'Well, go and have a look at yourself, and for fuck's sake, don't you smudge it.'

Amy got off the chair gingerly. She stared at her reflection. A pale-faced, rosy-cheeked doll stared back. Her eyes were blackened with kohl, her lashes long. Her lips were bright red. Amy's eyes flicked back and forth over the image. It fascinated her. She reached to touch the mirror. It was true – it was her. She smiled and was alarmed that the girl smiled too. Boy, would her mummy be mad if she saw her looking like this!

Suzanne's phone went off. It was Sunny, Amy could tell by the way she barked at him like a yappy dog. Amy stayed in the bathroom and continued to stare at her reflection. Something bad was happening. This wasn't the usual.

'Tomorrow morning it all kicks off. We move the merchandise over to the Filipinas' house, and then we start the auction.'

Suzanne hung up, and Amy waited for a few seconds before she called out from the bathroom: 'Suzanne? Have you got a different outfit? I don't think it really fits me.'

Suzanne laughed. 'It doesn't need to fit you. Come out and let me see.'

Amy stepped gingerly out of the bathroom. The white top clung to her fat pointy breasts. The rolls of fat around her stomach meant that the skirt, which was supposed to rest on her hip bones, got snagged above her waist and stopped where it met her stubby, shapeless legs – it barely covered her square bottom. Amy tugged at it but it wouldn't budge.

'Thank you for doing my makeup and bringing me these clothes. Shall I make you a drink, Suzanne?'

Suzanne considered it, then she looked at her watch.

'Why not? We have a long night ahead. Make it a weak one. I have loads to do tomorrow.'

Amy went into the lounge. She carried the bottle of gin and the tonic, a glass, a plate of sliced lemons all on a tray. Very carefully she came in; the tray was tinkling as the contents touched each other. Amy set the tray down.

'Then, please, Suzanne, can I brush your hair?'

She began mixing the drink the way she had learned. But, tonight was different.

'Pour yourself one too, Amy. Pour a gin out. Do it.'

Amy did as she was told. She made one drink for Suzanne and one for herself. She tasted it.

'Yuk – that's disgusting.' She shivered and stood with her stomach sticking out, making a face. She undid the skirt at the front and her stomach seemed to expand by six inches. 'I feel sick.'

Suzanne giggled. 'Do my hair now.' She sat down and waited for Amy to get the brushes. Amy poured another gin for her.

'You can drink, can't you, Suzanne, because you don't have to go anywhere this night. You have to sleep here.'

'Yes, fucking Sunny and that new guy who never says a fuckin' word, Pat, they've got something else to do – and I'm stuck here with you for company!'

'I am sorry.'

'So am I, believe me.' She downed her drink.

Amy filled up her glass again.

'And what the fuck have you done to that lamp?' Suzanne stared at the wire frame of the raffia lamp.

'Sorry, Suzanne, it just fell apart. I was touching it – I just noticed there was a thread – I started to pull . . .'

'All right, all right – you don't have to go into so much fucking detail. Thank fuck we won't have to stare at all this crap for much longer.'

'Can I go back to school, Suzanne?'

Suzanne laughed again. She was getting drunk, Amy could tell.

'You'll be learning something very important soon, believe me – now brush my hair and stop talking.'

Amy took long, even strokes as Suzanne closed her eyes and relaxed. Amy looked at the bottle of gin. It was two-thirds empty.

'Can I tie your hair up on top of your head into a bun, Suzanne?'

'Do what you want.'

'Here, Suzanne – you haven't had hardly any gin.'

Suzanne's eyes opened and she drank the rest of her glass. Amy filled it up again. This time with three-quarters' gin and a quarter of tonic water.

Suzanne tasted it. 'Fucking hell. What are you trying to do? That's way too strong.'

'Sorry, Suzanne.' Amy went to take the glass off her and put some more tonic water in, but Suzanne snatched it back.

'It doesn't matter. I feel like getting drunk anyway. This is a celebration, Amy. Tonight is the night that Lenny has promised to leave his ugly little wife and marry me.'

'Do you want to lie down, Suzanne? I can give you a foot massage.'

Suzanne looked at Amy curiously then kicked off her shoes.

'Okay, why not? There's nothing else to do. Here . . .' Suzanne fished in her makeup bag and found some almond oil she used on her cuticles. 'Use this, but don't waste it.'

'Thank you, Suzanne.' Amy put it carefully down beside her whilst she slid Suzanne's pop socks off. Suzanne had painted toes – so pretty, thought Amy.

'And get me some paracetamol out of my bag – give me four – I have a thumping headache.'

Amy looked around for Suzanne's bag. She found the pills. She gave four tablets to Suzanne, who swallowed them down with gin. Amy began to massage Suzanne's feet. She looked at Suzanne's handbag. The bottle of sleeping pills sat on the top. Amy kept her eyes on Suzanne, whilst she eased one hand gently across and tucked the bottle back inside the bag.

67

'Good evening, sirs.'

Comfort smiled. She looked around the table at the Colonel, Brandon and the Teacher. The Teacher's blue eyes rolled slowly up her body and settled on her face. He flashed a big sarcastic smile back, which stayed on his mouth as he spoke.

'Hello! Now bring me a beer and fuck off.' He turned to the Colonel. 'Where's Terry.'

'Terry is busy. He has a lot of things to coordinate. The end of the world is nigh. We must prepare.'

The Teacher studied him closely, a sneer on his face.

'You should lay off the stuff. You are beginning to look more than a little crazy.' He looked at Maya, who was slumped in the crook of the Colonel's arm. 'And you should put that little girl down. She looks sick.'

The Colonel leaned forward. His eyes bulged and his breath made the Teacher reel. Brandon sat watching.

'I will put her down when I please. You may be the big man's right-hand man, but this is still my world. I am God here, remember that.'

The Teacher shrugged and drank his beer.

The Colonel hadn't slept for three days. His body was so tired that he could hardly stand upright any more, but his mind raged on Shabu. He drank bottles of brandy and smoked weed, but still his eyes would not close. His leg tapped away involuntarily.

They were sitting outside the Bordello, Maya on the Colonel's lap. The little girl looked dazed. She had not spoken a word since she had watched her mother die. She hadn't done anything but stare. She was getting on Brandon's nerves. But then, Brandon was getting anxious full stop. He had become more of an undertaker than a bouncer recently, and Laurence and Jed had been friends of his. He didn't see why they had to be wiped out like that. Why couldn't they just have been moved on? Sure, they had been getting ambitious – Brandon had listened to them talk about their plans late into the night – but they were only dreams; what ifs. They were not realities. But his reality was that he'd had to take their bodies and throw them down the same ravine that he used to throw the women down – the ones that got sick, the ones that were discarded. No one wanted to fuck a sick-looking whore.

Usually it was the small runts. The Colonel liked to finish some of them off himself. He had a penchant for torture. If they were not finished, then Brandon slit the girl's throat at the edge of the ravine. Sometimes he just pushed them over the side. One or two had actually jumped. Brandon wondered what role he would have when the White Circle took over everything. He hoped that it would be a better one than undertaker. Hopefully Blanco would respect and need him. Blanco was a killer like Brandon, disciplined and clever. Blanco deserved big respect as far as Brandon was concerned. He had planned out the whole operation. He had coordinated Hong Kong, the UK and the whole of the Philippines. He had called in people that they would never have been able to access on their own. Even the government were working for them, and the DDS. The Colonel was fast slipping in Brandon's esteem. He was getting sloppy. He spent more time off his face than on it, and he was getting harder to reason with. Only Terry knew how to handle him. Terry was the master at it. Brandon watched the way he did it. He never lost control. Everything he said or did was considered first. Brandon saw how he watched the Colonel, letting him hang himself with his own rope, waiting till he was almost dead, then Terry would step in and slide a chair beneath his dangling feet and let him stand on it a while, until the Colonel decided to kick it away again. Terry would turn things around and make the Colonel look almost sane – Terry was fucking good at his job.

Today the Colonel looked a mess. Normally he was a meticulous dresser, he liked his chinos and his polo shirt, but he hadn't changed his shirt in days and the smell of stale sweat was sour and rank. He was drinking brandy chasers and looking up and down the street continually. His head swung back and forth as his leg jittered.

'When can we expect Terry, Brandon?'

'He should be here any time now, sir.'

'Teacher – is Blanco here yet?'

'No.'

'Well, how are we going to coordinate everyone without him here?' The Colonel was riled.

'Everyone has their part. They all know what that is. They have been told. We all do our job, Colonel – there shouldn't be a fucking problem. One of us cocks it up, and he effectively kills us all.' He sat and waited for Comfort to bring him his beer and leave again before continuing. She stood back, reached over and placed it in front of him. She wasn't going to make the mistake of standing too close. The Teacher was like the Colonel – never nice. When she had gone he sat back and glared at a group of passing locals who were not passing quick enough for his liking. 'But, what should I care?' He continued eyeballing them until they were out of sight. 'You can all be replaced.' He picked up his beer and raised it at the Colonel. 'Cheers. Go ahead and fuck up.'

The Colonel was shaking with anger. Maya squirmed as his grip on her tightened.

'I am a personal friend of Blanco's – you are just hired help. Don't forget that. If anyone is going to get replaced, it won't be me. Where is fucking Terry?'

The Colonel sat back and downed the last of his brandy. He banged on the table and Comfort appeared beside him with another brandy and two beers.

He caught hold of her as she was turning to go back inside the bar.

'Wait. Comfort, I need you. Go and wait for me upstairs. I need you to do something for me. You are my favourite, Comfort, always were. You know that, don't you?'

Comfort smiled and nodded her head. The Colonel watched her until she was out of sight. Reluctantly, she handed over her tasks to another girl at the bar and went up to the top floor, to the Colonel's apartment.

68

The Colonel sat on his bed in his shorts, his back resting against the rattan headboard. It would not let him sleep. His skin was bathed in old and new sweat. His bony chest rose and fell rapidly. He chewed the inside of his lips and they needed continually wetting. Comfort stood at the end of the bed, waiting. Maya sat in the corner of the room. He stroked his member as he sat watching Maya. It grew hard.

'What's the matter, Comfort? You look tense.'

Comfort had worked out who Maya was. After her meeting with Wednesday, her mind had been troubled, and slowly the pieces had fallen into place and she had remembered the face of someone she had called a friend. She had seen Brandon take the wrapped sheet containing Wednesday's body and she knew he was heading towards the ravine and that Wednesday's body was destined to feed the animals in the marshes. It would be devoured by the crawling creatures. Sadness consumed her now, sadness and desperation and a screaming anger that made her heart beat furiously. Comfort always had that anger in her, that's how she had been able to hurt Peanut. Most of the time she could shut her mind to it, but now memories came back of her horrible childhood, of her father who had beaten and molested her, and of the Colonel who had used her as a toy and then discarded her. The only sweetness in her childhood memories were the days when she had played with Wednesday, when the older girl had looked after her until the day she had been rescued and Comfort was left behind. Now she hated the Colonel more than she had ever done before. She looked at Maya and saw herself sitting in that chair all those years ago.

'You know who came to see me?' He smiled. 'You remember Wednesday?'

Comfort knew better than to try and lie to the Colonel. She nodded.

'Never thought you'd see her again when the priests took her, did you?'

She shook her head.

'No one ever escapes me, Comfort. You should know that. Now she has paid the ultimate price for disobeying me. Come here, Comfort. Come to me. It's been a long time since you slept in my bed, since I have a new little girl to play with. Does she look familiar, Comfort?'

Comfort turned and looked at the child sitting in the corner of the room. She nodded.

He laughed. 'And what will happen to little Maya now?' He looked over at her. She stared back. 'I suppose

I will have to bring her up like my own – but then I do own her. I own you all.' He laughed. 'I will have her like I had her mother and I had you.'

'Please – Kano, please, I beg you not to.'

As Comfort spoke the words, she knew she had overstepped the mark. It was like looking into the red-rimmed eyes of the devil.

He moved down the bed a little and made himself comfortable. He straightened his throbbing cock inside his pants. The Shabu gave him a hard penis like when he had been a teenager. It ached for relief, but it took him a long time to get it.

'I am feeling generous today, Comfort. Take off your clothes and come over here.'

Comfort did as she was told. She crawled naked onto the bed and knelt beside him.

'Turn around. I want to see if you taste the same as you did as a child.'

Comfort turned her back to him and swung her leg across his lap. She looked at Maya. Maya was hiding behind the chair. She saw Maya's eyes staring, horrified. The Colonel held onto Comfort's thighs and pulled her sex to his mouth. Comfort shut her eyes tight. His mouth was hard, always hard; even his tongue was angry and aggressive. He reached down and removed his shorts, kicking them off the bed with his foot.

'No hands.' He fed his cock into her mouth. He picked up a length of cord and pulled Comfort's hands together behind her back, tying them tightly. 'Just mouth.'

His cock was hard and huge in her mouth. Her mouth wouldn't open wide enough to take it in.

He pressed his hands to either side of her skull and held it in a vice. He kept her head straight as he forced his cock deeper into her mouth. Comfort began to struggle. She was squealing in pain as he began chewing her as if she were a juicy peach. He could taste the blood in his mouth. He pulled at her sex with his teeth. *Eeeee.* She sounded like a donkey as she tried to breathe and scream. Then *Awwwww* as her body shuddered. He had to hold her hard. She was strong and she fought hard against his grip, but she wasn't able to move more than an inch: her knees were jammed to his sides, her hands tied. *Eeeee Awwww Eeeee Awwww.* It made him smile. His balls twitched but he knew it would take him time. He held onto her head and pushed deeper. He could feel the back of her throat now, she was gagging, her teeth grated around his cock, but he wasn't all in yet. He wanted that hot mouth to be around the whole of his shaft. Comfort fought harder than ever. She was passing out. Hot pee covered the Colonel's face. It stung his eyes. *Fucking bitch.* He pushed her legs away from his face and knelt over her. Picking her head up in his hands he held onto it with a vice-like grip and glared at her – mad angry, but too excited to lose his way now. He had to finish it. He lifted her head from the bed and forced his cock deep into her mouth, pausing only to look at her. Her eyes bulged in her face, frantic. Her mouth was splitting at the sides – she stared at him in terror as he grinned back.

'So scared, aren't you, Comfort? I told you – you are worth nothing in this world. I own you. I can do whatever I want to you. You and that little girl over there.' He flicked his eyes towards Maya. 'You watching? It'll be your turn to please me soon. In fact, I think your time has come . . .'

He laughed. The thought of having the child made him much nearer to climax. He grinned down at Comfort, her face turning blue, her bulging eyes drifting.

'Just one more inch. Open wide.'

He held onto the back of her head, pushed hard and felt her teeth jam against the thick base of his shaft. *Just there – that's the place . . .* His cock was wedged inside her throat at an angle, its tip was touching the smooth sides of her trachea. He held onto her skull and squeezed it to him with both hands as he clenched his buttock muscles and thrust hard. He felt his abdomen tighten, twitch, spasm. It was coming now, relief, then he would be able to sleep. He lunged forward, pressed her head to him as hard as he could. Three massive thrusts and the Colonel threw his head back and bellowed to the ceiling in his painful ecstasy as he pumped his load into her throat. He rested there for a few minutes, breathing hard, sweat dripping from his forehead. He felt her motionless beneath him. Her head was heavy now in his hands. He relaxed his grip a little and looked at her. Her hair was wet with his sweat, her eyes were staring straight ahead. Her face was dark. Her mouth had stretched so that it had split in the corners and fresh pink blood was smeared on her face.

He held her by the hair as he tentatively eased himself out of her mouth. He was so sensitive now. Her teeth had hurt. It was a long way back. He lay down on the bed. Now he was so tired and so cold. It always took so much blood to fill that big cock, it left him as weak as a baby afterwards.

He lay there, his chest rising and falling at last, but still he was not to be granted sleep. He tried closing his eyes but they would not stay shut. The Shabu was not sated. He looked over at Maya.

'Come, princess, you will have your turn. Come here and lie with me.' He beckoned with his hand. Maya, still hiding behind the chair, shook her head.

'I said *come*.'

She slid out from behind the chair and walked slowly forward; her huge eyes were on Comfort. He pulled her onto the bed and laid her next to him. Comfort was in the way now. He had had enough of sharing his bed with her. He bent his knees towards his chest then pushed her hard with both feet. Comfort shot off the end of the bed. From the direction of the floor he heard her retching and coughing as she vomited.

'So, you decided to spit and not swallow this time?' His head went back and rested on the wall behind him as he laughed his lunatic laugh. 'Now get the fuck back to work.'

He left his head resting where it was, on the wall. He was exhausted, so spent, but still he felt the stirrings start. He ran his hand up Maya's leg.

'Come here, baby, come to me.'

He lifted her onto his lap. There was a banging at the door.

'Colonel, you need to come.' It was Brandon. 'The place is crawling with Chinamen. It's starting.'

69

This time Father Finn's office was next to his bedroom on the first floor at the front of the refuge. Mann sat listening to the crickets call and the mosquitoes whine furiously on the other side of the window net as they lined up to attack him when they got the chance. He was sat at Father Finn's desk, waiting for the laptop to fire up. Becky was resting in the next room – Father Finn's bedroom – which he had given over to her whilst he and Mann intended to share with Paulo and the boys downstairs, although no one expected to get any sleep that night. He waited with trepidation as the internet connected. He put in his password and his emails started to bounce up on the screen.

In the bottom right of the screen a message alert appeared.

You have a new message from BLANCO.

Mann clicked onto it.

PRESS. To sample the delights of Angeles.

Mann clicked on the sign and a photo appeared of Maya, naked, lying on a bed wrapped in a bloody sheet.

Tick Tock . . . Tick Tock . . . time is slipping away

Becky finished her conversation with Jimmy Vance, thanked him and hung up as Mann came into the room.

'Are you okay?' he asked. He could see she wasn't. She was sitting on the edge of the bed, her hands tucked beneath her legs, hunched over as if in pain. She kept her eyes glued to her lap as she spoke.

'Yesterday, in Puerto Galera, I checked a message left on my voicemail and found it was from a woman claiming to be having an affair with my husband, whom she called Lenny. She said her name was Suzanne. I thought it was just a mistake, nothing to do with me – wrong number. But when Jimmy Vance went round to check on things at my flat he found a woman there.' She looked up from her lap and stared wide-eyed at Mann. 'Jimmy's just rung me now. He's been at the flat. I asked him to look into it for me. He said Alex's PC is riddled with references to the Colonel, to Reese Pearce and to Terry Saunders.' She sighed heavily and shook her head as if she couldn't believe how stupid she'd been. 'Then I thought about it and I realised the names – Lenny is Leonard Cohen, his favourite singer, and 'Suzanne' is Cohen's most famous song. Alex is Lenny, and Alex is right in the middle of all this. What if he has something to do with Amy Tang as well? I married a monster, Johnny. He's been living a double life. He's capable of anything. I suppose he's not in Hong Kong?'

Mann shook his head. 'That much I do know. He left there just after we did.'

She was shaking her head in disbelief.

'You weren't to know, Becky. When you get too close to a person you just can't see it clearly.'

She stood and stepped away from the bed. Mann could see she was clearly reeling from it all. She looked at him, defiance and pain in her eyes.

'I'm ready,' she said. 'We came here to find out the person who has Amy Tang and to free her. If Alex is here and if he knows anything about it then, God help him, I intend to find out. I will do my job Mann, no matter what it takes.'

'Come on, Johnny . . . I mean it.'

Mann looked at her. The bruising and swelling in her face was livid now. She stood absolutely still, her shoulders tensed and her feet squarely planted – defiant as they faced each other beneath the fan that hung down from the apex of the high wooden-beamed ceiling.

'You can't come.'

She started to protest but he wouldn't let her.

'Listen to me . . . If you are right and Alex is involved in all this, then that's why you were targeted back at Puerto Galera. It's why you were attacked. It was retribution. Alex must be up to his neck in shit and he doesn't know the calibre of men he's dealing with – they will eat him alive. I don't want them to do that to you. They intended to kill you *then* . . . that's a certainty, they won't hesitate to do it now. I can't have that, Becky. I cannot go there knowing that you will be a target. We have to protect you and this mission. We can't afford to jeopardise any of it. Plus, Eduardo needs protecting. If the DDS are government-funded you can bet your life he's on their list, right at the top, joint first with Father Finn . . . I need you to stay here and protect them.'

Mann laid out his weapons on the bed. He stripped off his shirt and attached the shuriken knife belt around his waist and strapped the Death Star across his chest. He tied the throwing-spike sheath to his arm. The last time he had seen these weapons was when he had taken them out of the dead bodies of Becky's attackers. In the dim light of the room he could see how intently she was watching him. She was scared, he knew that. He looked at her.

'Someone down on Fields Avenue has the answer to why we came here. One of those men is directly or indirectly responsible for ordering the kidnap of Amy Tang. Our job is to try to stop the bloodbath that will follow a triad uprising if she dies. We have to do our part now. We have to see it through. We have no choice. If it turns out to be Alex then I will deal with it, not you, Becky.'

'What you're trying to say is that I might not be able to do my job, I might let him off, that I might not do the *right* thing.'

'I'm just saying that it's too much to ask anyone to do.'

She sat back on the bed, deflated.

Mann finished attaching his weapons. He put his

shirt back on, then he tucked Delilah into his boot. He pulled out a semi-automatic from his bag, and handed it to her.

'You okay with that?'

She nodded, it was one she was very used to. She had practised with it many times on the police targeting range. He fished out the ammunition and threw it down on the bed.

She looked at him, desperation in her eyes. He knew she didn't want to be left behind.

He put his hand on her shoulder. 'You won't be any good to me down there. I need you to stay here and protect the refuge and Father Finn.'

Father Finn appeared at the door. 'There's no way I'm staying here. I have a duty to that little girl. I am all she has now and I won't let her down. I'm coming with you. I will not rest until I have Maya in my hands. I owe Wednesday that much. I might have failed her in other ways, but I will die trying to get her daughter back.'

'Then it's down to you to look after things, Becky. Paulo Mercy and Ramon will stay here to help.'

Father Finn looked tensed and ready for the fight. His face bristled with sweat and his eyes burned. 'Yes. Please keep Eduardo glued to your side, he trusts you.'

'Never had a priest for a partner, Father.' Mann smiled.

'I won't let you down, Johnny. I *will* fight with whatever God puts in my hands. I will get that little girl back.'

'It might be one hell of a fight we find ourselves in

the middle of, Father. There's a whole army of Wo Shing Shing officers ready to engage war on the White Circle, although it might also provide the perfect opportunity for you to get Maya out.'

'What, if World War Three breaks out, you mean? I'd rather stop that from happening.'

'There's always a catch with you, isn't there, Father?' Mann smiled.

After Father Finn had left them, Mann and Becky looked at one another. She smiled.

'You look funny in that outfit.' Mann had borrowed one of the Father's blue gingham shirts.

'This is my camouflage suit.'

She looked suddenly lost, thought Mann. She would look like a little girl wearing flowery shorts and a red rose T-shirt from the refuge shop, if it weren't for the fact that she also had a semi-automatic in her hand. 'It all makes a horrible sense, doesn't it?'

'Yep . . .' Mann went over to her, took the rifle out of her hands and hugged her tight. 'I am afraid it does, Becky.' He kissed the top of her head. 'I will see you when it's over.'

Father Finn appeared in the doorway again.

'Is it time to go, Johnny?'

'Yes. It's starting, Father.'

'Okay. Then it must also end, no?'

70

It was two thirty in the morning when they parked up on the side road leading to Fields Avenue. Father Finn and Mann walked back up the avenue. Mann paused in an alleyway. Amongst the rotting garbage that lived on top of other rotting garbage a man's body lay in that awkward position that Mann knew was death. He was still warm, but already he had the smell of death and blood and faeces. His limbs were twisted. His throat had been cut. Mann bent down to look at him closely. His eyes were open wide. His head was almost severed from his body – a clean chop using a wide blade. Triad execution.

They passed a couple of small bars. Mann glanced inside and got his first glimpse of Wo Shing Shing officers. They were smoothly attired – fly-boy chic – with slicked hair and pale spotty faces. Their gold necklaces matched their teeth. But they weren't smiling. They were on patrol, moving in units, hunting in packs.

Mann and Father Finn crossed cautiously over to the darker side of the road. The pavement dipped and rose and was broken in so many places that it made their progress naturally slow. It was a busy night. The place was awash with whorists. The inadequate, the over-sexed, the fuck-ups, all congregated in Angeles. There was the familiar smell of fried seafood and garlic, with overtones of sewage. There were no streetlamps on Fields Avenue. All lighting came from the open-fronted shops and neon signs, or it seeped out in a flush of blue or an ooze of pink and red.

They stepped out of the way of a group of lads. One of them was carrying a tiny Filipina under his arm, who was laughing and squealing in mock protest, whilst another was shouting out obscenities to a group of GROs outside a club. The girls blew kisses back.

'See you later, boys,' they called.

The whole street was heaving. The neon hopped about the street like tracer fire, occasionally getting stuck like an electrocuted bunny. Father Finn and Mann moved stealthily up the road, out of reach of the bikini girls who might accost them, but watching all the time for the Colonel and Maya. As they passed Hot Lips, seven Wo Shing Shing members came out. They wore jackets in this heat, and Mann knew there would be many a chopper hidden beneath those. They didn't look like they had gone in for a drink. They didn't see Mann. He looked up and down the street, and spotted several more – all distinctive because of the general lack of Chinese on Fields Avenue. Chinese were not big visitors to Angeles. It was not upmarket enough for them.

Mann and Father Finn passed by almost unnoticed, only the tailor watched them walk by, and the old woman in the cafe. The old ghost of a beggar woman, who lived in the Viagra seller's doorway, stepped out from the shadows, put out her hand to them and watched them walk past. The Father pressed some coins into her hand, held on to it for a few seconds, then passed by. The begging children ran beside them for a few steps, took some coins, and then ran away to chase after others.

They stepped down from the pavement and crossed the road. Mann saw a back he instantly recognised. Alex Stamp was disappearing into Lolita's.

'There is someone I need to talk to, Father. He has just walked into the bar over there.'

'All right, Johnny. I will continue up the street and look for the Colonel and Maya. When I find them I will text you.'

Mann crossed the road and slipped past the bikini brigade almost undetected. He signalled to the mamasan that came to greet him that he just wanted a quiet drink, that he would find his own table. She bowed politely and stepped back.

To his right as he walked in was the elevated cage where a dancer gyrated inside. Her upper body, her small chest with its child's breasts, was painted as a butterfly. She wore a thong that showed all of her small flat bottom. She wrapped her leg around the pole of the cage like a hanging insect.

Mann spotted Alex Stamp. He sat at the opposite portion of the bar that ran around the cage. He was drinking fast. He saw Mann and the glass stopped at his lips. He looked around him, then at Mann, realised they were alone and relaxed a little. He swigged back his drink.

'Fancy seeing you here.' Mann sat on the stool next to him.

'Small world.'

'So it seems. Where is Amy Tang?'

'Where's my wife?' Alex Stamp looked around. 'Does she miss me? Or has she been busy screwing you?'

'She thinks about you, I'm sure. After you got her gang-raped, beaten unconscious and very nearly killed, I'm sure she thinks about you quite a lot.'

'There was nothing I could do about that. Tell her I'm sorry.' He looked into his glass, and for a second Mann believed he was sorry, in some way. But it was too late for remorse now.

'I'll tell her fuck all. What? So that you can make her carry some of your guilt, make her think you have a good side? You could have stopped it happening if you'd tried, but you were too busy playing Mr Big.' Mann felt the anger twist his stomach. But he couldn't afford to start a fight here, not tonight, and not in a place that was already a spark away from going up like a gasoline canister.

Alex Stamp checked his watch and looked up at the same time as four men appeared in the entrance to the club. They were the ugliest bunch Mann had seen for a long time. The one at the front looked like Castro. They were dressed all in black.

'You think you have been smart, Alex. But never underestimate CK. You will wish yourself dead if he ever gets a hold of you, and you can only pray that it will be quick. Tell me where Amy Tang is and I will do my best for you.'

'Amy Tang's predicament is out of my hands. My part in it is over. She was never meant to live.'

'You have made deals with people who would sell their own grandmother. All you have is hired help with a low integrity threshold. CK has his officers who have nothing to live for but him. Spot the difference, asshole.'

Mann's phone beeped. He snuck a glance.

Have found Maya. Come to Bordello.

'Got to go, Alex.' Mann slid off his stool. 'If I were you I would make myself very small. You are about to discover you're not such a big man after all.'

71

It was like the lull before the storm. It was past three when Mann walked back onto the avenue. He could see Wo Shing Shing everywhere he looked. Like meerkats, locals who made their living on the Avenue bobbed in and out of doorways, stared up and down the street. They were preparing to scramble for cover, bracing themselves for the force of triad terror. Bars were closing, girls were being taken off stages, bar staff had stopped smiling. He got out his phone to text Becky.

He walked past the Tequila Station and looked inside. There were a few guys playing pool, two or three around the bar. The bar staff stared out of the window and watched him pass. The bodyguard had stepped inside and stood ready to bolt the door when necessary. Those inside would be grateful for it, even though they did not realise it – they were the lucky ones, they were off the streets. The residents of Fields Avenue would protect their livelihood and stop them from seeing the trouble that was coming. Trouble was walking across the street from Mann in the shape of a squad of five Wo Shing Shing members systematically working their way up the street. Mann looked behind – there was another squad doing the same. There would probably be a hundred Wo Shing Shing on the Avenue tonight. But they wouldn't be just any old hundred, they would be the elite fighting squad.

Mann came within sight of the Bordello and saw what he most dreaded. At the front, by the tables, Mann could see Father Finn. A large white marine type was holding his arms behind his back with one hand; in the other he held a semi-automatic. The Colonel sat at a table. He had Maya on his lap and was holding the mobile phone in his hand. He waved it at Mann as he approached them.

'Texting – can't beat it. It's just like you – predictive. As you can see, we caught ourselves a prisoner.' He gave his lunatic laugh.

The Colonel threw the phone down and it smashed on the pavement. Still holding Maya, he took out a knife from a sheath in his waistband and held it up to the Father's throat and twisted it. Father Finn winced as the point of the knife drew blood.

'Give me your weapons, Mann. I know you carry a fancy Kung Fu belt. Throw them down now.'

Mann undid his throwing-star belt, then undid his spikes strap from around his arm, and threw them on the side of the road.

'I'm sorry, Johnny,' the Father said. His head was bowed. He was breathing hard. He'd obviously taken a beating.

'Shut the fuck up.' Brandon slapped him across the head with his rifle butt. The father's knees buckled for a few seconds then he drew himself up with dignity. Brandon pushed him back on to his knees. 'You can stay down there where you belong.'

The Colonel laughed. 'Do you know how many years I have waited for this moment, Father? Now, of all nights, you give it to me on a plate. You walk straight into my arms. You kneel before me and await your execution on a night when there will be so many dead that your body will be just one. Whatever possessed you to trespass here tonight, Father? Could it be this?' He held Maya aloft and shook her. 'Is it this small, ragged thing that you want? Well, she doesn't belong to you, Father. She is mine. You are in my world now, Father Finn. You will learn that you have no friends here. This is not a place for anything other than my type of religion. Who do you think all these whores pray to, Father? Who do you think?' He leaned across the table and spat his words. '*Me*, Father, that's who. I am their God here in this paradise.' The Colonel licked Maya's face. 'I am God here. I decide what happens here in my land. I say who lives and who dies.'

'Let the girl go. Do this one thing. Do not hurt an innocent child. Redeem yourself before it is too late.'

'Redemption?' The Colonel laughed for a full minute. Brandon shot a look at him and Mann knew that he was starting to worry – doubt was creeping into Brandon's mind. 'Why would I want that? She is not innocent. None of them are innocent. We live in a corrupt world, Father. You know that. She is just another whore born of a whore.'

'You have come to look at life that way because you

are sick, dead inside. But it isn't so. She is a little girl who wants to go and play with her friends. She is just a child.'

'Shut the fuck up.' Brandon kicked the Father in his back

'She is *mine*. I made her. I created her. Her life is mine for the taking, Father. Don't ever doubt it. One more word from you, Father, and I will snap her neck now.'

'Hey, Brandon?' Mann called over to him. 'You're a soldier, an ex-marine. You must be getting worried now. You are never going to make it out of here. Maybe you haven't noticed the place is swarming with Wo Shing Shing tonight. By now they will have disposed of half of your hired help.'

'Huh! I think not!' said the Colonel. 'We have sentries everywhere. We have set a trap for the Chinese. Let them make it so far up the street, then they will walk straight into it and be killed – all of them, everyone.' He made a gesture towards Brandon, who handed him the rifle whilst he took out a walkie-talkie from his pocket. 'Find out how many of our enemy are dead already, Brandon.'

Brandon punched in three different numbers, none of which responded. He closed up the walkie-talkie and looked up and down the street.

'Think we should get you inside, Colonel. I need to go and find out what happened to the sentries.'

'I can tell you what's happened,' said Mann. 'They are chopped into bits. The Father and I have already found one. He was dumped on a pile of rubbish. Didn't you realise you couldn't win? Didn't anyone tell you that you have been set up to fail? You made the classic mistake of underestimating your enemy.'

'We still have the government forces, Colonel. I will call them now. We made a deal, they have to be here.' Brandon turned away and dialled. He didn't speak, then he dialled another number and spoke to someone clearly. 'Get your men moving, now. Something's not going right down here. This is the time to put your plan into action.' He snapped the phone shut. 'Where is the fucking Teacher?'

'Let me guess? The Teacher is late thirties, blond, blue-eyed, a Brit?' Brandon stared blankly back at him. 'Thought so. I met the Teacher, Alex Stamp we call him. He's your double-crosser. He's made deals with everyone. He's left you in a weakened state just ready for the Chinese to come along and break you.'

Brandon flashed a look at the Colonel.

'You shouldn't have listened to him, Colonel . . . That's why he killed Jed and Laurence . . .'

'Don't you ever fucking tell me what I should or shouldn't have done.' The Colonel was spitting out his words. 'Now take this fucking gun and do your fucking job.'

Behind them the door of the Bordello opened and Comfort stood in the doorway.

'Get back inside, you stupid bitch!' the Colonel screamed at her.

She stood her ground. She looked a mess, dazed. Her hair was ragged and sweaty around her face. Her vest top stuck to her.

'Let me take the little girl, Kano. Let me take her, it is difficult for you to fight with only one hand. She is making a problem for you. I will look after her.'

He thought for a moment. The news that the campaign might be faltering made him edgier than ever. He was glad to get rid of the weight of the child.

White froth clung to the sides of the Colonel's mouth. His eyes were bulging out of his head and the veins stood out in his forehead and in his arms.

'Take her. Take her, and then get out of the fucking way. Brandon, get fucking Terry here NOW. I want him HERE.'

Comfort went forward and lifted Maya from his lap, placed her on the ground and gently pushed her to one side, away from the Colonel. Then she took out a small handgun from her pocket. She moved away from the table, so that she was standing in front of Mann. She levelled the gun at the Colonel's chest.

'Let the Father go.'

Comfort's eyes gleamed in the darkness. Her chest rose and fell.

'What? Would you shoot me? Ha ha! Get back inside, you worthless piece of rotten meat.'

'I am what you made me. I am a bad person. But I can do *one* good thing.'

'Get out of the fucking way! You're not going to fire that thing.' He turned his back on her and laughed.

Comfort's hand shook uncontrollably. She squeezed the trigger. The gun jumped in her hand as it fired one shot. She hit the Colonel on the shoulder. He lurched backwards in the chair, nearly knocking the table over as he did so. Brandon let go of Father Finn, springing forward and out of reach as he grabbed Maya. Then Brandon fired a round from his rifle into Comfort. She was hit seven times. At such short range some of the bullets passed through her as easily as if going through cheese. The rest sprayed her flesh over Fields Avenue.

Mann dived at the same time as Brandon fired. He felt a sharp pain but he also felt the opportunity and reached for Delilah, hidden in his boot. He threw her hard and strong and straight into Brandon's heart. He pushed Comfort aside and reached for her gun and fired at the Colonel – but nothing. Comfort's gun had run out of bullets. The Colonel stood over him, Brandon's automatic in his hand.

'It's Judgement Day, Sonny.'

72

'What, a street party and no one invited me? It's a good thing I was in the neighbourhood.'

Stevie Ho and ten Wo Shing Shing deputies were spanning out across the street. 'Check it,' he ordered; and they scattered to take up their positions either side of the Bordello. No one would pass down Fields Avenue again that night.

Stevie walked towards the Colonel. 'Put that gun down, old man.'

The Colonel stood panting like a rabid dog trapped in a corner.

'You may not have noticed, but your kingdom has been overrun by the enemy.' Stevie mimicked his accent.

'You have not seen the real might yet. The troops are on their way.'

'Which troops? Do you mean the government? They chickened out. We saw them driving away in a trail of dust. Your government took off in the other direction. We saw them when we were on the way in here. New day – new deals – get the picture? They decided this wasn't for them. The men in black got an urgent call back at the mother ship.' He sniggered.

Mann kept still. He was lying behind Comfort's dead body. He realised he had been hit. A bullet had passed right through Comfort and into Mann's side. It had lodged in the muscle there.

'And here we have – Johnny Mann. What about you? I bet you wish you were somewhere else right now? We seem to find each other wherever we go, don't we? Now I have come to tell you that you have failed your mission.'

'The time isn't up yet. I still have another five hours to find Amy Tang. The Teacher knows where she is, and so do others.'

'We believe that the little girl is dead.'

'Has CK ordered this strike?'

'No one will tell him it started early, and he doesn't care as long as he gets something out of it, and he will. He will take over all. It starts now.'

Two Wo Shing Shing officers held on to the Colonel. Stevie Ho spoke to a third officer.

'Tie the madman to the chair and keep an eye on Mann and that priest. No one moves from here until I say.'

Mann looked at Father Finn to see if he was all right. He nodded back an affirmation.

'Can I help Johnny? Is he badly wounded?' Father Finn asked Stevie.

Stevie looked Mann over. He knelt down beside him and lifted his jacket with his finger. He saw the splintered rib that was protruding out of Mann's shirt and he saw his side drenched with blood from the wound at his waist.

He got up, unimpressed. 'He's had worse. Stay where you are.'

Mann tore away the material that was frayed around his broken rib and pressed it into the wound on his side. He held it tightly closed with his fingers. He couldn't afford to pass out. He might never wake up. He stayed as still as he could. From his position on the ground he watched as Stevie walked away from him, past Comfort and Brandon, over to the Colonel.

'Strip him,' he ordered his officers. 'Make sure you tie him tightly.'

The Colonel began shouting – cursing and spitting out his hatred of all things Chinese and foreign. It was as if the act of tying him in, of restraining him, had finally brought his predicament home to him. His madness had reached full pitch now. He was dribbling and spitting and his eyes boiled in his head.

Stevie held out his hand to his deputy, who placed a rolled-up long leather roll into it. Stevie took out the long thin-bladed knife from inside. He came to the Colonel's side, reached across him and cut him, a long, smooth, precise cut across his chest with the blade. The Colonel let out a howl of agony as the flesh parted and the cut bled along its entire length in a smooth line. Large globules of dark blood peeled down his chest and spread around the folds of blanched skin on his stomach.

Stevie stood back to admire his handiwork. He was in no hurry. He took hold of a roll of fat on the Colonel's abdomen and sliced through. The Colonel screamed in his agony. Stevie dropped it from his hand.

'Now, I want you to understand what is happening to you,' Stevie said. He dug the point of the knife into the Colonel's shoulder, where Comfort had shot him, tugged it in an upward movement to open the wound further, then he twisted it until it scraped on the shoulder bone. The Colonel had to be held down. He was shaking the chair apart.

'You had the audacity to think that you could form your own triad society. You don't know the meaning of the word triad. You know nothing of its history or its sacredness. But, a triad you claim you are, and you will die a triad's death. I will bestow on you a fitting honour, ling-chi, death of a thousand cuts. It is an ancient and a ceremonial death reserved for traitors and motherfuckers and triad pretenders like you. I will carve your body up bit by bit. Until, in the end, when you are begging for me to end it, I will make a decision either to bury you alive or give one final piercing into your heart and end your agony. Lucky for us that you are a Shabu addict. Oh yes – I have studied you and your habits – it is well to know one's enemy. You will be with us to the end. You will be wide awake to feel every cut.'

He laughed, and so did his deputies.

'Do you think I fear you? Go to fucking hell you chink bastard,' the Colonel laughed. 'I fear no man. You want to kill me, go ahead.'

'Fighting talk, old man. Soon you will have less to say.'

He cut the Colonel again, ten neat slashes that

opened his back and crisscrossed the spine from across the shoulders downwards. Stevie slipped the knife beneath the skin and slid it along to separate it from the flesh. The Colonel began choking on his vomit. Stevie lifted sections of flesh from his back.

'I hope somebody's counting: fourteen, fifteen, sixteen, and let's make seventeen a good one.' He cut off his ear. 'The only place I will not cut is your vocal cords – I want to hear you beg for mercy, beg for the end.' Maya began whimpering softly.

The Colonel had the strength of a bull. He dragged the men with him that held him on the chair. The blood ran down his neck. His tendons stood out like tightened cables in his neck and shoulders. His face was a puffy red mash of anger as he screamed obscenities skyward. When he had stopped cursing he moved his head slowly back towards Stevie, breathing so hard that at every breath he sprayed blood and mucus out.

'Wait. Wait,' he said. 'We have only just begun here. We have the richest, most powerful, most corrupt contacts from around the world in with us. You can be a big part of it. I can share what we have.'

Stevie laughed cynically.

'We do not need *you*. We have followed your every move. We know every move you've made since the beginning. We have spies everywhere. You thought you had been so smart. The truth is . . .' Stevie cut deep into the chest fat as he spoke '. . . whilst you were busy raping children, we were busy buggering you.' He twisted the knife and scooped out the flesh. The deputies laughed.

Mann lay still. He had to keep movement to a minimum. He could feel the blood wet and sticky on his clothes. The pain was beginning to kick in. Mann watched the Colonel's world collapsing. His Angeles – a few dirty streets were his kingdom. The whores and the whorists were his subjects. Angeles – for the sad, the lonely and the screwed. The Colonel's world, was turning against him. His subjects were in hiding. His paid help had had a better offer.

'Do not forsake me!' he bellowed to the corners of his kingdom.

From a parallel road came the sound of girls laughing and dogs howling all to the boom-boom of the bar music. Father Finn started to pray.

Stevie went around to the front of the chair. He dragged a heavy wooden palm plant-pot with him. The Father scrabbled out of the way as Stevie rested the Colonel's leg on it. An officer came forward to hold it in position. He held his hand out to one of his men, gesturing that he wanted what the man held secreted in his jacket. He was handed a razor-sharp small chopper. The Colonel's face pulled and contorted as he screamed. He was snorting like a bull, chained and about to be castrated. Every sinew in his body fought the restraint and screamed with anger as he twisted and writhed.

Stevie came around to the front. He pressed the Colonel's foot flat onto the wooden rim of the pot and chopped off each of the Colonel's toes.

'Please. Please.' The Colonel's head was down.

'You beg too soon. You are a coward. What you fail

to realise, my white brother, is that the world is a small place and CK already owns a lot of it. You have only begun to scratch the surface. You think you have created this super-group of powerful allies. Think again. CK has been building his up for fifty years. He can call in any favour he desires. Whilst you, white boy, you are just a little boy wearing his big brother's trousers.'

The Colonel groaned. He had fallen quiet. His sweat and blood glistened in the lights from the Bordello. Kenny Rogers was singing about Lucille. The few people in the bar had the sense to huddle over their drinks and pretend that they did not hear the sound of a man being tortured to death.

Stevie reached over and tipped the Colonel's chair backwards. He tutted. He let the chair drop back. The Colonel shuddered. His body shook uncontrollably. Maya walked backwards away from the table. Father Finn beckoned her to him.

'This could be a long night.'

The Colonel began weeping.

'Please. Please. Please don't kill me. I had nothing to do with kidnapping CK's daughter. The Teacher is the one, not me. It was all his idea, him and Blanco's.'

'Who is Blanco?'

'I do not know. I only receive my orders by email and through the Teacher. He knows who Blanco is. I don't.'

'Is the Teacher here?'

The Colonel looked up at the windows and back at Stevie and nodded.

'Go through the rooms and find him,' Stevie ordered two of his men to go inside and search.

Mann waited – the pain had really kicked and he was losing his ability to concentrate. He mustn't pass out. He had to stay alert.

Ten minutes later they re-emerged.

'All gone, boss. The rooms up there?' One of the men pointed to the windows above them. 'Nobody in them.'

'Let the Father and me go, Stevie. I know what he looks like and I think I know where he'll be. We have a chance of finding him.'

Stevie stared hard at Mann. There were few people's word he could trust in this world but he knew Mann's was one of them. If Stevie wanted to break away from CK and the Wo Shing Shing he could not afford to have Amy Tang's blood on his hands. If it looked like they had acted too hastily and not waited for the agreed hour, if it came down to a matter of honour, CK would save his own face and Stevie would be sacrificed. He must be seen to do all he could to find her. He must let Mann fail rather than himself.

'You double-cross me, Mann, and this will look like a practice run for what I will do to you.'

'Save your threats for someone else. I came here to get Amy Tang released. Let me do my job. I will find him. I will keep him alive if I can.'

Stevie thought about it for a few seconds. He nodded to his deputies.

'Let him go. I am going to let you see this thing through, Mann. One of us will achieve his goals and CK will know I did all that I could. Besides, I haven't finished with the Colonel here yet. There are a lot more questions I want answered. I will have everything I need by the end. Fetch some Shabu for him. Stick it up his nose; make sure he gets a good load of it. I want him to stay awake now, right until the last minute, until he begs for the end.'

Father Finn picked up Maya and walked quickly over to where Mann was trying his best to stand. He helped him up.

'You find him, Mann, I want him alive. I want to parcel him up and give him as a present to CK – my goodbye gift,' Stevie called as Mann walked away, holding on to Father Finn for support.

They walked back along Fields Avenue. When they were out of sight, the Father stopped.

'Where will we go, Johnny?'

'I saw Alex Stamp earlier – he was with some heavily armed friends, they were dressed in black . They were DDS and their leader was a man I know – Fredrico. He used to be mayor of Davao. He's gone up the government ranks,' He'll want the boy. They'll be heading for the refuge.'

'Wait here, Johnny. Maya, you stay too. I'll fetch the car.'

Mann propped himself against the wall and waited the eight minutes it took Father Finn to sprint down the road and drive back up. Maya stood silent, unmoving. Mann winked at her.

'It'll be okay now.'

Her big eyes stared back, unblinking. Father Finn pulled up and put Maya in the front whilst he helped Mann to lie down in the back. As he started driving,

Father Finn began rooting around in the medical kit one-handed.

'There are some dressings and bandages in here, Johnny. We'll stop when we are on the edge of town and get you strapped up.'

There was a sharp intake of breath from the back seat as Mann bit the top of the dressing pack and gingerly peeled away the soaked fabric of his shirt as he pressed the new dressing on top of the cloth inside the wound. He pulled open another two dressings and covered the exposed rib, drawing in sharp breaths of pain as he did so.

'No, don't stop, Father.' He took the bandages handed back to him. 'Drive like hell.'

The Father was driving like he had never done before. He spun in and out of the night-time traffic, all hooting their horns and shouting out of their windows at the mad priest who was weaving around the road.

'Jaysus! I'm going to kill us all if I don't watch it.'

'Don't slow down, Father, you're doing a good job. Keep that foot flat to the accelerator pedal. We need to get there first and we need to finish it now, Father. It ends here.'

73

'Ma'am . . . ?'

Becky stood on the balcony and watched a dust trail make its way up the dirt road towards the refuge. Mercy stood behind her. It was dawn.

Two black cars were approaching, they appeared through the gaps in the greenery like images in a kid's flip book and in front of them were two motorcyclists. Their dust trails plumed above the green undergrowth.

Mercy let out a scream. She clutched one hand across her mouth, the other over her stomach as if to protect her unborn child.

'It is the Death Squad.'

'Get the children out, Mercy; take them to the workers' houses. As fast as you can.'

Becky ran down ahead of Mercy, who was met by Ramon halfway down the stairs. Becky ran past into the dorms and shouted to Paulo. Within minutes they had the sleepy ranks of children filing out of the back door and scampering through the undergrowth towards the other side of the hill and the workers' houses. She met Mercy, who was the last to leave.

'I cannot find Eduardo, Miss.'

'You go, Mercy. I will find him and follow. Go . . . Go . .'

Becky hurried Mercy out. She called out to Eduardo. She ran from room to room. In a panic she raced back up to her bedroom and found him there. He was hiding under her bed. She eased him out. She looked out of her window. The black car had turned into the drive and was nearly at the front door.

'Stay here.'

It was too late to leave now. She ran back downstairs and bolted the front and back doors. Then she tiptoed back up into the bedroom, picked up the gun and ammunition, held on to Eduardo, and they dropped to the floor to hide behind the chest of drawers. She heard car doors slam. There were voices coming from directly beneath the balcony outside the bedroom window. She heard the sound of men's voices and footsteps disappearing around to the back of the building. They would not be able to get in, thought Becky. This place was very secure. Father Finn had pointed that out to her on her tour. It had to be, he said. They were remote, at risk from bandits and government troops alike.

Someone was trying to break in at the front. Then she heard a voice she knew. Alex's voice came loud through the door.

'Becky, I need your help. They are going to kill me. Open the door. Let me in. I need your help. These men will kill me, Becky. I am sorry for everything. Please believe me, I never meant it to get out of control. I was just trying to make it, make money for us. I thought it would be okay.'

Becky closed her eyes. She didn't want to hear it. She could tell by every intonation, every inflection, every pause for breath, that the only thing he wasn't lying about was the fact that he was petrified.

'All they want is the child. I said I would deliver him. I made a deal, Becky. If I go back on that deal I'm dead. They are armed, they mean business.'

All the time her heart hammered. She wiped her forehead with the back of her hand. Eduardo didn't take his eyes from her face. In the dark of the shadows Eduardo's eyes were dark chocolate drops floating in saucers of milk – he clung to her.

Alex shouted again.

'Believe me, I am so sorry for what happened to you. I would not have hurt you for the world. I am truly sorry, Becky. Can you hear me? I will make it up to you. We can have children, how many would you like? Five? Six? Please, Becky. I will do anything to make it better.' His voice was beginning to break. At the same time as he was shouting Becky could hear him remonstrating with his companions. 'Becky, do you have a gun? For Christ's sake give me something to fight with. They are going to kill me. Open this fucking door. He's just one homeless boy. He knows no better. He's a beggar, an orphan. He doesn't matter, Becky. *We* matter. You matter to me . . . please, Becky, I am begging you . . .'

Becky moved the rifle onto her lap. From outside there was the sound of fighting, crashing, then Alex screamed. Afterwards there was silence before a man spoke.

'We have your husband, ma'am. You can save him if you wish. Give us the boy. We will look after him. No harm will come to him, you have our word.'

Eduardo clung to her harder. She drew him closer.

'It's my only chance, Becky. It's all gone wrong for me. I regret everything. Please forgive me. I never stopped loving you. It was everything else. Please don't let them kill me.'

Silence followed. She buried her face in her hands. Eduardo held on to her arm. She closed her eyes tight. There was the sound of a scuffle and someone being dragged, and Alex's shouting growing quieter.

'No. You can't kill me – please . . . Becky!'

Alex's voice was screeching. He was not near the door any more. Becky's heart pounded in her chest. She held on to Eduardo tightly and clamped her eyes shut. There came an awful silence. Then three precise, perfectly spaced gun shots: *pop pop pop*.

She drew in a breath and held it as she listened intently. The men were near the house again, but Alex's voice was not one of them. They were moving around the outside of the refuge. Fredrico gave the order:

'Torch the place.'

74

Amy lifted the wet necklace from the sink. She pulled either end of it as hard as she could. She put one foot on one end and stretched it. She wanted it to be perfect. Amy had woven many beads into it, the biggest, Suzanne's favourite colour – red – was right in the centre.

Suzanne was snoring heavily now. She had drunk the entire bottle of gin. Amy went back into the bathroom to retrieve her necklace. She dried it off a little and then knelt beside Suzanne. Suzanne's hair was still caught up at the top of her head where Amy had arranged it, out of the way. Amy fed the necklace carefully around Suzanne's neck and she positioned the big red bead right at the front. She pulled the ends to the front and tied them over the knot, as tightly and as carefully as she could. Amy went to the radiator, reached down the side and turned it up full, the way that Lenny had shown her she must do if she was cold. But Amy wasn't cold.

She washed her face, took off all the makeup and changed into her school uniform. She collected up her belongings and put them into her bag, neatly and quietly, and then she slipped the brace into her mouth and gave a few sucks of it to position it right. She smiled to herself – she liked its cold raw plastic taste – it was a welcome familiar sensation. It made her feel like she was halfway home. She took the keys and the phone from Suzanne's handbag and tiptoed out, gently closing the door behind her.

75

Mann and Father Finn saw the smoke from half a mile away. Neither of them looked at each other. Both understood what it was that they were racing towards.

'Our father, which art in heaven . . .' Father Finn prayed.

'What provisions have you for putting out fires?'

'We have just the hoses outside.'

'Can we expect help from anywhere else?'

'No. The local council have been trying to get rid of us for years. We are on our own, Johnny. I pray that everyone is out.' The air around was already carrying a hint of smoke in it.

They were getting nearer now. People were out of their houses on the side of the road. They were shouting at the Father, waving their arms for him to slow and hear what they had to say. He leaned out of the window to listen as they hurtled past, inevitably slower on the dusty road than they had been on the highway.

'The black riders came,' they shouted. 'Motorbikes and cars.'

Mercy met them as she ran towards the car as it spun into the driveway. She was screaming.

'Quick, Father. Becky and Eduardo are inside. We cannot get them out.'

She lumbered after them. Ramon was working the water hose. The older children were handing buckets of water to the adults. Mann looked up and saw Becky at the bedroom window. She was holding Eduardo. The wooden balcony was already alight. She was trying to open the balcony door. She was yanking it. Mann could see that she was panicking so much that she wasn't functioning. He knew what he had to do. He had no choice.

'I am going in the main entrance,' said Mann.

'No, Johnny. You are too weak. You'll never make it.'

'Ramon, point everything you have at the entrance. We will come out on the balcony. Father, get ready for us to jump onto something.'

'I will clear as much as I can here, Johnny. I have the sacks of rice in the Jeepney still, the ones we picked up in Manila. You can jump onto those.'

'Ready, Ramon?' Ramon's head nodded but his face was set in fear. Mann looked up at the window. He could no longer see Becky. 'Hose me down, Ramon.' Ramon drenched Mann with the water. Mercy handed him a wet towel and he put it over himself.

'Okay. Let's go.'

Ramon came behind Mann and blasted the front door as close to it as he could. Mann kicked it open. Clutching his side, he reeled back from the explosion of heat that hit him. Ramon hosed all around and the others threw buckets inside.

Mann kept the towel over his head and raced inside and up the stairs. The hot air heated his lungs like breathing in a furnace. Ramon followed him in and was keeping the flames in control as far as the upper landing. Mann beat the flames around the bedroom door with his wet towel and kicked it open.

Becky and Eduardo had passed out on the floor. Mann hit the floor himself, crawled towards them and dragged them back towards the balcony. He would have to be ready to get them out the second he opened the balcony doors. It would create a through-tunnel of air and the place would be a furnace in seconds. He was choking now. The acrid cinders were catching in his throat and making him retch. He cursed his useless side that stopped him pulling them both at once. He got them to the window and looked down. He saw Father Finn below, the children dragging the sacks towards the house. Father Finn saw him, his face said that they were ready, and Mann reached up, turned the handle of the latch, pulled it all the way down, gave it a good yank, and opened the window a fraction. He shook Becky. She did not stir. There was no way he could carry them both together and jump far enough beyond the balcony. He was going to have to do them one at a time. Mann picked up Eduardo, ready in his arms. He looked back at the door. It would be burning through soon. If he opened the balcony door it would be in seconds rather than minutes. He looked back at Becky; he had no choice, he had to do it. He steeled himself, then he opened the balcony door and threw Eduardo out over the burning balcony and onto the waiting sacks below.

A blast of flame from the balcony sent Mann reeling backwards The entire platform was fiercely alight now. For a second it eased as Ramon blasted it with the hose. Mann dragged Becky into his arms. The balcony was all but gone in flames. Ramon's hose ceased to have any effect on it. The heat was biting the back of Mann's throat. He heard the roar of the fire beneath him and the sound of glass shattering in the house. His skin began to scorch. He was clutching at the small amount of oxygen left in the room and he knew he was passing out. He looked behind him. The door to the bedroom was all but burnt through. He looked at Becky, he was glad she was unconscious. Hopefully she wouldn't feel the pain.

'I'm sorry, Becky, truly sorry, but . . .' he kissed her face '. . . but we are not going to fucking die here. Agreed? That's it then, no argument.'

With his last atom of strength he stood to his feet, wrapped the wet towel over his and Becky's heads and cradled her in his arms.

He looked back towards the door, any second now it would be too late. There was a huge roar all around them. The whole refuge felt like it was about to collapse. The glass was cracking and about to shatter in the balcony doors. Then it would be too late and they would be engulfed in flames. It was now or never. Better to die on the way out than be trapped here.

He took one last look at Becky, took a step back, and ran at the balcony doors, blasted them apart with a kick and jumped into the fire. It was like jumping into a lava flow. Mann threw himself and Becky forward straight into the mouth of the volcano.

At that second when his clothes caught fire and he felt them stick to his body, at that exact second when he felt the excruciating pain of death and he opened his mouth to cry out in agony, it was filled with a cold, hard torrent of water from above.

76

Morning had come to Fields Avenue. The cockerels that would die later that day in the cock-fighting arena, pitched against one another in a slaughter of blood and feathers, now stood proud and erect as they crowed their last ever morning salute from the confines of their crates. A weak sun turned the dawn sky milky blue. Fields Avenue was stupefied. Its occupants lay in a tangling of bodies, asleep in their beds, collapsed in spent lust.

The street children were awake early. Their pavement beds grew too hard to bear beyond a few hours. They were hungry and on the scavenge. The bins at the back of the restaurants would be a welcome source of breakfast. They had worked their way up Fields Avenue and now they gathered one by one in the place where a man was dying. The old woman was there too. She was watching silently from the doorway. Outside the Bordello the Colonel's journey was almost complete. Dismembered whilst still breathing, the Shabu had made the night a long one.

'*Finish it. Please.*'

Stevie Ho came around to the back of the Colonel's chair and held the point of his knife directly over the Colonel's heart. He rested the point between the exposed ribs and placed the palms of his hands over the hilt, one on top of the other.

'You were a worthy opponent. You died a good death. I will give you your wish.'

77

'You all right, Johnny?'

Mann awoke lying on his back, staring up at the blue sky with Father Finn's face blocking his view.

'I'm okay, Father. How are the others?'

'They're recovering, Eduardo is awake and he's fine. Becky is just coming around, the doctor is with her. Just rest now, Mann, you've lost a lot of blood.'

'What time is it?' Mann felt a pain in his lungs as he talked.

'It's three o'clock. You have been asleep for a few hours. You are very weak, Johnny. Mercy has cleaned you up, the bullet is out, but you need stitching. The doctor is on his way.'

Mann was on a makeshift bed under the trees in the garden. A gentle breeze fanned his skin. The sun flitted through the leaves and skipped across his face. The sky was blue, but ash and soot still floated past. He turned his head to see that the refuge was destroyed. Ramon was busy keeping the house dampened with the hose. Some of the staff were helping him, some others were making lunch in a field kitchen. The children were running

404

around shouting excitedly. They were splashing in the pools of water that had landed on hard ground and had not yet evaporated or been absorbed. Their arms outstretched as wings, they were re-enacting the moment Remy's plane dumped the lake on their heads.

'Thank God you all got out, and thank God for Remy. He managed to empty eight hundred gallons of water right on target.'

'He did a good job.'

'He's a good man, all right. He phoned me to say he's landed at Clark now, he's making his way over. I said we'd crack open that bottle of malt you brought over with you. We will need to camp out at the workers' houses until we can rebuild the centre. I've already started working on the designs. I have decided it was a blessing in disguise. Now we can build a bigger centre – specially designed for our needs. I have organised for you two to stay with Ramon and Mercy until we can arrange something else.'

'It will be just for a night for me, Father. I can't stay. I leave tomorrow. I have to get back to Hong Kong as fast as I can. It's not over till I make sure the trafficking ring is broken. We have to finish it off now that it's wounded, and I have to make sure CK sticks to his side of the bargain. I can't do that from here.'

Father Finn left to help Ramon and keep the flames from reigniting in the intense heat. Mercy and the others moved the children back and away to the cool of the gardens.

Mann stood, checked that he wasn't about to fall down, looked and saw that the others were too busy to watch him. He was looking for something that he hoped no one else would find. He had a hunch that the DDS would leave something behind. He looked around him and began searching.

He made his way across to the far side of the driveway. There was an area that Father Finn liked to call his garden shed. It was a cluster of small wooden structures, some used for storage, others just palm-thatched open-sided summer houses for tranquillity and a bit of peace. As he neared the space between two of the huts, he found what he was looking for – Alex Stamp.

Mann knelt beside him and looked him over. He had seconds rather than minutes left, thought Mann. His chest was saturated with blood. His face was grey. His breathing was so shallow that Mann couldn't be sure he was still alive. Mann checked for a pulse. As he pressed his fingers to the carotid artery, Alex opened his eyes.

'Come to gloat?' He could barely speak.

'No . . . death comes to all of us.'

Alex Stamp smiled ruefully.

'Yeah, well, don't let me keep you.'

'I'm not here to give you the last rites, but I will hear your confession. Where is CK's daughter? You do that and I'll do my best to keep you alive.'

'You're too late. She's already dead. Tell Becky I am sorry. Tell her . . .'

'I'll tell her nothing. She's suffered enough. Go to hell.'

Mann listened to the sound of death – the last gurgle

of laboured breathing as Alex's lungs became water-logged. He covered the body with a piece of sacking and then he moved into the shade of one of the summer houses. He sat down and looked at his phone. It was late afternoon. He had several missed calls. He phoned Shrimp first.

'Boss, you okay?'

'I'm fine.'

'I have some awesome news. Amy Tang walked back into school minutes before the deadline was up this morning.'

'How?'

'No one really knows. She said she got a taxi. None of the firms can confirm that, she said she thought it was a minicab that she hailed outside a flat. She gave a vague statement to the police. Said she just walked out. But, get this? Before she turned up we got an anonymous tip-off as to where she was being held. When we got to the flat, it was the weirdest thing. A Chinese woman was dead in there. Lying out on a bed in the back room. The autopsy is being done, but it looks like she died from strangulation. There was a string necklace type of thing around her neck – it had beads and stuff. The place was like an oven in there. Initial blood examination also indicated that she was heavily sedated – we found a half-empty bottle of sleeping pills in her bag. Apart from that the place was orderly. Clean, no sign of a fight. The woman had been drinking – there was an empty gin bottle in there. Nothing else, absolutely nothing else, and no little girl. Then I got a call from the school to say that she had just walked back in. She's been interviewed. She's drawn pictures of the suspects. One of them was definitely Alex Stamp, the other was the dead woman. She said that she was babysat by two other Chinese men – she drew one of them, London Chinese, named Sunny. He says he is a member of the White Circle. He's not saying anything else. She couldn't remember what the other one looked like, or even his name. She says she had put the necklace around the woman's neck as a leaving present. Strange child.'

'She's not strange. She's CK's daughter. She's *resilient*.'

'Another thing, boss. Information at the flat led us to another location. We found a group of six Filipinas, all of them under eighteen; all of them illegally trafficked in via Amsterdam in two lorries. They were in a bad state. It took them a month to reach the UK. It was a very slick outfit. They are being looked after for a few days and then they'll be flown home.'

'Do we know who is the head of the White Circle yet, boss?'

'He's about to show his hand, Shrimp.'

Mann made another call.

'You managed it then, Micky?'

'After I got the tip-off it was easy. Common goals, common aims, the Flying Dragons were keen for me to infiltrate the White Circle. I had to change allegiance for a while. But it worked and I managed to get myself hired as her bodyguard. I still don't know where the tip-off came from. That little girl – Amy Tang – she's smart. She said to me "Drop me off here at the end of the school driveway. I will tell them that I caught a taxi here. Don't go back to the flat." She was already changed into a school uniform; she had it all planned. She just got out of the car and walked up the driveway, her bag over her shoulder. She looked like nothing had happened.'

'Well done, Micky – thanks for your help, now get the fuck out from undercover.'

'You know what else she said? "One day I will be the Dragon Head of the Wo Shing Shing, Pat, and I will remember you."'

78

Mercy called Mann over to the Jeepney. It was his turn to see the doctor. Mercy accepted a push-up into the back of the makeshift ambulance.

Father Finn got in as well, just as the doctor was sewing Mann up. 'He needs to go to hospital, no?'

The doctor stopped his stitching, looked Mann over and shrugged as if he already knew it wasn't worth suggesting. 'He needs to rest and get his strength up. If he can do that somewhere here then he will be okay.'

'Do you hear that, Johnny? We will have your company for a few days here. You should have brought two bottles of scotch instead of one, no?'

'You're so ungrateful.' Mann grimaced and started to fidget. 'We'll see, Father. I have work to do. Anyway, the scotch would have gone up in the fire.'

'I didn't trust you with it. I hid it in the car. Now let the doctor finish stitching you up, for goodness' sake, and stop moving about.'

'It hurts.'

'Huh!' Mercy gave him an incredulous look and then

let her eyes slip to her swollen abdomen. 'Hurts? Ha! Don't talk to me about pain. You don't have any...' She was about to add something else when she stopped to listen. Someone was singing 'My Way' very loudly.

'Remy!' Father Finn grinned.

'Am I in time for lunch?' Remy poked his head through the flap that acted as sunshield and window at the side of the Jeepney. 'Looks like the BBQ got a bit out of hand, huh? Someone gunna be in big trouble for that, no?' Mercy giggled.

'Remy, you are just in time for lunch and an apéritif on the lawn.' The father got out of the Jeepney and shook Remy's hand as he passed him. 'I will go and fetch a drop of the single malt and we'll have a medicinal.'

'You never offered me that when I was in pain...' Mann called after him.

'I thought about it...' the Father shouted back over his shoulder as he marched off to his car to retrieve the scotch.

'Hey, Inspector, this a normal day for you Hong Kong police, huh? You spend your whole life escaping dangerous criminals and jumpin' from fires?'

'Yes, but what I always do first is make sure I have a reliable sidekick. Thank you, Remy, much appreciated.'

Remy shrugged, as if it was all in a day's work for him, but it was plain to see he was walking with a spring in his step and a definite swagger.

'No problem. Just target practice for me, no?'

Mann finished getting bandaged and went to see Becky. En route he had a quiet word with Father Finn and

411

arrangements were made to get Alex Stamp's body out of the heat and into an ice-cool morgue drawer. Becky was sitting beside Eduardo on the grass under the shade of a tree. She looked up and gave him a watery smile that barely tugged at the corners of her mouth. Her eyes said it all. She was scanning his face to see what answers she could find there. She wanted to know if Mann had found Alex. She had watched him go, even though he hadn't seen her, and she knew how his brain worked.

'Hello stranger,' she said as he got within range. Her voice sounded as if someone had filed away the inside of her throat.

Mann stood looking them over. They were sitting side by side, still covered in soot. Her blonde hair was now mainly black and her eyes were red-rimmed. Eduardo looked even worse than he had before. His thin little body was now soaked as well as soiled.

'You look like the two extras from *Les Miserables*.'

'Don't make me laugh . . . it hurts.' She began coughing violently. 'Anyway, you can talk – you are less than your usual immaculate self.' She patted the grass next to her.

'You all right?' He sat down beside her.

She nodded.

'Next time you rescue me, can you get here sooner . . . it was a very close call there.'

'You know me, I hate being late for anything, but sometimes you just have to make an entrance.'

She turned and her eyes locked on to his. He knew there were a whole lot of things that she wanted to ask, but she just sighed and rolled her eyes.

'Thank you, Mann,' she mouthed. She looked like she was going to cry.

He peeked around her to look at Eduardo, who was still sitting as close to Becky as he could physically get.

'If I give you a hug, will he attack me?'

'You're okay; he's not the jealous type.'

He pulled her close. She rested heavily on him and he stroked her arm. They sat for a few moments and watched the children making a happy event out of a near catastrophe.

'You're okay, it's all over now. Things will all work out. Do you want to hear some good news?'

She looked at him expectantly.

'Amy Tang is back safe and sound.'

'That's really fantastic . . . but Mann . . . what about Alex?' she said, almost in a whisper as if she were afraid of the answer.

'He's dead, Becky. I found his body.' Mann felt her shoulders stiffen as he said it. 'They are taking him to the morgue at the hospital.'

She gave a stifled cry as she buried her face in his chest. When she looked up at him, her eyes were full of tears.

She shook her head as the tears spilt over and rolled down her soot-smeared cheeks. 'I had to make a choice.'

He kissed her head. 'I know.'

79

Mann called Stevie Ho.

'I found him.'

'Alive?'

'No. The DDS got to him first.'

'Pity.'

'Better for him, I think. He wouldn't find a safe place on the planet; he double-crossed just about everyone. What about the Colonel?'

'He's keeping a flock of vultures in food for a week as we speak.'

'Did he tell you who Blanco was?'

'No. I don't think he knew. I have what I wanted from him, though.'

'It's not going to get you anywhere. CK's daughter is back in school, inside the allotted deadline. CK will know by now. Your dreams of having the monopoly on sex trafficking in Asia are over, Stevie. You'd better run back to Hong Kong. There will be questions to answer. I don't think CK is going to be best pleased with you.'

'I won't be going back to Hong Kong. I might be

left licking my wounds, but they will heal. I am not going back.'

'The world is too small to hide in, Stevie.'

'Maybe, Mann, but it's a changing world. A man must adjust. I have to make my own way in it now. I have plans. I have backers.'

'CK won't let you leave the Wo Shing Shing.'

'My allegiance was never with him, it was with Chan. I would never leave my master.'

'Your master died in the waters off Cheung Chau.'

'Maybe.'

'Are you telling me Chan survived? I watched him go under.'

'I am telling you that, in one form or another, his legacy lives on.'

'You were a good man once, Stevie. Now you have become as rotten as the man you served. I will hunt you down, just as I did him, if you pursue his aims.'

'So be it.'

80

In the morning, Mann got ready to go. They were due to leave in ten minutes. Father Finn was giving them a lift to Manila airport on his way down to see the charity commission about the refuge.

He looked up to see Becky standing there.

'You ready?'

'I think I might stay on here a bit longer, Mann.'

'Sure?'

'Yes . . .' She sighed and ran her fingers through her newly washed hair. '. . . and no. I can see to things at this end. I can write my report up, email it over. I will have to go back and give evidence soon enough, but I am due some leave. I think I will spend it here, help rebuild the centre. Maybe I will stay on afterwards, if the Father agrees.'

He appeared behind her. 'We need all the hands we can get, and you have a very capable pair. I will wait for you at the Jeepney, Johnny.'

She walked with him outside. They stood together at the back of the Jeepney whilst the Father finished off his preparations. Mann had already said goodbye to the rest of the staff. The breeze was fresh but the smell of the fire was still bitter in the air. They stared awkwardly at one another.

'Will you come back this way soon?'

'Yes. I have some things I have to do first – loose ends that need tidying. I'm owed a lot of holiday. I will come back and take you on a tour of the islands and you will see the real magic of this place.'

'I am going to miss you, Johnny Mann.' She stepped forward and hugged him.

'Ouch!'

'Oh, sorry.' She stepped back.

'I don't mean it. What's a bit of pain between us? Come here. I want to remember this hug, it might have to last me a long time.'

She pressed herself close to him and rested her head against his chest. Then she pulled back and looked up at him with a mischievous smile on her face. Mann looked down into the dark golden eyes, rimmed with eyelashes like coal.

'See! Jack the lad! I knew it.'

He grinned. 'Come here. It's nice to hear you laugh again. I am going to miss you, tough nut. You are one of the sexiest, brightest, sassiest women I know, and you have a great arse . . .' He slipped his hands around her waist, drew her to him and kissed her hard on the lips. 'When you are ready, call me.'

81

In five hours Mann was back in Hong Kong, changed and out of his apartment. He sat opposite CK in Grissini, the Italian restaurant in the Grand Hyatt Hotel, with its tall ceiling and beautifully patterned parquet flooring. It had panoramic views over a sunny blue Hong Kong.

'And the rest of the deal? Your little girl is safe, back at school, unharmed . . . I asked you for two more things.'

He waited whilst the waiter poured him a glass of perfectly chilled Muffio wine and they were presented with a platter of Italian cheeses and fresh honeyed figs to finish their meal.

'Do I have your promise that you will dismantle the networks you have set up and immediately cease all trafficking of human beings?'

CK put down his knife and wiped his hands with his napkin. He nodded towards the waiter who came to refill his water. He looked at Mann, studied him. Mann could see that his reputation as a poker player was well-earned. His expressions hardly changed. It was as though if he sat still for too long he would appear one-dimensional – a cardboard cut out: immaculately groomed, not a hair out of place, just the right amount of silvering at the temples. He was elegance and power personified. In answer to Mann's question he didn't so much as nod.

'Will Stevie Ho comply?'

For a second CK's eyelashes fluttered, but he kept eye contact with Mann.

'Stevie is ambitious.'

'Does that mean that you have lost control of him?'

CK pushed his plate to one side and waited whilst the waiter cleared it for him.

'Stevie's loyalty to me was always shared.'

It looked like Mann had hit a nerve. Although CK's manner hadn't changed dramatically there was a definite prickliness to the atmosphere.

'With Chan?'

'Yes, with my son-in-law, who, as we both know, has disappeared. But I will honour my side of the agreement. All operations that Stevie was engaged in, with or without my permission, are now ceased. I will restore the hotel ownership back to its rightful owners and compensate persons, as you have demanded. But Stevie himself has decided he will not be returning to Hong Kong. So, you have my word and that is good enough. And the last of your wishes, I cannot grant. The five men who took part in the killing have been retired, in different ways. It will serve you no purpose to pursue men who were only following orders. The man who ordered the killing . . . that is a delicate matter.'

'I have waited too long to find justice for my father. Can you tell me whether the man who ordered my father's death is still with us?'

'I will tell you one thing . . . you already know your enemy, but you do not recognise him.'

82

'Where is the child?'

'She doesn't speak, Father. She hasn't cried. She hasn't smiled. She doesn't want to talk about what happened to her. I am afraid for her. She has so much locked up in her young head.'

'I know, I know, Mercy. Don't you worry. I will give her to someone else to look after. You have enough on your plate, with this baby of yours about to pop and a toddler to look after.'

'No, Father. *Please*. I can manage. I want her to stay here. She needs us so badly. I just wish she would open up.'

Father Finn thought how tired Mercy looked. The exertion of the day before was still on her face. She had run around a lot more than was right for a woman in her final trimester.

'Where is she?' he asked, glancing around.

'Round the back, sitting on the steps. I asked her if she wanted to help in the garden but she hasn't moved from that step in three hours.'

* * *

'Maya?' Father Finn sat down beside her.

She did not answer.

'Come and walk with me.'

Father Finn offered her his hand. She took it and he led her past Mercy's house and up the hill. It was the other side to the refuge. It looked out over the sea. He walked slowly. The heat and the lush vegetation were not a climate to walk fast in.

'Maya, I knew your mother when she was a girl. A little bit older than you.'

Maya looked at him hard. Her little face was trying to make sense of everything he was saying.

'I did. And do you know what I remember?'

She shook her head.

'She had the brightest smile I had ever seen. When she smiled, you just had to smile too. That's a great gift, Maya, no? But she didn't always smile. When I found your mother she had had a terrible time, just like you have had. She was sad and angry and unhappy about what had happened to her and why it had happened. She didn't understand. But, after a while she made friends here and she became happy, and do you know what I remember most about your mother?'

Maya shook her head. Her large brown eyes never wandered from his face.

'Your mother was only here a short while but she was happy here. You know what she loved to do?'

Maya shook her head. Father Finn stopped to allow the child to rest a little.

'She liked to walk to the top of this hill with me and talk. "One day", she'd say, "I am going to graduate from high school and I will be a lawyer or a teacher." She was very smart, your mother. She didn't achieve that dream because something much more important came along that made her happier than she had ever been, happier than she could ever have thought. Do you know what that was, Maya?'

Maya gave a small puzzled shake of the head.

'It was you! Your mother loved you more than anything in the world. She didn't want to die, Maya. She wanted to live to see you do well in school, see you graduate, see you have children of your own, but sometimes life doesn't let us have the things we want.

'But the one thing that you can always hold inside is to know that your mother loved you more than the world. She loved you so much she gave her life for you. I know that you have seen awful things, Maya. In time you will remember your mummy smiling again, just like I do when I think of her. I am looking forward to seeing you smile, Maya.'

Maya wiped her eyes with the heel of her hand.

'You can stay here, Maya, live with Mercy and Ramon. They will be your family. Mercy will have the baby soon and you will have a new brother or sister who will need you. You belong here, Maya. Come. Let me show you something.'

They reached the top of the hill. There was a small cemetery, lawned and tended. Amongst the half a dozen graves there was a new plaque.

'Come, Maya. I know you can read and write because your mummy told me how clever you were. Come read this for me.'

They stopped at a new grave, covered in flowers. Maya read the words on the makeshift cross, written in black pen.

Wednesday, devoted mother to Maya.
Died 11 April 2004 at the age of 21.

'You can come here whenever you like, Maya.'

Maya looked back at the grave and let go of Father Finn's hands as she went to touch the cross. She pulled out some of the flowers from the bouquet that was left there and she knotted two stems together and draped the flowers over the cross.

Then she took the Father's hand and they started their descent back down the mountain.

83

Rosario and Tina saw the man standing outside the foot spa. They watched as their work mates, touting for business outside, pointed in at Rosario. They saw him look through the window at her and they saw the women's eyes fill with sympathy and their mouths give the Filipino smile as they pointed Rosario out to him. Rosario looked at Tina and Tina nodded. Rosario left her client and went outside to the man.

Tina watched them through the window. He was not a local man. He looked smartly dressed, he wasn't on holiday. He looked like he had come down from the city to see her: he was well-dressed but solemn. She watched Rosario talk to the man and her friend covered her face with her hands and nodded her head as she listened to him talking. His head was bowed. He stood close to her. He was not allowing others to hear. Whatever he was saying it was for Rosario's ears only. The man gave Rosario a piece of paper. Tina saw that Rosario was crying now. She was wiping away tears that fell so fast they fell onto her pregnant stomach and looked as red as blood on the pink

'Paradise' T-shirt. The man had finished talking. He was leaving and walking away down the lane. The piece of paper was still in Rosario's hands. Tina came outside to her friend, who had not moved from the spot since the man left. She stood and stared at the paper.

'What does it say, Rosario?'

Rosario wiped her tears from her face with the heel of her hand.

'It says they were taken to the UK, in a lorry. They were held prisoners. They were badly hurt.' She looked up at her friend and smiled. 'But they are on their way home.'

84

'Mum?'

Mann rang his mother whilst standing with Ng in Lantau Airport. It was mid-afternoon and Shrimp's flight from London had already landed, they were just waiting for him to clear customs. At the other end of the phone Molly answered with the cat in her arms.

'Are you home now, Johnny?'

'I'm back. I'll be over to see you tomorrow, if you're free.'

'Of course – I look forward to it . . .'

Molly hesitated. There was concern in her voice. 'I'm sorry about last time.'

'Don't be. I think you're right, it's about time I learned about Dad, warts and all. I can't keep hanging on to this childish memory. I'm a grown man, after all. David White sends his love, by the way.'

'I bet he misses the cat.'

'Ha . . . I told him he misses it a lot more than it misses him. See you tomorrow, Mum, love you . . .'

'And you, son.'

*   *   *

Shrimp emerged from behind the arrivals screen.

'Did you have a good flight?' Mann asked, and pointed to the enormous case he was pulling behind him. 'What have you got in there?'

Ng chuckled and shook his head.

Shrimp rolled his eyes skyward. 'Had to pay excess – bummer.'

Mann lifted Shrimp's case and groaned. 'I am not surprised.'

'I spent a fortune in the vintage clothes markets. Anyway, wassup? What are you two doing here? I was making my way in to do my report now. You didn't have to escort me.'

'We need to have a meeting before we face the Super,' said Mann. 'We thought we might as well have it here.'

They made their way over to sit on an empty row of seats in the huge open and airy terminal. Shrimp sat between Ng and Mann.

'There are a few things we need to get straight, to clarify,' said Mann.

'. . . to make sure we all understand it the same way . . .' said Ng.

'We need to leave someone who was involved out of the equation,' said Mann. 'We have to forget the role that someone took in this and look past it.'

'Ah . . . yes . . .' said Shrimp. '. . . Gotcha. I wasn't sure whether we would all come to the same conclusion . . .'

'At the same time . . . Yes.' Mann finished his sentence for him. 'We know that this person is fundamentally good, and I think we have to overlook this one incident.'

'A diamond with a flaw is preferable to a common stone,' said Ng.

85

Mann waited till he got back to his apartment to make the call.

'Why did you do it, David?'

He heard his old friend sigh deeply down the phone. He knew that he would have his eyes closed and he would be smoothing the top of his head with his free hand. For so many years Mann had watched him do that, sitting behind his big oak desk at Headquarters, surrounded by rugby trophies and family photos. Now Mann recalled one person on those photos that he should have recognised earlier.

'I knew you'd find my connection to him in the end. I swear to you that once I realised what he was up to, I tried to put a stop to it at once. I left a message for Micky. He's a good cop, I knew he'd manage to infiltrate them. Is Amy Tang safe?'

'Yes, she's safe. We never counted on the X-factor – the CK genes. She's more than safe as she killed her jailor. How did you get into it in the first place, David?'

'Alex Stamp is my nephew. I thought you might have recognised him. He came out to Hong Kong a couple of times when he was a lad. I had a photo of him and my sister in the office. I always had a soft spot for him. He didn't have much of a childhood; his father was a pig to him. He asked me for help to get some new business off the ground. I agreed to introduce him to contacts I had made over the years. One of them was Fredrico. From there it just snowballed. I think there isn't a villain that Fredrico doesn't know. It was only when I started investigating for you that I found out the extent of Alex's misdeeds. I am sorry. I will hand myself in.'

'You don't need to. Nobody else knows about this but me, Shrimp, Ng and you. They are too fond of you to see you put inside for it. By way of penance I have volunteered you to help Father Finn in his fight against the western paedophiles. It will mean flying out to the Philippines every few months, and quite a lot of hard work in-between. It takes him a long time to set up strong cases against these men.'

'Hard work is what I need, Mann.'

'Are you ready to trap Blanco?'

'Did you manage to do that thing I asked you to?'

'Yes, I did, sitting at a beach bar in Puerto Galera.'

86

A phone call came from Father Finn. 'Mercy had a baby boy. Two weeks early. They're calling him Johnny.'

'Ha! That's great. How is Becky?'

'She is doing fine. She's missing you already, I think. They are all helping each other through the process of healing. It will be a long route for some, but we will get there, no? I have heard from your friend – David White. He is coming out here in the next few weeks and we are going to start the clean-up all over again.'

'It's a thankless task, Father.'

'We are all going to have our work cut out to make a difference. Someone has got to put their hand up and say it's wrong. The world cannot just sit by and allow its children to live off rubbish dumps and be sold as sex slaves. Otherwise what happens when these children become adults? But, you know what, Johnny? Maya smiled today – so it's never thankless, Johnny, not in a million years.'

Mann smiled as he said goodbye to Father Finn and

headed off to the Cantina – he had a question for Miriam.

Amy had finished her interviews with the police and was allowed to go back to her room to sort out her things. It was good to be back. She unpacked her bag and put her new macramé equipment in the box with all the others. She would go downstairs and find her friends in the common room in a minute. She might have a game of pool or watch the television. There were only sports matches on that afternoon, and Amy was never in those. She wasn't good at sport, but she was good at other things – like macramé.

Terry sat in the Tequila Station. The place was quiet. Angeles was recovering from the death of the Colonel, whose body had been dumped outside Lolita's, in bits. All the Colonel's clubs had been temporarily shut down. The other bar owners had tried to take over his patch, but Terry had asserted his claim very quickly. The Colonel had signed everything over to him a long time ago, because Terry had a Filipina wife, so all the Colonel's clubs were in her name and therefore it all belonged to Terry.

Terry would give it a day, then he would open them up again. It wasn't up to Terry to settle everyone's nerves down. Sophia waited patiently for her father to finish his beer. She was playing with the pink pony he had given her. She combed its hair and held it in her small coffee-coloured hand as she trotted it along the surface of the bar.

Terry closed his laptop and drained the last of his beer.

'Come on, Sophia.'

'Okay.' Sophia clicked her tongue as she slipped off the stool and rode Princess Pony over the side of the bar, across the stool and into the air. She followed her father as he checked his watch and walked down the stairs past the toilets, past the dance floor, and into a back room.

It was Terry's office. It was a light, white-walled room with just a desk and a chair in the corner. It had a single bed in the centre and on the cover of the bed were pictures of Princess Ponies, like the one Sophia held in her hand, all jumping over a rainbow. Opposite the bed was a shelf with a webcam on it. Terry closed the door behind them. Sophia was still playing with her pony.

Terry sat at the desk. He opened his laptop and waited for it to fire up.

Mann sat in the Cantina enjoying a seahorse or two. He was checking his emails on his phone. He got one from David White.

You ready?

Yes.

'*La La La . . . Love Love Love . . . Kiss Kiss Kiss Me.*'

Sophia was singing as Princess Pony galloped in the air.

'Okay, we're ready, Sophia.'

She gave him that 'Do I have to?' face.

Terry clicked away on the keys of the laptop. It was slow today.

Sophia walked over to the shelf opposite the bed and stared up into the webcam. She put Princess Pony down next to the camera and turned its back to her, then she started unbuttoning the front of her school dress.

At the other end of cyber world, David White was waiting. The Trojan was searching.

'*La La La . . . Love Love Love . . .*' Sophia was singing as she made faces into the webcam.

Mann finished his drink just as Miriam appeared with a fresh one for him. She looked beautiful – she was pleased to see him.

'You doing anything later, Miriam?'

She shook her head and smiled. 'What have you got in mind?'

'You know the fancy dress party you had?'

She nodded. 'The one you never made it to, you mean?'

'That's the one. Do you still have the outfits?'

'Oh yes . . .'

Terry punched in the password. The Trojan lit up . . .

'Dance for Daddy, honey,' Terry said. 'Look at the nice man and smile.'

'Nothing's happening, Daddy.'

Terry waited. The connection was slow but the laptop

was working on it. He was through. Terry stared at the screen. It had one thing written on it.

PRESS–
Hello Blanco . . . *your time's up.*

Mann smiled to himself and closed his phone.

**Read on for an exclusive chapter of
Lee Weeks's new book,
coming in 2009.**

Mae Sot, Thailand, Burma border

'Bang, bang, boy!'

Saw Wah Say's men parted for him as he walked across the room towards the table where the boy was sat. Saw's head was shaved, leaving a long tuft of hair at the crown. From his right ear hung feathers and a lizard's foot. On his face he had smeared the blood of his victims. He leaned across the girl's naked body. Her blonde hair was matted with dark blood and her head twisted to the side. Through misting eyes she seemed to be watching the dawn as it filtered through the rank air and began its trespass into the long night.

Saw rested his gnarled hands on the table. They were disfigured from years as a Leth Wei, a bare knuckle fighter. Then he looked straight into the boy's eyes with a look of disgust. He called him a boy because Jake could not really be called a man. It was a month past his eighteenth birthday but his skin was still baby smooth, his voice still cracked and his thoughts were unsullied by loss, pain or death

Until now.

Saw spat a glob of sticky black phlegm onto the dirt floor. Grinning, he watched Jake squirm and cry like a baby. Saw had faced death many times. He enjoyed watching others die. He looked down and breathed in the mist of atomised blood and death from the girl. It caught in the back of his throat, he could taste it. He could taste her. Then a shaft of light hit him in the eyes and he turned his head towards the window. The corner of the make-shift curtain had dropped and the sun was rising fast. He knew that the game must end now. His instincts had kept him alive and out of Burmese hands for twenty-eight years. At this moment they were telling him to hurry. Someone would come looking for this half-Chinese boy.

'Do it. The world will know not to fuck with Saw Wah Say.'

Jake's face was stretched and contorted in terror, swollen from crying, with strings of saliva dribbling onto his T-shirt. There was a smell of stale urine coming from beneath his chair. He looked across the table at the girl. Two months ago when he arrived to teach English at the refugee camp, he had seen her walk towards him, laughing. A sound as clear as church bells, her hips swishing, her small breasts bouncing, and he had fallen in love. He had found passion in her arms. Now he wanted to reach out so badly and just hold her hand.

His arm shook so violently that the gun wriggled in the air like a snake let out of a bag. Saw's men whooped and yelped, moving in around Jake like jittery wolves waiting to finish off their prey. Their chests were bare, rank with stale sweat, sticky and thick with smeared blood. Their breath was heavy with stale liquor. Saw

438

had given them a night to remember. Now there was one thing left to do. They edged closer and looked back and forth from Saw to the boy, waiting.

As Jake looked at the girl he felt a terrible calm. He glanced up at the hovering men, waiting for his death like vultures, and then he stared hard at Saw's rattlesnake face. Jake stopped crying. A boy he might be called but he would end his life as a man. He reached out and touched the girl's cold hand. In the morning light her skin was grey and he knew she was gone. But her screams still rang in his ears. He didn't want to hear them anymore. He wanted to join her in peace. He held onto the gun with both hands and closed his eyes tight as he lifted it to his head. The cold steel found the dip of his temple and his forefinger squeezed the trigger.

WIN 2 FREE FLIGHTS TO HONG KONG!

Win 2 return flights to Hong Kong – the diverse modern metropolis steeped in Eastern and Western traditions.

To enter this free prize draw, simple visit www.avon-books.co.uk and answer the question below or send your postal entry to Avon The Trafficked Competition, HarperCollins Publishers, 77–85 Fulham Palace Road, Hammersmith, London, W6 8JB.

In *The Trafficked*, what is the name of CK Leung's kidnapped daughter?

A) Karen
B) Lucie
C) Amy

Terms and Conditions

1. This competition is open only to UK residents aged 18 or over. Only one entry per person is permitted. No purchase is necessary. Winners must be 18 years and over.
2. Only entries completed by post and via www.avon-books.co.uk will be valid. Any application containing incorrect, misleading or illegible information will be invalid.
3. The competition is not open to employees of HarperCollins and any other relevant company or its associated companies.
4. Closing date for the promotion is January 30th 2009 and entries must be received by the Promoter by 23.59 hrs on this date. The prize draw will take place on 2nd February 2009. The winners will be notified by telephone by February 27th 2009. The Promoter's decision will be final.
5. The winners will be drawn at random from all correct competition entries. The winner will receive 2 economy flights to Hong Kong. Flights will be direct. The return flight must be taken within seven days of landing in Hong Kong. This prize must be redeemed between 1st March–30th September 2009. The airline company used will be subject to availability, and the flights shall be subject to that airline's terms and conditions. Dates and times are also subject to availability. The winner will need to liaise with AVON about the exact timings of the flights, and shall supply various dates for travel. Final decision on the timing of the flight will be with AVON. This prize is non-redeemable for cash and cannot be deferred. No warranty is given as to the quality of the prizes. This prize is non-transferable and subject to availability.
6. By entering the draw the winner agrees to allow the free use of their name, photograph and general location for publicity and news purposes in connection with the Promotion.
7. Promoter: Avon, a division of HarperCollins Publishers Limited, 77–85 Fulham Palace Road, Hammersmith, London, W6 8JB.
8. Any breach of these terms and conditions by an entrant will void their entry. Misrepresentative or fraudulent entries will be declared invalid.
9. Proof of sending an entry via email or any other permitted means of entry is not proof of receipt.
10. Third party or bulk entries will be excluded from the competition.
11. No responsibility can be accepted for entries that are damaged, lost or not received by the Promoter.
12. The Promoter's decision on the winners of the competition is final and no correspondence will be entered into.
13. By entering the competition all participants will be deemed to have accepted and be bound by the terms and conditions and by any other requirements set out in these terms and conditions or any promotional material.
14. HarperCollins excludes all liability, so far as is permitted by law, which may arise in connection with this competition and reserves the right to cancel the competition at this stage.
15. These terms and conditions are governed by English law and are subject to the exclusive jurisdiction of the English courts.